"Intrigue, romance, and danger [...] tale of two sleuths on a secret m[...] [...]rely different motives. *A Noble Scheme* immerses you in English high society, where little is as it seems and love undergirds everything. Roseanna M. White's second book in THE IMPOSTERS series is as clever as it is glamorous."

Laura Frantz, Christy-award winning author
of *The Seamstress of Acadie*

"Two stories are mirrored in Roseanna White's *A Noble Scheme*—the mystery of a missing child and a heartbreakingly tender tale of grief and healing. With characters believable and unique, and a pace that builds suspense as the story unfolds, each thread is so compelling I couldn't stop turning pages."

Lori Benton, author of *Burning Sky*
and other historical novels

Praise for *A Beautiful Disguise*

"There are few things more joyous than stepping into the pages of a Roseanna White novel. *A Beautiful Disguise* has all of the hallmarks of this beloved author's resplendent fiction: pitch-perfect historical research, a thrilling setting and perfectly paced plot, and a love story that sparks as wonderfully as Lady Marigold's effervescent intelligence and charm. An unputdownable delight by a true master."

Rachel McMillan, author of *The Mozart Code*
and *Operation Scarlet*

"White's well-woven plot is engaging from start to finish with delightful threads of mystery, romance, and inspiration."

Carrie Turansky, award-winning author of *No Journey
Too Far* and *The Legacy of Longdale Manor*
on *A Beautiful Disguise*

A
NOBLE
SCHEME

Books by Roseanna M. White

LADIES OF THE MANOR

The Lost Heiress
The Reluctant Duchess
A Lady Unrivaled

SHADOWS OVER ENGLAND

A Name Unknown
A Song Unheard
An Hour Unspent

THE CODEBREAKERS

The Number of Love
On Wings of Devotion
A Portrait of Loyalty

Dreams of Savannah

THE SECRETS OF THE ISLES

The Nature of a Lady
To Treasure an Heiress
Worthy of Legend

Yesterday's Tides

THE IMPOSTERS

A Beautiful Disguise
A Noble Scheme

THE IMPOSTERS · 2

A NOBLE SCHEME

ROSEANNA M. WHITE

BETHANYHOUSE

a division of Baker Publishing Group
Minneapolis, Minnesota

Published by Bethany House Publishers
Minneapolis, Minnesota
BethanyHouse.com

Bethany House Publishers is a division of
Baker Publishing Group, Grand Rapids, Michigan

Printed in the United States of America

Library of Congress Cataloging-in-Publication Data
Names: White, Roseanna M., author.
Title: A noble scheme / Roseanna M. White.
Description: Minneapolis, Minnesota : Bethany House, a division of Baker
    Publishing Group, 2024. | Series: The Imposters ; 2
Identifiers: LCCN 2023045272 | ISBN 9780764240935 (paper) | ISBN 9780764242885
    (casebound) | ISBN 9781493445318 (eBook)
Subjects: LCSH: Private investigators—England—London—Fiction. | LCGFT:
    Christian fiction. | Dectective and mystery fiction. | Novels.
Classification: LCC PS3623.H578785 N63 2024 | DDC 813/.6—dc23/eng/20231003
LC record available at https://lccn.loc.gov/2023045272

Scripture quotations are from the King James Version of the Bible.

This is a work of fiction. Names, characters, incidents, and dialogues are products of the author's imagination and are not to be construed as real. Any resemblance to actual events or persons, living or dead, is entirely coincidental.

Author is represented by The Steve Laube Agency.

Baker Publishing Group publications use paper produced from sustainable forestry practices and postconsumer waste whenever possible.

24 25 26 27 28 29 30   7 6 5 4 3 2 1

To
Mike and LuAnn,
Justin and Karlene,
and too many others to count.
They're never forgotten.

ONE

*he Wedding of the Decade*. That's what Gemma would call it when she wrote her column for *London Ladies Journal*. Or maybe "of the century"? Was it too presumptuous to call it that when the century was only nine years old?

Oh, it hardly mattered. G. M. Parker wasn't known for her unbiased view of society and history. She was known for her clever turns of phrase and descriptions of exclusive events. She was known, mostly, for always "intuiting" where the fashion icon she'd dubbed Lady M would show up, and for writing up every detail of her latest *haute couture* ensemble.

Gemma sipped at her punch, smiling at Lady M now. It was really a wonder that no one had yet suspected that she did, in fact, know every place Lady Marigold Fairfax—now Livingstone, as of an hour ago—would show up, because she helped her plan her schedule.

And occasionally showed up in her place, decked out in her audacious and ostentatious frippery, head tilted down so no one thought to look at the face beneath the hat or mask or headpiece. All so that Marigold would have an alibi while she did Imposters work, usually spying on the very people who lapped up news about her like overeager puppies.

"Well. I know *that* expression." Aunt Priss planted her sturdy frame beside Gemma's, leveling one of those all-seeing glances on her before turning her gaze—if not her attention—back on the bride and groom too. "Plotting out what phrases to use in your column?"

Gemma grinned. Though the world at large had no idea what face paired with her *nom de plume*, she'd not kept her career a secret from her family. "I am transparent."

"You always have been." Her aunt's words sounded innocent enough, but Gemma's ears pricked with the current of unspoken things.

Things she had no desire to delve into at her best friend's wedding ball. She focused instead on Marigold and let out a sigh a few degrees happier than she really felt. As happy as she *should* feel. The fact that it was more imitation than truth was no fault of the bride or groom or their happy day. It was just . . . everything else. "She's radiant, isn't she?"

"Positively resplendent." Aunt Priss, being Aunt Priss, said it with a frown. "I don't know why she doesn't *always* let herself look so beautiful and instead insists upon all those outlandish, overshadowing fashions."

The overshadowing part was rather the point, but it was Imposters business that made it so. And while she'd told her family about her writing, she would never breathe a word about the investigative firm to anyone but her brother, James, who was stationed now in a corner, in deep conversation with Yates and Lord Hemming, their nearest neighbor.

If Aunt Priss ever got a whiff of it, she'd probably try to bully her way in and then try to solve all their cases by scowling at them. Gemma's lips twitched at the thought.

Formidable was the word Yates always used for her aunt. And she was. But it was all out of love.

Mostly.

"The house looks lovely. It's been too long since I've been here." Her aunt cast a scrutinizing gaze over the ballroom, and Gemma knew she'd be seeing more than all the pretty decorations—she'd be seeing the wear and tear underneath them. Most of the guests wouldn't, given the nonstop repairs that had been underway at the Tower ever since Marigold announced her engagement, but her aunt knew a bit of the difficult financial circumstances that had resulted from the previous Lord Fairfax's unchecked spending on every frivolity and entertainment known to man.

It had made for an enchanted childhood for them all. Circuses, theater groups, acrobats, musicians—they'd all peopled the Tower as surely as she and Marigold, Yates, and the Fairfaxes' distant cousin Graham had. Even now, the Romani circus family that had once wintered here wove in and out among the guests with serving trays in hand, playing the role of servants like it was one more performance.

By the time his lordship died, the estate had been on the brink of bankruptcy. The two siblings had been forced to dismiss all the staff, aside from the Caesars, who worked in exchange for retiring on the land—which meant that the stables now housed a lazy old lion, panther, and leopard in addition to the ancient horses.

More, Yates and Marigold had been forced to start the private investigating firm just to feed those animals and themselves.

Gemma chipped in too, from her earnings. As did Graham, though she had no desire to even think about him, much less search the room for his too-familiar face.

Things would improve a bit now that Marigold had married Merritt. One more income to help loosen the band.

His military pay wasn't exactly enough to rehire a houseful of servants, and he'd apparently refused the stipend his uncle—another earl, with considerably deeper coffers than Yates could boast just now—tried to give him. His argument was that he was only the heir *presumptive*, that Aunt Josie could yet present his uncle with a son, and Merritt couldn't abide anyone ever thinking he'd taken something that wasn't rightfully his.

That was fair. Even so, Gemma was grateful that he'd embraced the Tower as fully as the rest of them and was just as determined to see it through another year.

And until the Fairfaxes had well and truly righted their finances, the charade would continue. Lady M's applauded wardrobe would still come from the attic and be redesigned by the Gypsy seamstress who'd learned her trade in the circus. The Tower would still be run by the aristocrats themselves and those same retired circus folk. Yates would still attend the Sessions during the day and snoop on those same peers at night as an Imposter, solving their mysteries for them and taking a sizable chunk of their income for the favor. Gemma would still write about them in a way that made society *think* they knew them, providing the mask they could hide behind.

"I do adore a good wedding," Aunt Priss said. Yet another simple sentence with a world of complexity within it. The pointed look she sent to Gemma was superfluous. She might as well have shouted, *"How can you pretend you're not thinking about—"*

"Who doesn't?" Gemma took another sip of her punch and reached to pluck a cream puff from a circulating tray, smiling her thanks to Drina—an expert on acrobatics with silks but currently wearing the colorless uniform of a maid. Best to interrupt even her aunt's silent words. "I'm especially looking forward to describing what Lady M's attendant was wearing." She glanced down at her own gown, also remade from one of Marigold's mother's collections. "It isn't every day I get to talk about myself as if I don't know me."

"No?" From Yates, the question would have been amused and sardonic. From her aunt, it was a challenge.

Gemma bit into the pastry. *This* was why she rarely stayed with her brother, James—not that she didn't love her aunt, but every conversation had a thousand layers to it, and nine hundred ninety-nine of them were variations on accusation and critique. Priscilla Parks seemed to think that people were like papier-mâché—that one had to rip them to shreds in order to wrap them into shape. She only bothered if she cared about you, of course.

"What must you tell me for my own good this time?" *Lion-feathers*. Gemma really needed to learn to obey her own wisdom. The trick was not to argue. Not to defend oneself. And certainly not to invite the commentary about to come.

Her aunt's expression shifted into a thunderhead of a scowl. "You'll not take that tone of voice with me, young lady. You may be a grown woman, but that's no excuse to give up respecting your elders. When I think how I abandoned my own life to come and care for you and James after your mother died . . ."

Gemma was fully prepared to tune out the familiar refrain and was in the process of scanning the ballroom for something to distract her thoughts when her aunt went still, then shifted her posture to one of welcome instead of lecture, and a beaming smile graced her lips.

Gemma's spine snapped straight, and she pulled away by a step. Any number of guests could have saved her from the quiet tirade, but that particular smile was reserved for only one person in the world—the person Gemma least wanted to see.

"Graham!" Her aunt was a wily one, though. She reached out a hand toward the man who must be approaching from behind and to the side, but in such a way that she blocked Gemma's avenue of escape.

She half turned to try to escape in the direction from which Graham was coming, but she was too slow. Or he was too quick. He was already there, taking her aunt's fingers and giving her a warm smile.

"Aunt Priss! How it is possible that you're lovelier today than when last I saw you?"

Gemma rolled her eyes to fend off the warmth that always wanted to glow when Graham slathered flattery onto her usually immutable aunt. If anyone else tried such a thing, she'd cut them to the quick for the attempt. But for some reason, with Graham, her aunt laughed and flushed and patted the hair that was in the same utilitarian bun as it was every other day of her life.

It was a bit ironic, really, that Gemma earned a living describing fashions when she'd been raised largely by a woman who decried them all.

"How good to see you, Graham," her aunt said. *Gushed.* Her aunt gushed the words, sending another of her reprimanding gazes into Gemma. "It's been far too long."

Was it Gemma's fault she went stiff? After all, it's what papier-mâché did over time. The only way to hold its shape —to get dry and brittle and stiff.

"That it has. Though I've told you, haven't I, that you're welcome to drop by any time?" He'd always been good at *that* too—at spinning things around on Aunt Priss to remind her that the fault never rested solely on one person.

Except in this case, when it *did.*

Gemma cleared her throat, ready to mutter an "excuse me" and dart away the very second Graham released her aunt's fingers, which was about to happen. She could read them both as easily as she did the *London Ladies Journal.*

But unfortunately, they could both read her just as well.

Before Gemma could open her mouth, her aunt gave Graham's fingers a squeeze, told him to save a dance for her, and bustled off. The very moment she created that empty space, Graham shifted to fill it.

She could have—*should have*—spun and retreated to the rear instead of the front. But he had that soft smile on his face that took her instantly back to when he'd first arrived at Fairfax Tower as a lad, orphaned and terrified and trying not to show it to the distant cousins who had taken him in. Desperate to be independent . . . and yet to find someone to lean on. Brave but trembling. The exact sort of jumbled contradictions that made her heart go soft, both then and now.

"You look beautiful tonight, Gem." He'd given her more effusive compliments before, countless times. But he knew she'd turn away from the extravagant ones now. Knew that simplicity would stay her. His gaze swept over her hair. "I've never seen your hair like that. It suits you."

She'd tried a new style, one she'd seen in a magazine from Paris, for the wedding. And Graham had *always* been the first to notice the details. She was pretty sure the first moment she considered him a true friend had been when she was seven, he nine, and he'd sat down beside her in the schoolroom and said, *"A new hair ribbon! And look how perfectly it matches your eyes."*

No other boys she knew noticed such things. But Graham always had. Anything that had to do with color and shape and lines, be it on a person or in a building, caught his eye. Paired with her own predilection for fashion and story, they soon found they made a perfect pair. They'd wander about the countryside for hours together while his cousins practiced on the trapeze, him drawing and her weaving stories to match every ruin and landscape.

Then they'd rejoin Marigold and Yates, and they'd turn their attention to serious matters—like deciding on a name for their circus and deciding who would take what act. Gemma still had countless mock posters they'd created together. Graham had done the artwork, Gemma had written the copy, with the Fairfax siblings outlining all the spectacles they'd put on. The two of them on the trapeze. Marigold on the highwire, Yates as the strongman. They would stage a play that Gemma wrote and Graham designed the set for, but much like the Caesars' dramas, it would feature live animals playing some of the roles.

The Circus of Imposters, they'd called themselves then. Aristocrats posing as circus performers had been too much fun to dream up. A far cry, in some ways, from who the Imposters had become.

And not so far at all in others. The siblings still used their acrobatics. They all still played the roles Gemma wrote for them. Graham still took charge of their sets. It was just that their sets were real buildings and their costumes real clothes and the audience didn't know they were witnessing a performance as the four of them all gathered details to put into their files so that they could close cases and solve mysteries and collect tidy sums to feed their retired lion and provide shelter to their retired circus friends.

And while she was reminiscing, Graham had shifted to put himself at her side—the same side he always took, angled a bit so that his shoulder was behind her, their faces pointed the same way, yet he could speak into her ear without his voice traveling to the crowds.

"You all really got the old place looking shipshape again. Like it did in their father's day. I'm sorry I wasn't able to help more with the restoration."

He was just as deft at speaking to her as to her aunt—both praising their efforts and chiding her for being the one who'd forbidden him to help. Making it sound as though that "not able" was due to his own schedule instead of her command.

"It was a lot of work." A safe enough statement. "But rewarding." And a much-needed distraction as December loomed ever closer. As it arrived. As that date on the calendar, which so many looked forward to, made every bone in her body double in weight.

Leopard stripes. Papier-mâché wouldn't be enough to get her through this month. That's why she'd been carefully building a stone wall around not only her heart but also her memories.

"Well, everyone's efforts have paid off. The wedding is beautiful, as is the bride—nearly as beautiful as her attendant. I can't help but remember—"

"Stop." She'd meant it to come out as a command, brisk and brusque as if it had fallen from Aunt Priss's lips. Instead, it emerged as a squeak, desperate and thin.

He was going to bring it up. The very thing Aunt Priss had silently accused her of with a pointed look instead of words. *Of course* he would.

"What?" He leaned a little closer. "I was only going to say it reminded me of that first ball we snuck down to watch. Don't you remember? We were, what, eight and ten? We thought we were being so sneaky but were bored to tears within fifteen minutes."

Her shoulders relaxed. They'd snuck back out and had run with the wild abandon of children down to the shore—strictly forbidden to them after dark—and dipped their toes into the ice-cold water of the North Sea until they were shivering and laughing and convinced that the adults had it all wrong. Why choose a stuffy ballroom when they could choose a moonlight caper instead?

And this—*this*—was why she avoided him. Because this was what happened if she didn't. He slid too close, reminded her too quickly of what once had been, made her want to remember all the wrong things. More dangerous things, even, than the memories she was tiptoeing around. Happiness and hope and innocence and love songs.

That wasn't real. What was real was broken hearts and despair, betrayal and dirges.

She took a step away. "I don't want to remember. Not that. Not . . . anything." She couldn't. Couldn't let herself. Because calling one sweet memory to mind would bring more, and then she'd end up right back in the place she never wanted to be again.

Graham moved with her. "Darling, please. It's been nearly a year—"

She couldn't have said which of his words brought the fury rushing back, filling her veins and pushing her past him in one sweeping motion. The endearment? The plea? The reminder of those full twelve pages of the calendar that had flipped by since the world came to a screeching, shattering halt?

"You think I don't know how long it's been?" She hissed the words when she wanted to shout them, clenched her fist when she wanted to pound it into his chest. "You think I haven't counted every month, every week, every day, every hour?"

His face shifted from earnest and pleading to as cold and hard as the granite he favored in his work. "You think I haven't too? If you would just talk to me—"

"Why? You never listen. Had you listened a year ago—"

"You think I don't know that?" Somehow he managed to whisper his own shout, but the volume certainly didn't mute the fire in the words. "You think I haven't replayed that conversation in my head a million times? You think I haven't regretted it every single minute of every single day?"

Of course he did. But regret changed nothing. Sorrow changed nothing. A million apologies couldn't undo the damage his arrogance and pride had caused.

And if she didn't escape this ballroom right this minute, she'd ruin her best friend's wedding ball with a fit of weeping that was sure to garner the attention she wanted to avoid at all costs. With a shake of her head, she stormed away, out of the conversation, out of his presence, out of the ballroom.

She didn't stop until she'd walked directly out into the courtyard. They'd taken the trapeze down for the wedding so that Merritt's family and friends wouldn't wonder at it. Gemma had never had the skill on it that Marigold and Yates had, but tonight she could have done with swinging from the bar and letting the wind chase away the tears. Let it ruin her hair and replace the warmth of Graham's nearness. Let the rush of gravity and air pull her out of her head and away from the memories always lingering right below the surface.

Another rush of wind as the borrowed car spun out of control. Another squeak, not of guidewires, but of body panels.

No. *No.* The memories had gotten even heavier as the weather cooled again. When her foot crunched through the layer of ice on top of a puddle, she very nearly shattered too. But she wouldn't let herself fall into that. Not here. Not now. Not while *he* was right inside, when he might chase her out here.

"Gemma?"

At least it wasn't Aunt Priss. Gemma sniffed, telling herself her nose was running from the cold air and not from the tears burning her eyes. She pasted on a smile and turned back to the door from which she'd just run. The happy friend. The well-wisher. *Imposter.* "The bride shouldn't be sneaking away from her own wedding ball, Marigold. Get back inside."

She didn't. She came to Gemma's side instead, not even shivering in her gown of silk and lace, though Gemma was, she suddenly realized, quaking more than she ought to be from mere cold.

Marigold draped a shawl, colorless in the moonlight, over Gemma's shoulders. "We should have had the wedding in November. Or January."

"Don't be ridiculous." Marigold had always wanted a December wedding, filled with holly and ivy, yew and laurel, and the promise of eternity . . . before she'd given up on the idea of marriage when her father died. When Merritt resparked those dreams, they'd breathed life again into her old imaginings.

Marigold frowned. "I told you December was a bad idea."

"I wanted the distraction." And it had worked, as long as Graham was safely in London while Gemma, Marigold, and Yates were all here. She could ignore the gap his absence left, fill it with busyness and plans and laughter. She could write up extra columns and pen a few stories she'd never show anyone and read novels until her eyes went blurry and crossed and there was no room left in her head for reality.

Sighing, Marigold slid an arm around Gemma's waist and pulled her tight, resting her forehead on hers. They were the same height. The same size, had the same general figure. They'd learned to walk in the same way, had studied the same posture. They had worked for years to be interchangeable.

But never before had it been clearer that they weren't. There stood Marigold in her breathtaking wedding gown, the future spread out before her, filled with warmth and light.

And here was Gemma in the shadows, nothing but her words to keep her company, a lifetime of winter waiting.

"Come inside, Gem," her friend whispered after a long, pulsing moment of frozen silence. "You'll turn to ice out here."

She let Marigold tug her inside. But she didn't know why she bothered.

She'd turned to ice almost a year ago, and there was no fire on earth strong enough to thaw her again.

TWO

20 December 1909
London, England

Graham Wharton stared at the blueprint anchored down on his drafting table, but the weak winter sunlight that pooled on the paper had no hope of breaking through the fog. He knew very well that he needed to pull out his slide rule and a scrap sheet of paper and do some maths. He knew he had to sort out very practical questions, like how many support beams the tower would require and how far apart they could be.

But for the life of him, all he could think about was Gemma in that blasted evening gown at Marigold's wedding, standing there like one of these drawn support pillars, immobile and stiff.

She wasn't supposed to be like that. Gemma had always been the first one to take to the dance floor, laughter spilling from her lips, lamplight gilding her fair hair with gold. How many times over the years had he teased her about her enthusiasm? *Gemma-Gem, sparkling like a diamond. Gemma-Gem, gleaming like an emerald. Gemma-Gem, with her ruby red lips always ready to smile.*

The wedding ball was the first he'd seen her smile in

nearly a year. A *year*. It hadn't been for him, and it hadn't been sincere, and it certainly hadn't sparkled like a gemstone.

Even so, it had knocked the wind out of him. He'd seen it still in his mind's eye after she stormed from the room, and he'd been seeing it ever since.

And it wasn't just *one* smile he saw. It was a whole collage of them. All her smiles through the years, starting from the one she'd given him when he was a confused, lonely boy sent to live with cousins he'd never met. Her smile then had been the beacon telling him safe harbor waited there. It had been the beacon calling him home ever since.

And yet here he was. Home, but without Gemma.

Graham tossed his pencil down, squeezed his eyes shut, and leaned back on his stool. Tipping his head back showed him the rafters of his office, artfully dark against the white plaster of the ceiling. He'd unveiled them himself when he fitted out the garret for a studio, had enlarged the windows to let in the light, and had positioned his drafting table and desk just so. He'd worked from one of the bedrooms at the start, but that hadn't been an option for long—and this space had been one of the reasons this house had appealed. It had taken him nearly a year to complete the work. He'd been so proud—proud to have a position at a premier architecture firm, proud to have this house, proud to have the most beautiful woman in all of England on his arm.

Proud. Arrogant. Foolish. Those had become that woman's favorite words to apply to him. The fact that he'd admitted she was right didn't soften her stance either or inspire her to choose new words. No, they'd only gotten worse. *"You're the most arrogant, selfish man I've ever met. You've ruined everything. I hate you!"*

Graham stood, giving up on the blueprints for the new library meant to model an older one destroyed a century ago by fire. He had months before the plans were due anyway, since they wouldn't break ground until spring.

He moved over to the garret window, looking out at his tidy back garden. The house was on the edge of London, a short Tube ride from the firm's office, and perhaps more importantly, the National Archives. But the area was not so crowded that one couldn't stretch out and breathe. In the spring, herbs and flowers would nudge their heads up through the soil. In the summer, they'd provide a riot of colorful blooms.

Now it looked bleak and bare and brown. Lifeless, much like he felt more often than not.

The wind-bells spun in the breeze, dancing and singing all at once. He should have taken them in when the weather turned, but he hadn't. Just like he hadn't last year, though for an entirely different reason.

Last year, they'd stayed up because they brought laughter. This year, they stayed up because their every cheerful chime was a reminder of what he'd lost.

A different bell sounded, deep and throaty compared to the tinkle of thin tubes from the garden. Graham spun around, wishing he'd been standing at the opposite window, looking down on the street, so he'd know who was ringing for entrance.

If it was his boss, he'd let him in. Mr. Carter was set to leave Town to spend the next month with his brother's family in the country, and no doubt he had more instructions on the research he'd like Graham to do in his absence. If it was Yates, he'd welcome the distraction of a friend and cousin who always knew when to push and when to rest, who reminded Graham with his very youth that life hadn't really ended twelve months ago. If it was Aunt Priss, finally accepting his invitation, he'd play the gracious host and try to pry information on Gemma out of her. If it was James, he'd pretend he wasn't here, despite the light spilling from the windows.

It didn't really matter. Good manners had been too well ingrained. His feet were already taking him down the stairs, his voice was already calling out, "Coming!" He let himself steal only one glance at the darkened room that had been his first studio; the lavender scent drifting from the space nearly pulled him in.

Focus, Graham. He dragged in a breath as he neared the front door. He'd slam it in James's face if it was him, like he'd done last month. He'd always liked Gemma's brother—still did, as a man. But not as a vicar concerned for his soul, and that was all he seemed to be these days. Every time he'd dropped by lately, it had been to try to convince him that he ought to put his hand back into the Lord's.

Graham had given up on insisting he wasn't having a crisis of faith. Given up trying to explain that it wasn't that he doubted God's existence—it was that he doubted His goodness. It wasn't that He questioned for a minute whether or not He was Lord—it was that he couldn't believe the Lord loved them like James insisted He did. All evidence pointed to the contrary.

He really ought to have installed a peephole, or at least a window beside the door that would show him who stood out there. As it was, he felt a bit like a soldier prepared to charge blindly into battle as he pulled open the door.

Yates, with his boyish grin and hair flopping over his forehead under his hat. Graham relaxed and even pulled out a smile of his own as he held the door wide. "My lord."

His cousin—fourth cousin, if one were being specific—rolled his eyes and strode inside, giving an exaggerated shudder as he shrugged out of his greatcoat. "It's beastly out there. The Caesars predict a cold and snowy winter, so brace yourself."

He said it flippantly, but Graham's every muscle went taut. They'd had heavy snowfall last Christmas too. He'd let himself hope this winter would be mild enough to keep the memories at bay.

As if anything ever kept the memories at bay.

Yates turned, winced, and hung his coat on its usual hook. "Sorry, old boy."

Graham pulled a smile onto his mouth with sheer willpower. "No need to apologize for talking about the weather. And I've long ago learned never to question the Caesars' predictions. They're better than either the almanac or the meteorologists."

"Without question." Yates hesitated a moment more, as if debating whether to say something, then brightened. "Well. I have the list of likely buildings for this new job. I thought we could go over it while you offer me tea."

Maybe it was the way Yates tried so hard to be how he'd always been, or maybe it was his way of sponging tea or a meal from Graham each and every time he stopped by, but he couldn't help but chuckle. "How is it that you are *always* hungry?"

"I suppose I can't claim to be a growing boy anymore, can I?"

It had been his excuse for the last five years, but at two and twenty, he finally seemed to have stopped sprouting upward . . . though he was still getting broader, and every bit of it was solid muscle. Sometimes it was strange to look at the young man he'd always thought of as a boy and realize he was taller and stronger than Graham would ever be. A veritable circus strongman at this point—by design. "No, but I suppose you can claim you worked off your breakfast and lunch in the gymnasium."

"I did, at that." Too at home here to await an invitation, Yates aimed himself toward the kitchen. "Do you have any of that cheese you had last week? Where did you find that, anyway?"

"The shop down the street. And yes—and a fresh loaf of bread too, so help yourself." He would offer some of the biscuits or tart that he'd picked up from the bakery, but he knew well neither Yates nor Marigold ever ate sweets. They said it affected their performance in the gymnasium.

Graham said that it was a worthwhile trade. They could keep their trapeze and highwire and rings. He'd enjoy a biscuit now and then, thank you very much.

While Yates rummaged in the icebox, Graham put the kettle on and pulled down the tea tin from the cupboard, then reached for two of the teacups that Gemma had picked out. "What sort of buildings are on your list?"

"Couple private residences, a government building or two, a bank." Yates's lips quirked up again. "I imagine that last one will be simple as can be, right?"

Graham snorted. "Just don't ask for a way into the vault and we'll be fine. If it's offices you need to eavesdrop on, I don't anticipate much of a problem." And with any luck, they'd be in buildings of historical significance. Those he could almost always find schematics for in the National Archives.

"As I expected. Nothing terribly interesting this go-round, sorry."

"So you say." He watched Yates measure out the tea. "Though I'd remind you that I've found interesting facets of many a building you dubbed boring over the years."

"Hence," Yates declared, turning to cut a generous slice of bread, "why you're invaluable at this part of the research and I stick with climbing the walls and doing the necessary acrobatics."

"Which I don't envy you, so there we have it." The perfect team. Graham to do the research on the buildings and find the Imposters ins and outs and hiding places, Yates and Marigold to do the actual jumping and climbing and squeezing into tight spots to eavesdrop, Gemma to write up whatever articles they needed to provide them with alibis and paint the picture of the Fairfax siblings that they wanted society to know, and now Merritt to help with strategy and keep an ear on anything government or military related, which was certain to prove invaluable too.

"How's the library coming along?"

"Slowly, but there's no rush." He almost wished there were. Perhaps a looming deadline would have been a stronger distraction from All Things December. "Milk in your tea today?"

Yates pursed his lips. He was the only person Graham knew who took his cup differently from day to day. Now milk, now a single drop of honey, now black. "Not today, I think. Though I thank you."

He always did *that* too, thanking Graham for the luxuries neither of them had thought to question when they were boys. Luxuries they'd all had to forgo when they realized there wasn't so much as a shilling left in the Fairfax coffers after Yates's and Marigold's father died. Luxuries Graham could finally afford again in small doses, thanks to his career, while his higher-stationed cousins were still scrimping and saving every pence to keep the Tower running.

He gave them as much as they'd take. The Tower was *his* home too, thanks to the previous Lord Fairfax's generosity. He'd been only seven when his mother died, leaving him orphaned and alone. If his lordship hadn't taken him in, he'd have ended up in an orphanage somewhere, despite being from a good family. Instead, he'd entered the enchanted world of Fairfax Tower, where he had endless delights, ready-made friends, and the promise of connections that could lead him to whatever career or vocation he wanted to pursue.

There had never been any question, not since he first explored the ancient manor house he got to call home and the just-as-ancient Alnwick Abbey all but next door. Something about buildings—the way they merged beauty with functionality, strength with whimsy—captured him entirely.

His lordship had sent him to Eton even while Yates had opted to remain at home with tutors. Had seen he had the best mentors, had paid for university and made all the introductions. Graham had discovered that the thing he loved best—studying old blueprints, schematics, and drawings, and translating them into modern reality—was what set him apart. His proficiency in the Archives had landed him his current position, and slowly but surely, he was beginning to procure some of the top jobs in the country that involved recreating or borrowing inspiration from old, oft-forgotten buildings. It was an honor to be able to repay the Fairfaxes for their family's investment in him.

And, of course, it was pure fun to be an Imposter. He was rarely ever called to do any of the on-the-ground work, but he knew he was invaluable to the team. Otherwise Gemma would have convinced them to kick him to the curb a year ago, no doubt.

Something ricocheted off the back of his head, more startling than painful. "Hey!" He spun around, only to find that Yates had another almond ready to lob.

His friend pointed with his missile toward the kettle. Which was whistling. "I've warned you about getting lost in that labyrinth of a brain of yours."

And always found something to throw at his head to draw him back. Graham picked up the nut from the floor, brushed it off, and returned it to the bowl of them waiting by the nutcracker. "Some people snap their fingers or say my name."

"Because some people haven't the impeccable aim I have and risk breaking the china when they throw things at you."

Too true. Chuckling, Graham poured the water over the tea. "Have you seen Marigold yet since she got home?"

"They're coming over this evening." Yates sighed, his whole face drooping. "This bachelorhood thing isn't nearly so much fun without a roommate or two. I'm going to try to convince them to let their rented house go and move into Fairfax House while they're in London. I will solemnly swear not to bother them and give them all the space they need—heaven knows there's enough of it."

Ordinarily, Graham would have said that the chances of convincing a newly married sister to move back in with her brother were slim to nil. But Marigold and Yates were more tightly knit than the average siblings. They actually liked each other, even. They'd been a unit against the world for many hard years. "Just tell her you'll bar her from the gymnasium if she doesn't live there."

Yates snorted. "That might do it. She does get awfully irritable if she doesn't have her equipment for more than a week. I daresay she was such a pest by the end of the honeymoon that poor Merritt was ready to toss her into the sea."

"No question." He handed one of the cups to Yates and sat opposite him at the secondhand table.

For a long moment, silence reigned. Then Yates sighed again, turning serious eyes on him. "I don't know how you do it. Living here alone, I mean."

Graham took a sip of tea, even though he knew well it would be too hot. Better a scalded tongue than the slicing truth—this house had never been meant to be his alone. Living here with only echoes and memories to haunt him . . . sometimes it soothed. More often, it pummeled his heart anew every day. "You aren't totally alone, are you? Neville and Clementina are there—"

"Sometimes, but their rehearsals have been at odd hours lately."

The actor-slash-butler and his wife, actress-slash-cook, weren't really his intended topic anyway. "And Gemma's there."

Yates arrowed a glance into him that said *Don't think you can fool me. I know you're fishing for information.* "She's been staying with James since the wedding. Apparently I was 'moping' too much since I came back to London. Not that I wouldn't rather be in Northumberland, but this job . . ."

The downside of the business, to be sure. Northumberland was rarely a good base of operations—aside from the case Sir Merritt had hired them for last spring. "You? Moping?"

"I know! I haven't a moping bone in my body." He sighed again—which was so obvious a sign of moping that Graham had to hide another laugh in his scalding cup. "If the vicarage were bigger, I'd have threatened to go with her. Gemma and James are far better company than an empty house. But then—Aunt Priss." Yates gave an exaggerated shudder.

Graham chuckled. "You can always stay here if you're that desperate for company."

Yates brightened a bit. "Careful, old boy. I might take you up on that if I can't convince the newlyweds to call the House their home."

Graham found himself hoping they'd insist on their distance.

Solitude was seriously overrated.

THREE

21 December 1909

*Y*ates watched the lazy snowflakes twirling their way through the air outside the window of James Parks's church office and checked his pocket watch again. He'd left himself far too much time today before his appointment with another potential client because . . . well, because it had been too blasted quiet at home, and he was fairly certain he would be destined for the madhouse by Christmas if this kept up.

On the bright side, Marigold and Merritt had both wholeheartedly agreed that Fairfax House was too big for one lone bachelor, and they would be delighted to move in as soon as the lease was up on Merritt's rented house.

On the downside, that lease wasn't up for another two months.

Two months for newlyweds to be on their own was surely a good thing. He knew that. Intellectually. But practically, it didn't stop the house from being too blasted quiet in the meantime, when it *ought* to be filled with his sister humming Christmas carols and their skeleton staff making merry.

For that matter, he hated spending Christmas in London. Winters were much more pleasant, somehow, in the drafty halls of Fairfax Tower, where it was *supposed* to be cold and windy and damp—but happily so. It made him almost wish he'd declined this investigation that would keep him chained to Town for much of the winter.

Almost. Except for the fact of the thousand pounds sterling he'd collected for his trouble. That did weight the scale a bit in London's favor. A bit.

And perhaps it was best for them all *not* to be in Northumberland this December. Too many reminders of snowy tragedy waited to pounce on the icy roads of home.

"Ah, here it is!" James pulled a book from the shelf and presented it with a flourish. "I knew I'd put it here somewhere."

Yates accepted the tome with a smile and flipped it open to the title page. He'd been wanting to reread MacDonald's *At the Back of the North Wind* ever since the wedding, but he hadn't been able to locate his copy anywhere.

Apparently because he'd lent it to James a decade ago and never thought to reclaim it. Yates opened the cover, and there it was—the faint pencil mark of his initials in the upper right corner. "And right in the nick of time. It will keep me company in the confessional."

"Good luck with that. It's a bit too dim, if you ask me, to be reading without a lamp."

"I have my torch." He patted the pocket that was never empty of the tools of his trade—the small electric torch, the set of master keys, a file, and a pen-knife. Plus, of course, the irony of an earl who had a trade—he certainly never left home without an appreciation of *that*. "I'd better hurry along."

"Don't forget the choir will be coming in this afternoon. You'll want to make certain your meeting doesn't run more than an hour if you want to avoid the early arrivals."

"Noted." He nodded his thanks and strode out of the office,

soon taking his usual seat in the confessor's side of the old, otherwise-unused confessional booth, relic of an age gone by when this cathedral was Catholic rather than Anglican.

He still had forty minutes before the potential new client was supposed to arrive, but one couldn't count on potential clients to be on time. Sometimes they were late, other times they were frightfully early. Yates had always taken care to remain anonymous but especially since taking his seat in Parliament. He always slipped into his side of the booth well before schedule to avoid the possibility of being seen.

He didn't switch on the torch or open the book, though. Normally he would have, at least for a few minutes, but this time he pulled out the request for a meeting instead. He'd already read it a dozen times since it was delivered that morning, but something about it continued to niggle at him.

Need meeting as soon as possible. Of the utmost urgency. Today, if possible. Tomorrow at the latest. Lives at stake.

Drama? Yates was no stranger to such flair, living as he did with actors playing the roles of servants when necessary. And why would someone come to the Imposters if lives were on the line? They were investigators, not the police. If something were truly that urgent, they ought to be beseeching the actual authorities and not mysterious private investigators.

It had intrigued him, though. Urgent could mean easily squeezed in around the tasks for the other job, something quickly taken care of. Urgent could also come with a nice price tag that would allow him to purchase his sister and Merritt a fine gift for Christmas.

Urgent could be the distraction he needed to combat the empty house as well as the memories of last year's horrendous Christmas.

He'd written back straightaway, saying he could meet the man here at the church at three o'clock that afternoon, if it suited him. He'd sent the note, as he always did, via street urchin—and had gotten a confirmation far sooner than he'd expected. And so here he was, debating which of his arsenal of characters he would be, when he'd originally expected to be spending another boring hour with his barbells while he waited for Graham to get back to him with research on the buildings for the Ascot job.

He would go Cockney today, that was what. A grown-up version of Tiny Tim, given the season. That would do nicely.

The sound of the church's front door squeaking open and falling shut brought his brows down and his watch out of his pocket again. A full thirty-six minutes early. Either the potential client was one of the sort who hoped to get the drop on the Imposters and sort out who they were, or he was truly in a desperate situation.

Well, lionfeathers. Yates hadn't even had time to do his customary examination of conscience—a fitting rite, he'd always thought, before a meeting held in a confessional.

Quick footfalls sounded, even and only hesitating for a moment. Yates could imagine the man scoping out the scene, spotting the confessional, and then all but running along the side aisle, past the pews. His breathing was ragged, as if he'd run the whole way there from the Tube station.

Why, when he was so early as it was?

The penitent's door opened, closed, and whoever entered fell onto the bench with a huff that sounded nearer to a sob than a bid for oxygen.

Urgent. Definitely, honestly urgent. Yates took the time to say a prayer for whoever it was before he put on his Not-So-Tiny Tim. "Mite early, ain't you, gov'nor?"

The gasp-sob-huff caught in the man's throat, only to be cleared a moment later. "Praise God—you're already here. I prayed you would be. My shift begins at three thirty, but I was afraid if I asked for an earlier appointment, we wouldn't have time to confirm."

Shift? Yates shifted all right, frowning more than ever. Working men weren't their clientele. Working men couldn't afford their services. Working men wouldn't even *know* of their services. They'd made certain of that.

Not because they didn't sympathize with the pains of the working man, mind you—simply because what working men could afford to pay wouldn't allow them to feed and clothe the people who depended on them, few as they currently were.

Something else bothered Yates too—he knew the voice. He couldn't place it, but it was familiar. "Glad the Lord whispered in my ear, then. Shall we cut to the chase?"

"Please. Thank you." The man moved on his bench, leaning closer to the grate between them. "My name is Matthew Hart."

Hart . . . Hart . . . *Hart!* Yates nearly huffed out a breath of his own. Hart had a shift that evening, all right—at the Marlborough Club, where he was a waiter. Most assuredly *not* someone who could afford the services of the Imposters, even given the generous tips gents often left him for his truly conscientious service. But it did explain how he'd come by one of their cards, to know how to inquire.

"Good to make your acquaintance, Mr. Hart. Call me Mr. C." Usually he went by Mr. A—for Anonymous—but he'd tip his hat to Timothy Cratchit this time. "Now, why don't you tell me why—"

"It's my son." The words exploded from Hart's lips in a quiet blast. "He's been kidnapped."

All of the fun of a *Carol*-themed meeting evaporated. "Beg pardon?"

"My son has been kidnapped—on Friday last, the seventeenth. My wife and I—we've spent all weekend at the police station here or in Derbyshire, but the blighters have insisted they have no viable leads."

"Wait." His Cockney nearly slipped, but he pulled it back on just in time. "Derbyshire, you say? Why Derbyshire?"

Hart sucked in a long breath. "Perhaps I ought to begin at the beginning."

"Do." He even pulled out his notepad and pencil, which he rarely used in these meetings. Neville and the rest of the theater troupe had drilled him and Marigold both in memorization so that they could recall most of what they heard long enough to get to a private place after a meeting and dictate the conversation onto paper—preferably in shorthand, if Gemma was handy. But he had a feeling the details were going to fall like rain from Matthew Hart's lips, and he didn't want to risk missing anything vital. "Go on."

"All right." Another deep breath. "My wife shouldn't have married me—I was beneath her."

Yates let a grunt of protest fill his throat. "Maybe not back *quite* that far, mate."

"No, it's relevant, I promise. She was the daughter of a vicar who was in turn the second son of a baronet. A fine, respectable family. She ought to have married a gentleman, but we fell in love."

Yates leaned back against the wall. "As you do."

"We did. And we've no regrets, not about the life we've built together. Her sister, though—she fell in love too, but with a man who oughtn't really to have married *her*."

"A titled gent? Or a rich one?"

"Both. Lord Wilfred."

Wilfred? Yates pressed the tip of his pencil so hard against the pad that the tip broke—not that he needed to write that down. There was no hope he'd ever forget *that* name. He may not have been in Parliament long yet, but long enough to recognize that Lord Wilfred was one of the most coldhearted, cutthroat men in Lords. "I've 'eard of him. Never 'eard he married down, though."

"Of course not. He played up the respectable side of the family and pretended my wife and I didn't exist. Except that . . ."

"Yeah?"

"Our lads. We had sons the same age, and I was stationed abroad at the time of his birth, so my sweet Caroline stayed with her sister during their lying-ins. Wilfred didn't let it be known they were sisters and that our lads were cousins, just called Caro Nan's companion."

All right. So two sisters who still loved each other and shared company, though they'd chosen different lives. "Were you commissioned?"

"Enlisted. Royal Navy, until two years ago."

Ah. *Very* different lives, then. "Go on."

"Well, the ruse worked well enough. Caro and Nan looked nothing alike, you see. Any time I was gone, she'd go to Fellsbourne—that's Wilfred's country estate. The sisters would visit, and the boys would play together. More oft than not, Wilfred was away when she was there, in Town or off seeing to business."

He had a lot of that, Yates knew. Wilfred had come up peripherally in so many of their investigations that his dossier was nearly as thick as a case file.

FROM THE DOSSIER OF
Lord Philmore Wilfred, earl

HEIGHT: *6'*

WEIGHT: *12 stone*

AGE: *43*

HAIR: *Worn with a right-side part, pomaded into a heavy swoop toward the left. Short, cropped sides. Middling brown, darker with pomade.*

EYES: *Hazel*

STYLE: *Always dressed in impeccable suits—traditionally from Davies & Sons, but most recently has helped bring acclaim to the newcomer, Anderson & Sheppard. Favors the new drape-cut jacket (which is dratted uncomfortable) ^but flattering. Yates, you should wear it more often!*

OBSERVANCES: *Lord Wilfred keeps strict hours. He is always up at precisely six o'clock, will halt whatever business he's involved in to lunch precisely at noon, and will not meet with anyone outside of social reasons beyond six in the evening. He expects his world to run like a well-oiled machine, which is perhaps why he has invested heavily in a variety of industrial and mechanical companies.*

His wife died in childbirth in 1907, along with the baby girl. (After which his "friends" report he grew insufferable.)

One son, Horace (poor dear), who bears the subsidiary title of Viscount of Sheffield, born in 1899. Attends Ludgrove as prep for Eton (shocking!).

CASES IN WHICH HE HAS BEEN OBSERVED: *Adams, Grant, Worcester, Miller, Bligh, Fennwick, Josten, Rawlings*

IMPRESSIONS: *He's an arrogant prig, known as cruel and cold and cutthroat in business circles and not well loved by his tenants. Avoid him at all costs.*

So much for that closing bit of advice Yates had scratched into the file after his last observation of Wilfred during the Adams case. It seemed this one was going to encounter him again, perhaps more than peripherally. "All right, then. Your son and young Lord Sheffield are cousins and perhaps friends?"

"The best of friends. It was Horace's pleading that convinced Wilfred to pay for our Sidney to go to school with him."

Yates's stomach felt tight, and not because he'd spent an extra hour in the gymnasium this morning from sheer boredom. "I don't much like where this is going. Where was your lad stolen from, Mr. Hart, on Friday?"

"From the train station nearest Ludgrove, when he was coming home for his Christmas holidays. He ought to have been home within an hour, but when he didn't show up, his mum and I thought he'd missed the train or decided to pull a prank again."

"Again?"

Hart sighed. "He and Horace—well, Nan and Caro may not have looked alike, but the boys are near identical. They could pass for twins, and they've pulled the old Prince and Pauper gag enough times that all their teachers are wise to them. In his last letter, Sid mentioned that His Lordship was making Horace pay a visit to his grandaunt before he went home, and Horace didn't want to go. Sid likes the old bird, though. We thought maybe he'd gone in Horace's place—and sure enough, Horace apparently arrived at Fellsbourne directly. He didn't detour to Clareton Hall."

Using the least-obnoxious edge of the broken tip, Yates scrawled the estate names onto his paper. "But I assume your Sidney never showed up there either?"

"Nor at Fellsbourne, and certainly not at home, where he should have come. He just vanished."

Yates rubbed a finger against the crease between his brows. "How do you know it was a kidnapping?"

"Because a ransom note showed up—at Fellsbourne, for Wilfred. They thought it Horace they'd snatched. Because he was where Horace was supposed to be, while my nephew was happily chugging his way home, safe and sound."

Yates could hear the panic rising in Hart's voice with each word, and he could hardly blame him. "How much? The ransom, I mean?"

"Eighty thousand pounds."

A staggering sum that made Yates choke on his own saliva and cough a protest. "Beg pardon?"

"I won't make that in a lifetime, and Wilfred doesn't have that kind of cash lying about—and even if he did, he wouldn't give it, not for Sidney. He told us in no uncertain terms that we're on our own. He won't even pay for an investigator, only for a guard for his *own* son." Now his voice went taut, angry. "He wouldn't even show the ransom note to the police, though I've copied it out. He said if we told the authorities to talk to him, he'd claim he'd never met us and that *we* were the ones trying to get money from him. Which meant that the police began to even doubt we have a son who's missing. Thought we were after Horace."

Leopard stripes. Sometimes justice was anything but just. "Hence why they claim no viable leads, then."

Hart huffed. "If you ask me, His Lordship's not sorry it happened. He's been looking for a reason to cut us out of their lives entirely, and he'll take the opportunity now, despite Horace's distress over it."

For a moment there, Yates hoped that Wilfred was the one ready to foot the bill from the Imposters, if they took the case. But Hart's words dashed that thought to bits.

It didn't matter, though. This wasn't their usual fare of faithless spouses or underhanded business dealings or questionable identities. This really was a matter of life and death.

Because if someone thought they'd nabbed the pampered son of one of England's wealthiest lords only to realize they'd ended up with the nephew he didn't care a whit for, it could spell bad news for Sidney. And neither Yates nor any of the other Imposters could sit back and let that happen, not if they had even the smallest hope of stopping it.

"We'll take the case," he said, his Cockney rough and rasping. "Pro bono."

"Pro what?"

"It means for the good of doing it. No retainer. No fees. No charge."

"No charge?" Hart pressed a hand to the grate. "Are you joking? I know your fees are high. I work at the Marlborough; I've heard bits and pieces from the gents you've done work for before. That's why I know you're the best, sir."

"Then you know you can't afford us."

"I do—but we have a house, Caro and I. A gift from her grandparents. We'll mortgage it, sell it outright—"

"You won't. We'll not take money for this." Lionfeathers. Though his accent remained right, he'd slipped into the wrong cadence there. He cleared his throat and chanted *Timothy Cratchit* in his head three times. "Happy Christmas."

It wouldn't be, though. Not unless they managed to find his son. "Do you have any of this put down in writing yet?"

"Everything. All the reports we've made with the police, Horace's account of the prank, all the headmaster of Ludgrove could tell us, what the stationmaster saw—all of it."

"Good. Leave it. Get to your shift. We'll be in touch."

In the penitent's stall, Hart stood, and the sharp smack of paper slapped the bench. "Bless you, Mr. C. When? When will we hear from you?"

Yates's eyes slid shut. When indeed? "The very moment we have something to report."

FOUR

$\mathcal{G}$emma's arms, crossed over her chest, provided little defense against the bombardment of emotions flying around the room, waiting to catch her out. Yates had called an All Imposters meeting, which she knew from the start would be charged simply because of that "all." Stuffing her and Graham in the same room and forcing them to be civil was challenging enough. But the case?

The case made it a thousand times worse. Because she couldn't say no to finding a missing child, no more than Yates had been able to—no matter how much it hurt. Never mind the fact that they'd have to pay for every bit of it from their own pockets—thank heavens their pockets weren't *quite* so empty as normal, compliments of Sir Merritt. They couldn't say no.

That didn't mean her heart didn't feel absolutely battered after the first five minutes of the conversation. She still stood in the corner in which she'd planted herself when she arrived, as far away from Graham as she could get in the library of Fairfax House. She listened to every word as the others huddled over the mess of papers from Matthew Hart that they'd spread out over the table.

But part of her was on a cold, snowy roadside, the world

in pieces around her, and she couldn't bring herself back to the present enough to enter the conversation about finding Sidney Hart.

"We don't even know if it was him, though, at the train station in Basingstoke. That statement from the stevedore isn't exactly definitive." Marigold stood with her hands braced on the table, her left arm just touching Merritt's right in that way of a couple who found comfort in any small touch.

Without conscious effort, the statement flitted back through Gemma's mind. The distraught parents had flashed a photograph of their son at the likely stops between London and Sussex, with the thought that he'd boarded a train to visit this doting aunt who would ply him with sweets, thinking him her grandnephew, and then send him on his way with Christmas presents. Given the flood of schoolchildren returning home from their various boarding schools on the same day, finding anyone who remembered one rather average lad had proven all but impossible. One stevedore, though, had said, *"Aye, I saw a lad throwing a fit when 'is da dragged him toward a train, nigh onto six o'clock. Coulda been 'im, I s'ppose."*

When pressed as to why he called the man taking the boy his father, he'd only shrugged. *"Just 'sumed, is all. No reason not to think so, aye?"*

The Harts had recorded that and every other conversation they'd had over the weekend onto those pages on the table already, so Gemma had no reason to put the words down now, which was usually her job. Thus it gave her leave to go on standing in the corner, the bookshelf behind her digging into her back. Pain that was strangely welcome simply because it was minor. Because it anchored her here.

"It makes sense, though." Yates tapped a finger to the map he'd spread out. She didn't have to be able to read it to know he'd be indicating the southern coast of England.

"The ransom note demanded the cash be left at the church in Weymouth on Christmas Eve—and more, it said if it were, then the boy would be delivered to Midnight Mass."

"But it doesn't say he'll be delivered *there* at Midnight Mass. It could be to his home church," Marigold replied.

Her brother shook his head. "If the kidnappers will be there to collect the ransom, it's logical that that's where they'll deliver the child."

"Quite right." Merritt, though the newest member of the team, wasn't shy about offering his insights and opinions. "Any other time of year, perhaps, a kidnapper would be set on remaining far away and relying on communication from a hireling via telephone or telegram. But that won't be feasible on Christmas Eve since all the lines will be down. And with that much money being requested, the culprit himself will want to be nearby to receive it."

"Too true." Graham had pulled some book or another from the shelves ten minutes ago, but aside from noting that it had—shock of all shocks—photographs of old buildings in it, she made no effort to identify it. "You couldn't hire just anyone to collect it. It would have to be someone you trust implicitly."

"And we can't assume the motivation for the kidnapping is the ransom alone, not given how many enemies Lord Wilfred has." Yates had tossed his jacket and tie to a chair and had his shirtsleeves rolled up over his muscular forearms. He abandoned the map and the papers entirely and paced to the window. "This could well be a personal vendetta—revenge more than extortion."

Marigold sighed and leaned more into Merritt's side. "What do we know about the ransom drop location?"

All eyes turned to Graham at that one, even Gemma's. Perhaps it was because of the year in which she'd scarcely seen him, but looking at him now, bent over the books on the table, she saw Young Graham as much as Current Graham. She'd seen him just like that at age eight, age twelve, age sixteen. Always trying to unlock the secrets of brick and stone from an old drawing.

And he'd done it too. Always had.

Now he tapped a finger to the page. "St. Nicholas Cathedral is on the corner of Weywent Manor property—owned now by the Dowager Countess of Weymouth."

Yates pivoted back again. "What do we know about Weywent Manor?"

Graham flipped a page in the book. "It was originally built in the fifteenth century, over the ruins of a much older monastery and fortification against the Vikings. The central part of the house claims to be original, with two wings added on in the seventeenth centuries. Quite a few updates were made over the years, though this book is too old to tell me if plumbing and electricity are among them." He shot a playful glare at Yates.

Yates snorted. "You know well that it is *your* responsibility to update our books on heritage sites, Mr. Architect. If you have complaints, you have only yourself to blame."

Graham was already studying the book again in that way he had. His dark eyes so intent upon the words and photographs, seeking out details no one else even knew to look for, that he didn't seem to notice that one hand was lazily scratching at his head, disrupting the careful combing of his hair.

Her own fingers twitched. Once upon a time, she'd watched him ruffle those locks and then taken joy in smoothing them back down for him. Once upon a time, she'd have draped an arm over his shoulders and made a caricature of his study, pretending she knew what he was looking for, until he glanced over and smiled at her and she ruined her imitation with a laugh.

Once upon a time, he'd have leaned in for a kiss, and she'd have counted it a victory to have distracted him for even a moment.

She swallowed hard and looked up at the ceiling. Better to focus on what she could actually offer now, rather than those once-upon-a-times that would never be again. "Lady Weymouth, you say? Dowager W." That's what she'd dubbed her for her column. The lady had raised and married off three daughters successfully, making her a matron worth knowing in society circles. She was regularly called upon to sponsor other young ladies, and many of those she chose were darlings of their Seasons.

What's more, she was an avid reader of G. M. Parker's column and wrote in regularly about them. And even more to the point, she was one of the two dozen readers who had sent an invitation for G. M. to join her this Christmas season for a house party, "the report of which would be certain to entertain your dear readers."

She hadn't planned on going, of course. Gemma *never* actually attended events under her pen name—then people would be too careful of what they showed her and said around her. She'd found it far more effective to pose as a maid or as Marigold, so that she could move about without anyone guarding their conversations or actions. But this was a special circumstance. "I can get in—to Weywent Manor, I mean. If it would be useful."

Now all eyes flew to her, so she made a point of lowering her arms so that they looked less defensive and more comfortable. "Dowager W is hosting a holiday gala and sent an invitation care of the *Journal*. I could spend as much as a week there if it would be useful."

"Yes!" Graham straightened, his hand splayed over one of the photographs. "Yes, it would be useful. These fortifications against the Vikings—the area is riddled with them.

There could be tunnels, caverns and caves, all manner of hiding places perfect for concealing a kidnapped child. If we have a base of operations like Weywent, we could explore them all and get a feel for the area before the rendezvous, and if anyone knew who did or didn't belong in the town, it would surely be the people of the manor."

"We?" It emerged more as a breath than an actual word.

"The gala could even be the perpetrator's reason for choosing that location." Marigold tapped a finger to her lip. "Most of the people Wilfred has made enemies of are men of means. One of them could have been invited to the house party. Or at the very least, they could be using the festivities as a cover. Regardless, if the two of you are there, you're sure to be where the action is, and you may find Sidney ahead of time. In the meantime, the rest of us can go to Derbyshire and try to pry more information from Wilfred's household."

"The two of us?" This time the breath was at least a bit louder.

Loud enough to bring the others to a sudden silence that pounded in her ears like blood, and to bring concerned and guilty gazes her way from the others. Yes, she'd known that she'd likely have to work with Graham on this if she meant to do any poking about the manor house but . . . but they were making it sound far too cozy. "My invitation is only for *me*. I can hardly impose—"

"You won't have to impose." Graham slapped the book shut, his nostrils flaring. "You go on the invitation. I'll procure my own. You don't even have to admit to knowing me before we get there, *Miss Parker*."

He made her sound so petty for worrying over *him* when a boy's life was at stake. Worse, he was right. "And how will you do that?"

He flipped his fingers toward the book. "Her sort are always overeager to have their homes written up and studied in books like this. Prestige, you know. I'll tell her I'm working on a new book highlighting the most noteworthy manor houses in England and that I'm particularly interested in exploring the full history of her estate."

Lionfeathers, it would work. Dowager W was *exactly* that sort. "Over Christmas?"

Those dark eyes of his glinted. "I'm a working professional, darling. When else would I have the time to come but for when I'm on my holiday?"

She gritted her teeth at that *darling*. "Don't call me—"

"Don't start." Yates's voice brooked no argument, and the hand he slashed through the air was big enough, meaty enough, to remind her that he wasn't the baby of the group anymore. He was the earl. In Parliament. A grown man who had somehow become the leader of the Imposters even though he certainly hadn't started that way, given that he'd only been seventeen when they began their work. "There are more important things at stake right now than your anger with each other."

"Sorry," Gemma muttered, even while Graham slung his hands into his trouser pockets and said, "I'm not angry with her."

Yates looked from one of them to the other like a schoolteacher daring his pupils to interrupt again. "I know the timing of this is lousy and that none of us are in the best frame of mind with that anniversary looming. But our priority right now must be Sidney Hart. Are we all agreed on that?"

Gemma winced at even the mention of the coming date. Maybe this timing was, in fact, God-given. Heaven knew she needed something to think about other than her own pain.

"Yes."

"Of course."

"Absolutely." Marigold had left her new husband's side to move to the desk against the wall. "In fact, I believe we've received an invitation too. I know we can't get away for the whole time, but if you need us, we could all make an appearance for a day or two after we've done our research, perhaps."

Gemma's shoulders relaxed, even though she hadn't realized they'd gone tense during the exchange. Funny how much better she felt knowing that was a possibility. She wouldn't be alone with Graham the whole time. They'd have their friends as buffers at least a bit.

Well, and they would hardly be *alone* anyway. There would be dozens of people at the house party. And really, they wouldn't even have to communicate all that much with each other. He could do his searching of the site, she could do her listening among the people, and they could simply compare notes once a day or so.

She could survive that. For Sidney's sake. "Good to know, Marigold—though until we've learned a bit more about the situation, it's hard to say if that will be necessary."

"Well, we only have a matter of days to sort it all out. The ransom drop is Friday—tomorrow is Wednesday. You'll have to catch the first train south in the morning, Gem."

She nodded. "The invitation said a response could be sent up until the day of arrival, so I can send her a telegram in the morning and then be on my way."

Graham spun even then for the door. "I need to get a wire off to her too, before the office closes."

He'd barely make it—and chances were slim that it would be delivered to Lady Weymouth tonight. She wouldn't see it until tomorrow morning, wouldn't respond until afternoon, and even on the assumption that she would invite him, he'd be at least a day behind Gemma.

Her shoulders relaxed all the way. She'd have a full day to get her bearings there, on her own. Then he would show up as one more guest, who no one would expect her to know or interact with. And then Marigold and Merritt and Yates could all arrive on Friday, so they would be there for the ransom collection, which meant hardly any time at all when she'd have to face Graham.

She let out a slow, relieved breath. The only real problem was that she'd promised James she'd spend Christmas with him and Aunt Priss and be on hand to help him with all his parish duties, and she would have to renege.

Her brother would understand, though, when she said they had Imposters work that involved saving a child.

Aunt Priss, on the other hand . . .

With Graham gone, she finally sank to a seat in one of the reading chairs, smoothing her skirt with a damp palm. She didn't care to ask herself why her fingers were shaking.

Marigold probably noticed, though, as she approached and perched on the arm of Gemma's chair. Marigold always noticed *everything.* "We need to plan costumes."

Gemma grinned. "Clearly if Lady M is coming, she needs to wear something fantastically adorned in reds and greens and gold. You may have to spend the next few days sewing beads onto that burgundy dress Zelda finished remaking last month."

Marigold only arched her brow. "I was talking about *you,* G. M. Your alter ago has never actually had to appear in public, but you probably shouldn't go looking quite like yourself."

She probably *could.* It wasn't as though anyone cared that a steward's daughter made a living writing a society column, nor did she ever do Imposters work as Gemma. But then again, Gemma Parks was the daughter of *their* former steward, and no one needed to know that Lady M was old friends with the columnist. People might think it a bit unfair.

Moreover, she never tired of this game. Creating a character, choosing a wardrobe, deciding how she'd act, how she'd speak, who she'd be.

Someone else. Someone who could glide through life without that dark wall threatening to topple on her every single moment. Someone without the memories that she was so careful to keep packed away, where they wouldn't tarnish or tear from overhandling. Without the ruined life. Without the empty future. Someone who still believed stories could have happily-ever-afters and true love could prevail.

She pushed back to her feet. "Well, aren't we glad you didn't try to move your entire wardrobe to your new house?"

Merritt snorted a laugh. "I daresay the floor would have collapsed from the weight had we tried it. Our second room isn't big enough by half, anyway."

"I still say it's perfect for Leonidas, though." Yates flashed a grin every bit as joking as he'd been serious five minutes before. "It's bad form to leave your dowry at the bride's ancestral home, you know."

The thought of the old circus lion who made his home at the Tower bedding down in a London townhouse was enough to lighten the mood for them all.

Gemma pushed to her feet, grabbed Marigold's hand, and tugged her toward the door. "You gents can work out those arrangements. Lady M and G. M. Parker both have some costumes to put together."

A little breath of entertainment before the serious work began. A little piece of fun before she focused fully on keeping another family from falling apart. A little piece of peace before she had to deal with Graham for days on end—and *now*, of all times.

Marigold waited until they were closed into her room before asking, "Are you all right, Gemma?"

"You need to stop worrying about me. There are bigger things at stake right now."

Her friend gave her a long look. "I'll stop worrying when you stop pretending."

Gemma spun to the door. "It's what we do. It's our job."

"I'm not talking about playing a role at a stranger's house party, as you very well know. How long can you really pretend that Graham—"

"Forever. And a day." The very words he'd spoken to her once, swearing his everlasting love. She winced at hearing them fall from her lips now. "It's over, Marigold. It's over forever."

Her friend said nothing. And her silence was as haunting as the memories she refused to recall.

FIVE

22 December 1909

*L*eopard stripes." Graham gripped his bag in one hand, held down his fedora against the wind with the other, and ran toward the train as its whistle blew and its brakes hissed their release. By the time he reached the door, the locomotive was chugging slowly forward, the cars inching along the platform.

He'd known he'd be cutting it close, but when the telegram had arrived from Lady Weymouth that morning inviting him to come "as early as today," he'd grabbed the satchel he'd packed last night, locked the door, and hadn't looked back.

He could have taken a later train and been more leisurely about it. For that matter, he could have left from the depot closer to his house rather than first taking the Tube to St. Pancras. But this was the very train Gemma would be on, and if he had even the smallest chance of making it . . .

He leaped into the open doorway, grabbing hold of the handrail to steady himself as the train picked up steam. A glance over his shoulder showed him dozens of waving family members still on the platform, saying farewell to whoever they knew in the cars, a few children even running alongside them, shouting their goodbyes.

For a moment, he was taken back a decade, when it was the Fairfaxes seeing him off on a train to Eton. Yates—still a wisp of a lad—running alongside, waving with the enthusiasm of youth. He'd sought one last glimpse of Gemma Parks, standing there beside Marigold, waving with every bit as much enthusiasm as young Yates.

He could still remember the mix of emotions on her face. The pride in him for chasing a dream. The sorrow at his leaving. The flush of her cheeks from the quick, eternal kiss he'd finally worked up the nerve to give her before they left the Tower.

There was no Gemma on the platform now—but there was one somewhere on this train, and he turned to find her. She wasn't exactly the same girl who had waved him off a decade ago. He knew that. He wasn't the same boy either. But she was still *Gemma*. Somewhere under the layers of pain and anger and betrayal, she was still his Gemma. The first real friend he'd ever made. The coconspirator in all his childhood dreams. The only girl he'd ever loved. The woman to whom he'd pledged himself.

As he'd lain awake last night, very nearly praying in his desperation for a reply from Lady Weymouth, he'd come up with a plan. For the first time in a year, she'd have no choice but to be in his company for a week. She'd be playing a role, pretending to be someone else—G. M. Parker, writer. G. M. Parker, who had no reason to avoid him like Gemma did, who wouldn't therefore be able to demand he leave her presence like she'd done every time their paths had crossed recently.

And so, he would "introduce" himself. Remind her of why she loved him when she couldn't admit to hating him, thanks to her own self-written role. He would woo her like he'd never had to do before.

Gemma might have sworn never to give him the time of day again—but G. M. Parker hadn't.

He stepped into the aisle, surveying the occupied seats, looking for her familiar height and posture and hair. He had no idea what clothes she'd have decided on, and given the virtually unlimited options that made up Marigold's remade wardrobe, he couldn't rely on looking for familiar cuts or colors or fabrics. Those ladies dyed and redyed, sewed and resewed so often he'd long ago given up on keeping up with them. And hats! Lady M was especially known for her hats, which had proven convenient for them, since they could hide their faces beneath wide brims. Would Gem have opted for one of the oversized, concealing numbers today, or would she have chosen something smaller, given the close confines of a train seat?

He didn't see anyone in this car that made him look twice, as it was all families and businessmen, so he moved into the next, and then the next. In the third car, he very nearly continued onward but stopped in his tracks when a familiar movement caught his eye.

He frowned and gripped his bag more tightly. There was indeed a woman sitting alone to his right. She was the right size, boasted the same trim figure as Gemma. She was dressed in a well-tailored travel suit that was at once understated and elegant.

But her *hair*. It wasn't the mix of bright sunshine and honey that he loved. It was . . . *red*. Well, reddish. Strawberry blond, perhaps? Definitely not its usual color, and different enough that from behind, he'd immediately dismissed her as a possibility.

But it was Gemma—no. It was G. M. Parker. And beside her was one of the only empty seats in the compartment.

He would have breathed a prayer of thanksgiving if there'd been any point to it. Instead, he did what any traveler would do on his third compartment and slung his bag into the overhead before he even bothered asking, "Excuse me, miss, but is this seat taken?" and was already lowering himself to the cushion as he spoke.

For one second, recognition and frustration flashed through her summer-sky eyes. But she'd done far too much playacting in life to let it last longer than that single second. In the next, she was offering him the tight, polite smile of a stranger—for the sake of anyone looking at them, no doubt—but muttering, "In fact it is."

Nice try. "Beautiful day, isn't it?" She'd done something to her face too—no doubt cosmetics borrowed from Neville or Clementina. A powder of some sort on her face, and her lips—that perfect bow!—had changed their shape, making her bottom lip fuller. Only her scent was the same—a floral mix of rose and lily of the valley. And yet even that wasn't quite how he remembered it. There was no underlying hint of lavender anymore.

She must have seen him taking in every detail that had changed overnight, and no doubt she read the consternation in his eyes. Not that he didn't understand the need for a disguise—but her hair! Her *lips*!

She turned her face toward the window. "It's a trifle cold."

"To be expected this time of year. But the sun's out, and we can never count on that in December." He held out a hand, nabbing her attention again. "Graham Wharton."

For a moment she looked at his fingers, and he could see the debate inside her. She could snub him, turn to the window, and encase herself in the silence that was rather to be expected by strangers on an English train. Or she could shake, establish her role, get herself fully in the mindset she'd have to be in for the next several days, and embrace the festive air of the families chattering excitedly around them.

With only the smallest sigh, she lifted her hand and rested gloved fingers in his. "How do you do? Miss Parker."

He shook her hand like a professional rather than raising

it to his lips like a gentleman. "How do you do? Traveling to visit family for the holiday?"

"No, I'm afraid not. Business." She'd apparently decided on a different accent for G. M., and he wasn't surprised to hear she'd chosen the one she'd always been best at—not quite Brummie, but definitely Midlands.

"So close to Christmas?"

"Well, it's a Christmas house party that I'll be attending."

He made a show of looking surprised. "A house party—but for business?"

He could actually see the moment she resigned herself to the conversation . . . and the next moment, when she decided she might as well put it to good use. "That's correct. I'm a writer—a columnist—and the hostess has invited me to cover the event."

Graham pursed his lips and made himself as comfortable as he could on the bench. "Well, I hope you manage to enjoy yourself, despite it being work. You haven't left much family behind to celebrate without you, I hope?"

A perfectly polite question, and one she was certain to be asked over the next few days. Better that she hear it first from him, since he expected her little jolt. She smoothed it over quickly, though. "My aunt wasn't exactly pleased with the arrangement, but she'll be busy with my brother and his parish, so I don't imagine she'll have much chance to miss me, really."

A slice of truth to help her live the story, then. Wise.

"And you, Mr. Wharton? Are you traveling to or from family?"

He gave a little jolt himself. Turnabout, he supposed. "Neither. I have no close family of which to speak." The relation with the Fairfaxes was as much friendship as blood, given how distant their familial tie was. Distant enough that no one in society ever thought to make a connection between them. Why would they, when Graham had to trace the lineage all the way back to their third great-grandparents to find the common ancestor? He came from the branch that hadn't inherited the title, only the so-called dignity of gentle blood.

His family had been clergy, mostly, with a stray barrister or naval commission thrown in here and there. Mother had always told him the church would be his lot, too, simply because it was the most respectable option. He would be eternally grateful for the one clear memory he had of his father, who sat him down at age five and said, *"You'll be what you want to be, Graham. Find what you love and do it, no matter what anyone says."*

Advice he had clung to after Father died, and then Mother. Advice that, as an adult looking back, he wondered if Father wished someone had given *him*.

"What takes you south, then?"

He blinked away the past and focused again on Gemma, with her strangely red hair and too-full bottom lip.

And it was odd to hear polite, disinterested questions from the woman who arguably knew him better than any other on earth. Even though it had been his plan, still it gave him the strangest sensation to act like strangers. As though he were walking through a dream and could at any moment wake up, cold and lonely and ignored again.

"A bit of business myself, though the diverting sort. I'm an architect, you see, and working on research for a book on the most notable historic manor houses in my spare time. Since I've no family demanding my attention over the holiday, I'm taking the time off to do some traveling for the book. This trip, I'll be exploring Weywent Manor, near Weymouth."

She knew that already, so the widening of her eyes was only part of her script. "What a coincidence! That's where I'm going as well."

If any other guests of Lady Weymouth happened to be

in this train carriage, they would certainly be convinced by the note of surprise in her voice and impressed by this "coincidence."

Graham didn't have to force his smile. "Remarkable! What are the odds?"

Even though her own smile was only theater, it still tied a pleasant knot in his stomach, like it always did. "I daresay you're better at the maths than I am, Mr. Wharton, if you're an architect. If you actually care to calculate odds, I'll leave you to it."

"Quite all right. For the rest of 1909 I shall leave the mathematics at home and focus on the art and history side of my profession. Did you know that Weywent Manor sits on ruins dating back to the days of Viking invaders?"

When she tilted her head like that, so that sunlight from the window shot through her hair and set it on fire, he couldn't help but wonder again what she'd done to it. And pray it wasn't permanent. Not that it wasn't flattering— Gemma would be beautiful no matter what she did to her hair or clothes or anything else—but it wasn't *Gemma*.

The point, obviously.

She had a book in her lap, and the way she opened it to her marker and slid her finger into the pages clearly said that Mr. Wharton was quickly losing Miss Parker's interest. "Is that so?" Her voice was now flat, disinterested again. Even though he knew well that Gemma was fascinated by such things.

Had she actually decided that her character shouldn't be? Probably, if for no other reason than to have an excuse to ignore him.

He gave her the grin she'd always labeled as his most charming. "If you find yourself needing to hide from any Viking warriors, I can point you to several spots that saved the lives of the monks at the old monastery. They even built a few tunnels so they could escape from various parts of the grounds."

Her fingers twitched. She'd always been intrigued by things like secret tunnels and passageways—who wasn't? She had been the one to go with him each day to Alnwick Abbey when he was fourteen, measuring and diagramming and comparing the results with the old plans he'd dug up on his first trip to the National Archives, until he discovered an old priest hide from the days of Queen Elizabeth.

"If I remember my history correctly, the Vikings are already among us. Wasn't it their settling here and marrying the Anglo-Saxons that produced the current race of Britons?"

He made a show of considering. "I suppose that does explain our strapping figures and military might. Perhaps it's the Germans you'll need to hide from then. If one reads all the drivel from the spy novelists these days, secret invasions could come from any direction."

She chuckled. "I prefer a different sort of novel, sir." She tapped the cover of the one she held—*A Room with a View* by E. M. Forster. Graham had read it months ago, having little else to fill his evenings, and had wondered at the time if Gemma had discovered it yet.

Apparently she had now, at least. "Ah." He leaned forward to see where in the book her marker was. "Have you begun Part Two yet? Or are Lucy and her companions still in Italy?"

"Still in Italy on this read, but I've read it before."

Perfect. Something they could have an easy conversation about. He opened his mouth, ready to ask her whether she'd seen through Cecil from the start, but a family was coming rather loudly up the aisle and claiming the empty bench on the other side of theirs, and trying to talk would have required either shouting or leaning closer to her—not that he would have minded that, but she'd have objected.

A mother, three little ones, and a grandmother, from the looks of it. The mother was assuring the oldest child, a boy of perhaps seven, that Papa would meet them at the station in Basingstoke, and it would only be about an hour's ride. The three children squeezed into the space beside her, leaving the elder lady looking about for an empty seat.

There were a few throughout the carriage, but none nearby. The young mother had claimed the only full bench available, though, and who knew if other cars had any more, given the holiday-goers about.

Lionfeathers. He had been hoping for four hours of Gemma's company when she couldn't escape him and wouldn't dare to yell at him. But he could hardly let Grandmama leave Mumma with a fussing infant, a clinging toddler, and an inquisitive schoolboy on her own.

With only a bit of a sigh, he stood. "Here, madam. You can have this seat, so you're close to your family."

The woman faced him with wide, surprised eyes. "Oh! Are you certain, sir? I don't want to separate you from your—"

"We came separately," he interjected. "I'd only taken that seat beside her to leave the full one open for a group, knowing how busy it is. I can find another single seat somewhere else."

Both women looked ready to cry at the offer. "Very kind of you, sir. Happy Christmas to you," the grandmother said, sliding in as he slid out.

"Thank you so much," the mother added, bouncing the babe gently in her arms. "It's so gracious of you."

More than they knew, but still a small enough gesture. He tipped his hat to them, then to Gemma—knowing well she'd see the disappointment in his eyes that the strangers wouldn't—and wished them all a happy Christmas.

A minute later, he settled in beside another gentleman who had his nose buried in a newspaper and barely even glanced up to acknowledge him. Fine by Graham. If he wasn't going to spend the trip reminding Gemma that he was witty and charming and a fascinating conversationalist, he'd just as soon pass it in silent brooding.

Why could nothing ever go to plan anymore? He shouldn't *have* to convince Gemma of his charms. He never had before. He'd simply been himself with her, and *she* was the one who told him it was charming. If it was true, it was only because of her anyway. He'd shaped so much of himself based on her reactions as they grew up together. What made her laugh, he did over and again. What made her annoyed, he scrubbed from his behavior. What they could do together, he sought and learned. What took them apart, he eschewed—with his schooling being the one exception. But that separation he'd done *for* her, for them, for a future they could build together.

He let his eyes slide shut, his restless night catching him up. It had been a good future that they'd dreamed of, that she'd written countless tales about over the years. Marriage and children and brilliant careers for both of them, him at his drafting table and her at her writing desk. They'd holiday at home at the Tower and otherwise find some fashionable neighborhood in London for the first decade or two. Then, once he was England's most renowned architect and she was setting the literary world ablaze, they'd have put back enough to buy a holiday cottage somewhere. Brighton or Devon or Tynemouth.

A beautiful dream. One worth pursuing, worth fighting for, worth sacrificing for. One worth sketching out, taking care that every angle and measurement was to scale, one worth doing the maths for and choosing each and every construction material with care.

He hadn't known it could all come crashing down so spectacularly. He hadn't ever stopped to consider that one decision would turn her love to hatred and make everything he worked for turn to ashes.

Selfish. Arrogant. Maybe he had been. And maybe he'd

fallen right back into it with this plan, thinking it could be about wooing her again, winning her again, when the whole purpose of this trip was to keep another family's dream from forever shattering.

Sidney Hart. He called to mind the photo of the boy that Mr. Hart had given Yates. Ten years old, his face beginning to lose a bit of the soft roundness of boy and thin into the angles of adolescence. Sweet smile, mischief in his eyes.

Those eyes were likely full of fear now. They may even permanently lose a bit of their sparkle from this trauma. He may never again pull a prank, never again plot how to get extra sweets and gifts from his cousin's family, never again go off on a tear without even a thought to how he'd worry his parents.

Never again be a child.

Words sprang to Graham's tongue, to his heart. They wanted to emerge as a prayer, but he clenched his teeth together to stop them. God let children go missing all the time. He let them die. He let families be ripped apart, let tragedy happen. He let dreams turn to nightmares beyond imagining.

Why think He would stop *this* one?

Even worse was what James always claimed—that God had a plan. That each tragedy and pain was part of that plan.

What a cruel, cruel God He was, then. To do this to them *deliberately*. To not just allow but to *cause* the evils of the world.

If Sidney Hart was going to be returned to his parents, then it wouldn't be because of any mercy of the Lord. It would be because of the Imposters—and Graham would do all in his power to see that they succeeded.

He'd gone back to Fairfax House last night long enough to get a copy of the file, and though he didn't dare pull it out now on a crowded train, he pulled each item before his mind's eye and examined it again.

The ransom note, especially. It had been short but clear.

If you want to see your son again, deposit £80,000
into the poor box of St. Nicholas Church in Weymouth
at eleven o'clock on Christmas Eve night. Do it, and
you'll have him back by Midnight Mass. Refuse, and
your next visit to church will be for his funeral.

St. Nicholas Church. He'd tried to find a bit of history on it, but neither his home library nor the Fairfaxes' had given him anything useful, so he would have to discover what he could once at Weywent. All he knew at the moment was what he'd shared with the team yesterday—the church was on the countess's property.

What if Sidney was too? Old manors like that, ones built overtop ruins of previous castles and abbeys and fortifications, frequently had hiding places that the aristocrats didn't even know existed. But locals could. Men who had explored the area when they were boys, fishermen who saw something from sea that one couldn't see on land . . . any number of possibilities.

So who, then, in the Weymouth area would have such a vendetta against Lord Wilfred? It wasn't as though he lived nearby or even, so far as their dossier knew, had any particular business there.

No, that made no sense to him. It wasn't someone *from* Weymouth who'd had dealings with the earl from Derbyshire. The instigator *must* be someone coming *to* Weymouth, quite possibly to Weywent itself, perhaps with their own local connection, to know secrets of the area.

Or perhaps they were all overthinking things, especially him—seeing and seeking hidden passages and priest hides and caverns where no one else ever even *wanted* to. The boy was probably being held in a cottage or room somewhere, that was all.

In which case, he'd find *that* out once they arrived. Somehow. The stevedore in Basingstoke had said he'd assumed the could-have-been-Sidney was with his father. Graham could simply ask the workers at the station in Weymouth if they'd seen his nephew and brother come through yet. Show that school portrait Yates had let him bring with him, since Mr. Hart had provided them with several copies. Perhaps he'd get lucky.

Luck. Graham didn't believe in that any more than he did in God's mercy. He sank a little lower into his seat and tried not to pray as sleep overtook him.

SIX

Though the sun felt a bit warmer in Weymouth than it had in London, the wind whipping in from off the water was quite a bit colder. Gemma shivered the moment she stepped off the train, pulling her stole tighter against her neck and praying her hatpins held.

Praying, too, that her carrot-and-beet-juice hair dye hadn't permanently stained the band inside Marigold's hat. It was a conservative one, and hence one she didn't wear often, but even so.

She and Marigold had been up until midnight working on her tresses, with Neville and Clementina standing over them, sharing all the theater tricks they knew for temporarily altering one's appearance. The vegetable juices to tint her hair would wash out within a few days, so if she ended up staying the full week at Weywent Manor, she'd have to wash with it again, hence the bottle in her trunk. The oatmeal powder made her skin a bit fairer, to better complement the hair. A bit of rouge on her lips in a nearly natural shade filled out her bottom lip more than nature had done.

It wasn't enough of a change that anyone who really *knew* her would be fooled—just enough that near-strangers who met her here wouldn't immediately recognize her again in London if they passed her by on the street, when she was once more blond and wearing her own clothes and hat.

Not that it had stopped Graham. She knew where he was in the crush of debarking passengers—beyond the family of eight waiting for their trunks to be unloaded—but didn't look over at him. She certainly wouldn't have sought out a stranger who had sat with her for all of three minutes were it anyone else, after all.

She ought to have been relieved when his gallantry took him away from her so quickly—and she was. Sort of. It was only that she'd resigned herself to the conversation and convinced herself it would be quite helpful to have the chance to get into character verbally before her arrival.

And then there was the gallant act itself. Obviously he'd gone to great effort to take the same train and to find her in it. He'd looked quite pleased with himself when he sat in the seat beside hers. But even so, he'd given it up for the sake of a family. That was Graham.

One side of Graham, she reminded herself. Only one side of Graham. But the other side, the side that insisted on having his own way and doing what *he* wanted, what *he* planned, without any thought to the consequences for others, could just as easily have reared its head.

As the crowds cleared, she caught a glimpse of a man in livery and a chauffeur's cap, holding a sign in his hand. *Miss Parker. Mr. Wharton. Mrs. Horley.* That must be the driver Dowager W had promised would meet her train—and clearly the countess knew Graham would be on it as well, along with another guest.

Mrs. Horley . . . Gemma flipped the name this way and that in her mind but couldn't place it, nor assign a face to it. Probably not someone who spent the Season in London, then. Striding forward with more confidence than she really felt, Gemma drew near to the driver and greeted him with a nod. "Good day. I'm Miss Parker."

"Excellent, miss." The man looked to be in his fifties, and his smile was quick and bright. "Have you the tag for your luggage?"

She handed it over while he invited her to wait there with him until the other two expected passengers joined them. "I'll drive the set of you to the manor in her ladyship's auto, and my grandson will load your luggage onto the cart."

"Very good." She certainly couldn't demand that the man take her now and come back for the others so that she wouldn't have to share the limited space with Graham. G. M. Parker would have no reason to be so determined to avoid Mr. Wharton.

Though in the character profile she'd written up for herself, she'd had the foresight to come up with a reason for resisting the charm she knew very well he'd be pouring on. And it could prove entertaining to see how he'd respond when she waxed on and on about the fictional man she'd decided was courting her. Christopher Baldwin was sadly on the Continent for the next several weeks and couldn't make it home for Christmas, but she had a feeling he would have presented her with an engagement ring as a gift otherwise.

Without meaning to, she rubbed her thumb over the finger such a gift would encircle. The flesh was unadorned beneath her gloves, but even through the leather she could feel that slight dent. Would it never go away?

Catching herself, she made her hands relax before Graham could come up and see her rubbing her finger. She shouldn't want to make him jealous—she shouldn't want to make him *anything*. Her goal ought to remain what it had been for the last year: distance between them, as much as possible. All emotions folded neatly away. That was the only way to survive. So why had she felt that pang of disappointment when he'd given his seat to the grandmother and moved off?

A woman rushed their way, waving a hand in the air that had the driver clearing his throat and calling out, "Mrs. Horley, I presume?" well before the lady reached them.

She came to a stop with a little puff of breath visible in the cold air. "Indeed!" She turned to Gemma with a bright smile and sparkling green eyes. "Are you truly G. M. Parker? I absolutely devour your columns!"

Well, at least it was easy to remember to smile, even though Graham was coming their way now too. "I am, yes. How do you do, Mrs. Horley?"

"Oh, you must call me Carissa, if you're comfortable doing so." She held out a hand, clasping Gemma's fingers with enthusiasm. "And I'm quite well—quite well indeed! I despaired of ever meeting my husband's family, God rest his soul, only to receive this invitation last week from the countess herself. Can you believe it?"

"Oh . . ." Gracious, that was a lot of information to process about a stranger all at once, while said stranger was still squeezing her hands and all but bouncing on her toes. Should she express her felicitations over the invitation or her condolences over the widowhood? Given that Mrs. Horley wasn't in black or even grey, the loss couldn't have been that recent . . . though she didn't look a day over twenty-one, so how long ago could it have been? She opted for ignoring both the information and the question. "If I'm to call you Carissa, then please call me Gabrielle." She'd had to choose *something* other than her own name for that *G* to stand for, and she'd rather liked the ring to that one.

"How do you do, ladies?" Graham reached them, tipping his hat and spreading that charming smile of his between them and the driver. "It seems I'm the final member of our party." Though he'd clearly heard her new name, he didn't so much as flinch at it. Neville would be proud—clearly Graham had his actor-self in position too.

"Oh!" Carissa Horley actually batted her eyelashes, shifting immediately from avid reader to apparently eligible widow, turning toward Graham with a not-so-subtle shift. "How do you do, Mr. Wharton? What brings you to Weywent? Are you a friend of the countess's as well?"

Gemma's fingers clutched her stole more tightly than she needed to. It wasn't as though it was the first time she'd witnessed a beautiful young woman exhibiting clear interest in Graham. He was a handsome man. Women noticed.

It was just the first time she'd witnessed it when he wasn't *hers*. Perhaps she was the one to declare it so, but that didn't apparently keep the shaft of jealousy she'd imagined inspiring in *him* with her fictional beau from piercing *her*.

Leopard stripes. This was why she'd simply avoided him as much as possible since the moment she'd shouted, "*I hate you!*" and stormed out of the hospital room last year.

Graham took the hand Carissa Horley all but shoved into his face and bowed over it, but his gaze didn't linger overlong on her pretty face, framed by those perfect dark curls. "I've yet to make the lady's acquaintance, actually. I'm merely an architect, come to study her home for a book. And you must be Mrs. Horley. I've met the lovely Miss Parker already on the train."

If jealousy had been an arrow to pierce through her, it must have had a cord attached to its fletching that now wrapped around her and squeezed. Because he had absolutely no reason to do that—to make it clear with one well-placed word where his interest lay, to turn those few degrees to face *her* instead of Carissa Horley.

No reason at all, except the one he'd been insisting upon all along. She was the one he wanted. Only her.

It warmed her in one second and sent ice chasing after the

fire in the next. Loving her wasn't enough. Not when he'd proven in the worst possible way that he valued no opinion above his own.

She'd begged him—*begged him*—not to accept the offer of his boss's car last Christmas. She'd told him the weather was going to be too bad, the roads impassable. But he'd cared only for the prestige of arriving at Fairfax Tower in an automobile. Making a show, making a splash, proving himself.

His pride had killed her every dream.

The driver was asking for Carissa's and Graham's luggage slips, giving them the same explanation of auto for the people and cart for the bags, and then he was ushering them out of the station.

Graham stepped deliberately to her side, his elbow extended. "May I?"

If she didn't, Carissa Horley certainly would. But it wasn't to stake a claim that she tucked her fingers into the familiar crook of his arm. In fact, she shot the younger lady an apologetic smile. It was simply because G. M. would have had no reason to refuse, and she couldn't compromise her cover story so soon. Especially because they *would* have to compare notes now and then, and that would be best explained away, blast it all, by appearing to be taken with each other. Or at least not antagonistic.

For the sake of Sidney and the Harts, she would be friendly. But that was all. She'd have to deliver the news of her fictional all-but-betrothal soon and publicly, so that he'd have no choice but to let up on the interest.

Not that it had stopped George from *A Room with a View*, despite Lucy's all-but-engagement to Cecil. But hopefully Graham wouldn't think about that.

The car sat gleaming at the curb, the only one on the bustling street at the moment. She couldn't stop the tensing of her muscles as she drew close to it, much as she prayed with every step that this time she'd be able to draw near to one of the things without reacting so.

Because he noticed. The others wouldn't, but Graham did. When she tensed, he did too, and his fingers crept up to cover hers.

As the chauffeur helped Carissa Horley in, Graham leaned down and whispered, "I'm sorry, Gem."

"Sorry doesn't change it." She mouthed the words more than she said them, but he'd hear them regardless. She'd said them before, every other time he'd offered a meaningless apology.

Of course he was sorry. She hadn't for a moment doubted that. If they could turn back time, he'd make a different decision. He'd listen. Not because he respected her opinion, but because of what his choice had cost him.

They couldn't wind back the clock and undo anything. And so here they were. She let go of his arm and ducked into the car, choosing the seat beside Carissa so that he would be left to take the one opposite them, alone.

Carissa apparently wasn't one to let even a second slip by that she could use for conversation. She leaned close to Gemma while Graham was still outside and whispered, "Isn't he *handsome?*" in a tone that indicated her week had brightened considerably.

Smile, Gemma instructed herself. *Make a friend. It could be useful.* Obeying her own dictate took more effort than it should have, though. She shrugged. "I suppose, if you like that sort."

Carissa's eyes seemed to go wide more often than they were at normal size. "Who doesn't?"

She might have claimed she preferred her men ruddy and athletic—the description she'd decided upon for her dear nonexistent Christopher—but Graham slid into the car, and she wasn't about to say such a thing with him there.

At least they needn't worry about any awkward silences, not with their new companion. Mrs. Horley chatted about absolutely everything as they drove the five miles to Weywent Manor, including how her *late husband, God rest his soul,* was a cousin to the countess on his mother's side, and how she'd been hoping for an introduction to the fine lady ever since her wedding three years ago—to which the lady hadn't been able to come, though she'd sent her regrets and the most *exquisite* crystal vase as a gift—and that she'd all but despaired of ever making her acquaintance after her poor darling Marcus succumbed to consumption after a mere eight months of marriage.

Gemma didn't even attempt to get a word in, contenting herself instead with gazing out the window at the passing countryside.

She hadn't spent much time in the South. London was usually as far that direction as she went, and though she'd once dreamed of a seaside cottage somewhere along this shore, she found herself missing the rugged terrain of Northumberland. Marigold always said that that was what a coast should be—it seemed Gemma would have to admit to agreement after all. Not that there wasn't plenty of charm to the very different flora in evidence and the warmer sun.

"Nearing Weywent Manor now, ladies and gent," the driver announced a few minutes later. "Once we cross through the gates, all you see is part of the estate."

Gemma leaned a bit closer to the glass, though her breath fogged it up and made her retreat again. She could still make out the gate, though, and the stone hedgerow that stretched out from it in both directions as far as she could see. And there, beyond the copse of trees flanking the gate, she glimpsed the spire of a church.

She opened her mouth to ask about it, but Graham beat her to it.

"From my reading, I believe the church is part of the Wey-went estate as well, is that right?"

The driver half-turned his head, though he still kept his eyes on the road. "That's right, sir. There's an entrance to it from the village road too. St. Nicholas's serves the Weymouth family but also their tenants and all the residents of our village. If you attend services there on Christmas, you'll find it a sweet little chapel, I don't doubt. Built back before the Reformation, but it escaped Henry the Eighth's men by the wit of the clergy."

Graham, she knew, would be intrigued by the history simply because he was Graham, aside from any role the building might play in the ransom drop. He'd no doubt walk down first thing tomorrow and drop in, meet the vicar, hear the story of the priests' cleverness and every other tale linked to its hallowed walls. He would notice every flying buttress and grave marker. He'd ask question after question that would have the vicar going on in bliss.

But if what James said was true, he'd keep his eyes away from the cross. He'd talk about the church and its earthly builders but avoid all mention of the Church and its true Creator.

Thinking of that made her heart ache in a whole new way. Once upon a time, he'd spoken of Christ and faith and Scripture as easily as her brother did. Once upon a time, he and James had sat up until the wee hours of the morning debating the finer points of theology. Once upon a time, he'd trusted Him with their lives.

Another sad ending to what should have been a fairy-tale life.

Or sad interlude, anyway. This, at least, didn't have to be an ending. Her brother had told her months ago to pray for Graham, to pray fervently and tirelessly for a restoration of his faith.

She hadn't done it. Hadn't been able to, because she hadn't been able to hold any more hurt in her heart. But somehow now, in this moment, by seeing him trace the lines of a steeple with his gaze, it hit her.

Perhaps their hearts could never truly be mended. But his soul was not beyond the reach of God.

Forgive me, Father. Forgive me for letting my anger with him keep me from lifting him up to you. Forgive me for not realizing that my broken heart is not more important than his broken soul.

She'd gone eleven months without giving in to the tears that always wanted to overtake her, but these last weeks, her eyes had been burning almost constantly. The wedding, the approach of Christmas, this poor missing child and his desperate parents—and now this. Seeing Graham look at a church and close his eyes to the most important part of it. That was a new sort of tragedy.

Carissa Horley had turned to her again. "Will you be writing about Lady Weymouth's house party, then? Or have you struck up an acquaintance with Her Ladyship in London?"

Her Ladyship had sailed past Gemma, decked out in a borrowed maid's uniform, no fewer than a dozen times over the last few years and never looked twice at her. "We've yet to be introduced, but she was kind enough to invite me care of the *Journal*, certain my readers will enjoy hearing of the festivities."

Carissa clasped her hands in front of her chest, clearly in raptures. "Oh, how thrilling! How do you come up with the turns of phrase you use? Do you compose them then and there, while you're observing a ball or soiree, or do you have to ponder them later? I do hope it's while you're there—if I'm at your side, would you regale me with your descriptions throughout the night? I can think of little more diverting." She darted a quick glance at Graham.

Apparently she could think of *something* more diverting, but Gemma pretended she didn't notice the look. "I suppose it's a combination. Sometimes words and phrases do fill my mind as I'm witnessing something; other times I simply commit the impressions and images to memory and find the right terminology later. And always I keep a small notepad in my pocket in case the perfect idea flits through my mind and I need to grasp it firmly before it flutters off again. Words can be wily things, you know." She patted the pocket in demonstration.

Carissa giggled—and sneaked another glance at Graham, presumably to see if he noticed how endearing a giggle she had.

Graham still had his nose all but pressed to the glass, his eyes scanning the landscape like a schoolboy reading his primer, back and forth and back again. Looking, she knew, for evidence of the ruins over which the current manor had been built.

She'd gone with him to enough heritage sites to know that any bump or knoll could in fact be earth-covered history. He'd dug up—with the permission of rightful owners . . . mostly—more than his fair share of ancient walls and ruins buried for centuries under tidy gardens.

Carissa heaved a tiny sigh and focused on Gemma again. "Well, I can't imagine I'll be a popular addition to the party. I have no doubt the lady has far more important guests coming to whom she'll be paying most of her attention. So if you have need of an assistant, consider me your new right hand. I'd be delighted to fetch you fresh paper or pens or gather information that you need to fill out details, if you don't know anyone's name or title or what have you."

That could prove useful for this oddity of a trip. Usually she asked the servants, but that might not work so well when she was one of the guests. On the occasions when she'd attended as Lady Marigold, she simply hadn't described anyone's ensembles whose identity she didn't already know. "Thank you, Carissa. I may take you up on that if Dowager W doesn't introduce us to everyone at the start, or if more guests arrive for her Christmas Eve ball."

"I've heard *wonders* about her ball!" Another tinkling laugh. "May I ask, what will *you* be wearing?"

Gemma waved the question away. "Nothing worth noting—a simple gown in emerald green. My goal is never to get attention at such an event. The more I blend into the wallpaper, the more details I can observe."

And the more easily she'd be able to slip away with whomever among the Imposters was present to stake out the poor box at St. Nicholas's Church.

Carissa bounced a bit on her seat. "I can scarcely believe I'm here! How many guests do you think will be in attendance? At the house party itself, I mean. Or at the ball?"

To that, Gemma had no answer. "She gave no indication in her invitation, and I've never attended before, nor read another columnist's write-up of it. It's dreadfully difficult to keep up with all the holiday parties, you know. I wear my fingers to the bone with all the typing I do this time of year."

Except for last year, when she hadn't written a single word. Hadn't put either pen to paper or fingers to typewriter until the end of January, when her editor threatened to sack her and find another columnist if G. M. didn't reappear very quickly on the social scene.

G. M. reappeared. Perhaps she had mostly relied on Marigold to fill her in on the details her eyes still refused to pay attention to, perhaps her words were flat and unoriginal. But she'd written so that the paychecks continued to come in—more important than ever—and the more she wrote for her column, the more she could write for herself.

The more she wrote for herself, the more herself she became.

Words were wily things—but they were miraculous too. They created, they shaped, they breathed life. God had used them to form the universe, and Christ had come as a living Word to write Himself onto the hearts of humankind. Was it any wonder, then, that words had pulled her from the brink of darkness and delivered her, however slowly, back to the Light?

"I particularly enjoyed your recounting of the New Year's Children's Ball in York two years ago, Miss Parker." This came from Graham, who was still looking out the window even as he spoke.

Leopard stripes. Her throat went dry at the memories of that magical night. The event had been Yates's idea, when he was barely more than a tot. Lady Fairfax had been dressing for some holiday gala, and little Yates had pouted at having to stay at home in the nursery while his parents had all the fun. There ought to be, he'd proclaimed, a ball just for children.

His mother had made it so. She'd hosted it in York to draw more attention than she'd have been able to bring in Northumberland, and it had been a fundraiser for orphanages. More, it had been such a smashing success that first year that she'd kept the tradition alive until her death. Her husband had continued it after, and Marigold and Yates themselves had taken over the organizing the last five years, though at this point it had its own board of directors and all they really had to do was show up to lend it a bit of prestige.

A ballroom filled with children—little lads in miniature tuxedos, little girls in miniature gowns. Hobbyhorses and dolls and all manner of other gifts given to each attendee, laughing and happy squeals filling the air.

Her lips tugged up at the memory. "There is nothing like the Children's Ball." The one two years ago had been her favorite—and yet the one she didn't dare think about now. Because it had been her favorite because of *him*. The way he'd danced with her in the coat closet, dreamed with her of past and future, kissed her until her head swam.

"I read your account," Carissa said, pulling Gemma back to the present, "but I've never been. Is Lady M still attached to it? Will she still be there this year, do you think, now that she's married?"

"I can't imagine she'd miss it." She'd offered to skip last year's, to stay with Gemma instead, but Gemma had insisted she go, for the sake of the hundreds of children throughout Yorkshire and Northumberland who looked forward to it all year.

The car slowed, and Gemma turned for her first view of Weywent Manor. It sprawled over quite a few acres, bigger than Fairfax Tower's main house, though no doubt absent her home's particularly appealing outbuildings—the theater and gymnasium and what had basically become a zoological park. There were no zebras pulling the lawn mowers in the summer, she would wager, nor lions roaring from the stables. But it looked impeccably maintained, with evergreen shrubbery marching in ordered rows up the long drive and then around the main body of the house. It was built of golden stone, with towering pillars and banks of many-storied windows reflecting the sunlight.

Graham pursed his lips.

She shouldn't make it known that she'd noticed. Shouldn't ask the question that sprang to her tongue. But out it came tumbling anyway. "Does something not meet with your approval, Mr. Wharton?"

He sent her a look that smiled, though his lips barely hinted at it. "The wings aren't symmetrical. I've never understood such a decision. One more column of windows on the north side is all it would take, but no . . ."

That *did* explain the slightly lopsided look of the place. She'd thought it just their perspective, but he was right—of course. "Perhaps you should offer to remedy it for them."

He chuckled. "I've jokingly made the offer a time or two. It never seems to earn me either commissions or friends. Seems lords and ladies don't appreciate having the balance of their ancestral homes critiqued."

Carissa laughed, fingers covering her mouth. "Oh, you didn't! I can't imagine having such cheek. It would be like our dear Gabrielle here offering to remake a duchess's gown to be more flattering!"

She'd been tempted to do that a time or two, seeing what some ladies showed up in. But better sense had always prevailed. "I settle for polite critiques in my column and leave it at that." And always made certain to find something to compliment those ladies on at other times.

It really didn't do to make enemies of the aristocrats.

A lesson their fellow aristocrats would do well to learn too. If Lord Wilfred played a bit nicer in the business arena, his nephew wouldn't now be missing.

SEVEN

23 December 1909

*G*raham left the breakfast room only minutes after he'd slipped in, bacon-laden toast in one hand and a cup of tea in the other. His goal had been to be the first person through the doors the moment the servants set out the food on the sideboard at six o'clock, and then to be gone again before anyone else so much as came down the central stairs. He might have been eagerly welcomed onto the grounds of Weywent Manor, but he didn't need Gemma's or Marigold's experience with social functions to pick up in a matter of minutes on the fact that he wasn't truly a *guest*. Not like the others, anyway.

He'd been assigned a small bedchamber in the bachelor wing, but when he arrived without a valet, he'd received only a sniff of disapproval rather than the offer of a footman if he had need of assistance before the ball. Though he'd been graciously invited by the countess to join the party for meals, she'd also made it quite clear that the invitation did not extend to the other amusements she had planned for her friends and family. Though she'd made him promise he would attend the Christmas Eve ball, she also made certain that he understood that Christmas morning in the upstairs parlor was for her children and grandchildren *only*.

Understandable. He'd more or less invited himself—and had no desire to join in the hunt or the charades or the games of cards with which the other gentlemen would fill their afternoons, and certainly no desire to infringe upon the family's private celebration on Christmas morning.

He had ruins to find and explore. Secrets to uncover. A child to rescue.

Memories to be tormented by.

He opted for a side door rather than the massive front ones for his escape, not needing to hail a servant to tell him which way to go to find the garden exit. Though he hadn't been able to find much by way of detailed information on the manor house in the Archives, and especially not on the ruins over which it had been built, this central part of the house had been photographed for that out-of-date book in the Fairfax library, so he knew its general layout.

Gemma had always argued that seeing snapshots of rooms was no help in knowing how to stitch them together. She'd claimed that knowing what the drawing room looked like didn't tell her whether it was above or below or beside the sitting room.

He'd teased back that if not, it was only because she wasn't paying close enough attention and looking too much at the upholstery and not enough at what she could glimpse through the windows, or the position of said windows, or the dimensions of the room.

He had been halfway through his time at university before he realized that his mind was odd. That not everyone looked at photographs and came up with their own blueprint for a building. Who knew? He'd always thought it rather natural.

It had proven to be to his benefit that it wasn't. That, and his abilities in the National Archives, were what set him apart and earned him his position.

Though he slipped outside into the garden without any trouble, the sun was not in attendance this morning, unfortunately, and he quickly realized he ought to have taken the time to put on the scarf shoved into his overcoat's pocket and the hat he was holding rather awkwardly under his arm. Looking from his bacon sandwich to his cup of tea in search of fingers he could draft into use, he heaved a sigh that clouded the air before him with steam.

A poured-concrete bench sat a few feet away, tucked into the dormant garden, so he used it as a table to hold his cup, told his toast not to get too soggy when he set it as a lid over the tea for a moment, and quickly finished his bundling up. Then enjoyed his first bite of breakfast as he strode through the landscape.

He'd hated winter once, when he was small. Before Mother died, they'd been living about twenty miles inland from Bognor Regis, one of the sunniest places in England. His first winter in the wilds of Northumberland with the Fairfaxes, he'd thought he would freeze to death before spring finally showed its bashful face again.

At this point, with that Scottish border equaling home in his mind, what passed for cold in the South felt downright balmy as he finished his breakfast and tea. He kept close to the house until his beverage was gone, so that he could dart back inside for a moment and return the cup. Back out again, he pulled on his gloves and clapped his hands together, a smile tugging at his lips.

Time to get down to business.

He'd sketched a general map of the estate onto a piece of paper last night, which he had folded into his pocket now. As he walked, he noted the location of any bumps that could be earth-covered ruins, any man-chiseled stones scattered about, any indentations that could indicate where the ground had sunken into a collapsed tunnel below.

"Good morning! I didn't think anyone else mad enough to be out before noon."

Graham looked up from his map, where he'd added a small, oblong shape to represent this raised area on the south lawn, and smiled a greeting at the man leading a horse his direction. The horse had a touch of lather on his flanks, so the fellow must have had a nice ride. "Good morning. I'm never one to let the day get away from me."

"You're the architect, correct?" The chap—his riding clothes fine enough to proclaim him one of the gentry, without doubt—held out a hand as he approached. "Miles Fitzroy, nephew to the Weymouths."

Fitzroy. Graham had a copy of his dossier in his room even now.

FROM THE DOSSIER OF
Mr. Miles Fitzroy

HEIGHT: *6'1"*

WEIGHT: *11.5 stone*

AGE: *31*

HAIR: *Light brown, worn slicked back straight from his forehead*

EYES: *Green*

STYLE: *Better than he can really afford, usually from Anderson & Sheppard*

OBSERVANCES: *Fitzroy is the son of the sister of the late Earl of Weymouth; the title went extinct with the last earl's death four years ago, but they'd managed to break the entail on the estate before his death. He keeps close to the dowager, and gossip says it's in hope of a piece of the inheritance, though more likely she will leave the bulk of the estate to their daughters.*

His own family has descended into the realm of the shabby aristocrats (ah, our own kind!), his livelihood seemingly coming from shuffling debts from one place to another.

He is (too) often at the gaming hells and always bets on the wrong horse at the races.

CASES IN WHICH HE HAS BEEN OBSERVED: *Adams, Bligh, Fennwick*

IMPRESSIONS: *Amiable fellow, well liked, which is how he manages to sponge off his better-situated peers without anyone seeming to grow tired of him.*

Graham shook his hand. "How do you do? And yes, I am the architect—Graham Wharton. It was so good of your aunt to invite me for the holiday. I've been using all my free time this past year to do research such as this."

Fitzroy chuckled and surveyed the house, now rather distant. "Not to detract from your gratitude, but it was no great favor. She's been bemoaning for years that there are so few good books featuring the manor. I daresay you could spend months here and she'd be nothing but overjoyed."

"Good to know—though the town in Shropshire who hired me to design them a new library may object if I get too distracted."

"No doubt." Still grinning, Fitzroy looked over his shoulder. "It seems I well and truly trounced Astley in our race this morning. I'm beginning to think he's got lost."

Astley . . . Astley . . . Graham couldn't recall ever reading the name in their files, but he knew the countess had pointed him out yesterday. She had not bothered making broad introductions for any of the three who arrived yesterday afternoon.

Apparently columnists and architects and widows of distant cousins didn't earn that honor.

He was titled, though—she'd referred to him as Lord Astley. And he was a friend of Fitzroy, it seemed.

The question of his current location provided a perfect opening. Graham put on a smile of his own. "Let's hope he didn't fall into any old tunnels."

Fitzroy's head snapped his way again—rather suspiciously, actually. And he was now regarding Graham as if *he* were suspicious.

Perhaps not so great an opening.

"What do you know about such things?" Yes, his voice practically dripped wariness.

Graham parried it with a lifted brow. "Well, not much yet. But it's one of the things I'm hoping to study while I'm here. See?" He stepped closer and held out the map. With his pencil, he indicated the places he'd marked so far this morning. "Each of these places could indicate ruins of older fortifications or tunnels or buildings beneath the soil. The current manor was built overtop more ancient sites, from what I've read. Fascinating, isn't it?"

Fitzroy's demeanor relaxed again. "Indeed. I've always thought so. I've done quite a bit of exploring here when I was a boy. Found a few things I'll be happy to show you, though none are proper tunnels, per se. I don't doubt they're there, though. There are old stories abounding—you ought to ask the gamekeeper for a few of them. His family has been here for centuries."

"Gamekeeper. Excellent. What's his name?" Graham jotted it down when Fitzroy told him, but his mind was spinning more around his current companion than the local.

Why had he reacted so strongly to mention of tunnels if he'd never found any?

And more to the point—why did the cases he'd shown up

in sound familiar? He hadn't had time to review those, only Fitzroy's brief entry. Gemma may remember more about the cases, though. She had a mind for names and associations like he had for floor plans.

As he scribbled down where to find the gamekeeper's cottage, pounding hooves sounded, and a moment later another horse, this one with its rider still atop it rather than walking at its side, appeared from the direction of the coast.

The gentleman reined to a halt beside Fitzroy, his own chest heaving as much as his horse's. "Took a wrong turn," he offered with a lopsided smile, as explanation for his rather disastrous loss of the race. He dismounted, giving the horse a fond pat on the flank. Then he nodded at Graham with an inquisitive "Good morning?"

Fitzroy made the introductions. Lord Astley, it seemed, was a baron from Derbyshire. They'd gone to school together, putting the newcomer at around the same age of thirty-one, and tried to take their holidays together at least once a year still, since both were bachelors without immediate family whose demands must be met.

So far as Graham could recall, they'd never had cause to create a dossier on this Astley chap. It didn't necessarily mean he was upstanding . . . just that he'd led a quiet life and wasn't often in Town, more likely.

Yes, Graham had become a bit cynical the more cases they took on. They all had. The more they learned about society's secrets, the more he realized that James had one thing right at least: Humanity was composed of a bunch of wretches, and it was no wonder God had grown angry with them so many times throughout history.

Graham couldn't understand why He took His fury out on innocents instead of the guilty, that was all.

At a loud growl from Astley's stomach, Fitzroy laughed and nodded toward the house. "Well, we had better get in to breakfast. If you'd like me to show you what few ruins I've found over the years, Wharton, I'd be happy to do so later."

To actually show him something of interest . . . or to redirect him where he wanted him to go? Graham smiled, nodded. He'd have to revisit that dossier straightaway. "That would be wonderful, thank you. You'll either find me wandering about out here or, if I need to defrost my fingers and toes, I've scoped out a table by the fireplace in the library that I plan on claiming as my own."

"Excellent. I shall find you either inside or out while the guests are about their card games after luncheon."

"I'll look forward to it."

As the two gentlemen walked their horses back toward the house and stables, Graham continued his survey. He managed to cover about a quarter of the property by noon, at which point his breakfast had most assuredly worn off and he was more than ready for a spell by the fire.

He was eager, too, for a glimpse of Gemma—he'd be lying if he tried to convince himself otherwise. How had she passed her morning? In the company, listening to every word of gossip and sorting out the connections of each of the guests. Had she learned anything useful? Did she remember more about the cases Fitzroy had intersected?

How many of those bachelors—or for that matter, married cads—had noticed that she was the most beautiful woman present and would be angling for a flirtation or even a tryst?

"Good job ruining your own mood, Graham," he muttered to himself as he let himself back in the same side door he'd exited hours earlier. He tried to comfort himself with Yates's oft-repeated insistence over the years that Gemma wasn't *really* the most beautiful woman in England.

He'd never believed that claim, not for a second. It was obvious, wasn't it? No one else's blue eyes sparkled like hers did. No one else's smile made such a perfect rosy bow. No one else's cheeks rose to turn those eyes into half-moons when she laughed in quite that way. No one else was *Gemma*.

She could say all she wanted that it was over, that she wasn't his nor he hers, that the love they'd had since they were children didn't matter anymore—but she was wrong. He didn't even need to wonder where in this vast house she was, just let his senses go on Gemma-alert and his feet drift their way toward her. Did he hear her laugh? Smell her perfume? Catch a glimpse of her through an open door?

Probably some combination thereof, if one were being practical. All he really knew was that he ended up in the same room like he always did, and his eyes didn't have to search her out like they had on the train. They flew right to her.

The hair still gave him a jolt. More than yesterday even, given that she wore no hat over it. His fingers twitched with the desire to go and test the texture, see if the pigment came off on his hands. His feet very nearly pointed themselves toward her from long habit and inborn need.

Instead, he kept to the edges of the room, studying the magnificent plasterwork, and hoped that it wouldn't be too long before luncheon was announced.

He had to speak with her, though, at some point. Tell her what he'd discovered and the rather odd reaction of Fitzroy, see what she'd gleaned from the morning's indoor conversation.

Any other year, even had they been pretending they didn't know each other—which had been necessary a time or two on a case—he'd have simply caught her eye, raised his hand, and scratched twice under his right ear with his middle finger. Within a matter of minutes, she'd have made her way over to his side or followed after he left the room.

She glanced up, their gazes tangling for a heartbeat. Because he'd been staring. Perhaps he'd have tried not to, except that it really didn't matter if anyone thought Mr. Wharton was attracted to G. M. Parker. They all thought they'd only met on the train, so a bit of intrigue was par for the proverbial course.

Did he dare try to signal? No one, if they were looking, would think anything of it . . . but the risk wasn't in being seen. The risk was in the fresh pain he would experience if she ignored him.

He lifted his right hand and used his middle finger to scratch twice under his ear. He could always tell himself she couldn't get away from whatever conversation she was having with that lady in the horrible mustard-yellow dress.

To stay here or to leave the room? Sensitive conversations shouldn't try to be had anywhere they could be overheard . . . but at that very moment one of the gents sat down at the piano and launched into a rousing carol, providing a perfect buffer of noise.

He held his place, but for moving a few feet with his study. The plasterwork really was worth noting, if ever he wrote that book he kept talking about. And the hand-painted gilding on the rail was remarkable too. It looked bright and fresh, which made him wonder what artist the Weymouths had employed to restore it. He always needed new names, and a bit of gold scrollwork wouldn't go awry in the Shropshire library.

"Lovely, isn't it? The design reminds me of a brocade that Lady M wore to a masquerade last spring."

She'd come! Graham darted one glance over at her—which pulled to that unnatural hair of its own volition—and then looked back to the pattern on the wall. The glance had served to show him there was no one in earshot, not given the enthusiastic piano playing. "What did you do, anyway?" he murmured to the wall. "Soak your hair in carrot juice?"

"With a bit of beet thrown in. Do relax, Mr. Wharton. It'll come out in a wash or two, Neville says."

He would know. But still. "I suppose it's better than that walnut wash you tried three years ago." The goal had been to make her blond hair more the color of Marigold's light brown. The result had been a hideous near-grey.

She'd still been beautiful. But he'd teased her mercilessly about it.

"I assume you didn't signal merely to insult my hair?"

He turned to face her, tapping a finger to the scrollwork as if it was that he was telling her about. "I've made good progress on my map. I started with the section between the house and the shore, since it seems the most logical, if tunnels were built to escape Vikings. And I met two gents while I was out. Fitzroy and Astley."

"The nephew." Her lips in an easy smile, she traced a finger along one of the golden vines too. "I reviewed his dossier last night, after I heard his name. He's done business with Wilfred several times, it seems."

Wilfred's dossier—that was why those case names had sounded familiar. Several of them had overlapped. "I don't suppose you've done any fishing with the ladies?"

"They've proven quite a teeming stream of information." Her gaze wandered upward, focusing on other highlights of the room. "I had only to observe that Fitzroy was a fine-looking fellow and inquire as to whether he was attached to any of the ladies present, and I received no fewer than a half dozen warnings to keep my distance."

A professional question. A smart one, at that. Even so, his inner voice wanted to snap, *"He isn't that fine-looking."* "Oh?"

His blasé tone didn't fool her for a moment, given that little twitch at the corner of her mouth. "Debts, you see. Especially after that last venture with one of Lord Wilfred's machinery companies that proved a disaster."

"You don't say." He pointed up at the crown molding and moved his hand to the right as if tracing some line for her. "What sort of disaster?"

"The sort that involved a loophole in a partnership

agreement that left Fitzroy holding fifty thousand in out-standing debt while Wilfred waltzed away scot-free."

"Ouch." He turned to face Gemma fully, giving her the grin she'd once loved. "Motive?"

She turned her own face demurely down. "Could be. The ransom is more than that—"

"But he could consider it payment for pain and suffering, or to cover other debts from his gambling."

"Quite possibly."

He didn't want to think it of the cheerful chap he'd met that morning. Frankly, he never wanted to think such things of *anyone*. Who would really let a need for money convince them that kidnapping an innocent schoolboy was the answer?

His stomach went tight, and it took him a moment to realize it was because everything in him aside from that hard rock of fury told him to pray for the lad. Pray God gave them answers in time, that He led them directly to him, that He insulate that young heart from trauma that could turn into a lifetime of nightmares and brokenness.

No. What was the point? God would hear Him because He was God. And He would answer exactly like He always did: with a resounding, clanging *no*.

But they would find him anyway, even if Graham had to tear up every stone and board and block of Weywent Manor.

"Fitzroy reacted quite strongly when I mentioned the possibility of old tunnels about. Then tried to say he'd never found any, but that he'd show me what he *had* discovered as a lad. We're going to meet outside again this afternoon, if you wanted to join us."

A long shot, that. But maybe she'd be ready for a respite from all the gossip by then.

She tilted her head to the side. "I wouldn't mind observing him more closely, but it will depend on what the conversation is among the ladies at the time. Just make a point of inviting me—preferably not when our new friend Mrs. Horley is at hand, or she will most certainly accept as well."

At the smile she beamed, and the little wave of her hand, he glanced over and saw that said new friend was weaving her way through the crowd of houseguests, face bright. He nearly groaned. "She's insistent, isn't she?"

"She feels out of her element. Not that any of the gentlemen seem to mind the addition of another lovely face. Or will you tell me you didn't notice how pretty she is?"

The rock of fury burned like a coal. "Why would you even ask that? You know very well I never thought anyone else half as pretty as you."

"I know very little that I once thought I did when it comes to you."

The flames licked up, searing, scorching. "You know me."

"Do I? Where is your necklace, Mr. Wharton? The one I gave you for your eighteenth birthday?"

His throat went tight. "Around my neck."

The look she shot him was as scalding as the boil of his own blood. "I don't mean the chain. I mean the pendant."

He'd taken off the silver cross eleven months ago and had tossed it so forcefully into a drawer that it had chipped the wood—and replaced it instead with the golden promise she'd tossed back at *him* last year. But how had she known that?

James. Blast him. "The one has nothing to do with the other."

Mrs. Horley was nearly upon them. Another few seconds and their conversation would come to a halt.

But Gemma found enough time to deliver one final blow. Three little words he knew would echo in his mind for the rest of the day.

"Faithless is faithless."

It wasn't. It wasn't the same at all. Giving up on God hadn't ever, in his mind, meant giving up on *them*.

But she apparently didn't see it the same way.

EIGHT

*Y*ates had been hoping they'd escape London before Christmas, but he had to admit this wasn't what he'd envisioned. He'd had in mind a happy return to the Tower with Marigold and Merritt, perhaps a few visits to friends in the neighborhood, maybe a trip before the New Year to Merritt's family at their country estate, where he could make his new brother-in-law glare at him by flirting with his younger cousins. Then, of course, back to York for the Children's Ball.

In none of his musings had he thought they'd be in Derbyshire, scaling a frigid stone wall with numb fingers, wishing his close-fitting black leotard and trousers were fleece lined. Or had room for hot water bottles in the pockets. Or a nice furnace built into the cuffs. That would be delightful right about now.

"This is far more fun in the summer," Marigold muttered from her position to his right, her voice so quiet that he scarcely heard it over the moaning of the wind.

Or maybe that was the moaning of his own toes? He couldn't tell anymore. "We'll have some eggnog in an hour. Or—oh, even better. Mulled cider."

"Mulled cider." Marigold's echo sounded wistful. "Hurry up, then, will you?"

He had to flex his fingers to convince the blood to keep flowing through them, but then he fitted them into the next gap between the stones and worked himself up and over another few inches.

Fellsbourne's manor house was due for a repointing—the mortar had crumbled away between many of the stones, providing perfect toe- and fingerholds. Such deferred maintenance had come in handy many times over the last five years, but he'd been surprised to find it in evidence here. He'd rather thought Lord Wilfred the type to keep everything impeccable, as his house in London hadn't had so much as a smear of soot marring its white bricks. But then, that was where he spent most of his time, even when Parliament wasn't in session.

His wife and son had spent most of the year here, though, before Lady Wilfred died and young Horace—Lord Sheffield, technically—had been sent off to Ludgrove as soon as he was old enough. That alone should have been enough to bring Lord Wilfred home regularly, shouldn't it have?

The Fairfax family certainly had their share of secrets and irresponsibility. But the *family* piece they'd always got right, at least. He could be glad of that.

Another two minutes of climbing and they were finally able to pull themselves up onto the ledge that ran beneath the second floor, which made the going much quicker. Aside from the risky places where they had to pass in front of windows—all darkened, praise God—this was the easy part of the climb. They reached the one set of windows aglow up here right on schedule, and just in time to hear the muted voices of a child and a nurse coming through the glass.

". . . can't I ask him?" A young voice, no doubt Horace's.

"Because—" a female voice, which sounded middle-aged

to his ears, but maybe that was because he'd already learned that the lad's nurse was in her fifties—"you know how your father feels about Sidney."

"But he's my *cousin*! And my best friend. What if something's happened to him?"

"There's no reason to think that. I'm certain no harm will come to him. It's some lout thinking to get a bit of money from your father, that's all. When he realizes his mistake, he'll return Sidney to his parents and slink off into the night."

Interesting—so Horace knew about the kidnapping. They'd wondered if he did, hence why they'd sacrificed their comfort for this evening climb. But the nurse didn't sound nearly worried enough. He would hazard that the household didn't know the staggering amount of the ransom.

"But—"

"If you ask your father if the Harts have received any news, then he'll either know you were eavesdropping on his conversation with your aunt and uncle, which will land you in a heap of trouble, or he'll accuse the staff of speaking of it, and you'll bring trouble down on *everyone's* head. We'll have another Boxing Day with no bonuses if you do that."

Yates's frown was deep enough that he had to direct it toward his sister, just to see her matching one in the faint glow that spilled through the window. That seemed like a strange bit of guilt to saddle a ten-year-old boy with, especially when the boy would be the master someday.

A mighty squeak sounded from within—the unmistakable sound of bedsprings protesting when someone threw himself upon them. "I can't sit up here in the *nursery* and do nothing while Sid's in danger!"

"You're not doing nothing. You're praying for him like your saint of a mother taught you, God rest her soul."

"I ought to be searching for him. It was me they were

after, wasn't it? Yet here I sit while he's . . . while he's . . ."
The brave tone fractured, shattered.

A softer squeak of springs. "There now, dearest. Sidney
will be returned to his parents safe and whole, I have no
doubt of it. In time for Christmas even, I wager. It'll be
naught but an adventure for the two of you to brag about
for years to come."

Yates had to exchange another look with Marigold, whose
lips were pressed tightly together. Empty assurances from a
nurse who simply wanted to comfort her charge? Or something far darker?

It had taken them an hour to decode the telegraph Graham and Gemma had sent this afternoon—Merritt, they'd
learned, was the best man for that job—but they'd pieced
together the suspicions about Fitzroy, and the difference in
the amount of debt for which Wilfred was responsible versus
the amount of the ransom. Yates had only to make a few
calls to learn how much Fitzroy owed to the usual lending
houses and bookies, but adding those in still left a sizable
sum. Greed?

One could never rule it out. But Marigold had offered
another interpretation, whether Fitzroy was involved or not:
an inside man. Or woman.

It made sense. Someone would have to know what train
Horace was to be on, that he'd be boarding one for Basingstoke, not for Derbyshire. Someone had to know to send the
ransom note here to Fellsbourne instead of the Wilfred home
in London, where the earl was more often in residence, even
over his son's school holidays. Last Christmas, he'd never
bothered coming home; the boy had simply been brought
to London on Christmas Eve for an obligatory three days
together. Someone would be wanting to let the kidnapper
know if the money were being gathered.

If such a someone existed, then they might also let the

kidnapper know he'd taken the wrong kid, which could spell either relief or disaster for Sidney, depending on the nature and mood of the culprit.

And so here they were, eavesdropping now and making plans to infiltrate the household tomorrow morning and chat up a few of the servants before they boarded a train for Devonshire.

No sounds of outright weeping came through the glass, but a few sniffles reached his ears. "I don't want this adventure. I *want* to know that Sid's safe. What if they don't let him go when they realize their mistake? What if they hurt him because Father won't pay?"

"Oh, sweet boy. No one would expect him to pay ten thousand pounds for a child not his own."

Ten thousand? *False information.* Someone was giving out lies in the house.

"If he gets hurt because I didn't want to visit Aunt Ursula, I'll never forgive myself."

"He won't get hurt."

"You don't know that! He *could*! I have to talk to Father; I have to convince him to at least send *something*. Maybe if they get even a bit, they'll let him go." Another squeal of springs and then pounding steps away from the window.

"Horace Wilfred, don't you dare leave this room! If you go and bother your father with this now, he'll—"

The slam of a door cut off the nurse's shout. There was no telling when the two would come back to the nursery. They'd guessed from the routine they'd observed via binoculars last night that they would come up here after dinner at around the same time tonight, but now? There was little point to dangling about up here, freezing their noses and toes off. "Down?"

Marigold followed her nod with a quick scurry back the way they'd come. "Did we want to try to listen at Wilfred's study window?" she asked in a whisper once their feet had found solid—as in, frozen *solid*—ground again.

Yates rubbed his hands together to try to tease a bit of warmth into them. What he *wanted* was that mug of hot mulled cider back at the inn they'd rented two rooms from for the night. But at least listening to something on the ground floor could involve hunkering down in their heavy coats, with gloves back on their fingers and boots back on their feet. "Might as well while we're here."

At the corner of the house, they reclaimed their winter wear from the shrubbery in which they'd hidden them. Once back in the blessed wool, Yates drew his torch from his pocket and flashed a quick message to where Merritt was playing lookout for them by the stand of bare-limbed trees. Rather handy that his brother-in-law had already known Morse code. He spelled out *On ground; now study* letter by letter before returning the torch to his pocket. Merritt couldn't exactly signal back without risking someone from the house seeing the light, but at least he wouldn't be worrying.

The study was on the opposite side of the house. But the good news was that winter's darkness was thick enough that they could simply run through it, with little fear of being spotted. No staff were outside on this frigid evening, and few rooms were lit inside the house that they had to be careful of.

Five breathless minutes later, they crept to the space under the study's window.

All was silent within, though the golden light spilling out from the bank of windows promised the room wasn't empty. Yates settled silently onto the ground, trying to ignore the way the cold sank through his trousers in about half a second, and looked over at his sister.

She had that look on her face that said she was straining to hear sounds beyond her normal range, and he could all but see her mentally reciting the words they'd already overheard. Really, one of them probably could have handled this on their own. There hadn't been any jumps or swings that required two people.

But he didn't know how often she'd really be out here with him after this. She was married now, and married meant children, most likely. He certainly wouldn't be tossing her about on the trapeze or from building ledge to building ledge when she was with child. And once she was a mother, she could well lose her desire for such feats anyway. He'd have to take his act solo. Limit their surveillance to places he could reach on his own. Maybe even relegate her to office work, because he could only imagine the torture Merritt would inflict on him if she were ever caught in a questionable situation and arrested.

Leopard stripes. What a depressing thought.

Two minutes in, a cough from the study at least verified that Lord Wilfred was there. Though after another ten of silence, Yates was about ready to call it quits, and he suspected Marigold would be too.

Then he caught the sound of a soft knock. Yes!

Lord Wilfred called out, "Enter." And a moment later said, "Ah, Horace. Have you come to say good night?"

"It's only seven o'clock, Father." And the boy's opinion on being thought ready for bed at seven o'clock came through loud and clear, even with glass and stone between them.

"Hmm. So it is. Well, then. Shall we . . . ?" He faltered, apparently unable to come up with any pastimes to share with his son.

Sad, that. Not nearly as sad as parents not knowing where their son even was on this wintry night, but still sad, in a subtler way.

"I don't want to read together or play a game of cards or listen to that infernal record again. I don't want to show you what I've learned at school this term or have you look over my letter of apology to Aunt Ursula."

A scraping sound, like a chair being pushed across the wooden floor. "All right, then. What *do* you want to do?"

"*I* don't want to do anything. I want *you* to do something for someone else for a change!"

"What—"

"You can't sit here while Sidney is in danger! He's your nephew!"

"He was your mother's nephew. He's not my anything." Wilfred's voice was colder than the frozen ground and every bit as full of life.

"Well, he's my cousin, and I'm your son, if you recall. Or maybe that doesn't matter to you either. Maybe if they *had* grabbed me, you'd still be sitting here, claiming you won't negotiate with kidnappers. Maybe I mean so little to you—"

"That is quite enough." The snap of words was punctuated by a *thunk* of wood on wood. "This outburst does you no credit, and I would like to know who even told you of the situation, as I gave specific instructions that—"

"It isn't fair! They *ought* to have taken me, it wouldn't have mattered! But Sid . . . his parents actually *miss* him. They love him, they'd do anything to get him back, if they could. I saw them here the other day, I heard them—"

"Eavesdropping!" Wilfred shouted the word like it was the most serious crime ever to be discussed.

Ironic, given that he'd been eavesdropping about a kidnapping and extortion. And even more ironic, given that Yates was doing it right now. He sent a wink toward Marigold, who caught it with a grin.

"That! Right there! You are more concerned with controlling us all than with my cousin's *life* or my happiness!"

The scrape of a chair again. "Happiness," Lord Wilfred spat, "is an illusion. You'll do well to learn that now."

"It isn't! Not in *other* families, anyway."

The slam of a door signaled that Horace had stormed from the room, and Wilfred didn't so much as mutter anything for them to continue to overhear after that. So, after another five boring minutes, he and Marigold snuck away from the house and then ran across the dark lawn to the trees where Merritt waited.

With, God bless him, steaming cups of tea poured from the Thermos of it he'd brought. It wasn't quite mulled cider, but it would do. "Good man," Yates said as he took his. "I think we'll keep you around. Always said we needed a tea girl on the team."

"Careful, or you'll end up with it poured over your head instead."

"Sounds delightful right about now." He took a sip. It wasn't exactly *hot*, but it was warm enough by contrast to feel like bliss. "Ah. Heaven."

Merritt handed Marigold hers as well and then wrapped an arm about her. Possibly for extra warmth. But probably not. "What did you learn?"

"That someone had better be keeping an eye on young Horace." Marigold took a sip of her tea, and then a deeper drink when she found it not scalding. "He knows what's going on and is concerned enough to get himself into trouble trying to help."

She had a point. "Probably good that Wilfred hired guards."

"They're not very *good* guards. We got past them without any trouble, didn't we?" Merritt glanced toward the gate-house, where two of the four hired guards had been playing cards and sharing a fifth of something or another that made them jolly. The other two were inside the main house, but they certainly hadn't kept Horace from either listening in on the confrontation with the Harts or from confronting his father about it.

Still. "We're better at this than your average criminal, I like to think. Given that we're not. Criminals, I mean. If one squints at the trespassing bit, given that it's all in the name of justice and helping people in need."

The law might not say it was, but Yates's conscience was clear on the matter.

Merritt shook his head in the shifting moonlight. "What else?"

Between the two of them, Yates and Marigold filled him in as they hiked back to the village.

Much like Yates, he seemed especially concerned about the nurse's bad information about the demanded ransom. "Did Wilfred tell the staff that was the amount? But why? One would think that they would be more understanding, not less, of his refusal to cooperate, given the higher amount."

"I don't think we can assume she got the information from Wilfred." A cloud scuttled out from in front of the moon just in time for Yates to see a frozen-over puddle and sidestep it. "We have to ask the question—what if she's in on it? What if she was promised a cut by percentage, and so simply told a lower amount so they could pay her less?"

"Would she really give her own charge over to villains like that?" No moonlight was necessary to show Marigold's horror with that idea.

"Nurses have been found guilty of such things before—and worse." Not thoughts he cared to dwell on, and not crimes they usually investigated. "But I daresay she'd have been assured of his safety. She stressed that quite a bit, didn't she? That Sidney would be fine."

"I don't know." Merritt coughed into his gloved fist. The pneumonia that had made their paths cross to begin with last spring had cleared, but the cold air seemed to tease a bit of that nagging cough back to his lungs. "If she were the inside man—or woman, as it were—wouldn't she have already sent

word that they had the wrong boy? Or be trying to talk Lord
Wilfred into paying out despite them having the wrong one?"

Yates sighed and focused his gaze on the glow of light
in the windows of the town up ahead, now coming into
view. He doubted they would come to a conclusion in the
five minutes left of their walk, at least when it came to who
the traitor in Fellsbourne was, assuming there was one. But
he had a feeling Marigold's intuition about Horace himself
was accurate.

That boy loved and missed his cousin, felt guilty for his
inadvertent role in the situation, and was determined to set
things to rights.

Which could very likely spell disaster for them all if he
proved as slippery with the guards and his nurse as he and
Sidney had proven themselves to be at school.

NINE

$\mathcal{G}$emma eased her bedroom door shut, breath knotted in her chest at its squeaking hinges. She held the breath for ten long seconds, but no footsteps sounded from behind the other doors, and no curious faces peeked out to see who was slipping out of her room.

She'd never actually attended any house parties, but she'd been a society columnist long enough to know that everything wasn't all innocent fun at them, much of the time. It was not-so-secret liaisons and trysts, often with both wives and mistresses invited to keep powerful men happy. So far as she knew, Dowager W wasn't the sort to endorse such behavior openly.

And Gemma didn't want anyone thinking her the type to engage in them secretly either. Even if, technically speaking, she *was* slipping out of her room at midnight to rendezvous with a man. And even if she *had* once been quite at home in that man's arms.

This wasn't romance, though. It was rescue—at least, that was her prayer.

She tiptoed down the hallway, her boots cradled in her arms and ready to be put on once she was away from the other sleeping ladies. She already wore her black coat, and she'd chosen a utilitarian blue knit cap to cover her hair. Paired with the dark grey trousers she'd donned for the occasion—they'd been Yates's back when he was only her height—she was as ready for sneaking about outside as she could be.

The house creaked around her as she descended the stairs, but it was the comfortable, lazy sort of creaking of an old house holding its own against the wind. The *tap* and *pop* of pipes heating in the baseboards, the groan of boards cooling and contracting in the night.

She'd spent most of the afternoon outside with Graham and Fitzroy, and half of that time also with Carissa Horley and Lord Astley. It had proven to be more entertaining than she'd expected, even as she noted all the times that Lady Weymouth's nephew had seemed duplicitous or outright deceitful. She didn't trust him for a second—but he was clever and charming, anyway.

He had indeed shown them one little alcove of stone set into the hillside, which clearly went nowhere. And he'd also taken them down to the seashore and pointed out a cavern in the chalk cliffs, where monks had supposedly hidden from Viking invaders. Carissa and Astley had been with them for that portion, but her new friend had strayed a bit too close to the surf and ended up with a soaked hem and shoes, and Astley had helped her back to the house to change.

That was when Graham really got down to business. He had asked Fitzroy to show them some other parts of the property, and the hours-long tour was mostly Graham leading them about with his questions and Fitzroy doing his best to dodge giving straight answers.

Entertaining, to be sure. Especially since every time he invited them to look to the right, Graham was no doubt making a mental note of something to the left. Gemma had no clue what he might have discovered, but it was something, apparently. He'd slipped her a note after dinner telling her to meet him at the side door beside the billiards room at midnight and to wear her warmest and most practical clothes.

The clock even now chimed the changing of the day, and Gemma's heart pounded along with it.

Christmas Eve. Any other year, she might have spent it weaving a holiday tale or planning festivities of their own. This was their final day to find Sidney before the ransom was due. Twenty-three hours before that unspeakable sum was expected to be slid into the poor box, or . . . what?

She turned down the dark side hall, holding her breath yet again when laughter filtered through a closed door under which light seeped. Some of the guests, it seemed, were still at their whist game, which came as no great surprise. But they didn't seem inspired to retire by the chiming of the clock, and she slipped out into the cold night without anyone noticing her.

Only once out in the biting air did she bend to slip her feet into her boots, then pull her gloves onto her fingers before they lost their heat.

A band of pressure cinched around her chest as she stared out into the night. Clouds scuttled in front of the moon, playing hide-and-seek with the stars, and her breath made little clouds of its own to join them.

It should have been a peaceful scene. Quiet and lovely and full of promise. They were but hours away from celebrating the birth of the Savior.

But in London, a mother would be sitting at her window and looking up at this same sky and praying with every ounce of faith that her boy would be given back to her—the only gift she'd ever again want, Gemma knew. Her husband would be serving rich, entitled gents at the Marlborough Club, trying not to let a stitch of worry show on his face lest a patron complain about his inattentiveness and get him sacked.

And their son . . . Their son could be somewhere within a mile of her, held by strangers against his will. Could he see the moon and stars? Did he sleep? Did he even know that Christmas Eve had officially begun?

A soft hoot invaded the night, a near-perfect imitation of an owl. But not quite. Gemma turned in the direction of the call and searched the shadows for Graham's familiar form. She finally spotted the darker shadow of him, motioning her to follow him.

They didn't speak as they walked. Once upon a time, that wasn't unusual for them. They could spend hours in silence together, their fingers often woven together. But in the last year, she'd done her best never to be alone with him—and for the few moments they were, one or the other was always filling the silence with words.

Biting words, pleading words. Apologies or defenses. Accusations or deflections.

She'd missed this, more than she'd let herself realize. Just *being* with him, even when they were about serious business. In her place at his side, catching a whiff of his cologne, feeling his every familiar movement and hearing his every familiar noise. She missed it because it had been a part of her life for most of her memory, long before it meant romantic love. He had been her best friend, every bit as much as Marigold was.

That's why his betrayal had hurt so much.

"Faithless is faithless," she'd said that morning. But it had been meant to jar him more than to accuse him of anything. Because what he'd claimed was true—he'd never looked at other pretty girls. Only her. *That* had never been the sort of betrayal she had to fear.

A dip in the terrain, invisible in the night, sent her off-balance for a second. She stumbled toward him, and he reached out to steady her. Her pulse kicked up again, not from the trip or from the adrenaline of possible discovery, but just because he'd touched her.

She pulled away in the next step. But this time, she tried not to make a point of it. Even so, that was enough of the dangerous silence. Any more of it, and it would lure her into confronting all the things she'd sworn not to remember again. She cleared her throat. "Where are we going?"

"East end of the gardens." His whisper was warm against the cold. "Did you notice the odd bit of terracing that Fitzroy tried to direct us away from earlier?"

She'd noticed the behavior—not the quirk. "Terracing is odd?"

"In that spot, yes. There was no reason for it. I suspect there's something underground there, and after spending the evening with a few dusty old tomes I found in the library about the original house, I have a good idea of where an entrance to it might be, if indeed it's a chamber."

Gemma shook her head, though not because she doubted him. He had, after all, discovered several priest hides at Alnwick Abbey that generations of Hemming family and servants hadn't known about. "What exactly do you need me for?"

The fickle moonlight caught his face now, showing her the arch of his brow. "What, you don't want to come? Find a hidden room under the gardens?"

"Of course I do." Lionfeathers. She hadn't meant to *say* so, even if he knew it was true. "But it would arguably be easier for only *one* of us to slip out unnoticed."

"Exploring alone isn't nearly so much fun, though. Here— along that brick walkway now."

She'd been his exploring partner for far too long to bother arguing with that, so she settled for drawing her torch from her pocket when he did the same and directing the beam along the path. This part of the garden wouldn't be visible from the house, thanks to the slope of the ground and a few well-placed trees.

She didn't know what they were looking for, but she knew when Graham found it. He drew in a sharp breath, puffed it out again, and then rushed forward, toward a large, flat stone that looked as though it had been shaped by human hands into its arched shape. "A toppled standing stone?" That was her best guess.

Graham was shaking his head. "No, not that old. It's a Christian marker." He flashed his beam over markings she could scarcely even see in the scant light and through centuries of moss and lichen growth.

"Is that a cross?"

"A *chi ro pax*, I think."

She could see that now that he pointed it out. The long-stemmed *P* with the *X* through it, the early Christian symbol of peace. "Evidence that there was indeed a monastery here, then, but we already knew that. What makes you think . . . ?"

He knelt down, sliding a hand into the area around it, working his way around the stone. "In a few old sketches I found, monasteries in this area had a stone like that near the narthex. Ah!"

She lifted her torch a little higher to try to make out what he was doing and had to shake her head again when he vanished—just vanished—under the stone. "Have you found a portal to another world?"

"More or less" came his voice from the netherworld. Or perhaps, she saw as she toed aside the overgrowth of vines and saplings, from down those crumbling stone steps that were invisible until one looked at precisely the right angle.

Leopard stripes. This sort of thing was always far more alluring in daylight. "Tell me there are no spiders, at least."

"It's suspiciously tidy, actually."

"Good. On all counts." Tidy meant someone else had

been here. She stepped cautiously down each stone, careful to duck as she passed under the lip of the pax stone.

It was indeed a different world. All the normal night sounds from aboveground were instantly gone, and in their place came a faint trickle of water. No wind, no surf on shore, no animals foraging or swooping through the tree branches. It smelled like damp earth, and the darkness was so thick that their little torches barely made a dent in it. "How far do you think it goes?"

"I don't know." He turned his beam this way and that, following it a little ways to the right. "If this is the old monastery, it was a goodly size. But who knows what remains intact under here? I daresay much of it has caved in by now."

Not really tunnels, then. Halls. Corridors. Narthex and nave, transepts and presbytery. Cloisters and garth and range. She let out a slow breath. There could be bits and pieces of the monastery complex under the entire house and gardens. And if enough of it were still intact and accessible, it would provide uncountable places to hide.

Gemma followed Graham and his beam to the right, sending her own light along the floor as his tracked higher. She was tempted to ask him how he decided to go this direction rather than the opposite, but she bit her tongue. Sometimes those sorts of questions only served to showcase her own lack of observation. Better to look around. To note, as he had already indicated, the lack of cobwebs. The way the dried leaves were all gathered at the edges here, as if someone had hurried along and sent them scattering.

Someone had been here recently, that was beyond dispute. The question was who, and if they had a kidnapped lad with them. How, though, could they know that, aside from stumbling upon captors and captive?

They walked along in silence for several minutes, their steps slow and silent by unspoken consent. If Sidney was hidden away somewhere in this buried monastery, they certainly didn't want to alert his guards of their approach.

Guards. The thought of men holding the boy here by force made wariness sweep up her spine. Would they be armed? Her stomach went sick and tight at the memory of Yates nursing a knife wound six months ago—the first time in all their years of running the Imposters that anyone had been injured by violence.

She had no desire for that new disruption to their pattern of peaceful reconnaissance to be repeated. She was a writer, not a soldier or police officer. Perhaps the pen was mightier than the sword, but she had no desire to test its efficacy against modern firearms. And it wasn't as though Graham, with his slide rule and white pencil, would be any better able to handle ruffians.

What they had to do, then, was find the boy without being found in return. Survey the situation. Rescue him when the risk would be at its lowest.

They turned another corner, and for a moment Gemma thought Graham must have been working through the same thoughts, given the way he slowed. Then the way he moved his flickering beam over the space ahead made her realize that the darkness had turned solid.

A wall stood before them, and its presence seemed to surprise Graham.

She eased to his side, her voice the smallest of whispers. "Not supposed to be here?"

"I wouldn't have thought so." His voice was just as low, barely finding her through the foot of space between them. When his torch sputtered again and died, he slapped it against his palm. It flickered back on, but weakly. "Different stone, too, than the walls."

Was it? It looked the same to her eyes—dark and square, that is—but she was no expert. She simply nodded and swept her own beam of light around the floor.

A curl of white, bright as hope, caught the beam. She snaked out a hand and gripped Graham's arm, holding the light steady on it to show him what she'd seen.

He sucked in a sharp breath and took the two long strides necessary to put him at the fabric, then crouched down and scooped it up.

Her throat seized. Her first thought had been that it was some sort of bandage . . . but no. The cloth was too fine, the length and shape too distinctive.

It was a necktie. A small, boy-sized tie—exactly like the ones every Ludgrove student wore.

Graham stood again, his expression as stony as the wall behind him. He'd recognize the tie as surely as she had, which was why a million thoughts flashed through his eyes as he fingered the material and slipped it into his pocket, and why he sent his weak beam over that unexpected wall with renewed energy.

The torch went out again, and no amount of jiggling or muttering convinced it to come back on. Gemma handed him hers, even though relinquishing the light to him made her instantly aware of the darkness around her. But he only used it for a minute before sighing and handing it back.

"What?" she asked. That sigh had been of defeat. "Don't tell me you don't know where to go next. If Sidney was here—right here—then he can't be too far off now."

"I *do* in fact know where we need to go, unfortunately— back up. I need the library."

"What?" It took all her restraint to keep her volume low. "*Now?*"

Apparently. He strode off into the darkness, back the way they'd come. "There's no secret door hidden in that wall, Gem. They must have turned to the right back there where we continued straight."

"But they were *here*. Clearly!"

"Because they don't know their way around down here

either, I suspect. I think . . ." His voice had gotten a fraction louder, proving his confidence in his theory. "I think whoever has Sidney had a particular place in mind to hold him and that this would have been the most direct route to it, had it not been walled off. When it was, they'd have had to find another way."

"And on what do you base this theory?" Gemma scrambled after him.

He shot her a patronizing look that she had no trouble picking up on even in the dim light. "Do you have a better one?"

She huffed. She'd have *liked* to argue that there must have been a way through the wall—a door with a hidden latch or something. But he'd have known what to look for if that were true. No, far more likely was that the kidnappers had brought Sidney along this passage as he said, only to run into the wall. They'd have been upset, thrown off guard, and Sidney had likely tried to take the opportunity to escape. A scuffle well could have ensued, in which the boy's tie fluttered to the ground, unnoticed—or else he'd dropped it purposefully for someone to find.

But he wasn't there now. Obviously. Which meant they'd have taken him another way. "Fine, then. Where were they going?"

"I don't know. That's why I need the library. These corridors don't seem to be arranged in the typical fashion. If it was built in a different style, perhaps there's a text about it."

It was on the tip of her tongue to snap out that they hadn't enough time to spend hours scouring every book in the library for a sketch that might or might not even exist and to insist that they explore more now, physically.

Perhaps she would have let those words fly right off that tongue-tip, too, had her own flashlight not given a warning flicker.

Blast it all. That was what she got for bringing an Imposter-issued one with her, as Graham had no doubt done as well. Yates would have put the batteries in them at the same time, so naturally they'd die at the same time too. Drattedly inconvenient. She'd have a word with him about that when next she saw him.

For now, though, it forced her to agree to Graham's plan. "All right. The library, then—and we'd better hurry."

Out of this dark place before her torch died, yes, but they needed to find something useful in the library in a hurry too.

Gemma whispered an urgent prayer—and tried to ignore the way Graham went stiff beside her when she did. They had too much to do in the next day as it was. She hadn't time to worry about his faith gone cold.

TEN

Usually the hours Graham spent in a library were among his happiest, especially if he'd brought sketching paper and pencils and his slide rule along. Usually, he could spend hours upon hours bouncing from one text to another, taking notes and building houses, castles, churches, libraries, or other buildings in his mind and on the page, thanks to the words and diagrams found in all those helpful books.

But usually there wasn't a clock ticking its way down toward disaster. *Eighteen hours. Seventeen. Sixteen.* He paused to eat, to glare at the unforgiving mantel clock. He pretended that the sound of laughter and conversation that drifted down the hall didn't annoy him, and he told himself that it was good that Gemma was in there with the company instead of here by his side.

He didn't believe himself. Not for a second. Perhaps she was gaining vital information in the drawing room, but he wanted her *here*, with him. Leafing through any text that might mention the monastery, teasing him about the wrinkle of concentration between his brows, critiquing the sketch he'd made of what could possibly be hidden under Weywent grounds.

He wanted to glance up and see the cloud-filtered sunlight highlighting her hair. He wanted to catch a whiff of the floral scent she favored. He wanted her to catch him staring and look up and smile at him.

Instead, he had only the tyrant of a clock, the echoes of oblivious laughter, and an empty side mocking him. *Fifteen hours. Fourteen. Thirteen.*

He straightened from where he was hunched over his sketches and stretched, rolling his head about to try and loosen his stiff neck. Exhaustion made his eyelids heavy, but there was no time to sleep. How could he? There was a boy somewhere under the manor grounds, he was certain of it.

His best guess as to where the kidnappers had been trying to take him was the monks' cells. It made sense. They were small and clustered together. The close walls would have provided structure enough to ensure they hadn't caved in under the weight of the earth and buildings overtop them, unlike some of the larger chambers that well could have collapsed. And that corridor he and Gemma had traveled down could have led directly to them, had it not been sealed off. That wasn't the layout he'd been expecting, but his research thus far showed him it was an arrangement in use in the area at the time, so it was a perfectly valid theory.

He glanced toward the library door, willing Gemma to come sashaying through it so that he could tell her what he'd discovered thus far. When that failed, he stood and strode toward the collection of guests and, more importantly, the trays of tea things kept always at their disposal. A hot cup and a sweet biscuit might serve to revive him for another few hours of work.

The moment he entered the drawing room, his gaze tracked her way, like it always did. She sat by the window, its light reminding him that her hair wasn't currently glowing the right color—though the red tint had faded a bit, hadn't it? Mrs. Horley sat at her side, chattering and gesturing and laughing. Gemma smiled along, but she didn't look as though she'd gotten much sleep either, despite the fact that he'd sent her resolutely to bed when they reached the house.

It wouldn't have done for anyone to find them in the library together in the middle of the night, not if they didn't want to gain attention. He was familiar enough with society types to know that nothing set them abuzz quite like a perceived romantic liaison. It was perfectly ordinary for him to look her way and seek out her company when *in* company, and even to take walks together in the brisk winter air during daylight hours. But any nighttime meetings would cross a line into noteworthy.

He aimed himself for the refreshment table and smiled with heartfelt gratitude at the maid who was even then pouring a new batch of hot water into the teapot. He perused the offering of sweets while she finished and then poured a cup of blessed tea once she was gone.

"You look as though you haven't slept a wink in days."

The familiar voice didn't exactly make him jolt, but it did send a pleasant bolt of warmth through him. He angled a tired smile toward Gemma. "Now that you mention it . . ."

She frowned. "You'll be no good to anyone if you don't rest, Mr. Wharton." Her tone was light, easy. If anyone were paying them the slightest attention, they would hear only a friendly tone. But he could see worry and concern in her eyes.

For him? He wanted to think so, but the sad truth was that it was probably only concern for Sidney Hart, not for Graham. The lad needed him to be at his best.

But what good would a rested Graham be to him if he couldn't find where he was being held? With a sigh, Graham let his gaze wander the room. Fitzroy was there, along with his friend, frowning over a card game.

He still wasn't certain what to make of the lady's nephew. He clearly didn't want Graham snooping about the old monastery—but why? Because he was involved in the kidnapping? Or was there some other reason?

"Graham." Gemma's voice, quiet but demanding, drew his gaze back to her. Her expression brooked no argument. "Get some sleep. You know very well that you'll make better sense of everything once you've rested."

He also knew he had a bad habit of oversleeping and ignoring his alarm clock when he was tired, and *that* wouldn't do. But with no one to wake him up at a given time . . .

Clearly, she could still read his mind. Her eyes softened, and a bit of a smile even tugged up the corners of her mouth. "I'll send a servant up to rouse you at . . . one o'clock? Two?"

"One." That would give him a three-hour nap if he went up straightaway—ample time to clear the haze of exhaustion from his mind. Though it seemed a shame to waste the cup of tea he'd poured. He offered it to Gemma instead of lifting it to his own lips. "Here you are. I fixed this for you. Didn't know it at the time, but . . ." But it was how she liked it, milky and sweet.

She frowned. "Since when do you put milk in your tea?"

Since you stopped drinking yours with me. It had been one small way to feel like she was still there at his side. Not that he was about to say that here, now. He shrugged. "My tastes are ever evolving."

Her arched brow called him on the blatant lie—she'd always teased him about how he'd never outgrown his childhood preferences—but she didn't voice it. She simply accepted the cup with a vague smile. "Thank you for the tea. Happy resting."

"One o'clock." He held her gaze a moment more to make certain she didn't intend to be generous and grant him more time than that.

Her nod was somber and solemn. She understood the gravity of the situation as well as he did. "One o'clock."

He ate the biscuits as he exited the drawing room and traveled along the corridors that would deliver him to the bachelor wing, but he scarcely tasted them. Each step made him all the more aware of the fact that he hadn't slept in twenty-eight hours. His limbs were heavy, his mind foggy. The sounds from the rooms around him seemed tinny, distant.

He yawned as he let himself into his borrowed bedroom, his gaze falling happily upon the modest bed. Almost there. He wasn't about to undress just to take a three-hour nap, but he stumbled his way over to the window so he could toe off his shoes and leave his jacket and tie on the chair positioned beside it.

Clouds were gathering along the coast, and cold radiated from the glass. His fingers tightened on the silk of his tie. Snow? *No. Please.* He yanked the tie down, undoing the knot with more force than was necessary and tossing it to the chair when he realized his thoughts had sounded dangerously close to a prayer.

As if God would withhold bad weather this year any more than He had last. No, He had sent the storm last Christmas, so why would He refrain this year? It wouldn't matter that it could hinder their work to recover Sidney. It wouldn't matter if it would bring the horror back to the forefront of their minds—as if the day itself weren't enough to do that.

He wrestled the sleeves of his jacket from his arms and tossed it to the chair too, breath heaving with the effort.

He'd liked the snow once. Playing in it as a child, lobbing it at Yates, walking through it with Gemma. Now he was tempted to curse that first lazy flake that drifted down outside his window and anyone fool enough to be out in it.

Like that chap there below, striding through the garden. Graham frowned and stepped closer, blinking both the anxiety and the exhaustion from his eyes so he could squint down at the figure. Fitzroy? He'd been in the drawing room, but that didn't mean he was still. Perhaps he was going to the hidden monastery. Perhaps Graham ought to follow him. Perhaps he would lead him directly to . . .

No, not Fitzroy. The man paused, turned, lifted a hand in greeting to someone, and showed himself to be, rather, Lord Astley. And it was Mrs. Horley chasing after him.

Well then. Graham relaxed and pulled the curtains closed, then dropped onto the bed. For a moment, he worried that he wouldn't be able to quiet his thoughts enough to sleep.

Then something was pounding, calling him from oblivion, and he jerked from the arms of slumber back to awareness.

The door. Someone was knocking at the door. "Yes?" He croaked it more than he called it, proving he'd been asleep more than a few minutes.

"One o'clock, Mr. Wharton."

"Thank you." He pushed himself up before his eyelids could fall again, though it felt a bit like wading through molasses. Light—light would help. He rose and pulled open the curtains rather than reaching for the switch on the bedside lamp. Daylight would help convince him it was time for rising far more than electric would.

"Blast." A light dusting of white had covered the world, though no flakes were currently falling. He hoped the weather wouldn't keep Yates and Marigold and Sir Merritt from coming. If it was snowing at all here on the southern coast, chances were good that they were getting serious amounts in Northumberland.

Had they even returned to Northumberland, though? Probably not. London. And . . . wherever Lord Wilfred's estate was. His muddled mind wouldn't deliver that information.

Which wouldn't do at all. He needed his brain engaged and his senses on alert for the evening to come.

A bath. Fresh clothes. Then that tea—or its match, anyway—that he'd passed off to Gemma earlier. Perhaps food, if there were any set out.

Half an hour later, he felt marginally more human as he made his way back to the central part of the house and the bands of merrymakers making their merriment known to anyone within a half-mile radius. He cast one longing look toward the library but then ducked into the drawing room for sustenance.

"There you are. I was beginning to think you'd fallen back asleep."

Graham spun at the voice. He'd expected, perhaps, Gemma to greet him, but it was Yates who stood grinning at him. And, bless him, holding out a cup and plate. Graham took them with a smile. "Thanks. Are we allowed to know each other?"

Yates snorted a laugh. "I daresay there's no point in hiding it, since anyone who does a bit of digging would realize the connection. Not that we need to broadcast it, per se, but at the very least friendliness shouldn't be notable."

"Mm." That was all Graham could manage around a mouthful of sandwich. He cast his gaze over the room, spotting Gemma amidst a cluster of ladies who were looking at—but not speaking to—Marigold.

Even knowing that Marigold had cultivated such a response purposefully, it set his teeth on edge. How in the world could she tolerate being gawked at like she was? Without anyone ever bothering to be a friend?

Although, to be fair, she did look more like a fashion plate than an actual woman, with today's absurd dress and headpiece. Graham certainly wouldn't have had the gumption to approach her and strike up a conversation if he didn't already know that beneath the feathers and ribbons and silk was a girl as unpretentious as one could get, who preferred the stable with her retired circus lion to any ballroom.

And at least she now had Sir Merritt at her side. That had to give her some comfort.

He washed the bite of sandwich down with a swig of tea. "I do hope 'distract the company' was her stated goal this afternoon."

"Why else would she have chosen that headdress?" Yates grinned. "With her there grabbing attention and G. M. Parker observing it all cattily from across the room, I daresay no one will notice when you and I slip out and go exploring. Or whatever else we need to do."

Graham nearly winced. "We'll have to be careful. The snow will mark anywhere we go. And I still haven't quite sorted out where to take us. I could use a bit longer with my books in the library."

That, however, wasn't the cause of the disappointment that sank through him as he considered going out with his oldest friend. No, it was quite simply the thought that he wanted to adventure more with Gemma, not with Yates. Nothing against Yates, of course. But . . . *Gemma.*

His friend lifted his brows, clearly reading something of his hesitation. "The snow's already been well trampled by the staff. I doubt our steps would really clue anyone in as to what we're up to. Though if we need another hour or two in the library first, you know I'm always game for research."

Nodding, Graham glanced at the tall case clock in the corner of the room. Depending on how that research went, he wasn't entirely certain they'd have time both for that and outdoor adventuring before they had to dress for dinner and the ball. Speaking of which . . . "We should go over our plan for the night too. I imagine the ball will still be in full swing at eleven. How are we to all slip away? Or will only some of us?"

"Ah." Yates grinned. "We've already been making a big to-do about how tiring the trip was, and Marigold has braced our hostess for our early retirement, though we've promised we'll put in an appearance first. No one will think anything of it if we all 'retire' early. How long do you think we'll need to get to the church?"

"Probably between twenty and thirty minutes, depending on the snow and whether we have to avoid walking in areas where it hasn't been disturbed yet. And we'll want to be in position early." Better still if they could find Sidney *before* the time of the ransom drop. "I ought to be able to leave quite early. I haven't really been a crucial part of the party."

Mrs. Horley was the only one who'd made it a point to talk to him, other than when Fitzroy and Astley were leading him about out of doors. No one would think anything of it if he put in only a cursory appearance at the dinner and ball. The real question was how or if Gemma would be able to get away. Although if she couldn't manage an escape, she could still be useful inside. She could let them know if Fitzroy or anyone else disappeared, and when.

For now, though, the library. He stared at Gemma until she looked his way—which only took fifteen seconds—and nodded to thank her for sending the wake-up knock. He then motioned subtly with his plate between him and Yates and gave another nod, small and quick, toward the general direction of the library so that she'd know where they went.

She tilted her chin ever so slightly in response, in a way that would look like a simple acknowledgment to all the ladies flocked around her, then directed her attention back to the women.

A year ago, her look would have been lingering. Warm. Overflowing with love. A year ago, he could have left her side with confidence, knowing he could return to it at any moment. A year ago, she was the one person in the world he never had to doubt, not even a little. Even more than Yates and Marigold, she'd been his center. His family. His everything.

The ache stretched from the soles of his feet all the way up to the crown of his head as he led the way to the library. A year—a whole year without her, without everything that mattered most. Perhaps he ought to be glad that they had this work to give them purpose right now, to keep the memories at bay. Perhaps he ought to be grateful that they were at least in the same house now.

But it was hard to be glad or grateful when he didn't know to whom to direct it. He'd been trained all his life to give his gratitude, his praise, his joy to God. To whom was he to give it if he refused to acknowledge the goodness of the Lord? No one. Which meant, in some strange way, that he didn't even know how to feel that gratitude or gladness. Without a recipient, it was . . . empty. Meaningless.

Joy was meant to be shared. When it was closed up within him, it might as well not exist at all.

Not that he was exactly *joyful* right now, granted. How could he be, given the circumstances? But seeing her, hearing her, catching her scent again after all these months apart couldn't help but fill his heart. She was *home*. She always had been. Without her, he'd been left to drift, alone and lonely.

"I know this is a serious matter, old boy, but you look as though you might cry at any moment, and that's never a good idea when one needs to read." Yates nudged him with a familiar, familial elbow and sent him one of those looks that combined understanding with sympathy and encouragement. He was good at those looks. "I know it's a hard time—it is for all of us. But for you . . . It must be hard—and yet wonderful. Being together again, I mean, and yet not."

Graham sighed. "You have no business being both so wise and so young, Yates. It's annoying." And comforting. He was alone without Gemma, but never fully, completely alone. His family—however distant they might be by blood—would never abandon him. Even when he deserved it.

His cousin laughed. "My youth will vanish soon enough. Let's hope what wisdom I have only increases. So that I can annoy you all the more with each passing year."

Graham smiled too and strode through the doorway of the library with a feeling very nearly of peace. He had a few hours yet, renewed energy, and Yates's company. Surely the answers, then, would be forthcoming. He'd discover an alternate route to the monks' cells that aligned with the passages he'd seen below the manor, and they'd be able to explore with knowledge, not just a blind hope that they'd discover what they needed to without *being* discovered.

His smile faded when he looked at the table he'd been using earlier. The servants had assured him that he could leave out what books he was using, that no one would put them away so long as he was there.

Why, then, was his table all but empty?

Muttering a curse, he shoved his tea and plate onto the first flat surface he passed so that he could run over to the corner he'd staked out upon arrival. His pens and pencils were still there, and his slide rule. But his sketches were gone. The books he'd been reading and studying were gone. His pages of notes were gone.

"What is it?" Yates asked, but he must have guessed. His eyes tracked over the empty table with a frown. "Your workspace is never so clean."

"And it shouldn't be now either." He spat out another choice word that would have earned him a rebuke from Gemma or Marigold or James and spun toward the shelves. An over-tidy maid could have returned the books, having not been informed of his desire for them to be left out. She even could have thrown his papers into a rubbish bin somewhere, if she thought them discarded. In which case he had only to regather the tomes and find said bin.

Except that the shelves still had empty holes where the

books had come from. They weren't in the pile on the cart waiting to be reshelved either, with the novels and sermons and poetry other guests had read and returned. So where were they?

He spun in a circle, surveying the room and any likely place they'd have been stashed. And he would admit it—with each place he checked and found empty, his irritation and anxiety ratcheted up another notch, so that by the time he declared them absolutely missing from the room, he felt wound as tight as an eight-day clock.

Yates moved silently to his side when he came to a rest back at his too-empty table and clapped a hand to his shoulder. "Chin up, old boy. If the books you'd already selected were going to provide answers, you probably would have found them already anyway. Clearly the trick is to find a new book. One that our culprit hasn't got to yet."

"Right. You're right." At least in part. It wasn't as though Graham had gotten all the way through any of the books yet, but he *had* gone straight to the sections he'd hoped would be most helpful, so he already had that knowledge from them. There was a chance that helpful morsels of information were in more obscure sections of the books—that's what he'd been banking on. But Yates still wasn't wrong. Those morsels could just as easily be in other books. "Losing my notes, though . . ."

The meaty hand on Graham's shoulder squeezed. "Come now. Have you forgot your training? Neville would be appalled!"

Graham breathed a laugh. He had been trained in memorization and cataloguing things in his mind as thoroughly as the Fairfax siblings and Gemma—it was just that in recent years he'd had little call to put it to explicit use. *He* wasn't the one usually eavesdropping on conversations that he then had to record, with or without the aid of Gemma's shorthand.

Even so, the excellent memory that Neville and the other actors had trained him in had served him well in ways he probably didn't even pause to consider on a regular basis. He didn't have to refer back to texts nearly as often as his school chums; he could recall information far more quickly than any of his peers; and he cross-referenced and cited sources so easily that everyone in the firm tended to come to him for help with such things.

Another point in Yates's favor, then—his notes weren't *lost*. They simply weren't before him. He could re-create them, more or less verbatim if necessary. Or he could simply build on their foundation, knowing that the information was stored in his mind even if it wasn't handily before his eyes.

He gave a decisive nod. "Right. So then, back to the shelves. Some gem is surely still waiting for us."

Gem. Even saying the word made him think about Gemma, and the countless times she'd been the one at his side in a library or the Archives, scouring the offerings for that certain something that could assist them. Would her absence at his side ever stop aching?

It'll stop when she takes that place again. Hope? Dream? Faith?

No, not faith. That would imply prayer again . . . wouldn't it? Or did having faith in her, in them, exist somehow apart from his faith—or lack thereof—in God?

Blast it all, he needed more than three hours of sleep to be ready to tug on that particular thread again.

Books. Focus on books. The answers were there. They had to be.

"First things first," Yates said. "Are there any gaping holes you see for books you'd set your sights on but not got down yet? Let's determine how proactive our culprit is."

And testament to how well Yates knew his system. He never pulled down at once every book that *might* prove useful. He started with the three most promising, then moved on to three more, and so on. Otherwise he'd end up with tottering stacks on his desk that were impossible to manage. But he always knew which books he'd grab next, if necessary. And in this case, he had a list of nearly a dozen.

All of which were still on the shelves, thankfully. It took him only a few minutes to hunt them all down and pull out six—three for him and three for Yates.

"So *not* proactive. Merely reactionary. Noted." Yates took the books that Graham handed him and settled himself on the opposite side of the table. "Tell me what you've found thus far."

After fetching his cup and plate from the table inside the door, he obeyed while he finished off his tea—tepid now—and food. Yates nodded along, a crease in his brow to say he was not only listening, but actively thinking it all through. At the completion of the tale of their midnight escapade, he frowned toward the window. "Part of me wants to go down there again now with fresh batteries in my torch and explore, but you're right about the risk. We don't want to be seen or heard and risk them either resorting to violence or moving him, not this close to the rendezvous."

"Agreed. But I think . . ." He didn't bother finishing his thought, just pulled out a fresh sheet of blank paper and put down a quick sketch. It in part mimicked what he'd already sketched out, but not in full.

Because he'd been wrong. He couldn't see it earlier through his exhaustion, but he could see it now. Who knew if he would have, had the old sketch been still before him? He should perhaps thank the thief for removing that version entirely. Lips twitching at the thought, he quickly added wings and outbuildings and tunnels to his drawing.

Yates stood and moved to watch from over Graham's shoulder—something he'd been doing long enough that

Graham had long ago given up complaining about it. "Rather unusual design, isn't it?"

"Mm." Which was why he'd not thought to draw it this way before. But it was more in keeping with the indications he'd found on the property and with the history of this area in particular. "Viking invasions, you know. I believe they made changes to the building to provide an extra measure of safety. That's why they'd have built tunnels between the main building and the others on the property."

Gemma would have questioned him on that, demanding quotable logic on why he believed they made these *particular* changes versus some other ones, how he'd arrived at this exact image in his mind.

Yates, however, just grunted his approval. "You're a genius, Graham. And you think they're holding the boy . . . ?"

"Here." He tapped his new idea of where the line of monks' cells could be—still directly accessible from the corridor they'd explored last night. But the rest of the layout, and hence the alternate route, was vastly different from what he'd assumed at the time.

Even without turning, he could sense Yates's grin, wide and boyish. "Perfect. Now we have only to sort out the plan for retrieving him."

ELEVEN

ine o'clock. The chimes could barely be heard over the music from the string quartet set up in the corner of the ballroom, but Gemma had been listening for it. Waiting for it. At the first musical notes from the grandfather clock, her gaze flicked to Marigold and Sir Merritt, who were even then—right on cue—"hiding" yawns and exchanging a whisper.

Gemma's lips wanted to twitch into a smile at the very sight of Lady M in her Christmas finery. Zelda had outdone herself on the gown, awash now in silver beading sewn on in geometric patterns that at once flattered the figure and drew the eye ever downward, away from Marigold's face. It truly was a masterpiece, though it likely weighed about as much as old Eli the Elephant had.

Gemma's fingers itched to touch the taffeta and examine the beading more closely. She would have her chance. No doubt she'd don it at some point herself, to fill in for Lady M while Marigold was scaling a wall or jumping from building to building in a quest for information.

Gemma's emerald green gown was downright plain in comparison. "Simple, classic, and elegant" was how she would have described it for her readers, if her readers gave

131

a whit about what their columnist was wearing. And it had seemed so, in the privacy of her own chamber. But down here, among the plumage of the society ladies and the abundant Christmas decorations that now ornamented the room, she was scarcely more interesting than the garland draping the mantel.

Which was exactly as she had planned it. People noticed when Marigold, Sir Merritt, and Yates left the room a few minutes later, after saying their good nights to their hostess and her family. No one would bat an eye when Gemma slipped from her spot against the wall in another two minutes.

Graham had already left, and no doubt he'd have changed out of his tuxedo and into something more suitable to the night's waiting adventure. Gemma planned to do the same, and then rendezvous with him at the entrance to the monastery at exactly nine twenty. It wouldn't leave them much time to find Sidney, but they were operating on the assumption that if one of the guests of the ball were responsible for both his kidnapping and the collection of the ransom, they wouldn't slip out until close to the eleven o'clock meeting time, to avoid drawing attention to their own absence. The plan was for Gemma and Graham to find him before anyone else left the ball . . . and if they failed, then they would have enough time to return and see who *did* leave.

Thus far, no one else had left for more than a couple minutes, and none had gone anywhere alone. She'd been keeping Fitzroy under tight surveillance, doubly so after catching him slinking into the library that afternoon, clearly in search of whatever else Graham had noted down, though he'd left nothing to be found this time. The dowager's nephew had yet another glass of punch in hand and was laughing with a handful of other guests. He certainly didn't seem to be paying any attention to the time, and that punch wasn't exactly mild. Evidence that he wasn't involved in tonight's dealings, despite clearly working against Graham's research of the monastery? That he was sloppy? Or that he was so slippery she had missed something?

Five after nine. Time for her to leave. She made a show of jotting down a final line in her notebook, stowing it and her ever-present pencil in her small handbag, and turning to the door. No one would be watching, but if they were, they'd simply see a columnist who had recorded everything she needed and now was excusing herself from the company.

"Gabrielle! You're not leaving already, are you? The night has scarcely begun!"

Drat! She had spent a full hour with Carissa already, and she had thought that her new friend was now thoroughly engaged with the couple they'd learned over dinner were nearly her neighbors. Apparently not.

Gemma made sure to smile as she turned, brandishing her handbag and its notebook. "I wanted to take my notes back to my room and jot down a few ideas I had for the article while it's all fresh."

"Oh, but you'll miss the lighting of the tree if you leave now!" Carissa looked genuinely dismayed on her behalf and even went so far as to clutch at Gemma's elbow. "I'm told the children in attendance are going to join us for it, and that it will be an absolute delight."

"I intend to come back down for that." Keeping her smile in place, she glanced about the room. "I simply first need a few moments—"

"To regroup and get your thoughts out. I completely understand." Carissa looped their arms together. "You know, perhaps I should take a respite as well. It isn't often that I'm in such company for a length of time, and I daresay I look positively wilted already. Perhaps I could assist you in your notetaking? I've been making a point of observing everyone.

I've tucked a few details away that you may find useful, if you didn't notice them yourself already."

Bother. Her time for changing out of her gown and into Yates's old trousers was quickly ticking away. "That's very kind of you, Carissa, and I am grateful for any observations you've made—but I confess I'm a bit private about the actual writing process. I'm afraid I can't put words to paper properly if someone is watching. Perhaps you could jot your observations down on your own and give them to me in the morning?"

"In the morning?" Carissa looked horrified. "You said you were coming back down!"

"Well, yes . . ." If the situation worked out that way. With any luck, they'd have young Sidney in hand within the hour and would have to beat a hasty retreat in the Fairfax carriage. If not, then she would indeed make another appearance while Graham met up with Yates and Marigold and Sir Merritt. "But I certainly don't expect *you* to abandon the festivities to write anything down. Tomorrow—or even Boxing Day—is perfectly fine for you to give them to me."

Carissa looked somewhat mollified, but still she stood there, chatting, their arms linked together for half of eternity—or so it seemed to Gemma, who was keenly aware of the march of time. When the hall clock struck a quarter after, she had to forcibly disentangle herself. "I'm so sorry, Carissa, but I'm afraid I've had too much lemonade. Enjoy the ball while I'm gone! I'll see you again soon."

Carissa grinned. "Oh, I will. Perhaps I'll convince that handsome Mr. Wharton to dance. Have you seen him? I don't know where he's vanished to. . . ."

Gemma only shook her head and hastened from the room.

Dash it to pieces. That handsome Mr. Wharton would be at the opening of the monastery in five minutes, and if she wasn't there, he'd go in without her—that was their agreement. If she wasn't there at nine twenty, he was to assume that something had detained her and proceed on his own, and she would simply continue her surveillance here.

She wasn't about to let that happen, even though she had no time to detour to her room for a change of clothes or even a wrap.

Never mind. She'd grown up in the cold of Northumberland, after all. A little southern-coast snow was nothing. And besides, the ballroom had been so hot and close that a few minutes' dash through the wintery air would be a welcome respite, and once underground, she would be fine. Especially since she knew well that if she was chilled, Graham would insist she take his jacket. He was a gallant sort of fellow.

And luckily, she'd made certain to stash her electric torch—with fresh batteries—in her handbag, just in case. And she'd opted for stylish boots under her gown instead of slippers too.

When she slipped outside, she paused for a moment, captured by the magic of snow gliding gently down, the lights from the house shining off each crystal. It painted the world in shades of blues and silvers in a way that never failed to take her breath away.

She hadn't time to dwell on it now, though. She pulled a new breath into her lungs and prayed, *Dear Lord, help us. Help us to find him. Help Yates and Marigold to detain whoever will be there to demand the ransom. Amen.*

Then she ran.

The walkways had been cleared of the morning's snow, and the flakes falling now were beginning to add a new dusting to the pavement. Gemma hurried along the cleared path as long as she could, then lifted her dress a few inches when it came time to dash through the garden and to the hidden opening.

Graham was already there, and her torchlight illuminated

his frown the moment he caught sight of her. "Really? Those are adventuring clothes now?"

The snow was beginning to win out over the heat of the ballroom in her skin, so she brushed past him and into the relative protection of the stone passageway. "I was waylaid by Carissa Horley on my way out of the ballroom. I didn't have time to change," she whispered.

"Well, you shouldn't have come out like *that*." His voice was low but cutting.

She gritted her teeth, but it wasn't enough to bite back the quiet retort. "You wouldn't have waited."

"I couldn't—but you know well that you could slow us down in a dress like that, and the fabric rustles when you move."

She did know. It wasn't as though she had *chosen* this as her attire for the expedition. It was just that she wasn't about to let Graham go hunting for Sidney without her. "It will do. I'll keep it quiet."

He must have heard her unspoken reasoning, like he always had. He flicked on his torch and took off in a stride far brisker than what he'd used last night. "I realize you want to help find him. But putting the entire operation at risk because of your distrust of me—"

"It is hardly putting it at risk! My dress certainly isn't as loud as your accusations!"

His back was to her, but she could *hear* him roll his eyes, she was certain. "But you won't bother denying that you distrust me."

He turned to the right when last night he'd gone straight, and she came to a halt, frowning. She'd peeked at his sketches earlier, and in none of them had *this* been a viable route to where Sidney was most likely being held. "Where are you going?"

Graham halted, pivoted, and flashed his torch up enough

that its general glow caught her face. "What, can you not even trust me in this now? Don't you think I've mapped out our route with the utmost care?"

Her throat went tight. He'd never let the Imposters down when it came to architectural insights—never. He'd never gotten her lost when they went exploring—not even once. But he was exhausted. And no one could keep up so perfect a record forever. And what if tonight, when a lad's life was at stake, was the time he failed? "Tell me where we're going."

"There isn't time. I realized my mistake with the sketch, I corrected it. This is the way to the cells, Gem, I promise. Come on." He turned again, took several steps.

She didn't. Couldn't. She didn't know why, exactly. It was just that he'd pointed it out—that she couldn't trust him. Not anymore.

It was that it was Christmas. Which meant it had been a year, a full year, since the world had come crashing down around them—all because of him. Because of his arrogance, his pride, his determination to prove himself.

Apparently realizing she wasn't following, Graham paused and turned again. Even in the dim surroundings, she could make out the hard lines of his ticking jaw. "What is it? Do you think you know a better way?"

The passage up ahead that branched off to the left certainly seemed the sounder choice—like what he'd been planning earlier. It fit with what she knew of the layout of monasteries. With the research she'd seen him doing. It made all the sense in the world.

Which he knew already. And it wasn't as though *she* was the expert in such matters. Still, she shook her head, less in answer to his question than to the greater one—of whether she'd follow him into the unknown. "We can't let this boy down, and we will if we take a wrong path again. This is our last chance to find him before the rendezvous."

"Which is why we must hurry. Please, Gem—trust me. This is the way."

Trust me. He'd never had to beg her to do that before. She simply always *had.* Because he was Graham Wharton, the cleverest person she knew. Graham, who could find anything, who could create whole worlds with blue paper, white pencil, and a slide rule. Graham, who had brought an end to everything that mattered a year ago when he overruled her objections and bundled them into that accursed automobile for a drive through a too-snowy countryside.

"I can't." They'd already been whispering, but those words emerged as a choked gasp.

"You *can.*" He edged nearer, his tone soft . . . but in that forced way that said he was grasping at calm when he wanted to shout. "We're going to save Sidney."

The tears came out of nowhere. Tears she hadn't let herself shed all these long, interminable months. They burned, surged, and it took every ounce of will she possessed to swallow them down, blink them back.

She wouldn't let them loose here, now. With *him.* She wouldn't let him see the broken pieces he'd left of her. "How? How can I trust you to save someone else's son when you killed your own?"

She might as well have struck him. Graham stumbled back a step, his fingers tightening on the metal handle of his torch. Her words burning into his chest.

Words he had thrown at himself a million times. Words *she* had tossed at him a year ago in that wretched hospital room when she'd told him to leave, that she hated him, that she never wanted to see him again.

Words that hurt every bit as much now as they had then.

"It was an accident, Gem. You know that." Words *he* had been reciting to himself every day since, after everyone— Yates, James, Marigold, the constable, *everyone*—first said them to him.

A snowy, icy road. That blasted storm. *That* was the culprit in their tragedy. That was what had stolen Jamie from them—bad weather, the hand of God.

Funny, though. His own heart didn't believe that any more than Gemma's did. Because she was right. It was his poor judgment that led to their little family being in a car that day on those treacherous roads. She'd wanted them to take the train to Northumberland from London, like they always did. She'd stood there in the entryway of their house, little Jamie grinning in her arms, and begged him—*begged him*—to leave the car his boss had insisted he borrow for the holidays. She'd insisted the drive would be too dangerous.

He'd ignored her. And why? *Why?*

Because he'd wanted everyone at home to see him in his boss's fancy new car, that was why. His pride, his arrogance. She was right about that. He'd admitted it then as he sobbed in the hospital room.

Even thinking about it brought it all back—that horrid smell, the metal frame of her bed, the white bandages around her head. Her precious, beautiful face mottled and cut and bruised.

Her arms empty. Because their precious boy hadn't even made it to the hospital. He'd been gone when Graham blinked awake in the ditch, snow and crushed metal all about him, and that deep, gnawing panic as he realized what had happened. The panic that had never really vanished since, not completely. It had just knotted itself into a low, cold dread. Because every ugly fear had been reality.

He'd lost his family. He couldn't even remember the crash,

but he'd been driving, and he'd woken up, and they'd been gone.

Their son in the accident itself.

His wife because she couldn't forgive him.

Even now, she shook her head like a wild thing, edging backward. "You made your choices, Graham, and you can't undo them. I know you would if you could. I know you regret it. But that doesn't *fix* it. He's still gone!"

Did she think he didn't know that? That it didn't haunt him every hour of every day? "And I will carry that burden, that guilt, that loss for the rest of my life. I know I don't deserve it, but, Gem, I need you to forgive me."

Her larynx bobbed as she swallowed. "No. I can't."

He lowered the arm holding the torch, letting its glow fall to their feet. He could have sworn he felt his heart fall into shadow too, eclipsed by the mass of her hatred, even though she'd pledged before God, her brother, and all their friends and family that she would love and honor him through everything, good and bad, sickness and health. She'd sworn it in that church three years ago. Pledged her heart and her life to his for the rest of their days.

Was it anger that bubbled now in his veins? Pain? Despair? Exhaustion with it all? Perhaps it was some vile amalgamation of them all. He took another step back, shaking his head. "I was an arrogant fool. I won't argue about that. But you, Gem—you value words so highly, yet you've turned your back on the ones you said to me before God."

Perhaps her face was largely in shadow now, but enough light touched it to show the quick flash of rage. "You would accuse *me*?"

"You're the one who left! Who turned your back on our marriage vows and tossed your ring at my head at our son's *funeral*. You won't even use my name anymore, *Miss Parks*, as if you can erase the fact that you're my *wife*!"

"I would if I could! I wish I'd never even met you!"

It felt as though every muscle in his body tightened. "And yet you dare to preach to *me* about God's love and demand I trust in Him? Are you really doing any better than I am? Doesn't He demand you forgive?" It wasn't a gracious thing to say, he knew that. She wouldn't *hear* it, not from him. But the words tumbled out before he could stop them. And he didn't take them back. How could she claim to cling to her faith when she refused its most basic tenet?

She said nothing. She didn't have to, not now. She'd already said it yesterday—words that could be applied to her as easily as to him.

He lifted his chin and tossed her words back at her. "Faithless is faithless, Gemma."

He swung back around and strode off down the corridor. She could follow or she could not. That was her choice. It always had been.

He couldn't bring their son back. He couldn't save him that day a year ago. He couldn't wind back the gears of their lives' clock and undo it all.

But he could dratted well do all in his power for Sidney Hart, and he wasn't going to waste another minute trying to argue her into trusting him again.

No light footsteps echoed after him. No too-rustling dress chased him down. By the time he made the next turn, resignation had sunk deep into his bones.

She wasn't there. Not behind him now, not ever. Because if she couldn't trust him in this—even though she'd always granted that he was the expert in such things—if she couldn't trust him with the task of restoring another family, then she would never consider entrusting him again with her heart. With *their* family.

His nostrils flared, the scent of musty stone and damp earth punching him in the nose and churning his stomach.

He reached up to where the necklace she'd given him hung under his shirt and touched the warm gold ring he'd put on the chain when he'd taken off the cross. The ring he'd slipped onto her finger three years ago. The ring she'd thrown at him like an accusation.

Somewhere deep down, always in the back of his mind and heart this last year, had been the hope that she'd come home, and he'd get to slide it back into its place on her bare finger. That they'd cry together, finally mourn together. Reminisce together. Remember that bright little life who had made them laugh and sigh and exchange so many smiles during the nine months of his life outside the womb, and the nine months before within it. That *Jamie* would be a name they could speak again, and that by speaking it, healing could come.

He'd hoped. At the start, he'd prayed. He'd waited. He'd let himself dream, now and then, of holding her again. Convincing her that though they would never forget their little James, they could still accept the gift of another child, the brother or sister they'd been hoping to give him before the accident stole everything.

Before *God* stole everything. Because even that hope was dead.

He saw it now. He'd been a fool to cling so long to what would never again be. He was a husband who would never again hold his wife. A father who would never again hold his child. A Christian who would never again trust in the goodness of the God he knew was in heaven.

God was love, the Bible said. But love was gone, at least for him.

Musty stone, damp earth, and . . . something else stung his nose too as he dragged in deep breath after deep breath in an attempt to push it all back down. *Waste.* Unpleasant to his physical senses even as it kicked his emotional ones up in a whole new way.

That particular smell all the way down here could only mean one thing. Someone had not only been down here, but someone had been *kept* down here long enough to need a chamber pot.

Sidney. He knew it down to his core, and it made his pace increase, though he was careful to keep his steps silent on his rubber-soled shoes.

Doorways appeared now from the shadows. They were empty of the wooden doors that had once filled them, but his light hit on evidence of hinges and iron fastenings, and when he flashed the beam into the first of the chambers, his heart pounded its agreement.

A monk's cell. The size and dimensions would have been enough to prove it to him. The broken basin in one corner merely confirmed it.

He had found it, just as he'd told her he would—and with relative ease and speed too. A glance at his watch told him it was only nine forty. Despite the time wasted arguing with Gemma, he'd arrived exactly where he wanted in better time than he'd dared to hope. No obstacles on this path, no unexpected walls or obstructions. Which meant that all he had to do now was find the one that held Sidney.

Only three of the double line of doorways had doors still in them, which narrowed it down considerably. The lad *must* be behind one of them, and deciding which was a simple matter of following the wrinkling of his nose.

Poor boy—held here for days, and apparently left with his own chamber pot. Or at least Graham hoped he had a pot. Surely his captors would grant him that, wouldn't they? And food and water.

This one. The fourth room down on the right. This was definitely where the smell was coming from. Graham paused outside the closed door, listening. He heard no rustling, no heavy breathing, but that didn't mean much. The lad could be asleep, and those sounds wouldn't travel well through the heavy door. But it did likely mean that his captor wasn't within.

A prayer sprang by old habit to his lips. He bit it back . . . then thought again and mouthed it. Perhaps God wasn't good to him. Perhaps He'd taken everything He'd once given. But maybe He still cared about *this* boy. It was worth the petition if there was even a chance.

Then he held his breath, wrapped his fingers around the cold iron ring, and tugged.

The hinges creaked, but they didn't groan. A wave of stench rolled out, but Graham ignored it. He stepped inside, light shining and reassurance on his lips, ready to spill out for the boy.

It died on his tongue. The room was as empty as his own house.

TWELVE

*T*he church hunkered down in the darkness, a white-blanketed giant slumbering against the hedgerow. No lights yet glowed in its windows, though soon enough the vicar would be coming to send out the golden beacon and welcome the parishioners for the Christmas vigil. Soon enough, carols would be spilling from the panes of glass along with the light and villagers would be welcoming the Christ child into the world once again.

The question in Graham's mind was whether another child would be here soon.

The snow fell quickly now, handily obliterating his footsteps and saving him the effort of either wiping them out or needing to stick to a road. He'd checked a few other possible places of hiding he'd determined in the underground monastery, but when those came up empty, he'd retraced his steps and hastened to join Yates, Marigold, and Sir Merritt. He hadn't come across Gemma anywhere in the corridors, so he had to assume that she'd reverted to her part of the plan and had returned to surveilling the ballroom.

He hadn't even cleared the shadows and stepped toward the church when his cousin's hulking frame materialized at his side seemingly from nowhere and made him jump.

He shoved Yates in the shoulder and muttered, "Don't *do* that."

Even without the aid of moonlight, Graham could see Yates's grin flash and then fade. "No luck, I take it?"

"Some luck. I found where they'd been keeping him. He wasn't there anymore." He'd wanted to simply turn and run back out after his first glance, but had Gemma been with him, she would have forced him to question his assumption that it was *Sidney* being held in that room. And so in a silent nod to her, he'd searched the chamber for some identifier of its occupant. There hadn't been any other boy-sized tie, but what he'd found had been curious.

First, the room had been . . . outfitted. He didn't know what else to call it. Where he'd expected a bare pallet on the floor and an overflowing chamber pot, there had instead been a real bed with blankets aplenty, along with toys and books. There had been a box of chocolates—uneaten—and sugarplums and a plate with the remains of a real meal, and what looked for all the world like a complete child's nursery transferred down to that monk's cell.

Yet there had also been a silver button from a Ludgrove uniform, placed deliberately beside a stone with *Help* scratched into it.

All the proof he needed, personally. Sidney had been in that room—recently. His captor had been trying to care for him, which was reassuring, but Sidney knew well he wasn't a guest.

"He can't have been taken far. I don't suppose you saw tracks in the snow?"

"It's covering them more than revealing them right now." Graham nodded behind him, where his own tracks through the previous dusting were little more than smudges, quickly filling thanks to wind and snow. "I did look, but I didn't see anything." He wasn't as good at noting such things as Yates and Sir Merritt were, but his cousin was gentleman enough not to point it out.

"Well, we'll simply have to follow whoever shows up here back to him, then. Marigold and I have scouted out positions inside the church, and Merritt volunteered to watch the northbound road, if you wanted to take the southbound. I can show you to the most advantageous spot we found for observing."

There was little point in arguing. While he might prefer an indoor location given the weather, hiding inside was usually trickier, especially in a church whose vicar and parishioners would be arriving soon. They might need to make a quick exit, and Graham hadn't their particular skill in doing so, even if he was generally the one to provide them with their escape routes. Theory he could do. The actual acrobatics required . . . not so much.

He followed Yates back toward the manor house, but along the road rather than through the land. "So our plan is to follow whoever comes? Not to apprehend him?"

Yates snorted a breath. "We're hardly constables. We discussed it, but it seems wisest to stick with our strengths and simply discover where the boy is now and free him. We'll then alert the authorities for the apprehending portion."

Graham nodded, though part of him would prefer to do to this kidnapper what he'd wanted to do to God after He took Jamie—grab him by the arm, give him a good shake, and demand answers.

But the kidnapper, much like God, could simply refuse to give him information. More, someone could have been hired for this part who wouldn't even *have* the answers. But he'd have to report to someone, and surely that someone *would*.

"Did Gemma make it out of the ball?"

The very mention of her name made the muscles in his shoulders bunch up. When he blinked, he saw her again, clothed in green and snow crystals and rage. In so many ways still the girl he'd loved all his life. Except for the one way that mattered.

She didn't love him anymore.

"Graham? Are you all right?"

He wasn't. How could he be? But now was hardly the time to discuss it, so he answered the first question instead of the second. "She was a bit late—got waylaid by Mrs. Horley—but she made it in time to question my sanity over the new route."

Yates chuckled. "But you proved yourself right."

"I did." She just hadn't been there to see it. No matter. She'd realize it eventually. No doubt she and Marigold already had a time scheduled to catch each other up on what they learned from their respective tasks that night.

"Well, here's your hiding spot." Yates indicated a place where one of the few trees stood sentinel beside the hedgerow, providing a good portion of darkness and strange shapes into which his could blend.

"Perfect." He vaulted over the low stone wall. "See you soon." As Yates melted back into the night, Graham got as comfortable as he could in the snow, positioned so that he'd see anyone who approached from the direction of the village—and not surprised that Sir Merritt, Coldstream Guard as he was, had taken the outlook toward the manor house, from which they assumed their kidnappers likely would come. Of the two of them, Graham was definitely lesser trained for this sort of work.

In the quiet of the snow-bright night, his gaze drifted away from the road and toward the little stone church. He'd popped in quickly yesterday, hoping to catch the vicar and get those stories the chauffeur had mentioned, but had found the place empty and the vicar not in his home either.

It had been the first time in a year he'd stepped foot in a

church—or nearly a year. The last time had been the funeral. And he'd sworn in that moment it would be *the* last time, at least as a worshiper.

But that was before Gemma had stood before him, accused him of killing their son, and refused to forgive him.

He'd thought the moment of the accident the one that would forever define him—that everything from then on would be either "before Jamie died" or "after." But something deep down in his aching soul said this would be another such moment—the moment he knew that Gemma was lost to him forever. If she hadn't forgiven him before, she wouldn't now, not when he'd said the things he had. And in the shadows of "after Gemma," that church, standing as it had done for centuries, its steeple pointing up toward an eternal God, called to him in a way he didn't want to admit.

He couldn't be alone for the rest of his life. He couldn't. He'd *never* been alone, not until this last year, and he couldn't bear it forever onward. If he hadn't his Gemma, then . . . what?

He wanted his Lord back.

No . . . he wanted the trust that his God was *good* back. He wanted to go through a day without questioning that, without this bone-deep anger burning away at his soul. He wanted . . . he wanted again to be the man who could believe.

His fingers extended from the warmth of his palm, reaching out toward that still-silent building. Soon, carols would sing out. Soon, bells would toll. Soon, those villagers who had fortified themselves to greet the arrival of Christmas would begin arriving, smiles on their lips and joy in their eyes.

How many of them had lost children? Some, without question. Many. In much of history, the answer would be *most*. How did they keep coming, keep praising the God who stole their little ones from them? How did they go on loving and worshiping Him?

He didn't know. But for the first time in a year, he wished he did.

He sat there longer than he'd expected to have to. In his mind, the kidnapper or whatever courier he'd hired would have shown up early to wait for the ransom drop. But a quarter inch of snow had accumulated around Graham before the muffled *clop* of horse hoofs tickled his ears, along with the low owl hoot that he knew was Sir Merritt's signal rather than an actual bird.

At nearly the same time, another snow-muted *clop* reached his ears, this time from the direction of the village. He peered down the road in both directions, not surprised when a whistled version of "God Rest Ye Merry, Gentlemen" drifted through the night from the stretch assigned to him. That would be the vicar, coming to get the church warm and bright for his flock.

From the other direction, the pace of the horse picked up, and then came the sound of boots hitting the ground outside the church building.

Graham strained his eyes but couldn't tell who was yanking open the door. A man, clearly. One bundled from head to toe, masking his features. By the shape and size, it *could* be Fitzroy.

Curling his fingers back into his palm, Graham made another silent promise, here in the shadow of the church. *You won't get away with this, whoever you are. We're going to find that boy. And we're going to return him to his parents, safe and sound.*

The internal clock in Yates's mind kept ticking and tocking, counting down the seconds before he knew the vicar would arrive. With every minute that seeped from future to present to history, his stomach went a little tighter.

Why wasn't the kidnapper or his compatriot here? Had someone been watching the place to have seen that no one came with money?

Even as he wondered it, he assured himself that no one had been. They'd checked every possible vantage point, even the ones so far away it would require a good pair of opera glasses or field binoculars or a spyglass to spot them. No one had been watching all evening, and no one had come since.

Why? Why, if the whole point of this kidnapping was ransom, was the culprit not champing at the bit for the money to be delivered? Why was *he* not camped out here like Yates and Marigold, Merritt and Graham were?

It didn't make sense. And that set his teeth on edge.

By the time Merritt's signal hooted quietly through the stone and to his ears, Yates had decided they were missing some vital piece of information. No wonder, given how quickly they'd put everything together.

Urgent cases, he decided as he made himself as small as possible in his hiding spot, were *not* their forte. They excelled at research, at careful planning, at complicated execution. Two days were not enough to do all those things well.

As the door creaked on its hinges, Yates cast one look toward the patch of darkness in which he knew his sister resided, though no one else would ever know it. She would be watching that poor box as intently as he would be, and there was comfort in that. If he missed anything, she would see it.

Though there was precious little *to* see in the darkness. He'd been in here long enough that his eyes had adjusted as much as possible, but he was no lion. He couldn't discern any details of his prey as the masculine figure entered the church.

Some clue, Lord, he prayed silently, with every single cell of his being. *Give us some clue.*

His lips twitched when the figure flipped on an electric

torch. No doubt their villain didn't *mean* to be the answer to Yates's prayer, and the irony of it was absolutely delicious.

The man flicked the beam around the narthex, landing on the poor box after a long, searching sweep that said he wasn't entirely certain where it lived.

Yates frowned. If it was Fitzroy—whom he'd met briefly that day—shouldn't he know its location? This was, from all accounts, his home parish.

Though from what Yates recalled from his files, Fitzroy wasn't the type to darken the doors of any church all that often, and he certainly wasn't the type to ever have put money in the poor box. So perhaps it made sense.

Yates shifted a bit, slowly and carefully, to avoid making the beam on which he perched groan. From up here, at this angle, he could see only the snow-dusted crown of the man's hat, not his face, even though the torchlight would be reflecting upon his features at least a little.

Marigold should have a decent view, though. She, with her much-slighter frame, had been able to squeeze in behind a wooden frame with a bid for donations posted to it.

His ears, however, picked up plenty of information that his eyes couldn't. The quick squeak of the poor box hinge—shouldn't it have been locked?—the smack of its wooden lid hitting the wall behind it. And then the snort of disbelief.

That, Yates had expected. What utterly surprised him was the breath of laugh that followed it.

"You *are* predictable, Wilfred," the man whispered, his voice a low threat. "Have it your way, then."

Yates's brows knit. This was no hired courier—he clearly knew Wilfred. And he hadn't, it seemed, been expecting any money to have been delivered. Which meant . . . what?

In the next moment, the man had flicked off his torch and charged back out into the night. Yates waited ten seconds before lowering himself from his beam and jumping with only a soft sound to the stone floor again, the leather soles of his acrobatic shoes aiding his silence.

Marigold materialized at his side, pressing a bundle of cloth at him—his coat, scarf, and whatnot. He slid them on without a word, even as from outside came a cheerful, "Happy Christmas, friend! Not going already, are you?"

The vicar. Yates went tense, praying that his coming upon the man wouldn't spur their villain toward any violence.

Even if he tried it, Merritt would be on alert. He was likely crouched nearby even now, ready to pounce. It was rather handy having someone with such excellent military training on the team.

"I'll be back," the man said, sounding jovial and friendly. "Forgot my offering in my hotel room."

"Ah. Well, who am I to interfere, then?" The vicar laughed and resumed his whistling.

Yates ducked with Marigold behind a stone wall. Logically, the vicar should aim himself toward the lamps in need of lighting—the church hadn't yet been wired for electricity—and would hence give them ample opportunity to slip out unnoticed.

Even as he hid himself again, he gave their mystery villain credit for the quick, clever lie he'd told. Given Merritt's signal, the man had come from the manor, not the village. But he'd immediately planted in the vicar's mind the notion that he was visiting the area, and that he was therefore a stranger with only a hotel room to claim him. The vicar, then, wouldn't be trying to place the voice.

Clever indeed. Drat it all.

The door opened with another gust of cold air, and the cheerful sounds of the clergyman filled the narthex. The happy whistle, a clapping of hands and stomping of boots to remove snow. As the door fell shut with an unabashed *bang*, the man turned his whistle into a full-throated baritone and sang out the same hymn he'd been sharing with the night. His step sounded nearly like a jig as he vanished into the nave.

Wordlessly, Yates and Marigold slipped out of their hiding spot, cracked the massive exterior door open just enough to squeeze through, and then eased it shut again behind them.

Not until they'd reunited with both Graham and Merritt did Yates dare to breathe the question foremost in his mind. "Who was it? Fitzroy?"

Marigold, her arm linked through her husband's, shook her head. "No. I'd expected it to be, but . . . no. I think it was that friend of his, Astley—though I'm not altogether certain. I didn't see enough of him earlier to compare."

"Whoever it was, he returned toward Weywent. And at a fast clip." Merritt indicated the road toward the manor house and pulled Marigold along with him. Not toward the road and its winding but straight across the land. The quicker route back to the house.

As they went, everyone compared what they'd observed, and Yates could tell from the other men's silence that they were as struck as he had been by what the man had muttered upon finding the poor box empty.

"How good of friends are this Astley fellow and Fitzroy?" Marigold asked as they hurried over a knoll. "The man in the church—perhaps Yates will disagree, but he sounded as though he knows Lord Wilfred. And is furious with him. The cold kind, not just bluster over not getting the money he'd wanted in that moment."

"Yates will not disagree," Yates said, wishing he'd taken the time to put his nice, thick wool socks back on rather than putting his leather-slippered feet back into his hefty boots. The socks were in his pockets, but they weren't doing him much good there.

No time to stop, though. If they hurried, they would arrive

back at the house not long after their chap on horseback and be able to identify him with certainty.

"Maybe Fitzroy owes him money, and this payday was supposed to return it?" Merritt sounded far from convinced, but they knew so little of the Astley chap . . . who was to say? "Not that this theory would explain any anger with Wilfred, other than perhaps his having cheated his friend out of what profit should have been his."

"Cheated him?" Graham leaned forward a bit, no doubt trying to see Merritt past Yates and Marigold. "How so?"

Ah, right. Given his friend's exhaustion and need to concentrate on the monastery, Yates hadn't filled him in on other details they'd discovered before their arrival. "When you sent the names, we did a bit more digging through our files. You remember the case Fennwick hired us for? That business conglomerate he wanted to sound out before joining?"

"Vaguely. Was that the ballroom with the Reuben-painted ceiling? The James I baroque feasting room?"

Leave it to Graham to remember a case only by what room and building they'd set up surveillance in. He chuckled. "One and the same. We discovered Lord Wilfred's schemes in time to keep Mr. Fennwick from getting disastrously involved, but not before Wilfred managed to finagle all the profits his direction and push all the losses toward his other investors. All strictly legal—but far from courteous. All the others suffered considerably, including Fitzroy."

"And what of Astley? I didn't recall reading anything about him."

"We don't have a dossier on him. Yet." Marigold's voice had that sharp edge to it that said she would take a bit of pleasure in creating one now, and in putting some particularly scathing personal notes in it that he'd have to cross out. Eventually.

"We need to get back to London as soon as we reasonably

can." Yates increased his stride a bit, as much because of how cold his toes were growing as because the extra seconds they would gain would make that much of a difference. "Discover what there is to discover about him."

"I don't intend to leave yet." Graham's voice was tight and dark. "Not until we know for a fact Sidney is no longer here. He must be, at the moment. Somewhere. Perhaps not on Weywent property anymore but *somewhere* nearby. Or in some other hidden place I don't know about. The caves, perhaps. That the monks hid in to evade the Vikings."

Yates shivered at the very thought of the boy being held in a drafty seaside cave on Christmas Eve. "Let's hope our 'friend' back there really does have a room at a hotel, then."

Soon they were within view of the manor house again, and they all fell silent and picked up their paces still more. A hand motion sent Marigold and Merritt around the back— Marigold had to rendezvous with Gemma—but Yates hurried toward the stables, Graham close behind.

Just in time to see the familiarly mysterious man charging from stables to house.

Good timing, as he'd hoped. Though while he was hoping, he'd prefer the man go to wherever Sidney was being held rather than straight back inside. But perhaps he meant to report to Fitzroy.

"Come on." They hurried through the night, Graham aiming for one side door while Yates followed their quarry toward another, closer to the central part of the house. Whoever he was, he seemed to know his way about the manor. Yates crept close as the man went through the door, peeked in through the glass to watch him stride down the corridor, then slipped inside himself.

Yates was hardly dressed to rejoin the ball, though at least he had regular trousers on instead of the pajama-style ones he usually wore for his acrobatics. But if necessary, he could spin a yarn about wanting to welcome Christmas in among the snow and any stars that peeked through the clouds. He'd certainly chosen to do so before, so he could make it sound believable. He ran down the corridor—on his toes to keep his moves light and silent—and got to the end in time to watch the man go into the ballroom.

Definitely Lord Astley, given the half-drunk greetings he heard. Which brought a new frown onto his face.

Why on earth would a peer, a lord, get himself involved with *kidnapping*? Was he so desperate for funds?

Possibly. Yates knew better than anyone how desperate a nobleman's situation could grow without it looking obvious to the outside world. Perhaps he'd given money to Fitzroy for that business venture in hopes that it would save him. Perhaps when Fitzroy was instead left holding the debt, it had been his ruin too. Perhaps they both blamed Wilfred for what they'd see as his cheating them and had concocted this scheme together.

Perhaps in their minds it was innocent enough. They wouldn't have intended to hurt the boy. Nor even to scare him. Just to get at his father.

Graham stood at the door to the library, clearly having watched Astley go back into the ball as well. He glanced once at Yates and then turned into the library, shrugging out of his overcoat.

Yates did the same and hastened over into the comfortable, firelit room. "What do you make of it? Being Astley, I mean?"

Graham shrugged. "I haven't any idea. You?"

Yates sketched out the thoughts he'd been musing on, though he knew well they were no more than theory. They couldn't know Astley's motivations until they knew more about him and his situation. Which, again, brought him back to the need to return to London and do some research as soon as was feasible. Should they leave now?

Even if they did, everything would be closed for the holidays, blast it all. And he didn't know what snow they'd encounter on the way. Better to have daylight on their side, at least. No, better to keep a hawk-eye on Astley and follow him anywhere he went.

Surely, *surely* he would check on Sidney again. All they'd have to do was watch where he went, then return there once he'd gone. Yates repositioned his chair so that he had a direct view of the ballroom door. Once Marigold returned with her report from Gemma, Yates would go and change back into his tuxedo and rejoin the party, claiming he hadn't been able to sleep after all. He would trail Astley everywhere he went. The man wouldn't leave his sight again.

"I imagine Gemma can fill out our files on him a bit," Graham said. "She can direct all the drawing room gossips while we're still here. I think up until now she was focusing on what she could learn about Fitzroy."

"Good. I—" Yates broke off with a frown when the sound of footsteps, quick ones, invaded his perception. Familiar ones, at that. He wasn't surprised when Marigold rushed into the room . . . except that she rushed in alone, with a frown on her face. "What?"

"I can't find Gemma. She isn't in the ballroom, nor is she in her bedroom."

Well, it was a large house—there were any number of places she could have gone. Only, she wouldn't have, not if she was to meet with Marigold five minutes ago. "Hmm" was all Yates could think to say.

"What's more, that Carissa Horley woman who's befriended her saw me in the corridor and helpfully informed me that Gemma never returned to the ball at all."

Graham washed pale as the snow. "She . . ." But he didn't say anything more. He simply scooped up his coat and dashed from the room.

THIRTEEN

*H*ad she really thought, as she'd hurried out into the night in her ball gown without even a wrap, that she was too warm to ever feel the cold? That the cold of the South could never harm a Northumberland girl? Gemma's teeth chattered as she flashed her electric torch's beam down yet another—or perhaps the same?—underground corridor. *Cold* didn't begin to describe how she felt right now.

Perhaps in terms of temperature, Northumberland had the southern coast beat. But in Northumberland, she'd always been able to grab a coat or a blanket or a hot water bottle to ward off any chill. In Northumberland, her outdoor winter excursions had been in thick socks and winter boots and wool clothes. In Northumberland, she'd always been able to loop her arm through Marigold's or Graham's and snuggle in for warmth.

She had most assuredly gone down this same blasted tunnel or corridor or whatever it was. There was the same bit of crumbled stone she'd nearly tripped over ten minutes ago. Or was it an hour ago?

Drat it all. She tried to hold the image of the monastery—any monastery—in her mind's eye long enough to know where to go, but this had never been her strength. It had never *needed* to be. When had she ever gone exploring in an old building without Graham, to have to find her own way about?

All she really knew to do was make a different choice than the one she'd made last time she reached this juncture, so instead of turning right, she turned left. It looked like only a service corridor, but perhaps that was what she needed? Even though she'd most certainly never entered it before, so it wasn't the way out. Or wasn't the same way out that she'd come in, anyway.

It could lead to another entrance, though. Couldn't it? A monastery would certainly have more than one door, and quite possibly more than one had survived and reached its fingers up into the modern world.

Maybe. She hoped. Prayed. "Please, Lord."

The words echoed back at her, cold and hard and empty. They slapped and clawed.

She had prayed, this last year. She had prayed like she always had. She had said all the right words, hadn't even doubted them. Her faith had never come into question.

Graham was wrong. *Wrong.* About that as about everything else. She wasn't faithless. Not to God, and not to Graham. Perhaps she had left—she had *had* to leave! But it wasn't as though she'd gone into the arms of another man. It wasn't as though she ever intended to.

It was just . . . it was just . . .

Empty. Hard. Cold. The echo, the tunnel—they rather perfectly summed up all her life had been this last year. She had gone through all the motions of living. Of praying. Of being.

But she wasn't. Not really.

She'd been wearing a theater mask, that was all. One that seemed now to fall to the stones at her feet, piece by piece, with every shiver and chatter.

Were the walls narrowing? No, that was only her imagination. It only felt that way because of the way her light jittered and jumped in her shaking hands. It was her life that was narrowing, growing heavier and closer with each day. With each word she'd spewed at Graham. With each thought she refused to speak, each memory she refused to hold.

Jamie.

No, no, she couldn't think about him, not now. Just as she hadn't been able to think about him until now. Every time his memory tried to overtake her—a thousand times a day—she pushed it down. If she handled those memories, she would change them, bruise them, lose them, like pages too often turned or clothes too often worn. That wouldn't do. She had to preserve each memory. They were all she had.

But it was more than that too. To look on it would be to break. To give it voice would be to come undone. To feel the loss would be to admit, once and for all, that her precious baby was gone.

She stumbled on some unseen something or another, lurched forward, flung out a hand toward the wall to steady herself.

It was far closer than it should have been. Dirt instead of stone. How could that be? Maybe it wasn't dirt. Maybe it was some sort of ancient, crumbling plaster or mortar. She didn't know.

It didn't matter. The ground was sloping upward now; she could feel it in the burning of her calves if not see it with her eyes. Whatever little service hallway she'd chosen, it was slowly making its way up toward open land, praise God. Then she would merely have to discern where it put her out and where the house was in comparison. Walk back. Return to the ball. Watch the guests as she'd promised to do.

Find other things to think about. Other problems to solve, ones she actually could solve, or help to do.

A cup of hot tea. A blanket. Her borrowed bed. No, she must return to the ball—ah, that overheated ballroom! She could certainly find a cup of something hot there. Do her part. Help find Sidney.

Why did this blasted tunnel go on forever? She went up and up and up, on and on, but it never led anywhere! She rubbed a colder hand over her cold arm, trying to ignite a bit of warmth in one piece of flesh or the other.

Maybe Graham was right. Maybe she'd lost her faith as surely as he had. Maybe God had drawn her into the very bowels of the earth, buried like Jamie, in her own personal hellish labyrinth where she'd wander for the rest of time.

Lost. You're lost, Gemma. You've been lost all year. You'll be lost all of eternity.

"I'm not. I know where I am." Her words lashed back at her, mocked her. She'd been stumbling through life just as she stumbled through this underground maze. Thinking she knew best, that she was in the right, never in doubt . . . until she ended up absolutely nowhere, cold down to her bones, her arms so heavily empty.

"You're the one who left!"

Graham's words must have been absorbed by the walls, because they seeped out of them again now and traveled from the fingertips she'd been trailing along them into her veins, straight to her heart.

"I can't go back." Those were the words she'd said to Marigold, to James, to Aunt Priss. She couldn't go back into their empty house, without its baby laughter and coos. She couldn't see all Jamie's things, couldn't face the toys strewn about the floor or see the memories caught in every corner like dust. She couldn't stand to look in Graham's eyes and feel that horrible, wretched flame again.

You. You did this. That had been the first thought she'd had when she woke up in hospital and saw his face hovering over her. She hadn't had to ask where Jamie was. She had known it the moment her bruises and aches found a mirror in his shattered expression.

She'd known without a word that their son—her son—was gone. Gone because Graham had refused to listen. Gone because he'd cared more for his pride than his family.

Hate was a horrible thing. It blazed through her and consumed her and left nothing but rubble in its wake when it left again. She couldn't keep feeling it. She couldn't go home, back to London and their house, where every time she looked at him, she'd lose a little more of herself to that wretched fire of bitterness.

It hadn't been leaving. It had been staying, staying where he'd put her with that accident—on the other side of the abyss from him. She'd stayed for months in Northumberland with the Fairfaxes and the Romani staff who loved her and never tried to force the issue. She'd eventually gone back to London when work demanded it, but to James's vicarage or the Fairfax townhouse. Safe places. Places where she wouldn't have to face him so much and feel that sharp stab of flame again.

It hadn't been a matter of breaking her marriage vows. It had been a matter of preserving what little of herself she had left in the wake of their son's death. It had been a matter of protecting him from that hatred.

No. That was a lie she dismissed even as she thought it. She hadn't cared about protecting him. She had even wished, in a few of her darkest hours, that he'd been the one to die instead of Jamie. The arrogant instead of the innocent. Then she would have mourned that he'd not listened to her, but there'd have been no one to hate.

It made her a horrible person. She knew that. She didn't need her brother's sermons nor Graham's accusations to tell her that wishing such things on her husband, refusing him forgiveness, was a sin as black as this winter's night.

She knew it. She felt the frost climbing ever outward from her heart to her muscles to her bones. She knew that the longer she stayed in the cold, the more impossible it would be to ever be warmed again by the fire of God's love, and of Graham's.

She knew it. It was just that she'd been as helpless to escape it as she was now in this claustrophobic tunnel.

Her toes bumped against something, and she realized that she'd let her torch hang limp at her side, illuminating only where she was instead of where she was going.

Another metaphor.

But she shone it now upward and drew in a chattering, relieved breath. Stairs. Stairs! She ran up them, not pausing to worry about whether it would lead to a dead end or a barred door or—

Freedom! She surged out into cold, blustery, stinging snowflakes. And darkness that spread out with the heavens instead of closing in with the walls.

Spinning a circle, torch flashing over the landscape, her relief plummeted into dismay. This looked nothing like the part of the estate she'd explored with Graham. The slope of the land, the crowding trees . . . where were the open expanses that tumbled down to the cliffs and the sea? The carefully manicured gardens? The copse that ended quickly in path and lawn? These trunks seemed to march on into eternity in all directions.

But they couldn't. She knew that. How far away from the house could she really be now? Not very. It was simply a matter of choosing the correct direction.

"Think, Gemma. Think." The ground sloped upward to the left of her, down to the right. She knew that, generally speaking, the manor was situated uphill from the village, and from Graham's drawings, the monastery stretched toward the house and perhaps onward, away from the village. If she ended up beyond the house, then she needed to go downhill to return to it.

Right. Downhill it was. She had no particular direction beyond that, but once she cleared the trees, she would be able to reassess. The manor house would be lit up to guide her.

Within a few steps, the mounting snow had found its way into her stylish half-boots and made her gasp out an objection as it immediately penetrated her silk stockings. There was no point in stopping to clear it as it would only keep coming in. "Northumberland girl," she reminded herself. "You can handle a bit of snow."

She had to hurry, though. The very depth of the snow accused her of wasting far too much time underground, walking in circles and silently cursing Graham.

Her throat went tight as she trudged past another tree. This particular incident wasn't Graham's fault. She was the one who had decided to go off on her own to look for Sidney rather than simply turning around and stomping back to the house and the ballroom, like she should have done. She'd thought at the time that she would simply follow his first, sounder plan. Find the monks' cells. Find the boy. Then she could deliver not only the child to safety, but a lovely I-told-you-so to Graham.

Fool. She sniffled, telling herself it was from the cold and not the fact that she was out here alone and freezing because she'd refused to trust Graham when she should have. He had probably found the cells straightaway—and, she prayed, Sidney.

Why had she resisted his direction? It had seemed obvious at the moment, but now . . . now she was failing them all. She was failing to do her part of the surveillance. She was perhaps missing the opportunity to gather a piece of information that would help them crack the case.

Maybe she still had time. The snow could have simply accumulated fast. Maybe it had only been twenty minutes, or thirty. That would still give her ample time to get back to the ball and keep an eye on Fitzroy and the other guests, as she was supposed to do.

The next sweep of her light found no trees to obscure her path, praise the Lord. She picked up her pace, surged out into the open, and let out a laugh when she spotted the manor house down below, glowing merrily in the night. Not so far. Not exactly close either, given the weather, but another ten or fifteen minutes and—

Ding, dong, ding, dong . . .

She froze, the distant sound of the church bells shattering the last vestige of her mask. Those bells didn't ring out every quarter hour, not during the night. They would only ring at midnight—midnight on Christmas Eve, calling all the faithful who were awake to celebrate the birth of Christ.

Midnight. An hour past the scheduled ransom drop. Five minutes past when she was supposed to rendezvous with Marigold.

She had missed everything. Failed everyone.

Her throat, still open from the laugh of a moment before, convulsed in a sob, the kind that tore through her whole shivering frame and took every last bit of strength with it. She didn't realize her knees had buckled until she felt the cold of snow on her legs, on her hands.

What had she done? She had stood in that tunnel and accused Graham of arrogance that led to their son's death, and then she'd turned around and made her own arrogant choices, putting another boy in more danger. She had let down her team. Her oldest friends. The child who needed her, needed all of them, to be at their best. The parents who would be pacing their home, waiting for word, trapped in the teeth of the unknown.

"Forgive me." She sobbed it out into the snow, aimed at God, at Sidney, at the Fairfaxes.

And she heard in her spirit the same words she recited daily, the very ones Graham had tossed in her face.

Forgive us our trespasses, as we forgive those who trespass against us.

Why would God forgive if she refused to? How could she hope to receive from the divine what she refused to give on earth? No, not even why, not even how . . . that, her brother would say, assumed God was standing up in Heaven with forgiveness in His hand but refusing to pour it out on her. That He, like an angry mortal, would withhold His affection until she had earned it.

That wasn't it at all. As the heaving sobs racked her, bent her forward until she could feel the cold of snow radiating onto her face, she knew that down to her core. God wasn't refusing her anything. God wasn't withholding love or forgiveness.

But her heart was too cold to receive it. She had become ice, unable to receive the cleansing flow. Blocked off, frozen over, paralyzed in her soul. She had let the winter into her heart, thinking she was protecting herself from that flame of hatred.

But it had won. Because she'd been too much a fool to realize that ice burned as much as fire.

The bells stopped tolling. The wind picked up. Gemma's feet went numb in her snow-packed boots, her fingers from piercing pain to tingles as she gripped her skirt as if it could anchor her. Otherwise, time seemed as frozen as she was. She ought to get up. Walk back down to the manor house. And she would. But . . . why?

She had let down the only people who mattered. She had looked her husband in the eye and told him she wouldn't ever forgive him, had all but declared she could never love him again. She had no son to work for, to smile over, to watch grow up.

Her sobs redoubled. No Jamie. Her son, her sweet little love, was gone, buried in the cold, frozen earth of Northumberland beside her parents. He was gone, and no amount of turning away from that truth this last year made it any less real. He was gone, and she'd gone with him, in some vital way. She wanted to reach for the memories, gather them close, live them—but she couldn't. She couldn't recall the vision of his face in her mind's eye.

"No. No!" She couldn't have forgotten him—that was the very thing she wanted to avoid!

The memories must be there. They must! Fumbling with her numb fingers, she reached into her handbag and pulled out her ever-present notepad and pencil. Dropped them, but only onto her lap. Opened to a fresh page and tried to steady her shaking hand enough to write. Perhaps the pictures wouldn't come, but words would. Words always did.

He was the most beautiful boy. He had blond hair like mine, but I wondered if it would darken as he grew up—Graham was blond as a child too. He had his daddy's eyes and that grin I fell in love with, first in Graham and then in our Jamie. The same grin, in miniature. How many times did I laugh because of how precious they looked, grinning together at each other? I would rush over and kiss them both and

No, this was no better. Her fingers curled around the pencil so tightly it snapped, and she had to slap the notepad closed to keep snow and her tears from blurring those few words she'd managed.

"I'm sorry." She didn't even know who she whispered the words for this time. God? Jamie? Graham? The Fairfaxes, James, her aunt? Her own frozen-over heart? "I'm so sorry."

The snow devoured her words, the silence the only sound. The only answer. Reminding her that she was alone. Just as she'd chosen to be.

Her shivers now so bad they should rightly be called shakes, she wrestled the notepad back into her handbag.

"Gem?" The word came from somewhere in the trees and brought her head up.

She fumbled for the torch she'd dropped into the snow. "Graham?" Her own voice was more a weak croak than a voice proper, but it and the light must have been enough.

"Gemma!" He came running toward her, a black form against the night-white of the snow. His own torch flashed over her face, but then he switched it off and in the next moment he was on the ground beside her, pulling her into his arms and against his chest that seemed as warm as a hearth.

Shouldn't she have run out of tears by now? But they surged again, all the ones she'd stifled and tamped down for the last year. Because it felt so right to be there in his arms, and so wrong, all at the same time. The thud of his heart, the sound of his breathing was as familiar to her as her own pulse, and yet hearing them again made her all the more aware of the year it had been since she last had. All she'd lost.

All *they'd* lost. "He's gone." The words were more gasps than words. Her fingers, still so cold, fisted in his coat. "Our baby is gone, Graham. He's *gone.*"

"I know. My sweet love—I know." His arms tightened around her, and his head came down until it rested against hers. His tears dripped down, mixed with hers.

And she could have sworn one frozen place inside of her began to melt.

FOURTEEN

25 December 1909

Warm was too much of a stretch, but by the time she slipped back into a side door of Weywent Manor, Gemma wasn't nearly as cold as she'd been. She still had the blanket wrapped around her that Graham had apparently grabbed on his way out, and he had given her his gloves too.

She was a wreck, she knew that. Her hair was crusted with ice and snow and drooping in its pins, her dress was ruined, her feet were still blocks of ice, and her boots had rubbed blisters onto both ankles. She was exhausted and emptied and chapped from the crying, and she was leaning far too much on Graham in order to mitigate the pain in her feet.

But somehow the internal ache felt . . . good. Like the feeling returning to her too-cold limbs. It hurt, pierced, cut, throbbed—but it meant life. It meant the healing flow of blood.

"Oh, gracious me! What's happened, Gabrielle?"

Perhaps her mind was still a bit numb from the cold or overtired from the emotions, but it took Gemma a long moment to realize that Carissa Horley, who was even now rushing toward them from the main part of the house, was

170

talking to *her*. She found herself casting her gaze around in search of this Gabrielle.

The way Graham squeezed her waist and cleared his throat brought the reality back into focus.

She managed a weary smile. "Nothing to look so worried over, Carissa, I promise. I . . ." She had the story all planned out, the lines ready for her character to deliver. Nothing she hadn't done countless times either upon their stage at the Tower or about Imposter business. *I went outside to refresh myself and decided to explore the gardens in the snow, but then I got turned around. . . . Thank goodness Mr. Wharton found me!*

Only the words wouldn't come as she looked into Carissa's genuine, concerned eyes. She sighed. "I ought to tell you that G. M. Parker is only my *nom de plume*."

Carissa blinked, pulling up a step away. Not, she suspected, because the news itself was at all distressing, but because she wouldn't know what that had to do with G. M. Parker coming inside crusted with snow and looking like she'd been stuck out in the storm for hours. "Em . . . all right?"

Gemma kept moving, wanting dry clothes and a warm pair of socks too much to delay. She motioned with her head for Carissa to walk with them, unwilling to let go of her fierce hold on the blanket. "I chose the pseudonym so I could retain my anonymity and thereby better observe the social scene. Though it *is* based on my real name—Gemma Parks."

She felt Graham stiffen at her side, no doubt like he had every time this last year when she'd made a point of using her maiden name.

She'd done it to hurt him. She'd done it to cling to who she'd been once, before she became a mother without a child. Gemma *Parks* had no reason to feel so empty. She had the future ahead of her. She was nothing but a friend and writer and sister and niece—not a wife, not a mother.

But she wasn't that girl anymore. She glanced up at Graham's clenched jaw, then back to Carissa. Perhaps she would confess that Parks was her maiden name too. Though if she did so now, it would prove a distraction.

"Gemma." Carissa smiled. "It suits you. You are certainly a gem."

Another something to be debated another time. "I need your help. Were you in the ball all this time?"

Carissa nodded, though she was still giving Gemma's appearance a worried look. "I was. I was taking note of everything I could for you—mentally, I mean."

Praise God for Carissa! "You can't know how relieved I am to hear that. Did you note when Lord Astley left and returned? Did Fitzroy leave at any point?"

Her friend nodded, eyes bright. "I did. One of the ladies left around the same time, and I had wondered if perhaps Astley wasn't so high of character as I had hoped. But she was only gone a moment, and he an hour. Fitzroy stumbled out rather merrily, if you catch my meaning, during the same stretch but returned before him. He was absent perhaps twenty minutes."

Twenty minutes. Not enough time to leave the manor and make it back. If he'd been moving Sidney during that time, it must have been within the property.

But Sidney, Graham had said, was already gone when he got down there, before either man had left the ball. They must have moved him before, earlier. Fitzroy could have gone to check on him, though, while Astley went to the church. She exchanged a look with Graham, knowing he'd be thinking the same thing. Sidney could be *here*, somewhere within the manor house. Some closed-off wing or attic room, too far removed from the rest of them to be heard.

She suddenly felt as though she'd stumbled into a Brontë

novel and had to shake it off. "What about when Lord Astley returned? Did he and Fitzroy have any sort of exchange?"

Carissa was clearly a natural at reconnaissance. She grinned. "As a matter of fact, they were in conference in the corner for perhaps five minutes, and Astley looked positively grim. Not at all what one would expect at the toll of Christmas bells."

No indeed. Though exactly what one would expect of coconspirators. "And Fitzroy? How did he look?"

"Shockingly sober—and then suspiciously drunk again after they parted ways." Carissa leaned close. "I found it quite odd, especially given the number of cups of punch I'd watched him consume. Which was when I noticed that the same waiter was all the time bringing him a refill—he never took any from other passing trays or went to the bowl. So I took the liberty of slipping his glass off the table while he was dancing again and took a sip. Nothing but cranberry juice and lemonade! The drunkenness was put on, though *why* I cannot fathom."

Gemma didn't know whether to laugh or gape or offer her a position. "Carissa, *you* are the gem. You can't know how helpful you've been."

Graham turned them all toward the stairs.

Carissa cleared her throat, came to a halt, and leveled a glare on him. "My dear Mr. Wharton—given Gemma's clear distress but seeming comfort with you, I will graciously assume that *you* are not the one responsible for her current state. But that hardly means you can accompany us up these stairs. You will return to the bachelor wing now, or to the ball."

Graham stiffened again, and the arm around her went tighter instead of loosening. He'd always been protective—exactly as far as she wanted him to be, after which he encouraged independence. She could feel the process working through him now, the way he drew in a breath, loosened his grip after a long moment, and looked down at her. Asking with his eyes if not his lips if that was what she wanted.

Maybe it was the screaming of her blisters, but the thought of bidding him adieu brought something akin to panic instead of relief. She sighed and turned her face toward Carissa's. "About my pen name—it was based on my *maiden* name. But if we're truly going to be friends, you should know that my name now is actually Gemma . . . Wharton."

She hadn't said it in a year. As if by not speaking it, she could undo the truth of the matter. But it didn't feel strange on her lips. How could it, when she had said it so many times in the years before, practicing it long before Graham ever proposed, even?

"Wharton." Her friend's eyes went wide, and she glanced from Gemma to Graham and back again. "No! You're . . . *married?*"

"We've been estranged." Yes, she felt Graham flinch at the word, but she couldn't very well leave this helpful new acquaintance angry with her for the deception. "And when I realized he was here, I intended to keep it that way."

There. Graham clearly caught on to her angle. He grinned. "And I intended to win her back. Not that I've altogether succeeded—but I do beg your indulgence in letting me help my wife up to her room. Her feet are blistered and numb, and I'd like to make certain she isn't in need of a physician."

"Oh!" Carissa looked down. She wouldn't be able to see Gemma's feet, but she could see the ruined hem of her dress, still caked with snow that now melted into drips and puddles, and the toes of elegant boots clearly not meant for a snowy adventure. "Gracious, Gab—Gemma. What were you about?"

Gemma sighed and exchanged another look with Graham. She'd already proven herself a useful ally, and though she wasn't about to entrust her with any Imposter secrets, perhaps a bit more information would result in her being an even greater help.

For the sake of Sidney, it was worth the risk. She cleared her throat and nodded toward the stairs, leaning unabashedly on Graham as they climbed. It seemed her boots were rubbing the blisters more with each step. Or perhaps she could feel it more, the more she warmed up. "I didn't come here to observe the party for my column, Carissa. I've come because some friends of ours have asked for help. Their son is missing, and they think Fitzroy may have information."

Perhaps it was a stretch to call the Harts her friends, and they didn't know anything about Fitzroy, but those bits of truth would have to do.

Carissa gasped again and pressed fingers to her mouth, a perfect portrait of horror. "A missing child? Oh, but surely Mr. Fitzroy wouldn't . . ." Her fingers fell away, and her frown deepened. "Though he *is* often in bad company in London, I hear. What do they hope he knows? Have you questioned him? Tried to discern if he's acquainted with whatever shady character would do such a horrid thing?"

"We've tried to be subtle," Graham said. "We don't want to cause any offense or burn any bridges. But we've caught him in a few lies and have wondered if perhaps he's even . . . thought to warn these characters he knows. So we've followed him a bit."

"I was attempting to retrace an earlier path and look for a clue when I got turned around," Gemma added. True, even if not exactly what Carissa would think. "Had Graham not found me, I may still be out there shivering in the snow."

Carissa shook her head, lifting her skirt a few inches so she could dart up the stairs. "Perhaps you'd better carry her, Mr. Wharton, so we can get out of these open halls the faster and get her warmed up."

Graham lifted a brow, angled it down at her.

With a sigh, Gemma nodded. Her ankles were screaming so loudly it was a wonder they couldn't hear them over the caroling in the ballroom. "It would be quicker."

All the invitation he needed, apparently. He scooped her up like he'd done countless times before. This time she didn't laugh, didn't squeal, didn't pretend a protest or rest her head against his shoulder—the range of her usual responses. But she rested there, in the familiar cradle. She let her eyes slide shut for a moment, knowing he would see her safely up to her room. She let the pain of blisters rubbed raw throb its way through her, join with that other, deeper pain, and fill her. She let the comfort of his nearness soothe it away again, just a bit.

She'd missed him. How could she both have hated him and missed him so much? How, even now, could she both want to shove him away, claiming nothing could ever be the same again, and beg him to hold her until Christmas turned to Boxing Day and the horrible anniversary of Jamie's death was well and truly over?

A few minutes more and Carissa was taking Gemma's room key from her hands and opening the door. A lamp was still lit, one of the many windows glowing into the night, making it easy for them to slip inside and shut the door again behind them.

Graham eased her into the chair. "There we go, darling. May I take your boots off?"

She nodded. Her fingers, encased as they still were in his gloves, were probably warm and nimble enough now that she could have managed it, but exhaustion had her in its teeth.

He unlaced them, pulled the first gently off, and winced. She braved a peek and saw the bloodstains over her throbbing ankles. "I suspected as much. Lovely as they are, those boots were not made for hiking through the countryside."

Carissa sank to a seat on the floor in front of Gemma,

a towel in hand and the basin and pitcher beside her. "I still cannot believe it—a missing child, and Fitzroy knowing something about it. Why, do you think? Ransom?"

Gemma nodded.

"I do hope your friends have contacted the authorities."

"They have, yes. And hired an investigator." Gemma offered a small, tight smile. "But when they mentioned the connection to Weywent, to which I'd been invited . . ."

"One can't help but try to find answers. I completely understand." Carissa positioned the basin under one of Gemma's feet. "Are the stockings stuck to the wounds? We can rinse first, if so."

Graham gave a gentle tug on the silken toe. The wet fabric clung far too much to pull free, but it did move enough from her ankle to prove it not stuck there. "Will I scandalize you, Mrs. Horley, if I help her take her stockings off?"

Carissa arched her brows. "You're truly married?"

"Three years," they said in unison.

"Then there's hardly a scandal. And I'll remind you I'm a widow myself. It won't shock me to realize you've seen your wife's legs."

Even so, Gemma felt heat stinging her cheeks as Graham removed the stockings—Gemma helping as much as she could—and Carissa commenced cleansing the blisters with lukewarm water that felt hot as a bath. Surely this wasn't real. Her estranged husband and a woman she hadn't even known for three days working together on her feet while chunks of melting snow slid down her neck.

And then came a knock on the door—the knock Marigold always used. Gemma sighed. "Come in—but brace yourself, we've got company."

Marigold didn't look surprised to enter and find Graham there, though she gave a minuscule start upon spotting Carissa. It only lasted half a beat. Marigold was an expert in sizing up a situation. She'd know that Gemma had known it was her at the door, but she'd invited her in anyway. Which meant that she trusted Carissa. Which meant, apparently, that *she* would trust Carissa, at least a bit. "Lionfeathers, Gemma. What happened?"

"Well. It seems I'm rubbish at finding my way around in the dark without Graham to guide me." She tried for a self-deprecating smile and nodded at Carissa. "Did you officially meet my new friend yet? Carissa Horley. Carissa, Lady—"

"I daresay 'Marigold' will suffice under the circumstances." She wasn't exactly in her Lady M persona, but she wasn't her preferred casual self either. Her hair was still done up from the ball, and though she wasn't in her gown, she wasn't in the trousers she'd have worn outside. Just one of the day dresses she'd brought for the party. That wouldn't be shocking.

The shocking bit would be that she'd come to Gemma's room and greeted her by name.

Carissa paused with the towel hovering under Gemma's right foot, her own cheeks now going pink. "Lady Marigold! You—you know each other?" Yet another widening of her eyes. "You *know* each other!"

Marigold grinned. "We're old friends. Gemma's father was my family's steward for most of our childhood, and then she remained as my companion after he died."

That would perhaps answer part of Carissa's question, but she could see others brewing. Gemma smiled. "We built our careers together, one might say."

Marigold chuckled. "One might. Gemma helped create Lady M in the columns, and knowing my whereabouts guaranteed she always had a subject to write about. Perhaps a bit unsporting, but it worked to our mutual benefit."

And wasn't *so* big a secret, really. Marigold's identity had never been in question. It was only Gemma's that had been a bit secret, and she'd already told Carissa that part.

Graham snagged everyone's attention when he stood, her bloody stockings in his hand. "You need some salve on those ankles, Gem. I'll go and see if I can find something somewhere. Would one of you ladies come with me in case I need an escort back into this wing?"

"I will," Marigold said before Carissa could volunteer. No doubt she imagined she could get more information about what happened from him than from Gemma. "We'll be back straightaway, Gem."

"Thank you." She sighed as the door closed behind them, praying she hadn't made a grave mistake by confiding in Carissa. What if she was involved with Fitzroy or Astley? What if—?

"Well, I feel the fool." Carissa pressed her lips together and gently patted the water from Gemma's foot. "All those things I said about how handsome he is—your husband!"

A bit of the knot eased. Gemma was no novice at reading people, and Carissa Horley had no guile. "You needn't feel foolish. He *is* handsome. It's a simple fact."

Carissa stilled, and then met her gaze. Held it. Her eyes were more serious than Gemma had yet seen them. "But you're estranged?"

Her own eyes slid shut. "We . . . lost our son. A year ago. In a car accident. Graham was driving, and . . . and I couldn't . . ."

"Oh, Gemma." There was a shifting and a sloshing, and then Carissa's arms came around her shoulders. "I'm so sorry. How old was he?"

"Nine months. Just nine months. Starting to crawl, and to chant 'ma ma ma' and 'da da da' at everything." She choked on another rising sob, tried to swallow it down. "Christmas Eve last year."

The arms went tighter. "Today—no, yesterday now. And you said nothing."

"I didn't want to think—"

179

"Of course not. I understand. I . . . I lost a baby too, when she was only two days old. A month after my husband . . . She came too early, and though I prayed, there was no help for it. But I held her, those two days. I loved her. I've missed her every day since." She said it softly yet fiercely. As if it were a secret she didn't dare share with anyone.

Perhaps it was. Perhaps she belonged to one of the families that told her to put on a stiff upper lip and get on with life, who was accustomed to handing one's infants off to a nurse for the first three years anyway, who couldn't understand growing attached until one knew the child was out of the danger of simply being an infant.

But Gemma wasn't that sort. "Of course you have."

For a moment, they simply clung to each other, letting their individual griefs mingle. They weren't the same—no two griefs were. Carissa mourned the life that had been all she had left of her husband, a sweet little someone she'd not carried long enough and only been allowed to hold for two short days. She mourned all the would-have-beens and what-ifs. Gemma knew some of those two, but differently. Her grief involved months of watching and knowing and loving and dreaming. Nearly a year of having her son, only to have him stolen from her.

Carissa pulled away after a long moment, wiping at her eyes. "Your husband—he's a good man?"

Gemma's throat didn't want to work. She could still hear in her mind the litany against him that she'd been chanting to herself all this last year—*arrogant, selfish, refuses to listen, proud, haughty, ambitious.*

But she'd known Graham Wharton most of her life. She'd seen his weaknesses, yes, but his strengths too. His heart. His soul. And she'd chosen to love him not because of either his flaws or his virtues but because of who the combination of them created.

He wasn't perfect. His choices had ruined her life. But he was no monster like whoever had kidnapped Sidney for financial gain.

She nodded.

"And he loves you—I could see at the start he was enamored, but watching him carry you up here, the way he looked at you . . . Not every man loves his wife like that. But he does."

It was true—both that he did and others didn't. One couldn't observe society as much as Gemma had without knowing that the vast majority of upper-class marriages were made for reasons other than love. Sometimes affection came . . . sometimes it didn't.

But she and Graham weren't high society. They'd had the freedom to choose each other for love, and she'd never once doubted his feelings for her. Not even this last year. He'd made it clear in their every short interaction that he loved her, that he wanted to be with her still. Even after the horrible things she'd said to him in that tunnel, as hurt as she knew he'd been, he'd turned around and come in search of her. He'd held her. Cried with her. Protected her.

Her throat was still too tight, but she forced words through it anyway. "I know he does."

Carissa smiled, lifting her brows. Somehow it looked all the more friendly in contrast to her red-rimmed eyes and damp cheeks. "So then? Are you going to let him win you back?"

She wanted to. Sort of. Almost. She wanted that desire to be enough to overcome the pain and the bitterness and the year of brokenness between them.

But even that was progress toward that seemingly unreachable forgiveness, wasn't it? A few hours ago, she simply would have said no. Now, a refusal seemed as ungraspable as full healing.

She drew in a long breath, let it back out. "I don't know. Honestly, I don't even know why he's trying. I've been nothing but horrible to him since the accident."

Carissa reached for her fingers and then gave them a squeeze. "I know why. You've lost your child, Gemma—I know how empty that leaves you. But you don't have to lose each other. You can still have your husband. And I hope that, from someone who has lost both, you'll hear me when I say this. Don't lose him too."

Gemma squeezed her friend's fingers back, but she made no other response. She didn't know what to say. She didn't know how to forgive him, how to be healed, how to heal the wounds she'd deliberately inflicted. She didn't know how to take the pieces of their ice-shattered lives and put them back together.

Forgive us our trespasses as we forgive those who trespass against us.

She felt again that crack in the ice of her soul, where the trickle of God's flowing waters had broken through.

Maybe it wasn't that the ice of her unforgiveness kept her from receiving His. Maybe . . . maybe His forgiveness, as it broke through the barriers and melted her heart, would flow back out of her. Toward Graham. Perhaps she didn't need her *own* forgiveness.

Perhaps she could rely on His.

FIFTEEN

He'd slept some—after he'd snooped through every unlocked door in the house that he and Yates could find, after Astley had retired. He'd been exhausted when he finally climbed into bed at four in the morning, but the kind that often prohibited sleep. For what seemed like an eternity, he'd lain there, worrying for Sidney. Wondering where he was, if they'd walked right past him, if they ought to have forced every lock.

There simply hadn't been time enough, and eventually exhaustion had won out. That one nap in the last forty-eight hours simply wasn't enough to go on. But perhaps two of them would suffice, since that's all this sleep had amounted to.

Graham turned off the alarm clock pulling him from slumber, rubbed at his eyes, stretched his sore muscles, and levered himself up in his borrowed bed in the bachelor wing. He'd left the curtains open, and a glance toward the window showed him that the sun had cleared the horizon, and that the clouds had broken up and were currently set ablaze in a glory of color that never ceased to call to the artist in him. For a long moment, he stared at it.

Christmas morning. The second Christmas in a row that

he'd woken up neither in his own bed in London nor his usual one at the Tower. But waking up *here* certainly beat the cot in the hospital ward last year.

A glance at the clock verified that it was five after eight. Only three hours of sleep, after he finally convinced his mind to still, but it was something. Enough to fuel him in the next hours of searching for Sidney. After he checked on Gemma.

Graham might never recover from the sight of her collapsed in the snow like she'd been, sobbing. It had whisked him back to that Northumberland road. To the panic of opening his eyes and realizing she and Jamie weren't in the cabin of their crushed car anymore. To clambering out, searching, seeing her crumpled and still against the stark white.

He'd thought he'd lost them both, in that moment. And while nothing—nothing—could ever eclipse the pain of losing his firstborn son, there had been joy when he pressed a finger to her neck and discovered she was still alive. He hadn't lost his Gemma.

Except that he had. He just hadn't known it yet.

Last night had, in some ways, been the reverse. He'd finally realized she was lost to him, down in the monastery corridor, only to find her again in the snow.

She'd let him hold her. She'd let his tears mix with her own. For the first time in the last eternal year, he hadn't been alone in his grief. Even if he was always, in a way, alone in it. They both lost the same son, and yet a mother's loss was different from a father's. Graham had his guilt coloring it; Gemma had her anger.

Different, but still they grieved the loss of the same little boy. Crying together was still crying—but it was *together*.

He rubbed at his face again. They would have a few hours of quiet to search this morning. The other guests, he knew, wouldn't rise until ten or eleven or even noon, and the servants might have even been granted a few hours' extra respite after the ball kept them all up until the wee hours.

He wasn't entirely convinced Gemma would feel up to hauling herself out of bed, but he hoped she would. A bit of restorative sleep and the salve he and Marigold had found for her ankles would, with a bit of luck, have her feeling at least somewhat human.

He'd told Marigold all about their argument, and how he'd found her. His cousin, her eyes wide, had been so shocked she'd nearly stumbled—which was saying something indeed for the graceful acrobat.

"*She was* crying?" she'd said. It hadn't been disbelief in her tone—it had been wonder. And maybe something even deeper, closer to gratitude. She'd pressed a hand to her lips and blinked back tears of her own. "*Oh, praise God. She hadn't, not once. Not this whole year. Perhaps now she can finally begin to heal.*"

Graham had only stared at her. She hadn't cried over Jamie? Over their broken marriage? Gemma, who had always worked through her emotions with tears? Gemma, who cried over wilted flowers and injured rabbits—she hadn't cried over their *son*?

A flash of anger had rippled through him, but it had vanished as quickly as it came. In its place surged compassion. Understanding.

She hadn't cried because she hadn't mourned. She hadn't cried because that would have meant accepting that he was really gone. She hadn't. She couldn't. She had clung instead to her rage.

But rage could never last, and last night it had finally turned to dust in her fists. Last night she had finally been hit by the truth. She had finally felt it. Maybe, as Marigold had said, it was the first step toward healing.

The first step on a long, long road. He'd been walking it alone all these months. But if he could walk it with her . . . that would make a difference.

"Don't get ahead of yourself, old boy," he muttered as he pushed himself to his feet. He shouldn't get excited because she'd admitted to a stranger that they were married. How pathetic was it that he *wanted* to be excited by that? For all he knew, her admission of being his wife could lead her to contemplate divorce instead of just ignoring his existence.

He squeezed his eyes shut. Even thinking that word sliced him through. *Divorce.* She wouldn't, would she? Her brother would be horrified, Aunt Priss would threaten to disown her. Divorce wasn't something that respectable, God-fearing people of society considered.

No, respectable, God-fearing people of society simply lived in separate houses and had affairs when their marriages failed. They didn't divorce.

Cynicism he would tuck away along with the fear.

Hope. He would hope. Why not? It was the season for it, or so everyone said. So he'd once believed.

Marigold had thought there was cause to hope. Marigold had been quick to credit God for the change in Gemma. Marigold had given him a fierce hug and whispered that God still loved him even more than he still loved Gemma.

"He's waiting," she'd said. *"He's waiting just as you've been. Don't give up on Gemma—God hasn't given up on you."*

Graham splashed warm water on his face—a servant must have been in already with fresh—and toweled it dry, then hurried through his dressing. Tea. He needed tea to soothe the throat that felt rather dry and scratchy all of a sudden. Giving his tie one last adjustment, Graham slid his room key into his pocket and let himself out into the quiet corridor. He wasn't the least bit surprised to find Yates locking up his own door too and lifting a hand in silent greeting.

He'd wanted to snap that God could keep on waiting—that he wanted no part of a deity so cruel. If God was a father, He didn't seem to be the kind Graham had wanted to be—He was more the sort Lord Wilfred was. A strict, unfeeling disciplinarian.

Maybe He'd taken Jamie as punishment for the very sins Gemma had accused him of. Maybe his loss was Graham's fault on a whole different level than he'd assumed.

"Are you quite all right?" Yates had somehow appeared at his side and clapped a big hand to his shoulder.

Gemma would never forgive him. Never.

"Graham?" A little shake. "Do you need to go back to bed? You know how you get with too little sleep."

"No." He pasted on a smile that probably looked about as convincing as the faux wainscoting in his room. Wouldn't fool anyone with a drop of experience, and Yates had buckets-ful. "I'm all right. Just need some tea."

And to find Sidney. It may not inspire Gemma to forgive him, but perhaps it would be one tally mark in his favor, anyway. With her, with God, in his own mind. Something.

Yates opened his mouth, clearly about to call him on the lie, but paused. His eyes went narrow as he looked at something past Graham. Then he muttered, "Leopard stripes," and brushed past him. "Excuse me. Miss?"

Miss? Graham spun about, frowning when he saw that his cousin was addressing a maid who was bustling between two open bedchambers, a pile of linens in her arms. The maid had come to a wide-eyed halt, clearly alarmed at being addressed.

Graham chased after Yates with a shake of his head. His cousin was an *earl*. He had been raised in society. And for

part of his life, at least, his own home had run like a traditional nobleman's estate, complete with a full staff of people
not counted as family. He ought to have known the rules
about engaging—or *not!*—with staff.

But Yates, the baboon, went right up to the nonplussed
chambermaid with a smile and waved a hand at the room.
"Pardon me, I don't mean to interrupt. Only, isn't that Lord
Astley's room?"

Oh. The room that now stood open and was being stripped.
A sure sign that its occupant had either left or ordered, for
some reason, a full cleaning.

The maid dipped a curtsy. "It was, my lord, aye."

Was. Blast. They'd pressed an ear to that door when they'd
returned from their fruitless hunt the night before and could
hear Astley breathing within so had dared to grab a few
hours of sleep themselves.

A mistake, clearly. And they'd been sleeping too deeply to
hear him leave. Failure weighed heavy on Graham's chest,
and he knew Yates would feel it too.

His cousin produced a look of disappointment that would
have fooled anyone, unlike Graham's smile of a moment
before. But then, Yates had embraced the lessons of the
theater troupe far more eagerly than Graham had. "Has he
left already? I was hoping to enjoy his company later today."

"Two hours ago. Sorry, my lord." As if she were responsible for anything more than obeying the orders to clean up
after him. "And Mr. Fitzroy with him."

"Well, blast." Yates spun, that look still on his face, and
pursed his lips at Graham. "There goes our foursome for
whist, Wharton. Shame, that. I was hoping to win back yesterday's losses."

Trying to call up every acting lesson Neville had hammered into him as a child, he went for a lopsided grin. "I
suppose you'll have to hunt them down in the gaming hells

in Town, old boy. Or else find your recompense from some other saps later today."

"I suppose so." Yates didn't thank the maid—proof that he *did* know the way things were done and was showing her the kindness of letting her go back to her expected invisibility. Even though Graham could see his lips twitching, wanting to say the words. He pressed them together and started down the corridor again, toward the stairs.

Graham might have chuckled if the news the girl had shared didn't have such grave implications.

They were gone—both of them. Two hours ago, while Graham and Yates had been sleeping.

Blast it.

"That changes our plans for the day," Graham muttered as they jogged down the stairs. "If they're both gone, they must have Sidney with them."

"Agreed." Yates managed to pack urgency into the single word. "We need to try to discern where they've gone and by what means. Carriage? Train?"

"If train, they'd have had to have their tickets already— not only theirs, but Sidney's too. Would they have thought to have one for him?" Graham already had *his* return ticket, as did any other passenger intending to travel over the holiday. The train lines encouraged everyone to purchase one of their flexible-date tickets for Christmas travel, when trains would run but the offices were closed. He'd been assured upon its purchase that it was good for any return to London between December 20 and 27.

"Quite possibly. Astley didn't sound surprised by the lack of ransom last night. Though that doesn't guarantee travel by train. There are an awful lot of people around, even on a holiday."

True. Was it instead more likely that they'd be going by carriage or automobile? That would make them harder to track but going more slowly. More able to be overtaken if they could narrow down which road they were on.

Yates must have been thinking the same. "We'll have to split up. You and Gemma, if she's willing, take the train station and see if anyone was about who saw them. We'll take the road. I daresay they were headed generally north, wherever else they were going, as there isn't much other choice down here. Perhaps the stable boys know something, or someone along the way."

"Leopard stripes." He would have liked to spit out something a little stronger, but he knew better—especially since they were even then arriving at the main part of the house, and the ladies and Sir Merritt were already gathered.

Marigold was dressed in one of her ridiculous outfits. Mrs. Horley had shown up again, to which he had no argument, and Gemma stood in a dress of blue that matched her eyes, with gold trim that matched her hair more than it should have—the dye was wearing off. Seeing her there, looking out one of the arched columns toward the snow-covered landscape, made his heart contract. She didn't hold herself like she was in pain, so that was good.

Yates went straight to them. "Well, my plans for the day have been trounced." His voice was cheerful to match his expression, but his eyes were anything but. "Seems Fitzroy and Astley have left already. They must have known my plans to win back what I lost to them yesterday and made a run for it."

Anyone listening, be they the staff bustling about or the two other early-rising guests Graham could see in the drawing room, would assume he meant gaming losses, but their group would know better. Well, Mrs. Horley might not have full comprehension, but enough that she didn't look surprised when Marigold pronounced, "Well, then. Home?"

"Home." Yates turned to Gemma. "Not that you need to

leave, Miss Parker, but if you wanted a ride to London, we'll be going that way. Or I believe Mr. Wharton was catching the train today and would be happy to accompany you to the station."

Graham watched Gemma struggle to keep her easy, G. M. Parker mask in place and knew that if the struggle was even that visible, it bespoke an eruption of thoughts and feelings she *didn't* show. Gem had always been a natural at the actress's roles. She wasn't one to slip, but her Midlands accent scarcely made an appearance as she whispered, "When did they leave?"

Yates shot her a quick warning look and glanced around, seemingly to see who else was up. "Two hours ago, apparently."

"Lionfeathers," Marigold muttered under her breath.

Carissa Horley looked from one of them to another, settling on Gemma. She rested a hand on Gem's arm. "You'll want to go too, I imagine. Start your write-up? I can keep my fingers on the pulse for you here, if you like. And write to you with anything I see or hear?"

Gemma's smile was genuine. "That would be perfect, Carissa. I'm in your debt. Let me jot down my direction for you. And then . . . Mr. Wharton, I'd be pleased to share your ride to the train station if you're arranging one."

He supposed he'd better. There wouldn't be enough room in the Fairfax carriage for the five of them, and besides which, it would look odd if they all left together. He'd have to request the car that had brought him here, much as he hated to pull the chauffeur away from his Christmas. "I'll see to it now."

He knew they'd have to have a true conference before any of them left, one out of hearing of the other guests of Weywent. But that could wait until they had the wheels of their departure in motion.

The gents had two hours' lead on them. They couldn't afford to waste any more time dilly-dallying about for the sake of appearances. Graham shoved a hand into his pocket, his fingers finding that silver Ludgrove button he'd taken from the cell the night before.

Sidney had been there. He'd scratched *Help* into the stone. Graham hoped that those out-of-place comforts meant he was cared for, but what of the cold fury Yates had reported hearing in Astley's tone? What if it turned to violence?

What if . . . what if they finally realized they'd nabbed the wrong boy? What would they do then?

Graham's stomach went cold and hard as a ball of ice as he left the group with a nod and went in search of a servant who could help with their departure. Yet again, for Sidney's sake, he found himself lapsing into old habits and praying.

Save him, Lord. Keep him safe. Help us to help him.

Saying the words silently in his mind didn't convince him God would hear and answer with anything kind. But when one was desperate, one appealed to the King. Even if the chances of help were slim, one had to take the chance anyway.

He was out nothing but the chafe to his own pride to try it. And he'd already learned the price of his pride.

SIXTEEN

Yates knew his way around a stable yard—more, truth be told, than anyone would ever think. At the Tower, he helped muck the stalls, harness the horses, and care for the retired circus animals. He still counted among his best friends the young men who had once been stable hands for the Fairfaxes and now worked at the neighboring estates, since he couldn't afford to pay them a fair wage.

Which meant it was easy to look comfortable as he lounged against the stall while his carriage was being prepared, easy to smile and look around as if merely cataloguing ideas he could implement in his own stables—as if he'd ever again have funds to improve his stables. Easy to strike up casual conversation with the men working on Christmas—they'd have tomorrow off, he hoped.

He'd found one in particular, who answered to the name Cap, to be blessedly chatty. Yates had already plied him for ten minutes with subjects completely benign, asking about breeds of horses he'd recommend, and which carriages were best sprung, his thoughts on automobiles, and whether Her Ladyship intended to have electricity strung out here any time soon.

Chatty Cap didn't blink an eye when Yates then said, "I was disappointed to see that Astley and Fitzroy left already.

We'd been talking autos over our card game yesterday. Did Lord Astley have his here, by chance?" He had no idea if Astley even had a car, or if he'd come by horse or carriage or train. But Cap might know.

Cap did. He shook his head. "Oh no, the only ones what came in cars were the Wrens and the Foresters. His Lordship musta taken the train. We hain't had his carriage in here, but Geoff was rousted before daylight to make a run to the station."

Geoff must be the chauffeur. Yates made a disappointed noise. "Shame. I was hoping for your opinion on it. What does Geoff say about Lady Weymouth's choice in automobile? I'm still debating the options."

Which he was—intellectually. Neville was after them to buy one, insisting they'd be giving away their secrets soon if they didn't, since all the other aristocrats were buying them. But they all knew that money could be better spent elsewhere. Still, dreaming and debating the pros and cons of each new model to hit the market was free.

It didn't sound like the model Lady Weymouth had chosen would be in his someday plans, though, given what Cap related Geoff saying. Troublesome engine, didn't drive well. He listened, nodding along, before grinning. "I bet Fitzroy hates it, then. He seems to favor racing cars."

"Fitzroy." Cap apparently didn't think anything of snorting his opinion of his employer's nephew for a random guest to hear. "He *would* waste money on such a thing—if he had it to waste. Her ladyship keeps that one on a tight budget, and wisely so, if you ask me."

Yates let his lips twitch. He could probably teach her ladyship a thing or two about tight budgets—and her wastrel of a nephew about how to keep to them and still enjoy life. "So no racing horses either? No high-sprung carriages? Was he relegated to the train for his holiday visit too?"

Cap chuckled and switched from the curry comb to the

brush on the horse he was grooming while Yates lounged outside the stall. "Couldn't even convince his aunt to send her private train car for him. He had to come with Lord Astley, and probably convinced him somehow to spring for his food and drink along the way. You want my advice, your lordship, you'd do well to steer clear of that lot and find your friends elsewhere."

"Oh?" The back of Yates's neck tingled in anticipation. "I admit I've heard a warning or two about Fitzroy, amiable though he may be. But no one said anything about Astley. And they were both quite a few years above me in school, so I don't know them much personally." He hadn't actually gone away to school, but they would have been nine years above him, had he gone.

Cap's strokes slowed, and his face went thoughtful. "Cain't imagine folks know what to say about him. He don't say much, hisself, that I've seen. But it's how he looks when he ain't talking. Brooding, me mum woulda called him. Me sister, Mag—she works in the house—she says he spent his whole stay here demanding extra this and that, like he was too good to eat with the rest of the company or some such. And always snappish about it too."

The tingles danced a jig. That sounded very much like he was requesting things he could deliver to an extra mouth he had to feed—and was on edge about it. Yates gave a sober nod. "I do thank you for the warning, Cap. I certainly don't need friends who behave so. My own staff is as dear to me as family, and I hate to think of any guests I invite treating them so poorly."

Lionfeathers, he was making himself miss them, and it didn't look as though their journey home would be able to be *all* the way home to Northumberland. Not quite yet.

No, London would have more information on Astley and Fitzroy both. So to London they'd go.

Cap beamed. "Maybe you *should* befriend young Fitzroy. He could do with a good influence. And a bit of growing up, besides."

Yates laughed and pushed off the stall when he saw the groom who had been hitching up his horses to his carriage come back in with a nod. "Well, I'm not opposed to my virtues rubbing off on my acquaintances, but I do tend to be rather choosy about who moves from *acquaintance* to *friend*."

"Wise lad." Cap chuckled and gave him a salute that indicated a life in the military before he came here. Maybe "Cap" was a title from that earlier life, not simply a nickname. "Happy Christmas, my lord. And safe travels home."

"Happy Christmas, Cap, to you and Mag both, and whatever other family you share." He strode away, tipping the groom who'd prepared his carriage and adding a matching one with a quiet instruction to give it to Cap. He wished he had something more generous to give them, but his tip budget was nearly gone, and they still had a few stops they'd have to make between here and London.

He looked up to where Hector—a lion tamer by trade and a wanderer at heart, who had jumped at the chance to play driver for them on the trip south—secured the last of the trunks. "Is that everything?"

Hector was the youngest of the Caesars, the family of Romani who had retired at Fairfax Tower, but he still had a good thirty-five years on Yates. He grinned. "Unless you left something in your room, my lord."

He'd gone over it three times, but the very suggestion made him want to take another peek. Which Hector would know, blast it. Yates scowled. "You're a cruel man."

Hector laughed and climbed from the top of the carriage to the driver's seat. "You getting in now or walking back to the house?"

He walked, since he'd have hours enough in the carriage, and folding himself into the box for long periods always felt a bit like playing at contortionist. Maybe they should have spent the money to keep up Father's private rail carriage. It would have been nice to be able to stand and move about on a long trip.

Irrelevant. He strode back to the house, let his sister and Merritt know they were ready to leave, said his farewells to the handful of guests who had deigned to greet the morning thus far, and then, finally, they were all in their carriage. No one to overhear them but Hector, who he'd trusted with his life more than once.

He leaned forward and shared what he'd learned in the stables.

Marigold pursed her lips. "Should we go to the train station, then, with Graham and Gemma? See who might have seen them?"

Her husband shook his head. "They can handle that, I think. We need to get back to London as quickly as possible. We'll already be arriving hours later than they will be, and we'll need to reconvene to plan next moves at the first opportunity."

"I agree with Merritt." Yates leaned back, blustering out a long breath. "I have a bad feeling about all this." Something about the tone of Astley's voice in the church, the devil-may-care attitude of Fitzroy, the cold reception of Wilfred . . . they all added up to an explosive situation.

And Yates could all but hear the hissing of the dynamite's fuse.

Gemma nearly wept with relief when she finally, finally found a stevedore who gave an affirmative nod when she showed him the sketch of Fitzroy, Astley, and Sidney that she'd forced Graham to make. He claimed he was rubbish at drawing people. Their lines, he'd always said, weren't as comprehensible as a building's. But he made perfectly passable portraits. Perhaps they lacked the soul that, ironically, his architectural studies had, but they didn't need something worthy of the British Museum. They only needed something to point to as they shouted their questions over the noise of steam locomotives and countless holiday-goers calling out greetings or farewells to their families.

Gracious, but she hated traveling at Christmas. They'd done it every year since their wedding, and it was always chaos, even on the holy day itself.

She caught the thought mid-think. Realized how *normal* a complaint it was. How small a one, given the tragedy of last year's journey.

Remembered, for the first time, the frustration in Graham's eyes when she'd begged him to take the train, given the weather forecast. *"You hate the train at Christmas,"* he'd said. *"I only wanted you to enjoy the trip this time."*

Gemma had to swallow past the sudden tightness in her throat, force a smile past the unbidden memory. Focus on the sweaty, exhausted-looking stevedore who was looking from the drawing back to her. His nod was in answer to her question of a minute before, some variation or another of, "Excuse me, sir. Would you by chance remember seeing any of my family here this morning? They apparently meant it when they said they'd leave without me if I wasn't up by six."

It was the story she was acting out for each person she spotted who looked either like they worked here or had been waiting too long for their train. His was the first positive answer in a dozen queries.

"You do?" Relief tasted giddy on her tongue, and she let out a little laugh that seemed perfectly in character. "Oh, thank heavens. All of them? My brother and his son and our cousin?"

At that, the man frowned. "Well now. I don't recall seeing this one." He tapped the drawing of Fitzroy. "Your cousin, you say? He looks a bit like the countess's nephew."

Gemma gave an enthusiastic nod. "Yes, quite. Our cousin Fitzroy—we're from the other side of the family, but her ladyship was kind enough to have us all for the holiday. Never mind him, though. I'm far more concerned with my brother and nephew." She gave him her best grin. "If he shows up at our parents' and I'm not close behind, I'll never hear the end of it."

The man grunted what might have been a laugh, had it been a bit more energetic. "Sorry to say, madam, that he was on the only train to Matlock today. Though if you take the next one to London, I daresay you'll find a connection there if your ticket will cover it."

Matlock? In Derbyshire? Gemma was careful to keep from her face the fact that his destination was news to her—and instead thanked the Lord for His guidance in choosing a Midlands accent for her stay here, which was totally appropriate to the region she'd inadvertently claimed to hail from. "I think it will, thank you. Though I'll miss passing the trip with my nephew."

The man eased back a step, squaring his shoulders and clearly ready to find his next passenger to help. "The lad looked as though he'd sleep the whole trip anyway. His da was carrying him like a rag doll. Must have been up till the wee hours to welcome Christmas?"

Gemma made herself laugh. "We all were. Hence my oversleeping." She pulled out a coin and pressed it to his palm—the usual tip for the job she'd cost him in time. "Thank you for your help, my good man. And Happy Christmas."

His eyes brightened a bit. He slid the coin into a pocket

with one hand and tipped his hat with the other. "Happy Christmas to you too, madam."

Leopard stripes. She didn't know whether she wanted to shout in victory or weep in frustration. The train to Matlock had departed at 6:45 that morning, according to the schedule she'd already studied, and the stevedore was right that there wasn't another going there from Weymouth today. Not that they could dash off to the Peak District without letting the Fairfaxes know and planning their next move, anyway.

Graham. She needed to find Graham. The next train to London—there were three more of *those* today—would leave in fifteen minutes. They needed to be on it. They could wait to leave until noon and still arrive in Town around when the Fairfaxes would, but more time there meant more time to research and plan.

She half-ran to the other side of the station, the side Graham had said he'd cover with his own copy of the drawing. It took only a cursory glance over the crowds to spot him. His familiar fedora over the hair she'd run her fingers through countless times. The overcoat she'd helped him pick out two years ago. The form she'd long ago learned to spot in a second with that unerring gaze that called out *mine*.

A year apart clearly hadn't changed that. She rushed toward him, not taking the time to wonder at it now. And just like always, he turned a half-second before he should have heard her quick approach over the din, sensing her somehow as she neared. And he smiled.

Jamie's smile. It punched her in the stomach even as it pulled her closer. She wrestled the emotion down, though. It was about Sidney right now. Astley. Fitzroy.

She slipped her hand into the crook of his arm and stretched up on her toes to put her mouth close to his ear. "I found a stevedore. He hadn't seen Fitzroy, but he saw Astley board the train to Matlock carrying a sleeping Sidney 'like a rag doll.' Said he looked as though he'd sleep the whole journey."

"Drugged." Graham covered her hand with his opposite one and pulled her toward the platform for the next London-bound train. "I suppose I ought to be glad he carried him on as a passenger and didn't try to put him in a trunk or something."

She shivered at the very thought. And wondered, not for the first time, how they'd gotten him here and into that underground prison to begin with. "Any luck over here?"

"Fitzroy went to London. First train of the day."

Good. Or at least it was good that they knew where everyone was going—or had gone. She nodded but didn't try to say anything else above the increased noise.

Graham handled getting the luggage loaded, just as he'd always done, while Gemma held their place in the line of laughing families and a few sisters singing carols as they waited. By the time boarding began, Graham was back at her side.

He didn't ask, this time, if he could sit with her. For that matter, he followed behind her down the aisle like he'd always done, with a hand touching the small of her back. And it felt . . . right.

Right enough that she didn't take one of the open single seats she passed but kept looking for space for them both. Right enough that she didn't mind that they'd look like exactly what they were to anyone looking at them—a married couple, as comfortable with each other as with themselves.

Funny how it could still be true, even when it spoke more of how uncomfortable she was with herself than of how comfortable she was with him.

Regardless, she didn't want to be alone right now. Perhaps she'd be working through the same thoughts whether he was at her side or not, but they seemed somehow less likely to crush her if his shoulders were beside her, holding them up.

He must have known it, like he always had. After he stowed

their bags in the compartment above them, he sat down. And he turned his hand palm up on his knee, his fingers toward her. An invitation he'd given a thousand times. An invitation she'd accepted just as many.

She had to swallow, draw in a deep breath that felt more like prayer than air. Tears burned the backs of her eyes, even though she'd begun to think, until last night, that she'd never cry again.

She slid her fingers into his. Rested her palm against the one wider, longer than her own. And couldn't stop the tear that slipped out at how much it felt like home.

Graham lifted their hands and pressed his lips to her fingers. "We're going to find him, Gem. We will."

Would they? In her mind, their deadline had been the ransom drop. She had been thinking ever since they took the case that they *must* return the boy before the chime of the Christmas bells, or they'd have failed.

They'd failed. But maybe, if Graham was right, they could succeed too. Maybe this first failure didn't mean all hope was lost.

Another tear chased after the first, and because she didn't want to be an absolute ninny crying on a public train on Christmas Day, she turned her face into Graham's shoulder and tried to sniffle her composure back into place.

He leaned his head against hers. "How are the ankles holding up?"

The non sequitur teased out a laugh that fought back the tears. "I won't dare to wear those boots again until they've fully healed, but they're fine in my regular shoes that don't touch the blisters." The pair of silk stockings had been fit only for the rubbish bin, given the holes that had run all the way up her legs, and that was a shame. But she'd had a spare pair to don today.

"I still can't believe how useful Mrs. Horley has proven to be. I thought her nothing but fluff and nonsense."

Her lips settled into a smile as the tears retreated, but still she left her head on his shoulder. Just for a moment more. "There is definitely more to Carissa than empty chatter. I think I'll be glad to count her as a friend from here on."

"Good. One can never have too many of those." He said it with the tired, flat tone that said he hadn't enough of them.

She lifted her head so she could look at him. And wondered, for the first time, what else *he* had lost, besides Jamie. And her. James, who had always been one of his dearest friends. She knew her brother continued to visit, but she also knew the visits had become less about friendship than James trying to cajole Graham into a return of faith. Yates, who would never abandon him even if he tried to make him.

But who else was there? He'd had endless acquaintances through the firm, but all their socializing had been as a couple. Had he gone to any dinner parties or outings alone? Somehow she doubted it.

Which meant that while she'd walled herself off at her brother's house or the Tower with Graham's only family and had refused him entrance into that haven, he'd been in their silent London house. Alone, but for the haunting memories.

She tightened her fingers around his. Perhaps it wasn't much of an apology, but it was the only one she could offer. She'd meant to cause him pain—a sliver of what he'd caused her—but now she looked at his handsome face and regretted that she'd stolen the smile from it.

Jamie, crawling about on the floor with wild laughter as Graham chased after him, crawling too, grinning like an utter fool and laughing just as wildly.

The words, the memory, pummeled her as the last one had done, coming out of nowhere. Her breath caught, and she had to cough to cover it. Even so, he would notice. He always did.

He lifted a brow but didn't say anything. Just repositioned himself a bit against their bench as the train let out a shrill whistle and then began to move. He closed his eyes and said, "Sleep?"

She snorted a laugh. "You can never sleep on a train." Neither could she, even when she wished she could.

A corner of his mouth turned up in acknowledgment. Still. He kept his eyes closed as the train gained steam and pulled away from the station. He roused to hand the conductor their tickets but then went right back to pretended rest.

Gemma would have thought he wanted to avoid talking to her, had he not kept a firm grip on her fingers. Had his thumb not taken to stroking over her knuckles in the way he knew she liked.

He was thinking. Turning something over and over in his mind. Worrying it. Gemma settled in, knowing he'd speak when he'd fit it all into whatever neat, orderly compartments he'd built or found for each piece.

It took twenty minutes before he did. Before he squeezed her fingers, shifted again, and rolled his head to face her.

She turned hers toward him too. And waited.

She expected something about Sidney. Or Fitzroy. Or Astley. Something about their first steps when they got back to London.

Instead, he said in a voice so quiet she could barely hear him over the *chug-a-chug*, "Do you think you can ever forgive me?"

She didn't pull her fingers free from his. She didn't turn away again. But she couldn't quite keep a few blocks of the ice wall she'd lived with for so long from trying to shield her heart.

That wasn't who she wanted to be, though. If she wanted forgiveness to flow in—which she did—then she had to let it flow out.

It was just so *hard*. She couldn't quite find any words. Not because none seemed right, but because she simply didn't know her own answer.

An eternity later, she finally said, "I don't know."

SEVENTEEN

I don't know."

If someone had asked Graham what the worst words were in the English language, he probably would have chosen something far more pointed than those three innocuous syllables. Something that was only despair with no window for hope, perhaps. Because *I don't know* didn't mean *no*. It didn't.

Not knowing was more a torment than a decisive negative. He could fight a negative. He could sort through the debris from a total collapse. He had made his career of taking other men's *no* and doing the research that allowed an *if* that would turn the client's dreams into a *yes*.

But Gemma's words were still echoing in his ears as they hailed a cab outside St. Pancras and both climbed in, as they were driven to the Fairfax townhouse whose address she'd given the cabby, as he helped her out again at the familiar, stately abode on Grosvenor that the Fairfaxes could neither afford to keep up nor afford to sell, given what it would cost their reputation to do so.

No, not just Gemma's words. His own too, when she'd flipped the question around on him a moment later. When she'd looked earnestly into his eyes, her own still shining with those few tears, and had asked him if *he* could ever forgive *God*.

Forgive God. A phrase so bizarre that for a moment he'd only been able to gape at her. One didn't *forgive* God. God, by the very definition, did nothing wrong—or nothing mere mortals could accuse Him of in any heavenly court. Wasn't that what James had lobbed at him left and right? That God made no mistakes. God was the very definition of good. If God did it, it must be for a purpose, it must be right, it must work out for the good of those who follow Him.

And everyone knew that humankind wasn't asked to forgive *rights*. They were asked to forgive *wrongs*. Therefore, forgiving God was a logical fallacy. Or something like one. Impossible. Unnecessary. Irrelevant.

And yet the moment she said it, he realized that these twisted-up, tangled feelings that wound tighter and tighter in his chest every time he thought about the Almighty taking his son were the exact same sort of anger he would feel at an unjust judge. An intemperate king. A cruel aristocrat. Graham hadn't decided intellectually that a good and gracious God couldn't exist.

He was furious with Him. Hurt by Him. And in that light, Gemma's question made perfect sense. Whether or not the wrong was real or only perceived, it still required forgiveness by the hurt party to move beyond it.

He'd been pondering her question most of the train trip to London, and he still had no better answer than the echo of her own that he'd stuttered out. *"I . . . I don't—I don't know."*

He wondered, as they climbed the steps while the cabby moved to get their luggage out for them, if Neville and Clementina would be at home or if Graham would have to fish out the key he had somewhere on the ring of them in his pocket.

He wondered, as Gemma rang the bell and the old actor's face soon appeared, wreathed in a smile, if she'd let him come in to make use of the Fairfax library and records or spin around and bid him an uncompromising farewell.

He wondered, as she sent a small smile over her shoulder at him and inclined her head in silent invitation, if all this hope her every non-hateful word and gesture pumped into him would mean a worse crash into the abyss of despair when she decided that *I don't know* was really *no*.

Probably. But he followed anyway, smiling at Neville and exchanging the expected holiday greetings as the actor looked over his shoulder, into the house. Probably expecting his wife to come running out too.

Gemma was unwinding her scarf from her neck even as she asked, "Have we beat the others home? They had an earlier start in the carriage, but our train was no doubt faster."

Neville chuckled and held the door open for the cabby carrying their bags, still darting glances inside. "I haven't seen them yet, though they did warn me before they left that they may be arriving sometime on Christmas." He sent them a question, spoken only in his brows. *Good news?*

Graham shook his head.

Neville pursed his lips for a moment, though he was all smiling graciousness as he instructed the cabby where to put things, tipped him, and then closed the door. "Well, now I had better warn you that—"

"Gemma? Is that you?"

The voice came from the corridor that led to the kitchen, but it wasn't Clementina's. It was, without question, the voice of Aunt Priss. But what was she doing here in the Fairfaxes' empty house on Christmas?

Gemma spun, the same question in her brows and the set of her lips, though she didn't dare utter it aloud, given that her aunt was barreling toward them with all the velocity of a locomotive, her arms outstretched and a look on her face that combined the deepest pain with a hint of relief.

"Oh, my girl! I knew you couldn't stay away the whole holiday. I *knew* you'd be home." Her gaze focused solely on her niece, Priss didn't stop until she'd folded Gemma into a tight embrace and squeezed her eyes shut. "My darling. Are you all right? I couldn't fathom when James told me that you'd left, now of all times. I know you want to distract yourself, that you don't want to let the grief in, but on the very anniversary . . ."

The few times Graham had witnessed an embrace between the staunch Priss and her niece, Gemma had remained stiff in her aunt's arms. Not so now. Now she clung, her own eyes shut too. "I . . . it has been . . ." She sniffled, choked on a sob.

"There, there." But her aunt wasn't trying to soothe. She was crying with her. "I know. I know how it hurts. We all hurt with you. We *all* lost Jamie. Your children are the closest I will ever have to grandchildren, Gemma. You know how I loved him too. How I love *you* and your brother. You're all I have."

"I know," Gemma said. But from the way she squeezed her eyes shut, and the grimace on her face, he realized that she *didn't* know, or hadn't let herself consider that *everyone* mourned their son, not just them. "I'm sorry, Aunt Priss. I'm so sorry. Sorry I didn't let you mourn with me—or that I didn't mourn with you . . . or whatever the way is to say it."

Graham stood there, still clutching his coat and hat and scarf in his hands without the wherewithal to hand them to Neville—who hadn't the wherewithal to reach for them either. They both watched the exchange, silent and sober. Graham wondered if Neville's throat was as tight as his.

After a long moment, Priss pulled away, wiping at her cheeks with one hand but still holding onto Gemma's shoulder with the other. He'd never seen quite that expression on her face—vulnerable and open and more than a little broken.

Then she spotted him, standing there with Neville, and her eyes went wide. "Graham!"

He mustered a smile. "Happy Christmas, Aunt Priss."

Her arms were about him next, squeezing the life out of—no, into—him. Then she stepped back, eyes shining with both tears and hope as she moved her gaze between him and Gemma. "You're . . . together. You've spent the holiday together?"

"A bit," Gemma said. "We were in the same place. And . . . we're working on it."

Aunt Priss looked as though her niece had handed her the most exquisite gift in the history of Christmas. She clutched her hands before her, eyes wide, mouth caught in a shape too in awe to be a smile. She embraced Graham again, then Gemma, then turned to Neville, who looked afraid that she was about to hug *him* too.

But no. She merely said, "My coat and hat, if you please!" Then she spun back to them. "I don't want to impose on your reunion. You two talk. I only wanted to be here when Gemma got home."

Neville jumped into action, mumbling something that resembled "Oh, *now* she doesn't want to impose, does she?" which made Graham grin. He returned a moment later with the lady's things, having put Gemma's away. Graham finally thought to hand over his own for a final exchange as Priss bundled up.

Gemma gave her aunt one more long hug. "Thank you," she murmured. "It . . . it means the world. That you'd come to wait for me. I'm sorry I . . . that I haven't been myself." She pulled a tremulous smile onto her lips. "I'm afraid I rather forgot how to be, without my precious boy."

"I know you did." Priss pressed a kiss to Gemma's cheek.

"Grief can do that. But you're not alone, dearest. You're never alone. You have me, you have your brother. And you have a husband who loves you more than life itself."

This part she said while sending Graham a wink—a wink! From *Aunt Priss*! Graham smiled, nodded. "She does."

A moment later, the older woman bustled out the door Neville opened for her, and they all gave a collective exhale in her wake.

Neville's butler mask fell neatly away the moment the latch caught, and he was all frowning protector. "No word, then, on the boy?"

"Word, yes. Heroic rescue, no." Gemma sighed and smoothed her hair back down where the hatpins had tugged it out of place.

"Well." Neville echoed the sigh, then rallied. "I imagine you'll want to await Lord Fairfax's return. And Lady Marigold and Sir Merritt will be here for the meeting as well? I'll make certain Clementina has dinner enough for everyone."

Graham nodded, still more relief seeping in when Gemma motioned for him to follow her. He trailed her along the darkened corridor and into the library, moving to the unlit but ready fireplace while she turned the knob that brought up the lights. It only took a minute to have the fire blazing cheerfully, but Clementina must have had water already on in the kitchen, because he no sooner turned around again than Neville was wheeling in a tea tray.

"Bit of Christmas cheer for you? We've fruitcake and biscuits that Clementina made because she says it isn't the holidays without them, but we all know neither Lord Fairfax nor Lady Marigold will have more than a bite."

A quirk neither Graham nor Gemma had ever shared— and Clementina's fruitcake was the stuff Christmas dreams were made of. He all but ran to the tray. "Now that you mention it, we skipped breakfast."

"And luncheon. And tea." Gemma swarmed the offerings alongside him, choosing a plate and cramming it full of treats—and a sandwich quarter, just for balance, he knew.

Neville chuckled. "There's plenty more if you need to make a whole meal of it. Enjoy. And if I may say so again, my dear—you did make a charming ginger."

Gemma laughed around the bite of fruitcake she already had in her mouth. "I would have had to retint it today, had we not decided to leave."

She was right about it having faded, unlike that walnut-shell wash she'd once tried that had lingered for weeks. He'd been glad when she finally declared defeat in the quest to look more like Marigold. Their disguises always worked well enough without their hair being an exact match anyway. And then Gemma had been with child, so they'd had to resort to other forms of alibis for a few months.

And then she'd been a mother, and he'd wondered if she'd perhaps want to forgo that side of her work entirely—stay home with Jamie and write her columns. But she'd missed it. Missed the rush of excitement, the challenge, and quite likely the feeling of pulling one over on the society so quick to snub her as *less*. He hadn't made any objection when she mentioned filling Marigold's hat and gown again. He'd simply said he'd stay at home with the baby, if it was in the evening.

He sank down into a chair at the library table, his plate and a steaming cup before him instead of books or files. For now. He'd start pulling out his research soon, anything he could find that touched on Lord Astley or his home or Matlock. But first . . .

"Do you remember . . ." Did he dare? Would it chase her away? He took a sip and decided he had to risk it. "Do you remember the way he laughed every time the wind-bells sang?"

Gemma went still, though she was mid-reach for her own chair across from him.

Graham swirled his spoon through his cup, though he hadn't added any sugar. With her there, having her light-and-sweet tea, he was free again to go back to his own black version. "The set your brother gave us, the ones that had that verse etched onto them." A line on each of the chimes. *But I will sing of thy power; yea, I will sing aloud of thy mercy in the morning; for thou hast been my defense and refuge in the day of my trouble.* "The first time you went to that musicale as Lady M, when he was four months old. He was missing you, crying, so I was walking the house with him. I paused at the window. It was open. The wind was blowing, the chimes going. And he *laughed*. His first laugh I'd been there for, and it came up from his soul, it seemed." He set the spoon down and stared into the cup. "We stood there for hours, until you got home. Watching and listening and laughing."

Gemma eased into her chair. "You forgot to feed him. I was so annoyed—it meant I had to rush to do it and bathe him and get him into bed. But then he laughed again, and I couldn't be angry."

His lips turned up. Just a little. Just for a moment. His eyes slid closed. "I never could bring myself to take them down. They're still there, in the back garden, even though Mr. Potter points out every single Sunday that I ought to take them down in the winter."

"Mr. Potter is a busybody." There was no heat in the words, though. Just the quiet pain of memories they could never replace with new ones. She blustered out a breath. "How do you do it? Stay there?"

How can you not? The words were on the tip of his tongue, but he warded them off with a bite of biscuit. "It . . . helps me to keep him close. To remember. When I can't sleep, I can go into the nursery and sit in your rocking chair and . . . and remember. That once, I was a daddy. Once, I was a husband. There's proof of it. I didn't imagine it. He was real, and he made me something I wasn't before. Something no one can take away."

"Graham." Her voice sounded like glass shattered on stone, but she reached across the table, leaving her fingers there in the middle, as close to him as the width of wood allowed.

He wanted to reach. Take. Hold. Instead, he looked her in the eyes. "I'll always be Jamie's father. Death can't steal that."

Would she sneer now? Lash out? Tell him he didn't *deserve* to be father to the baby he'd killed with his bad decisions? Last night she would have—all but had.

Tonight, she stretched a little more, pushing her fingers a little closer. "You will. It can't."

He moved his hand from where it rested against the edge of his plate and stretched it out until it brushed hers. "I don't want to be his father without him. I don't want to be your husband without you. But, Gemma, I can't change anything but the future. I can't wake us up from this nightmare. I can't—"

"Stop." The command fell from her lips as she pulled her fingers away, and in that heartbeat, he knew he'd overstepped, overspoken, pushed her back into whatever netherworld she'd been living in, where he was never permitted to follow.

Except that in the *next* heartbeat, she was sitting in his lap and her arms were around him. Her face was buried in his neck, and he held her as tightly as he could, his fingers no doubt digging into her back. He couldn't convince them to gentle, though. Couldn't do anything but hold on.

"Tell me more," she whispered against his neck, her voice tight now with the tears he felt warming his collar. "When you sit in the rocking chair—you remember? Can you . . . can you still smell him in there?"

"Talcum and lavender powder." He closed his eyes again,

smelling it even now. "There's still that new jar of it. I open it sometimes. Sprinkle a little." He squeezed his eyes shut, but it was no use. It never was. And though he might hesitate to admit it to anyone else, he *needed* to say it to her. "I sit there, most nights, and cry. Miss him. Miss you. Scream at the injustice of it all."

Her arms went tighter. "At whom? At whom are you screaming? If not at God, I mean?"

He breathed a mirthless laugh. "It *is* at Him, I suppose."

"Because you still know He's there."

"I know He's there. I . . . can't believe He cares. He took my son."

"I know." She pressed her lips—actually pressed her lips—to his neck, and she reached up and wiped away his tears. "He took mine too. But He gave His own."

Her brother's words—words he should have been able to dismiss. Though he couldn't. Not entirely. Not from her. "Jamie died."

"So did Jesus."

"But Jesus lived again!" Another belief he couldn't stop believing, not entirely.

"And so will Jamie. So *does* he." Her hand still on his cheek, she sat up enough to hover there in front of him, her gaze locked on his. "I have to believe that. I have to. Don't you? Believe our baby's in heaven?"

"I do." And he did—something he'd said to her brother a dozen times. It was just Graham wasn't there with him. And that's where he was supposed to be—*with him.*

Gemma's gaze went soft. She nodded. Then she leaned over and pressed her lips to his.

It was over before it even began, before he could react. That was probably a good thing, or he would have crushed her against him, begged for another touch of her lips, another chance.

She spoke again before he could think of anything he wanted to say. "How long will you love me, Graham?"

It could have sounded sad. Angry. Frustrated. Longing. It sounded, instead, patient. "Forever," he said, as he'd always said. "And a day."

She gave him a smile that looked exactly like she'd sounded. "Even if I can't forgive you?"

Was his love dependent on hers? No. This last year, when she'd declared hatred in place of love, he'd loved her still. Would he wait forever, was that what she was asking? Wait her out? Watch the road for her return every day? Keep the lights on for her, even if she never came back? He would. Until he was old and grey, if that's what it took.

He nodded. "Even if. I'll still love you. I'll always love you. I'll always—I'll always be waiting for you to come home. Whenever you're ready."

Her face shifted, and she clearly fought back tears. But she won the battle. Leaned over again, kissed him again— another brush so soft and light it could have been the greeting of a relative instead of a wife.

Then she whispered against his mouth, "You sound like another Father I know."

EIGHTEEN

26 December 1909
London

Gemma rubbed at her eyes, strained and tired after too many hours poring over every document and book they'd been able to dig up in the Fairfax library, and files that might tell them something about either Fitzroy or Astley. Christmas night had drifted away under the mountain of paper and binding, and Sunday had drifted in amidst yawns and clattering teacups and too many exclamations of "lionfeathers" and "leopard stripes" as they all started making errors in their notetaking, dropping pens, and staring at words without comprehension.

Eventually, Yates had declared sleep more pressing than the next pages and sent them all off to bed. No one left the house—Marigold and Merritt didn't return to their own, nor did Graham. The goal, as they'd all known it, was simply to snatch a few hours of slumber and then return to work as soon as they could.

Gemma wasn't entirely certain the slumber had worked its magic. When she'd risen, she'd found that Graham had gone to the National Archives for research, intending to beg one of the security guards he was on good terms with to let him in, despite it being officially closed until Wednesday. He returned in time for the traditional cold Boxing Day luncheon with rolls of papers in hand, praise the Lord.

The rest of them had continued the work of the previous day, looking through any book that might mention the Astley family or its estates, and perhaps more importantly, any case of theirs whose business he might have been involved in.

She never could quite focus. It was partly the mountain of work that felt tedious and dull when every nerve in her body screamed that they needed to *move*, needed to *act*, needed to hurry to Matlock and *do something*.

It was partly the memories that kept slamming into her every time she sneaked a glance at Graham.

The way he'd looked cradling their newborn—he, who had never held a baby, holding that tiny little life as if one breath out of turn might shatter them both.

The way he put aside all semblance of composure and made every funny face he could think of to earn a baby laugh.

The way Jamie would clap his hands and chant "da da da da" every time they heard a noise from the street.

"I'll always be Jamie's father. Death can't steal that."

She had tried to, though. She'd tried to take that from him, that distinction that had made him into the man he'd never known he wanted to be. She'd taken it, moreover, from herself. The only way to protect herself from the harsh realities of her son's death had been to protect herself from the blessed reality of his life.

She'd gone back to Gemma Parks, who was neither wife nor mother. She'd denied the sweetest, deepest part of her existence in some misguided attempt to stop herself from falling to pieces. She'd failed to see that sometimes people needed to shatter. Sometimes the pain needed to have its way with them. Sometimes that was the only way to remember what the sacrifice of praise really meant.

The Lord giveth, and the Lord taketh away. Blessed be the name of the Lord.

She rubbed again at her tired eyes, stretched her sore muscles, and stole a glance across the room, where Graham had claimed his usual broad table and had a blueprint underway on it, based on whatever plans he'd copied or studied at the Archives. A slide rule in one hand and white pencil in the other, he was making lines with that precision and surety that had always baffled her.

How did he know at exactly what fraction of an inch to make each line, when being off even a sixteenth meant feet or yards in reality, depending on his scale? How could he calculate angles with only a protractor, compass, and the workings of his own mind? How could he build something on flat blue paper with white pencil and know what it meant in terms of wood and stone, brick and mortar?

Missing him was an ache in her bones that she was only now beginning to realize had been ever-present this last year. The fear, the desperation had been too loud and bright for her to sense the deeper pain beneath it, but it was as familiar as the habit of reaching for her teacup.

He glanced up, not for the sake of glancing up, but for the sake of working through something in his mind. She recognized the inwardly focused look in his eyes that said he was peering at the world he sketched on the page, not the one around him. If she had the skill with drawing that he did, she'd have tried over the years to catch that look. That look encapsulated *Graham*.

It was why the opposite one, when he totally left his own mind and focused on Jamie, had been equally striking to her. He had taught her, through his love for her and their baby, that a person was never one thing. A person was contradictions and contrasts, silence and noise, exterior and interior.

He blinked, caught her looking at him, and sent her that self-satisfied start of a smile he'd been giving her since they were children. The one that only occupied one corner of his mouth but all of his eyes. The one that said, *"I see you seeing me."*

She'd missed seeing him. Not simply looking at him when their paths crossed but *seeing* him. She'd missed knowing someone else so fully. She'd missed how doing so meant knowing *herself* so fully.

She managed only a ghost of a smile back at him—not because of him, this time, but because of her. That's all she'd let herself be lately. A ghost. A phantom. A faded echo of the woman she should have been.

Yesterday, before the Fairfaxes returned, when she'd gone to him and even pressed her lips lightly to his, she'd thought for certain she pressed too hard. Wasn't even certain, honestly, why the words about God kept coming to her lips. They'd been her brother's words, in some ways. Words she'd needed to hear as much as he did. She'd feared even as she gave them voice that they'd make him turn away instead of toward her, harden instead of soften.

But it seemed the Holy Spirit had known better than she what Graham needed—an obvious statement that made her smile go self-deprecating as Graham turned back to his blueprint and she pulled forward the next business document to review. She regretted none of the words. Nor did she regret the minutes in his arms, the chaste kisses she'd given him.

They hadn't been the kisses of her own love, her passion, her desire for him as her husband. They'd been the kiss of Christ. A reminder that he was loved by One far more perfect than she. Far better at that love. Far more faithful.

Humbling, that. For all her recitation of creeds and prayers and Scripture, for all her tossing his doubt in his face at

Weywent, that might have been the first time in her life she was aware of acting on Christ's behalf instead of her own.

"Lionfeathers." Yates tossed his pen to the table and did his own stretch, making his shirt strain against his muscles. "I wish more was open today. We simply don't have enough information about this chap. Nothing here tells us what we need to know—where he went to school, how he met Fitzroy, what connection he may have to Wilfred *other* than Fitzroy, if there is any."

"We need more on Fitzroy too." Marigold shoved the stack of folders from their own records away from her. "We've never looked into him in anything but a peripheral way. We need a case file, not a dossier."

"We at least know what clubs and gaming hells he frequents." Sir Merritt picked up a piece of paper and let it drift back down to the table. He looked from Yates to Graham. "They'll be open still. We can go."

Yates made a face, but he nodded. "Unfortunately a good idea, though never my first choice in places to spend an evening. Graham?"

"Mm?" Graham had clearly not been listening and likely wasn't listening now either, given the way he didn't glance up.

Yates, of course, knew his cousin well. "Graham!"

"What?" He jerked to attention, straightening from his bend over his desk.

Yates smiled. "How are you coming along with the study of the Astley manor house?"

Graham blinked a few times, looked down at the technical drawing underway, and then back up. "I found old schematics of Derwent Hall at the Archives—that's the Astley ancestral estate. Named for the nearest river. I doubt it's entirely accurate still, though. There was mention of a fire in the 1810s in one of the texts I found, but I've yet to find reference to what was rebuilt and how, or what additions there may have been. But I daresay the foundation is the same. It was stone, so it's unlikely the whole place burned to the ground and they started completely over."

"Do we have enough that you're comfortable traveling to Matlock tomorrow?" Gemma asked. She had wanted to book tickets first thing this morning. They *knew* Astley had Sidney there, so they needed to go.

Only, they hadn't known quite where, not until they'd done some research. Without knowing where he resided, they'd known only that he'd boarded a train to Derbyshire. He could have taken another one from there. He could have had rented rooms somewhere. He could have debarked anywhere along the way and gotten into a carriage and gone who-knew-where.

Now, though, they knew that Matlock was the closest town to where he lived—making it highly likely that he'd taken the boy to his own house, risky as that seemed. Now, Graham had at least a rough idea of where Derwent Hall was in relation to the towns and villages, the roads and rivers and fields. They could sort out where to enter the manor lands, and perhaps even how to sneak into the house.

Graham studied his blueprint for another moment, pulled forward a map, and only after a long sigh, nodded. "I'll have enough, I think, by tomorrow. I hate to have held us up—"

"You haven't." Yates squinted at the windows and pushed to his feet. Something outside had caught his attention, though whether it was a bird or a passerby or a cloud that looked more interesting than another sheet of paper, Gemma couldn't guess. She didn't see anything when she followed his gaze. "It's the fact that everything's closed for Christmas that has really delayed us. But we'll trust the Lord's . . . timing."

Knocking—so quick it practically tripped over itself—began on the back door during Yates's pause. Which meant that he spoke *timing* with a grin. And was rushing from the room even as he said it. "I thought that looked like Rabbit loping along."

Gemma pushed to her feet along with the others. Rabbit was one of the band of street urchins they employed to play courier for them—he or another member of his gang always kept an eye on the Imposters' drop locations so that the moment a client left a message for them, someone was bringing it to Yates.

The children didn't know what the messages were. They only knew that every time they showed up with one, they got a coin and some food for their trouble.

Gemma told herself not to get too excited by a message coming on Boxing Day. It was likely the Harts replying to the update Yates had dispatched to them yesterday evening as soon as they were back in Town.

Her racing pulse ignored her logic.

By the time they arrived in the kitchen, Clementina had already let the boy in and put a piece of fruitcake before him. He was shoving it into his mouth with a grin. "Ain't you supposed to be off work today?" he asked the cook. "Boxing Day and all? Or do cooks take Monday or Tuesday like the bankers?"

Clementina, once a leading lady of the stage before an illness had reduced her voice to a permanent whisper, laughed. "I've been on holiday enough. Milk?"

The boy nodded, eyes lighting up. Gemma had no idea how old he was. He was small, but that could be from malnutrition instead of youth. His eyes were old, but that could be from experience on the streets rather than age. Eight? Twelve? She could never guess. But she'd learned years ago that there was no use in trying to coddle him or any of the other boys he ran with. They were happy enough for a bite and some coin, but they had no desire to be tamed by the likes of the Imposters.

Yates pulled out the chair opposite the lad and smiled. "Is it only cold out there, or was your urgency for a greater purpose?"

She knew Yates had offered his young couriers refuge from the weather whenever they needed it, but they never took him up on it. They had their own places, they said. On their own terms.

Rabbit didn't bother swallowing his current mouthful before answering. "Bloke was in a hurry. Antsy too. Never left the corner, though he turned his back once, so we could get out the note. Waitin' for an answer, I reckon." He reached a dirty hand into a ragged pocket and pulled out an envelope.

Yates took it with a smile that didn't quite cover the tension around his eyes. "Have a sandwich too, then. We'll read it over and write our reply."

Knowing Yates would be charging back through the kitchen doorway, Gemma backed up out of it—straight into a solid form that her every sense recognized as Graham seconds before he chuckled in her ear. His hands cupped her elbows, directing her back another step. With him. Still no more than the breadth of a hair between them.

Leopard stripes. That melting that had begun in her soul on Christmas Eve seemed to be extending to her limbs. Her stomach. The old familiar tingles he'd always ignited raced over her anew—all the faster, it seemed, for their year of dormancy.

The moment Yates was past, she pulled away. Not because being pressed against Graham was unpleasant, but because it was *too* pleasant. Scarily so. It seemed that in the sudden absence of her hatred, all the old feelings of love and attraction were back in force—but the cracks in the foundation of their marriage couldn't be patched up with warm embraces.

And rebuilding—deciding if she *could* rebuild—would

require attention and prayer that she didn't have right now. Sidney first. Graham later.

Back in the library, Yates already had the envelope open and the sheet of paper it had held unfolded. "From Mr. Hart, as I expected. It reads, 'Dear Mr. C, My wife and I do thank you for your update and your efforts to recover Sidney, even though you met with no success in the ultimate goal. We scarcely slept last night, as you can imagine, and have been talking in circles about what the reasonable next step would be. But our musings were cut short by the arrival of a tele-gram minutes ago from Lord Wilfred.'"

Gemma sucked in a sharp breath—and she wasn't the only one.

Yates blustered a breath out instead, apparently having glanced ahead. "Not good."

Marigold moved closer to her brother's chair. "Another demand? Or—please tell me it isn't Horace."

"It's Horace. He's gone." Yates muttered something Gemma didn't catch and ran a frustrated hand through his hair.

Marigold, however, was shaking her head with all the fervor of denial. "That doesn't mean he was kidnapped. You heard him as well as I did, Yates, that boy wanted to find his cousin with or without his father's help. He could have given the slip to the guards and—"

"He did. That's what the telegram said. That he got away from his guards, and that apparently the kidnappers found him. A new ransom note was delivered, saying they now had *two* boys, so the price had doubled—one hundred and sixty thousand, due on the twenty-ninth."

"Blast." Sir Merritt turned away from the table, paced to the fireplace, and pivoted again. "And Wilfred's response?"

"Hart doesn't know, exactly. The telegram demanded that both the Harts and 'that investigator you said you hired' report to his estate in Derbyshire."

"Derbyshire." Gemma frowned. She'd known that was where his estate was, of course, but she hadn't yet pulled out a map to see how close Wilfred's estate was to Astley's. "Are they neighbors?"

Yates shuffled a few pages. "Depending on your definition. They're about an hour's drive apart, so not exactly near enough to pay daily visits. But closer to each other than to most other peers."

"Divide and conquer, then." Graham strode back to his desk. "Gemma and I can go to Derwent Hall, as planned. Yates, you can go with Hart in your Mr. A costume, and Marigold and Merrit can either go separately, with you in other costumes, or stay here and continue the research as offices open up again."

"Is there anything else? In the note?" Even as she asked it, Marigold simply leaned over her brother's shoulder to look for herself.

"Just the train schedule and a plea for me to join him, if I would deign to do so." Yates shuffled things about until he came up with a fresh sheet of paper. "Which of course I will—though it's Mr. C this time, old boy, not Mr. A." He turned to his sister. "What would you two rather do? Come with me, or stay and research? I think Graham laid out our options rather succinctly."

"Come," Marigold and Sir Merritt answered in unison. She went on to add, "Research is all well and good, but if any acrobatics are needed to infiltrate one of those estates, you'll need me there."

"And I highly doubt anyone would recognize me, if you felt the need to have me along as a second." Sir Merritt's expression would have been amusing if the situation weren't so dire. "I suppose I'd even allow a bit of costumery—for the sake of the boys. If necessary."

Marigold's lips twitched into and out of a smile. "I can go

225

to the kitchen at Fellsbourne and inquire about work while you two are meeting with the gent. See what the servants are saying."

Gemma nodded her approval of the plan. "I can do the same at Derwent Hall while Graham is scoping out the exterior and comparing it to his blueprint."

Yates scrawled his pseudo-signature onto the page and set his pen down with a slap. "We'll have time this evening to sort out the details, as we've already missed today's trains to Derbyshire and will have to wait until tomorrow. I'll—where are you going?"

That last was directed to his sister, who was already making for the door. Marigold snagged Gemma's wrist on her way by. "Costumes, first of all. And then the gymnasium. If I'm going to be hours on a train after hours in a coach, I need to exercise while I can."

Gemma let herself be tugged along, knowing that the men would take care of the technical arrangements while she and Marigold were upstairs taking care of the creative ones. If her every muscle felt tense and on guard, it wasn't over that typical delegation of tasks. It was over the fact that she knew an inquisition would be coming the moment they were well and truly alone.

She'd been wanting time to talk to her best friend, yes. But she was hoping it would come when Sidney was safely back in his parents' arms, and she could give herself room to explore her own thoughts and feelings. Now, that band of urgency that held her captive also stole too much of her attention. And likely skewed her outlook. It was Sidney and Horace, after all, who must be found quickly. Her relationship with Graham could be examined at their leisure. There was no rush.

Except . . . one never knew which day would be one's last. Jamie's death had taught her that. And they were about to put themselves in another potentially volatile, dangerous position.

What if it turned violent? What if Graham were killed? What would she do, how would she ever forgive herself, if she lost him without first having found a way to repair these broken pieces?

Marigold pulled Gemma into her bedroom, through to her enormous dressing room stuffed with everything from maids' uniforms to evening gowns, and nudged the door closed with her toe.

She didn't give Gemma an arched brow or silly smirk or an I-saw-that-exchange look. She simply drew her in for a long embrace, held her tight, and whispered in her ear, "It's good to see you again, Gem. It's been too long."

Gemma could only squeeze her back and nod.

NINETEEN

27 December 1909
Fellsbourne Manor, Derbyshire

Moustaches were terribly itchy things—at least when one had only glued the hairs in place instead of growing them oneself. No, he'd tried growing one once too, and his opinion held. They were itchy. Full stop.

Yates didn't worry about being discreet as he lifted a finger and scratched his upper lip. He watched men with actual moustaches all the time, and they made the move frequently too, seemingly without being aware of it. It wouldn't look odd for his character to do so now.

The real challenge was to keep the slight stoop to his spine when he was accustomed to impeccable posture, and to change his walk as if his every joint were aching and arthritic instead of primed by daily exercise and a diet specifically designed to support it. He shuffled over to a window, his eyes tracking over every inch of the room to which he, Merritt, and the two Harts had been shown.

Not an informal drawing room—a formal parlor. Every piece of furniture was expensive and uncomfortable, arranged with mathematical precision that would have made Graham proud. No tea or other refreshment had been offered, and the door had not been left open to allow them a view into the magnificent entryway of the manor house.

Wilfred was making it clear, even before he entered the room, that they were not guests. They were business associates, here to answer his questions. Nothing more.

The sun shone today, the light blinding as it reflected off the snow that had fallen over most all of the country on Christmas. Perfect. That meant that if he stood here throughout the meeting, with his back to the window, he'd be in such sharp relief that the details of his face and figure would be hard to make out. No one would be able to tell that the white dust on his shoulders was flour from the greying treatment they'd applied to his hair, not dandruff. That the lines in his face were cosmetics rather than age.

He and Merritt had taken the early, predawn train here as opposed to the one an hour later that the Harts had used, so that he wouldn't be subjected to the long ride under their perusal. Though really, he doubted they'd have noticed the small oddities in his costume, not given their distress.

He wasn't willing to gamble on the same inattention from Lord Wilfred.

In general, people saw what they expected, what they *wanted* to see. No one would be expecting the investigator who answered to Mr. C to be a young lord of two and twenty, so no one would think to look through his costume.

Lord Wilfred wasn't no one, though. All they'd learned of his business tactics and maneuvers had proven that. He saw what others didn't. Planned what no one else even considered. Made the least-expected move.

If anyone were to see through his disguise, it would be Wilfred. So Yates would have to mitigate that possibility as much as possible and trust that even if he realized the grey and wrinkles weren't natural, he wouldn't recognize Yates as Lord Fairfax.

The clock on the mantel tapped out a painful litany, seconds dragging into minutes. The Harts, both pale and drawn, their hands tangled together, kept shifting on their uncomfortable settee. Merritt, on whom Marigold had glued a full beard, poor chap, had rather opted to sit with perfect stillness in his chosen chair, an ankle hooked over the opposite knee. His military training peeked through, but that was all right. Plenty of men had it—well, some of it. Not many could claim to be a Coldstream Guard. But he knew that under the bushy brows they'd pasted on, Merritt would be cataloguing every detail he could find.

Good. Yates did the same, but he knew they'd come out with different observations, different information. Merritt would be noting all the facts; Yates would be working out how to use them. Entrances, exits, hiding places. When combined with the data his brother-in-law was no doubt amassing on pounds invested in each piece of furniture and whatnot, they'd leave with a very thorough view.

Lionfeathers, but he was glad his sister had fallen in love with such a good, useful chap who'd demanded to join the Imposters to be with her. He made a most excellent addition to the team.

Yates's well-trained ears picked up on the steady, forceful footfalls several seconds before the Harts' seemed to do. A few more seconds, and the parlor door swung open. Lord Wilfred strode in, closing the door behind him again.

He didn't look pale. Didn't look drawn. Didn't look as though he'd failed to sleep last night in his son's absence. He didn't look furious. Didn't look distraught. He looked . . . well, that was interesting, really. His face looked so utterly empty of emotion that it would be easy to think he didn't feel any. That his only son's disappearance didn't affect him at all. It would be easy to think him just as heartless as he was reported as being.

Perhaps Yates would have thought it, too, if he didn't catch the tremor in the lord's hands as he shut the door. The single second he took as the latch clicked to close his eyes, draw in a breath. When he turned, he was blank again.

But it was too late for that. Yates had seen the truth in that split second of fortification. No one paused to fortify themselves unless they were weak and needed to appear strong.

Everyone paused to fortify themselves. Because they were all weak. Just pretending to be strong.

Wilfred did a bang-up job of hiding it as he turned and glared down on his guests. "Matthew. Caroline." He didn't say it with the familiarity that came of being family. Rather, he made it sound like he was addressing servants. His gaze flicked to Merritt, to Yates. "And you two are the investigators, I presume?"

Yates nodded, though he made no attempt to move forward and offer a hand for shaking. Wilfred made it quite clear he didn't welcome such a move. Which suited Yates fine. He nodded. "Mr. C. And my colleague, Mr. Smith."

Merritt mumbled a how-do-you-do that Wilfred summarily ignored. "And to what firm do you belong, Misters C and Smith? I will not have ne'er-do-wells employed on any case concerning my son."

Ah good. A bit of feeling slipped out in that line. Sounded more like anger than fear, but the two were traveling companions more often than not. He smiled under his itchy moustache. "The Imposters, Limited."

Watching other people react to their name never failed to entertain him. Sometimes they'd never heard of them, and the oddity of it made them laugh. Sometimes they *had* heard of them, and their brows jumped up in surprise. Sometimes they were intrigued and leaned forward, eyes dancing.

But Wilfred scowled. "Poppycock."

Well. That was a new one. Yates gave a lazy blink. "Beg pardon?"

Now twin blooms of pink crept into the man's cheeks. "I don't know what the point of this charade is, but I have heard of the Imposters, and there is no possibility under the sun in which Matthew Hart could afford to hire them."

"Quite right." Yates grinned, showing off the teeth he'd yellowed a bit. "I told him as much when he came to me. But what can I say?" He shrugged, making the movement stiff and creaky. "It's Christmas. Missing child. We took it on pro bono."

"Without consulting his colleague, I might add," Merritt added, sounding none too happy about it.

Who knew the Guard was such a natural at acting? Yates nearly grinned. But didn't. He muttered, "Have a heart, old boy. Good will and all that rot."

Merritt grunted.

Wilfred studied them a moment, then looked at the Harts—who both wore looks of humility and gratitude— and pursed his lips. "I happen to know the Imposters were hired by an acquaintance of mine, George Adams—"

"Upon his proposed consolidation of ventures in Canada, yes." Yates lifted his brows. "Not that you came out smelling of roses in that case, Lord Wilfred. Keep burning business associations as you've been doing and soon no one in the empire will do business with you at all."

Rather than looking insulted—or chastised—Wilfred looked satisfied. He nodded once, curt and quick, and took a seat. "Very well, then. You are, it seems, the Imposters. I'm flattered at the honor of actually seeing your face as so few have done."

He wasn't, and that suited Yates fine too. "I've found flattery to be a waste of time. If we could cut to the chase? Your son is missing now, we're told, along with his cousin."

"I went directly to the authorities—the fools." He added a choicer word to their description and pulled a sheaf of folded papers from his jacket pocket, slapping it to the nearest end table. "They seemed to find my lack of cooperation with the Harts' report but a sudden report of my own to be suspicious. They actually dared to propose that the two boys are simply off on a lark—and then suggested that the Harts grabbed Horace when they failed to find Sidney."

Matthew Hart went pale. "We'd never!"

Wilfred's glare was scathing. "I'm not an idiot. I know that. Perhaps I'd suspect a more ambitious brother-in-law to arrange all this for his own advancement, but you are certainly not *that*."

A convoluted insult, but it served to bring the color back to Matthew's cheeks. "Some of us value living a moral life above lining our coffers."

"Let's not dissolve into squabbling, gents." Yates raised both hands, palms out. "The note you received yesterday— was it in the same hand as the original?"

"To my eye, yes." Wilfred motioned to the papers. "You're welcome to look. I've included a copy of the constable's report too, such as it is, and the statement from the guards I'd hired, incompetent as they've proven themselves to be."

"To be fair," Yates said as Merritt reached for the papers, "they wouldn't have expected their charge to give them the slip. They thought the threat would be coming from without, so that's where their attention would have been. They'd never have considered that young Lord Sheffield would try to escape, to be on guard against it."

Wilfred's snort didn't sound inclined toward mercy. "I accept no excuses in this. The guards have been sacked, as has Horace's nurse."

Leopard stripes. Yates took half a step away from the window. "Sacked! You haven't let her *leave*, have you? She is quite possibly in possession of key information about your son!"

For half a breath, regret fluttered over Wilfred's face. Then it was gone. "She is no longer in the house, but I daresay she only went to the village."

"And the guards? Did you have the presence of mind to keep them nearby, or did you scare them off with your threats and vitriol?"

The faint flush grew darker. "Now see here. I don't know who you think you are, but—"

"Who I *am* is the bloke who's going to find your son—in spite of you, if not because of you." Yates was careful to keep the Cockney in place, to keep his fingers curled as if with arthritis as he slashed a hand through the air. "Who *you* are is a lord who thinks that title and wealth means value and worth—but you're wrong, and I pray to God that you begin to see that before you taste the true cost of your ambition and lose your son for more than a day or two."

Wilfred's jaw ticked. "You know nothing about me and my son."

Yates leaned back against the window frame, as if the outburst had cost him precious energy. "I know every business deal you've struck, manipulated, and reneged on in the last five years. I know that you spend more time away from your son than with him, even when school is on holiday and Parliament isn't in session. I know that Horace resents being viewed still as a baby, and that he begged you to intercede on his cousin's behalf. I know when you refused, he resolved to save Sidney himself."

Wilfred rose from his chair—and not steadily. His eyes flashed, but his voice emerged in only a choked whisper. "You can't know that. How *could* you know that?"

Yates twitched his itchy moustache in his best impression of an omniscient smile. "We are the Imposters, my lord. We are everywhere. We hear everything. And that is how we're going to find your son—both your sons. Now." He clapped his hands together, held them there. "Tell me about your association with Miles Fitzroy. And then with Lord Franklin Astley."

At *Fitzroy*, Wilfred began to sneer. But at *Astley*, the haughtiness collapsed into genuine surprise. "Astley! What has he to do with anything?"

"You know him?" Merritt had his whiskered chin tucked down as he read through the pages he held. He'd taken from his pocket the pair of spectacles Marigold had given him and hooked them on, though the lenses were nothing but regular glass.

"Of course I know him. He lives an hour south of here, at Derwent Hall—the next estate of any size in the region."

Yates pulled a notepad from his pocket, along with a pencil. "Were you aware that he and Fitzroy are friends?"

Wilfred frowned and sank back down into his chair. "I . . . no. Though Fitzroy is everybody's friend, so it isn't exactly surprising. Still, he's the sort of friend that people invite to dinner parties and let stay overlong afterward, perhaps the kind one seeks out when one desires a night of clubs, gaming dens, or brothels. I didn't think Astley inclined toward any of those things."

"Our information on your neighbor is slim, I confess." Yates jotted Astley's name onto the top of the first blank page. "He isn't often in Town, even for the Sessions, from what we could gather. But what research we've done said that the two of them went to school together."

"I suppose they *are* of an age," Wilfred granted with a tilt of his head. "Though Fitzroy always seemed younger to me. I certainly haven't ever seen them together. All my dealings with Fitzroy have been in London. He was . . . shall we say, too eager to toss his few winnings into the business arena without a bit of thought or research."

"And you were too happy to take the funds and use them for your own means." Merritt delivered it without judgment. Somehow. "And Astley? What are your dealings with him?"

The bafflement returned. "I don't *have* dealings with him. We are invited to the same events from time to time, but we never both seem to show up to the same ones. I've seen him in passing a few times in Derby or Sheffield. We're cordial. We have no history, either good or bad."

That made precious little sense. Yates lifted his pencil from the page, frowning. The motive had to rest with Fitzroy, then. But the same old question kept nagging—why would Astley go along with it? What did he have to gain that he would risk such a crime? It wasn't a prank, a bet one made over too many drinks. It was a felony. *Kidnapping.*

"Again, I must ask," Wilfred continued, "what has he to do with any of this? I haven't so much as seen Lord Astley in a year or more."

Merritt pulled out a paper of his own from his pocket, one of the sketches Graham had made. "He was at a house party with Fitzroy this last week in Weymouth—where you'd been instructed to leave the cash for the ransom. We noticed how chummy they were and began to pay attention. It was Astley who showed up at the church on Christmas Eve. And then Astley who, the next morning, was seen in the train station carrying an unconscious Sidney."

Mrs. Hart squeaked out a protest and covered her mouth with her hand. "My poor Sidney."

"We have every reason to believe he was well, Mrs. Hart." Yates gentled his voice, infused as much comfort as he could into the syllables. "We know he was being fed, and though he was certainly drugged to stay quiet on the train, it bodes well that he rode as a passenger. There has not been any violence." Yet. He hoped that meant there wouldn't be. He just couldn't make that promise.

"And he's clearly a clever lad. He left clues for us to find—his necktie, a button from his coat. He even scratched *help* into the floor where they'd been keeping him—in considerable comfort, you'll be happy to know."

Yates nodded along with Merritt's encouragement. "Quite right. A lad like that who keeps his head and thinks things through—I wouldn't be surprised if he found a way out of this even before we can get to him. Especially now that his cousin's with him." Assuming the boys were kept together, which could well be a misstep on their captors' part, but one he prayed for. Together would be so much better for them than alone.

Wilfred's gaze burrowed into him. "Astley had Sidney? On a train? To . . . ?"

"Matlock." Yates knew he needn't add that it seemed likely, then, that his destination was his own home.

Wilfred made the same connection. His frown said so. "This makes no sense. Why would he get involved? Why would he risk the consequences? Especially by taking him—them, perhaps—to his own estate? That leaves him no plausible deniability. No excuses that he didn't know what Fitzroy was about. And he has no blighted *reason* to do such a thing! I've never had any business with him."

"But you have with Fitzroy." Yates flipped to an earlier page. "According to our records, he lost a pretty sum in that last deal of yours, while you made off like a bandit. Our theory—only a theory, mind you—is that Astley put up the funds for Fitzroy. Perhaps he thought that if *you* were the partner, it was a safe investment. All of England knows you rarely make bad ones."

Wilfred muttered a curse. He turned his face away, closing his eyes, clenching jaw and fists and perhaps wrestling a few demons. He sat like that for an eternal minute, so silent that no one else dared to make a peep.

When he looked up again, fire lit his eyes. He stood, though he didn't come nearer. "Find my son, gentlemen. Find his cousin. Whatever it takes, whatever it costs—forget pro bono. I will cover all your fees, both from before today and moving forward. I want everything you have, every resource and contact, focused on this. Do you understand me? I will cover all fees, pull any strings you need, whatever it takes. Only find my son."

Yates flipped his notebook closed and slid it back into his pocket. It would be useful to have Wilfred's cooperation— more, to have his weight fully behind them. It would open doors before Yates could even fish out his master key. Oil a few cogs.

Clog up others.

He would take the man's help. But that was all. "We'll find your boy, my lord. But we don't want your money."

Merritt coughed. "We don't?"

Yates didn't look away from Wilfred's gaze. "If money was enough to solve this, you'd pay the ransom."

A crack formed in Wilfred's composure. "I can't. Not all of it, not in cash, not in the amount of time they've given me. Eighty thousand would have been difficult without liquidating a few assets—but a hundred sixty?" He shook his head. "I'd have to sell half my holdings. There's no way to do that in forty-eight hours, which is all we have left at this point."

Yates nodded. It was a staggering sum, and Hart had said Lord Wilfred wouldn't be able to pay it . . . but a part of him had thought it must be doable. Why set a ransom so high it couldn't be met?

It was about more than the money. It had to be. Yates just didn't know what the other thing was, not yet.

He shook his head. "Perhaps from your point of view, we're simply the more affordable option. But I want to be clear: We're not helping for the money—and I suspect your two lads weren't kidnapped for it either, or a more reasonable price would have been named."

"Greed is blinding, though. Unreasonable," Mrs. Hart murmured. "They overreached. That's all."

"A hundred and sixty grand is more than an overreach, madam." Merritt pushed to his feet. "They don't have any expectation of receiving the full amount."

"So then you think if I give what I can scrape together, they'll return the boys?" Wilfred lifted a hand, though he didn't seem to know what to do with it. He let it drop again.

It was possible. Possible that Astley and Fitzroy wanted to humiliate him, to bleed him dry. Maybe they set that ridiculous ransom amount just to guarantee they didn't aim too low. But that still didn't sit right. "I honestly don't think so. I think this is about something more—and I want to discover what that is before he's given the chance to demonstrate it."

Wilfred nodded and started for the door. "I'll have the nurse brought back, and the guards. My entire staff is at your disposal—for interviews or assistance, whatever you need. And even if you refuse fees, I hope you'll use my car, coach, or private train car for any travel you require. I can arrange rooms here or at the inn in the village, if you prefer. Whatever you need. Let me do that much. Please."

A glance at Merritt verified his own thoughts. They'd have to be careful what they accepted—maintaining their anonymity remained, as always, a top priority. But they'd be fools to say no altogether. "Thank you, my lord. We'll get started on those interviews straightaway."

TWENTY

The gates were barred. Graham had no intention of letting that stop him from his quest, but it was worth noting. He and Gemma had arrived in Matlock in late morning, had played the role of holiday-goers interested in seeing all the sights of the area, and thus had asked the locals about the nearby manor house. Was it open to tours? Could visitors walk the grounds?

They'd received smiles and assurances from the friendly locals. Lord Astley was always gracious to visitors, they'd said. There were walking paths through his property available to the public. And he always opened parts of the house up for tours during Christmas week—a tradition dating back generations. Eight to five every day until New Year's, they'd said. The cook always had biscuits and cakes and punch set out, they'd said. Derwent Hall decked out in its red-and-green splendor was a sight to behold, they'd said.

But the gates—plural—were barred. All of them. On the main drive, on the secondary one, and even on those supposedly public walking paths.

"Well, that's not suspicious at all," Gemma huffed from his side, planting her hands on her abnormally ample hips. Her disguise today was a well-padded walking ensemble that

240

made her look considerably curvier than she was . . . and reminded him a bit too much of how she'd looked the week or two after giving birth, before she slimmed back down to her usual size. She'd donned a dark wig, kohled her eyebrows, and had seemed to be having quite a bit of fun with it until this last locked gate.

Graham had been bullied into a wig too, though he maintained it was pointless under his hat. He'd also been provided with a padded-out outfit . . . which might not suit his vanity but certainly kept him warm during the trek through the snowy terrain. "A fellow has a right to close off his own property," he said. And then vaulted over the gate.

Gemma laughed and opted for a hop onto the brick, a swing of her legs over to his side, and another hop down. She pursed her lips at the crunch of snow. "This could be a problem. Tracks."

"Mm." The trail itself had plenty of footprints already upon it, but he didn't intend to stay on the trail. "He must not have ordered everything closed until he arrived with Sidney, or even after. Looks like quite a few people were wanting a Christmas stroll."

"Or else we aren't the only ones who ignore the gates." She squinted into the glare of sun on snow, her gaze tracing the path. "Useful in the short term, anyway. We'll sort out the long term later."

Chances were, they simply wouldn't worry about it. They'd get what they needed, then scurry off Derwent land, hoping—praying?—no one noticed their presence or their tracks until long after they'd gone.

"Better not dawdle." He checked once over his shoulder to be certain the country lane leading to this gate was as empty as it had been a minute ago and then took Gemma's hand and hurried them forward. Her ankles, she'd promised him, felt fine in the high boots she wore today, which were well suited for a hike. He intended to keep a close eye on her expressions, though, to catch the first hint of pain.

He would feel better once they'd passed the little outcropping of trees ahead, which would block the view of them from the lane. At least after that point, they would only have to be wary of being spotted from a single direction—that of the house. In the picnic hamper he carried were his paper, pencils, slide rule, and other tools. Well, and a Thermos of tea. And the two scones Gemma had bought. All the things they'd need for this particular outing, whose purpose was to give him a glimpse of the actual house to compare to the image he'd put together based on nothing but books and those old drawings in the Archives.

"This does change *my* plans, though," Gemma said once they were into the trees. "I can't exactly knock on the kitchen door and inquire about positions if the whole place is locked up."

A good point. Not that he minded a revision of plans that would include them staying together instead of separating, but . . . "It begs the question, doesn't it—where is his current staff? Are they locked in here with him, or did he send them all away?"

"That much we ought to be able to answer with a few more questions in town." She frowned. "Not that anyone seemed to know that the place had been closed up."

"Must be a recent development. I daresay word will soon make its way to all the inns and pubs that tourists frequent. If he wants it closed, he probably also doesn't want a bunch of strangers coming repeatedly to his gates and making a fuss."

"It isn't a very good idea, is it?" The path tracked up a hill, and Gemma slid her arm through his when the path got icy. He didn't complain about it. "Closing it up, I mean? It gets far more attention than preserving the status quo would have done."

Her words put a lens on the very unease that had been niggling the back of his mind ever since they came upon the locked main gates half an hour ago. "I was thinking the same. It's a large house, built of stone. Two boys could scream at the top of their lungs in an old basement room and not be heard in any of the places the public are allowed. Why draw attention to himself?"

"He clearly has no experience at being a criminal."

He chuckled, but it wasn't a cause for comfort—it was a cause for concern. "I don't like it. First the train ride with Sidney out in full view beside him, if asleep, and now this? He's being irrational. And irrational—"

"—is dangerous," she finished for him. An observation they'd set down as a tenet of the Imposters within their first month in business. "If we were to obey our own rules, that would mean we avoid engagement at all costs."

Graham sighed and held up a holly branch drooping with snow. "I can't see that being an option. Because Sidney and Horace are in there."

"We *think*." She was always a stickler for not assuming things . . . but she didn't sound as though she really questioned it. "It could all be a ploy. A cover. We've yet to find anyone who saw him return on Christmas—maybe he didn't. Maybe he took Sidney elsewhere and had the manor locked up to throw off anyone sniffing after him. He could be in Scotland by now for all we know."

"He was in Derbyshire yesterday if he took Horace."

"We don't know that was him either. And being here yesterday doesn't mean he still is." She sighed, though, and watched a bird flit from limb to limb overhead.

They knew Fitzroy hadn't nabbed the young lord. He'd spent all of Christmas and Boxing Day at his favorite club, seen by dozens of people, and had still been there when they left Town that morning, according to the last report from the waiter they'd tipped to provide information. If it wasn't Astley either, that meant a whole other party they knew nothing about.

Possible. But he favored the simpler answer. "There's no evidence to assume a third party and plenty to point to him. He had opportunity, means, and we *know* he was the one at the ransom drop. We *know* he had Sidney on Christmas."

"But motive. I still don't understand his motive if it isn't the money."

"We'll find it." The path cleared the copse of trees, and Graham drew Gemma to a halt. They were still a good distance from the house, but this prospect gave them a fine view of it.

"What a beautiful home."

It was, especially with the blanket of snow draping the landscape. The manor house was the sort he appreciated most—graceful, tasteful. A large central part that had been the original building, with matching turrets on each flank, and then a wing going off either side at ninety degrees. It didn't sprawl like some of them did, wasn't so enormous that one's mouth gaped open. Well, at least not when one was accustomed to manor houses. The garden between the wings was even visible from here. He couldn't make out details under the snow, but the placements of its bumps and stretches made him think it well designed.

He swung the hamper forward, unlatched its lid, and reached inside. "Not too far off from my guess. Though the wings are longer than the description I found. Or more windows have been added, which I'd find odd."

"You and your window counting." Gemma took a step away, planted her hands on her waist, and studied the scene. "There's smoke coming from three different chimneys. *Only* three."

Using the lid of the hamper as a makeshift desk—though an awkward one—Graham made a few minor adjustments to his sketch. "That lends credence to the idea that he sent the staff away. It's too cold for them to simply be going without heat if they're there and working." He glanced up to see which chimneys.

None in the central part of the house, which was interesting. That was where the kitchens were, and the rooms in which one would entertain or, if Astley was like most gents he knew, spend his own leisure hours. But there were two puffing away in the eastern wing, and one in the western.

"Any idea what rooms are there?"

He blustered out a breath. "In 1790? Certainly. Today? I can only guess."

Gemma turned back to him and leaned close to look at the drawing. Close enough that he could smell the cinnamon and cloves from the cider she'd had with luncheon. "When it comes to houses, your guess is usually better than anyone else's knowledge. So I'll take it. Enlighten me."

"All right. These two in the east—one of them is where a billiards room was reported in one of the descriptions I found. The other is near enough that I wouldn't be surprised if there were a gentlemen's domain set up there. Billiards, perhaps a smoking room, hunting trophies. Astley's ancestors were famous for their hunts."

"And in the west?"

He shook his head. "Just the normal rooms for guests, so far as I can tell. Bedrooms, small sitting rooms."

"So then he could have the boys there, in a random bedroom. While he's brooding in his favorite places, as far from them as possible."

He hadn't seemed the brooding type during their brief meetings at Weywent. But perhaps he was simply good at the façade. Heaven knew plenty of nobility were. Plenty of *people*, in general. They all learned to put on a smile and get on with life, no matter how much it hurt.

He rolled up the blueprint and slipped it back inside the hamper. "Good enough for now." And they hadn't even had to leave the path. "Let's get back to town before someone spots us."

"Wait." Gemma crouched down, brushed aside a clump of snow, and pulled up something in a faded yellow. It took him a moment to realize it was a wooden duck, the sort with feet that padded along if one pulled it by a string, though half of the string was missing.

His throat went tight. It was similar to one of the toys they'd bought last year for Jamie for Christmas—only, he'd never had the chance to pull it along. "It's . . . someone must've dropped it. A family out for a stroll. Probably months or even years ago, given the state of the thing."

Gemma, face pale as the snow, only nodded. But she didn't drop the duck back to the ground. She clenched it tight in her gloved fingers and led the way back along the path.

It was just a toy. One with a thousand twins in England alone. A little wooden duck like countless other little wooden ducks in the country. No doubt some mum or papa had seen it in the store window and parted with the coin to bring it home for their little Tommy or Jane. Or some grandmum had thought to spoil her sweetling with it. Maybe some child had fussed and screamed and pointed until a harried nanny had handed over a slip of discretionary spending money for the trinket.

Just a little wooden duck, indistinguishable from any other. But Gemma couldn't convince herself to let go of it. Graham was right, that it looked as though it had been there a long time. The wear of the paint looked less like chipping from play and more like fading from sun and rain. The string ended abruptly in a frazzle. One webbed toe was altogether missing. Whatever child had dropped it, they weren't likely to come hunting it down at this point. No, if it had been missed, it had likely been replaced. Or forgotten altogether.

She could tell from the looks Graham kept sending her as they hurried back toward the locked gate that he was remembering *their* little wooden duck. The one they'd seen in the toy shop window while they were out together, Christmas shopping for Jamie. His first Christmas, and he was old enough to delight in anything they gave him. They'd left their son with James and Aunt Priss for the evening, and a night out, just the two of them, was rare enough to feel special. Magical.

But this little duck didn't strike her so soundly because of that other one—at least, she didn't think so. She had more memories of finding the thing, after all, than of Jamie with it. Oh, he'd clapped and laughed and crawled along with it when Graham took it for a walk on Christmas Eve morning, when they'd let him unwrap it before they left for Northumberland. But then he'd gone back to the paper and string, which was infinitely more entertaining to him, for whatever reason, than any toy.

Maybe it was the sadness of a lost toy that had nabbed her attention. The forlornness of it.

Or maybe it was the words carved into the base that she'd spotted as she stooped to pick it up. She hadn't been able to read them then, covered in soil and rotted leaves and snow as they largely were. But she rubbed the spot clean with her gloved thumb as they walked, not even looking at it as she did so. And then, when Graham was jumping over the gate again, she looked down and read the inscription.

For my sweet little duckling. Papa

"Gem?"

"Here." She handed him the toy, bottom side up so he could see the words.

Graham frowned at them but didn't seem to find it odd. "We ought to leave it here for another child to find. Or perhaps even the original, if the family who lost it is local."

Gemma hopped up onto the bricks as she'd done before, not entirely certain why she wanted to argue with him on the matter. But she did. "No. There's something . . ." She didn't even know how to finish her sentence, and the look Graham sent her—half incredulity and half pity, like he suddenly questioned her sanity—made her press her lips together against any attempt at a rambling explanation.

For a moment, frustration tempted her. It would be so, so easy to snap at him, to accuse him of ignoring whatever feminine instinct might be at work, to point back to the last time he'd ignored her hunch. To let *this* small little splinter of discord turn into *that*.

But she didn't want to. She didn't want to be that Gemma who had been filled with anger. She had learned too well that anger, rage, bitterness, and hatred didn't ever fill you. They emptied you. Emptied you of life and goodness and the ability to love. And that emptiness left no room for anything else, even the sweet memories.

Feet on the ground again, she closed her eyes, breathed in a prayer, and sighed out the dark temptation. *Don't let me be that person again, Lord. Please. Save me from myself.*

When she opened her eyes, she directed them to Graham. "I know it doesn't make sense. I can't put words to it. It's . . . something about it has caught my attention, something more than the fact that we got one so similar for Jamie, and I'd like to show it to Marigold. Perhaps she can spot what it is."

He hadn't been expecting that—the rational attempt at explanation, the casual mention of the gift. He blinked a few times, but the words must have convinced him she wasn't teetering on the brink of madness. He nodded and motioned with the toy. "Do you want to carry it, or shall I put it in the hamper?"

"The hamper is fine, unless you don't want it touching your drawings. It isn't exactly what one would call clean."

He brushed a few more bits of dirt from it and shrugged. "I'll put it on the opposite side from the papers."

"All right. Graham?"

He paused with his hand on the hamper's latch, brows up. He looked at once like *Graham*, with that face she knew so well, the features she'd memorized and traced and kissed, had watched grow from boy to man, had seen in every expression . . . and *not Graham*, with the clothes he'd never have chosen, filled with stuffing to make his figure not his own, the wrong color hair peeking out from the wrong style of hat.

He looked like some future Graham, or some could-be Graham. Like the stranger he could have become had she continued down her path of ignoring him, of hating him.

The thought squeezed her heart, twisted. When she thought about forgiving him, being his wife again, moving back into their house, that white-hot panic that tasted like the deepest mourning still seized her. Being his wife would mean more children, and the very fact that she could want that felt like a betrayal to the child they'd lost.

But the thought of *not* forgiving him, of drifting away until she'd scarcely recognize him on the street, of living the rest of her life alone . . . that terrified her even more, lit an even deeper flame of grief.

She moved closer, until the familiar scent of his cologne eclipsed the deceptive look of him. She watched his eyes track her, watched them fill with love and longing. She knew he loved her, just as he'd said. Despite her every horrid thought and word, despite her absence. He loved her like the Father loved him. And she wondered if maybe, in some way, accepting that love from him would show him that he could accept the same from God.

She didn't know if it would. But what she did know was that her soul yearned for the love *he* offered, for the healing it would bring. She slipped a gloved hand onto the back of his neck and pulled his head down to hers.

His lips were cool from the winter air, warming quickly against hers. His arms slid around her, comfort wrapped in wool. His breath eased out with a little hum at the back of his throat that said, *"I've missed you."* And as she kissed him, she felt for the first time in a year as if she were *her*.

Complete? All the pieces back together? No—there would always be a piece missing where Jamie had been. But as he pulled her close, as that one gaping hole closed, it changed her perspective on the others.

The loss of her son, of her father, of her mother . . . The loss of old dreams, the disappointments, the failures . . . They left holes, yes. In her and in everyone. Life wasn't about escaping them, though.

It was about who they made her.

She could choose to be nothing but a moth-eaten rag fit only for the rubbish bin . . . or she could let God work her into lace, the holes left by pain and sorrow every bit as beautiful as the gossamer threads of faith and love that held her together. She didn't quite know how the Lord would make such artistry from her ruins—but she caught enough of a glimpse of the result that she knew she could put her life in His hands.

After a long moment, she pulled away, caught her breath. Met Graham's gaze again even when part of her wanted to squeeze her eyes shut and wonder what she'd done, what she'd restarted. She didn't honestly know the answer to that. But she determined not to regret it.

She moved her hand to his cheek, the beginning of stubble

rasping against her glove. "I still love you, Graham. I never could have hated you as I'd done if I didn't love you."

Amusement, and something steadier, danced in his eyes. "That's a strange sort of comfort."

"Will you take it anyway?"

He smiled and framed her face between his palms. "With both hands."

TWENTY-ONE

Gemma held her steaming cup of tea between her hands, the crumbs of a delightful Victoria cake on the plate before her. She still wore the dark wig she'd decided would remain her identity while in Matlock but had changed from the walking outfit into a tea dress—still too large and then padded out.

Across from her, Marigold sat, looking a far cry from the fashion icon London knew. She could never manage a wig, given how voluminous her waist-length hair was, but she'd donned plain, matronly styles today, including a broad but boring hat that no one would look twice at. Her own cup sat half-full, her plate still had half a cucumber sandwich on it—no sweets for Marigold, even when she was in disguise, silly girl—and she turned the wooden duck over in her hands to examine the inscription.

Her lips pursed, and her brows pulled down in a way that had Gemma scooting forward onto the edge of her chair. Marigold saw something too—she could tell by the way calculation ticked through her friend's eyes.

"Something grabbed my attention. I can't put a finger on what it is," Gemma murmured.

"The handwriting." Marigold traced a fingertip over the elaborate capital *F*, and then the *P*.

Perhaps that was it. "It's elegant. Which bespeaks an educated man. I suppose there have been any number of those who have traveled through the area and may have taken his family for a promenade on Derwent property, but—"

"No, more specifically." Brows still knit, Marigold set the duck down on the table and reached for the bag she'd brought with her, which was larger than her typical handbag but every bit as nondescript as the rest of her ensemble. She pulled out a stack of papers and slid one over to Gemma.

A glance showed her that it was the ransom note—one of them, anyway. The second one, she saw as she scanned the words.

Perhaps now you'll take me seriously. Thanks to your son's determination to rescue his cousin, I now have them both in my possession. Two boys, then, equals twice the price. Bring one hundred and sixty thousand pounds in cash to the foreman's office of Matlock Textiles at dawn of the 29th. Fail to show up, and you will never see Horace again.

Gemma's mouth went dry, despite the tea she'd sipped. This was the first she'd seen the actual wording of the second letter, and it made her stomach want to reject the cake she'd enjoyed. She had to read through it again to look beyond the words and their meaning to the script in which they were written. "Is this the original?"

"We made a couple of copies with a roller press, to preserve the handwriting, much like the copies Hart provided of the first one."

Gemma nodded. It would mean fading out the original a bit as the press stole some of its ink, but if they wanted to

253

compare the writing itself to the first letter—or to anything else—that part was crucial. She had to assume that the others had already affirmed that it was in the same hand as the first letter.

Not just that, though. The capital *P*. The *F*. Both letters carried the same distinctive flourish in the ransom note as the ones on the base of the duck. Knowing her kohled brows were knit, she looked over at her oldest friend and stared at her, trying to make the pieces all fall into place as she moved the duck off the table again, down to her lap where it was hidden from view by the table. Suddenly it seemed far too important to leave out for all to see. "This makes no sense. Does it speak to someone other than Astley?"

Marigold shrugged and looked around the crowded tearoom, lifting a hand to signal the girl who had served them. For a moment Gemma thought she suddenly had a need for more hot water, but no. The way her friend smiled and turned her face into one of the many masks they'd learned to don said she meant to engage on a different level. Gemma took the hint to refold the letter and slip it from view too.

The tea girl approached with a smile. She was nicely dressed, her cheeks pink and her eyes merry. If she was anything like the employees of the tea houses Gemma frequented in London and Northumberland, she was a daughter of a respectable family, taking on this position for the pocket money because it was one of the few jobs deemed acceptable for someone of her station. "Can I get you something, miss?"

"Information." Marigold made her eyes sparkle and grinned the sort of grin that invited one to become her conspirator. She leaned closer to the girl. "I'm trying to remember all I've heard about your local lord, that Astley fellow, but I'm coming up dreadfully dry."

The girl chuckled, not seeming at all put off by the prospect of gossip. "His family has always kept to themselves and lived rather quietly. None of us have any complaints. He's fair to his tenants and generous with his neighbors."

Marigold's nod somehow acknowledged and dismissed that all at once. "But his personal life—that's what I'm trying to recall. He isn't married, is he? Yet I could have sworn I saw him once with a child. . . ."

The girl looked once over her shoulder, lips pursed, and then edged a bit closer to their table. She dropped her voice to a whisper barely audible over the chatter of the room. "Never married. And so he doesn't *officially* have any children, if you catch my meaning."

It would be hard to miss. Marigold widened her eyes, nodding. "Perhaps it *was* him I saw then. Though it was several years ago now, I think . . ."

"It would have had to be. Sad thing—he doted on the girl, had a whole floor for her and her mum at his house, everything a child could want. But when he and her mum had a falling out, Agatha went with her mother. And then . . . well, I daresay he regretted that after the accident. He never saw her again after they left."

Something caught the girl's eye that had her straightening, clearing her throat, and pasting a professional smile onto her face. "I'll be back directly with that fresh pot of water." She darted away, taking their current pot with her even though it was only half empty and probably still warm enough.

The gaze Marigold slid to Gemma could only be termed *careful*. She was waiting for the words to strike—*"the accident."* Waiting for the implications to rip her to shreds.

Another child lost to tragedy.

Gemma waited too. Waited for the denial to try to wrap itself around her, for the fury to gnaw at her, for the pain to suck her down into its abyss. And she felt all those things. They were there, in their respective places. But only *there*.

They didn't overwhelm her completely this time, didn't overtake her.

She lifted her cup, took a long sip, and gazed at that sad little duck in her lap. *His duckling.* His daughter. An illegitimate child, but one he'd clearly doted on—until, it seemed, he didn't any longer. She'd been cast out with her mother.

Another page in the tragedy that was the human story. She sighed and let her eyes move toward the letter again. "Does it have anything to do with this, do you think?"

Marigold picked up her sandwich. "If I've learned anything in our work," she said, pausing to take a nibble, "it's that everything has to do with everything. The trick is sorting out *what*."

A trick indeed. Gemma handed the ransom note back to Marigold and checked the watch pinned to her bodice. "Perhaps Yates and Merritt will have learned something that will help. Or perhaps this will help them make sense of something."

"I ought to get back before I lose the light." Marigold put the letter back in the bag, but then handed the whole thing to Gemma. "These copies are for you and Graham. Did you secure rooms at the hotel?"

Gemma nodded and slipped the toy into the bag too. "Where are you staying?"

"A hotel in Sheffield. My brother decided to take his lordship up on his offer of rooms at Fellsbourne, though my husband declined, for some reason." Her lips twitched.

Perhaps because they hadn't yet been married a month. Gemma stood, looping Marigold's bag over her own shoulder. "Why am I surprised he offered?"

Her friend blew out a long breath and led the way back out into the blinding winter sun. Not until they were on the pavement did she say, "I think . . . I think even Lord Wilfred didn't know how much he loved his son. Not until he realized that all the money in the world couldn't keep him safe."

A whole different sort of tragedy. The tragedy of regret. "I'll pray he learns the lesson well—and that we can return his son to him, so that he has the chance to choose a different path with young Horace."

She would pray, too, for the strength to stand by her own decision to avoid the same.

Though he'd been an investigator for five years, Yates wasn't the sort of investigator who usually had a line of witnesses queued up and awaiting an interview. He was accustomed to having to find his information through subtler means. Eavesdropping. Seemingly innocent questions asked while undercover. Endless hours of reading.

Sitting at a table in the steward's office while that man showed out yet another employee made him want to squirm in his borrowed chair.

"This is downright unsporting," he muttered to Merritt, who hid a chuckle behind a cough.

They'd been at it for several hours already today, after quite a few put in the night before. They'd started with the guards, who had both been duly abashed at letting their charge slip by them. They'd been otherwise moving steadily through the other ninety-five members of the staff—domestics, gardeners, upper staff, grooms, everyone. Marigold's asking about in the kitchen yesterday had yielded little more than a quick dismissal, but they were certainly getting their chance now to hear from each and every servant.

It was all wrong, though. Instead of appearing as a commiserating face who could be one of them, they looked like authority figures. Which meant everyone was either mum or defensive. Too quick to declare their loyalty to the Wilfred family and household. No complaints. No plans to leave. No desire for more pay.

Rubbish, the lot of it. He already knew that Wilfred was an unloved landlord and a harsh taskmaster. He cared nothing for those in his employ in general and even less for the staff here at his country house. All his efforts were focused, it seemed, on his London dwelling. That was where he entertained. That was where he negotiated business deals. That was where he spent every moment he could.

"Mrs. Christianson, sir," the steward was saying now as he held the door open for the next interviewee.

And this time, Yates perked up. Mrs. Jill Christianson was the nurse, the woman Yates had heard young Horace speaking with when he and Marigold were playing spider. The woman who had mentioned an incorrect sum of a ransom demand. The woman Wilfred had been so quick to dismiss, and who had been so quick to leave that it had taken this long to bring her back.

He'd given strict instructions for her to be delivered to him at once upon her return to Fellsbourne. Given her pink cheeks and wind-tossed hair under her hat, he was willing to grant he'd been obeyed.

He gave her a tight-lipped smile that meant absolutely nothing and indicated the chair set far back from his desk. "Have a seat, Mrs. Christianson."

She did so in a way that made it look as though there was a bed of nails on the chair. "I did nothing wrong," she said, gripping her handbag with white knuckles. "I told his lordship that, and I'll say it again."

Well, at least he didn't have to work to get her talking. Yates flipped to a fresh sheet in his notepad. "Excellent. Please do."

Her knuckles went even whiter. "Master Horace slipped

out while I was in the necessary. I can't be expected to never leave him for a moment, can I?"

"Certainly not." But she was lying. Her eyes were darting all about. Yates scratched a few words onto the paper. "The necessary, you say. How long were you away from him?"

Her cheeks went pinker. "Only a few minutes."

"And you didn't ask someone else to—"

"He's a strapping lad of ten, not an infant! I'm kept on more to provide company and consistency for him than anything." The pink went red. "Besides, the guards should have stopped him. They were right outside the door."

"Yes, we've already spoken with them." This from Merritt, in the chair he'd pulled up beside Yates's.

"Then I don't see why you need to speak with me. As I told his lordship, Horace had made noises about rescuing his cousin, yes, but I didn't expect him to actually run off!"

"Of course not, of course not." Though she ought to have. He and Marigold had suspected he would try something after one overheard conversation, and they didn't even know the boy. "Though to be honest, I was a bit surprised. That he escaped from *you*, that is. On Boxing Day. Shouldn't you have had the day off?"

Mrs. Christianson went still, with the kind of stillness that shouted, *"Careful now, Jill."* She wet her lips. "I haven't got the day since Master Horace started school. Haven't asked for it. Hardly makes sense to take a day off when I've only the two weeks to work during his holiday."

Yates made a few noises of agreement. "And were there Boxing Day bonuses this year—or was it another year with none?"

The stillness went pointed, her gaze suddenly drilling into him with equal parts incredulity and confusion. Did she remember throwing that possibility out at Horace as a means of keeping him in line? Did she wonder how he knew of it?

"I wouldn't know," she finally said. "Master Horace escaped at first light, before the boxes were handed out, and I was dismissed immediately."

"And where did you go upon leaving Fellsbourne?" Merritt asked, pen poised over his own paper. "The village? Sheffield? Do you have people near here?"

She had *not* been in any of the neighboring towns or villages, they knew—otherwise she'd have been brought in yesterday. "My husband and I lived in the village until he passed, God rest his soul."

"Which doesn't answer the question in the slightest," Yates pointed out with an easy smile. "But you have children, I assume?"

"Four. All scattered about." Her response came neither too fast nor too slow, nor with any tone that said they were relevant to the discussion.

Someone would be, though. She had to have been *somewhere* the past two days. "Sister? Brother?" *There.* "Sister."

Merritt lifted a too-bushy brow. "Does she live in or near Matlock, by chance?"

Interesting. Yates wouldn't have thought to ask that, but Mrs. Christianson blanched, proving Merritt onto something. Yates glanced at his paper to see what clues he'd picked up on, but his brother-in-law had only scratched *Call it a hunch* onto the page.

A good hunch.

Yates made a show of repositioning himself over his paper. "What's your sister's name? Spell it for me, if you please."

"No! You won't go harassing poor Hannah. I won't have it!" She flew out of her chair, lurching forward to slap a hand onto the desk.

He nearly said something trite, something about her sparking his curiosity. But he looked into her eyes and saw something more than fear in them, more than guilt. He saw the sort of pain he'd seen far too often lately, in far too many other sets of eyes. "We have no intention of harassing anyone, madam. I promise you. We only want to find the boys. I trust you heard that a second ransom demand was sent?"

She sank back to her chair. "He won't pay it, though, will he? The miser."

Finally. A bit of true feeling from someone. "Perhaps he would if he could afford to. But a hundred and sixty thousand in cash is asking too much even of Lord Wilfred."

"A hundred—what?" Horror now in her tone. "But . . . no."

"You thought it lower—ten grand or so, perhaps? Is that what Lord Astley told you?" Merritt scratched at his beard, which was no doubt as irritating as Yates's moustache. "We know he's the one who sent the ransom notes. He was seen in Weymouth, boarding a train with Sidney on Christmas."

"Did he offer you a cut in exchange for a bit of information, perhaps? Something to make up for the bonuses Wilfred likes to withhold?"

"You think this is about money?" Her handbag slipped from her fingers, slid all the way to the floor, and she didn't notice. "I'm not so base. I did it for *them.* Lord Astley would never hurt the lad—neither of them. But Lord Wilfred—*he'll* hurt them, like he's hurt so many others, if he isn't brought to bear."

Interesting. He wasn't entirely certain he believed her rationale . . . but she had admitted to conspiring with Lord Astley. Which unfortunately meant she'd have to be taken to the constable, to be questioned officially and likely arrested.

Yates sighed. Merritt had spoken with the authorities yesterday and had verified what they all knew already—no one had any intentions of knocking on the door of Derwent Hall and accusing one lord of kidnapping another's son. It was unthinkable. Perhaps they'd begin to change their minds if

Mrs. Christianson admitted to them that he had hired her. But would she? Or would she button her lips?

Or, for that matter, would she end up taking all the blame while the nobleman's involvement was glossed over? It happened more often than not. He pursed his lips. "I think it would be in your best interest to stay here with us until this is all resolved, Mrs. Christianson."

She seemed to only just become aware of what she'd said—what she'd confessed. And perhaps, too, of all it implied. "I only meant—that was why I didn't do more to talk Horace out of his plans. That's all I meant. I should have, but I thought if he were missing for an hour, it may strike a bit of fear into his father's heart. I certainly didn't think anyone would take the boy."

"And yet you're certain Lord Astley wouldn't hurt them. Most people would question our assertion that a local baron has stooped to kidnapping."

"*If* he did." Her fingers flexed, and she looked wildly around, then bent and retrieved her fallen bag. "That's all I meant. *If*, then the boys would be well. Everyone knows Lord Astley's a good chap. Wouldn't hurt anyone, especially children."

"And yet you showed no fear for them. You would, I presume, if you thought some greedy ruffian the one who'd stolen your charge." Yates shook his head, almost pitying her. At this point, she was digging her own grave. "You might as well come clean, madam. It will be better for you. What did Astley tell you was his reasoning? How can we get the boys back to their parents without harm?"

"Either you tell us," Merritt said, "or we'll be forced to go and see what your sister knows. I daresay someone in the village can tell us where to find her."

"She'll not be able to tell you anything." This she delivered so flatly that Yates believed her. "And I have nothing else to say. I've given you the truth—that I turned a blind eye when I shouldn't have, but it was because I want to see this family put to rights. That's all."

It wasn't. But gone was the panicked look. Gone were both the blush and the pallor, gone were the heated feelings about either lord in question. She knew she'd said too much, and her answer would be to say nothing more at all.

For now. So be it. She'd given them more than he'd really expected . . . and perhaps if they pressed her later, something else would slip out. He called the steward back in and asked him to show the nurse to a room where she would be safe and protected until the boys were recovered. The steward no doubt thought he meant "where she can't get away." And there was that, it was true. But his spoken words held too.

She might be convinced that Astley wouldn't harm anyone, but Yates had no reason to think so. And hired lackeys who turned on their coconspirators, even unwittingly, had a bad habit of ending up dead.

The moment the door closed on her, Yates turned to Merritt. "We need—"

"The sister." He stood. "I'll discover her full name, and then we'll send one of the ladies."

Yates scratched at his moustache and scowled. "I was going to volunteer to do that."

"No, no. You're the senior partner, Mr. C. It's more important that you stay here. Conduct the rest of the interviews." He was already rushing toward the door, blast him. Though he paused to shoot a victorious grin over his shoulder as he let himself out.

"Lionfeathers." Next time, he'd have to be a little quicker on his feet. Keeping ahead of a Coldstream Guard was no easy task.

TWENTY-TWO

Matlock Textiles was a dark, foreboding smudge against the pristine white landscape behind it. Graham stood outside the barred iron gates and wanted to find some beauty in the brickwork, in the design, in the neat symmetry of the lines.

Half a century ago, when the building was first constructed, it would have been a point of pride for the region. A factory, yes, but one that cared what it looked like to passersby. He imagined that when it opened, locals lined up to fill the positions, to put Matlock on the map, to take part in this revolution of industry that would allow their children to stay nearby instead of running off to some other factory in some larger city.

He would say that the intervening fifty years hadn't been easy on the place, but he knew it was only the last two that had forgotten it. No, not forgotten. Perhaps the bricks in disrepair pointed to negligence, as did the vines creeping into every seam. Perhaps the condition of the roof spoke of too many blind eyes turned.

But the graffiti smeared on the bricks was far more purposeful than neglect. The smashed windows said no one had forgotten this place—even if they wanted to. And for good reason.

He remembered reading about it—had remembered the moment Gemma showed him the ransom note and he'd seen the new drop location, though he'd given it no thought in years. Matlock Textiles had made the news nationwide, and not for the cloth it was producing or even the strikes held here like they were in so many other factories.

Matlock Textiles had made the news because of the collapse that had killed twenty-three workers and rendered the entire building unstable.

They'd studied the initial report at his firm. "A structural catastrophe," the reporters had called it. New machines had been installed, more efficient ones—heavier ones. No one had checked the support beams. No one had done the maths. No one had thought to make certain the fifty-year-old building could withstand the new equipment. One day, in the middle of the shift, there had been a groan, and then total collapse as the main floor gave way and fell into the basement used for storage.

It could have been so easily avoided. That was the real catastrophe, his boss had said. A few added supports. Some crossbeams. Perhaps a new floor, steel girders instead of the old wooden ones, and the machines would still be humming along. The workers would still be alive.

Two men, fifteen women, and six children would still be alive.

Graham shook his head and walked along the wrought-iron fencing, looking for the same way in that the locals must use to keep the walls and windows so consistently vandalized. He found it along the southern fencing—a place where the iron rods had been hammered apart, making a gap big enough for even a grown man to slip into, provided he went sideways.

While Gemma and Marigold had focused on the hand-writing of the letter, he'd been intrigued by why Astley would have chosen this factory for the ransom exchange. It made sense in a way, he supposed. It was infamous. Easy to find. But also abandoned.

Though architectural firms across the country had submitted bids on restoring the place to working condition—his own included, though he'd not been called on to help with the proposal and heard little of it after the initial news report—it didn't look as though any of them had been hired for the task. He couldn't remember reading about it after that initial report. The London papers hadn't run much by way of follow-up, and he hadn't sought information out elsewhere. He'd had a new assignment he was working on, and this catastrophe hadn't ranked as needing his attention.

Perhaps the insurance money hadn't been enough to cover the costs of fixing it. Perhaps the owners hadn't had insurance. Perhaps the factory hadn't been profitable enough to warrant the time and energy to set it to rights.

He looked once over his shoulder to make certain no one was watching and then ducked through the fence, hurrying to the cover of a few scraggly bushes. The vandals probably opted to do their work under cover of darkness, but he'd wanted to make use of the daylight to do his reconnaissance. If this was where Lord Wilfred had been commanded to bring his entire fortune tomorrow at dawn, then they needed to know everything they could about the place beforehand. How to get in, how to get out, where the foreman's office was located. Where Astley was likely to be waiting.

Part of him would rather try to sneak into Derwent Hall, but the gossip around the pub last night hadn't only been about the local lord's sudden decision *not* to open the house for holiday tours. It had been about the appearance of armed guards that afternoon at every gate, path, road, and door.

The people were all abuzz about why in the world kindly Lord Astley would need a veritable army around his house. Had he been threatened? Or maybe—finally—gone completely mad?

He and Gemma had exchanged a few looks over those musings, to be certain.

"He never was quite right after the girl died, you know," one woman had whispered to her husband—a whisper loud enough to be heard by the whole room.

"Maybe he's finally filed those legal accusations he's been talking about, and he fears it won't go over well." That from a diminutive man in the corner who downed pints of ale like they were water.

They'd fished for a bit more information from that man after buying his next pint. All he'd known, though, was that Astley had kept harping on about justice needing to be served for the accident that killed his daughter. When Graham had asked how the daughter had died, the man had gone blubbery. *"Sad, sad thing,"* he'd said over and again. *"Terrible shame. Senseless loss."*

The death of a child always was. Graham knew that firsthand. He strode to a side door that was hanging on one hinge and clenched his teeth. All of life, truth be told, was one tragic shame after another. Disease, accidents, violence, natural disasters, industrial catastrophes. There was no shortage of ways for people to be stolen from their lives.

He'd never before thought it proved God unloving. Not until life was stripped bare. Graham had always been able to find words to explain it. The rains fall on the just and the unjust . . . they lived in a fallen world . . . God had a plan . . . it was merciful for the Lord to take them . . . they were in a better place.

None of those words meant a thing anymore. Not a thing. He followed the drift of dried leaves and melted snow through the gaping doorway, knowing that he wasn't the only one to think so. The slogans painted on the bricks outside said many other mourning families found it all as senseless as he did.

"I can't see the sense of it."

It was Gemma's voice in his ear, so clear he had to stop, spin around. She wasn't there, of course. He knew she wasn't. Marigold had come to Matlock again this morning, and the two were going in search of the mother of Astley's child. But she'd come to so many other old buildings with him.

She'd said those words before, though not today. Countless times. He'd be rambling about the design and the decisions, the purpose of each stone and crenellation and gap, and she'd get that little smile on her lips. *"I can't see the sense of it."*

One time in particular, he remembered they'd been touring old ruins near Land's End. He'd said they were walking on part of an old wall, and she'd laughed and pointed down at the old square stone, massive yet worn. Crumbling, moss-covered. *"That? That's no grand castle wall, darling. That's a rock."*

"You have no imagination." He'd been able to make the accusation because it was so blatantly untrue. She could imagine worlds, stories, wardrobes, whatever backgrounds they needed for the characters they played in the Imposters.

But when it came to understanding these sorts of architectural details, she really was hopeless. Stubbornly so, he often thought. She *chose* not to see.

That day, she had shaken her head. Climbed up on the time-worn rock and declared it just as likely to have been a giant's table. A Druid altar. A meteor fallen from the sky. He'd laughed, grabbed her by the waist, and twirled her around. Insisting that if she could view it like an architect, she would understand.

"*View it like an architect.*" His own words echoing now, repeating over in his mind as he waited for his eyes to adjust to the dim interior.

Shapes started to emerge from sunspots, light from the broken panes falling in sharp angles on metal and wood. This door had opened directly onto the factory floor, giving him a heart-thudding view of the collapsed machinery. The broken floorboards. For a long moment he stood there, trying to sort out the gut reaction from the intellectual one.

His stomach churned at the loss of life. His chest went tight at how this affected countless local families and would do for generations to come. His mind calculated the weight of machines versus the weight-bearing load of each girder. His eyes searched out visual clues—trusses, beams, spans.

When he'd come home from the office that day and saw the same news story on the front page of their own paper, he'd gone from commiserating with the families in one beat to trying to solve the architectural dilemma in the next. "*Choose a reaction, darling,*" Gemma had said. "*Emotional or logical. You set my head spinning when you bounce from one to another.*"

He'd laughed. And shaken his head. And insisted that he *could* have it both ways—he was, after all, both a man with a heart and an architect. The two aspects weren't at war. They were what made him *him*.

Senseless. That was the human, heartfelt response he had as he looked at the buckled boards. But they made perfect sense. Mathematical sense. Scientific sense. Logical sense. Someone had made choices, knowingly or unknowingly, and this had been the result.

You made choices.

He turned away, keeping close to the wall where the floor would still be structurally sound enough. He knew he'd made choices. He'd regretted them every day since. He chose to borrow the car. Chose to ignore the weather forecast. Chose to make the drive. Chose when to stop for petrol and food, when to get back on the road. A thousand small choices that had led them to that icy patch at that particular moment when the ice and snow and temperature all coalesced into tragedy.

But God made it snow. God could have stopped it. God could have protected Jamie's fragile little body. It was senseless, God. Senseless!

He had no way of knowing which office of the three belonged to the foreman, but he made a guess and went into the one closest to the factory floor. What he found made him frown.

The place looked as though it had been used just last week. There was still a bowler hat hanging on a hook, an overcoat draped over a chair. Books and files were stacked on cupboards and the desk, papers still strewn across the top.

He knew the property had been condemned, that the workers had been barred from returning, so it was no surprise to see items left behind—everyone would have evacuated as soon as they could when the collapse occurred. But wouldn't the man have taken his things with him that day? Wouldn't the owners have gathered the files, at least, when they made their decisions about what to do with the building? Although the owners no doubt had their own copies. Perhaps they hadn't deemed collecting these worth the risk of entering the unstable building.

Two men.

Two men had died, though the machines were mostly run by women and children, hence the higher proportion of them. The men would have been overseers. Managers. Skilled technicians, perhaps.

Foremen.

A chill swept up his spine, even though it was nothing

more than a hypothesis. A decent one, but only a guess—that whoever the foreman was, he'd never come back into this office that day. And no one had braved the condemned building to collect his personal effects and send them home to his family.

Had Astley known that when he chose this particular room? Was it, for some reason, *why* he'd chosen it?

The single window remained unbroken, and the sunlight filtered through the two years of dirt and grime. Graham had no trouble seeing as he eased into the room, nor of making out the words on the papers on the desk.

He sucked in a breath as a particular heading caught his eye, familiar enough in style that it could have come from his own firm.

It was from one in Sheffield, dated six months before the accident. A professional evaluation of the structural integrity of the building. Graham scanned the words, knowing which paragraphs he could skim or skip altogether and still understand the final recommendation.

Building structure cannot support proposed machinery upgrade without substantial fortifications. For an estimate on replacing the structure in question with steel girders, see page 2.

They'd known. Graham swallowed hard and eased to a seat on the corner of the desk as he flipped the page.

This firm hadn't inflated the costs, high as they were. They weren't proposing anything unusual. In fact, their estimate came in a good deal lower than what his own firm would have suggested, probably due to costs being lower here than in London. Eighty thousand pounds. It was a fair estimate. A reasonable one.

It had been rejected. That note was clipped to this one, its decision a few typed lines that had destroyed twenty-three families. *Taken under advisement. Proceed with machinery installation as planned. No changes to structure will be contracted at this time as it would delay production.*

He tried to view it logically. The owners had contracts to fulfill. Being in breach of them could carry significant penalties. Work to the building would mean a delay not only in installing the new machinery they no doubt needed to meet new output requirements; it would mean halting current production on the old machines too. That meant lost money.

But logic couldn't bear up under hindsight.

They'd known. They'd done it anyway. And it had cost them far more than those contracts, those days or weeks or months. It had cost them everything.

He flipped through the other papers on the desk, all dated within a week of the accident. That made him frown. Why was this one out when it was so much older? Had the foreman been bothered by it? Or needed to refer to it, perhaps to defend a decision? If so, all he would have to do would be show that memo on the official letterhead of . . .

Graham sucked in a breath and moved the paper into the light. The logogram in the corner was familiar.

It ought to be. He'd seen it on countless entries in the files he'd been reviewing all week. *Wilfred Enterprises, Ltd.*

Wilfred. Wilfred had been the one to make this choice. Calling him here, then, for the ransom drop . . . that was no matter of convenience. It was a slap in the face. A reminder of failure and bad choices.

Eighty thousand pounds . . . the cost of the renovations he hadn't done.

After a moment's debate, he folded the papers and slid them into his pocket. Moved back to the doorway. Surveyed the destruction.

Senseless. But it wouldn't have seemed so to Lord Wilfred. He made business decisions every day. He probably cut corners left and right without any dire consequences. To him, it had been a balance sheet. A ledger. A review of contracts and schedules. He had made a bad decision that had seemed like a good decision at the time, based on his expertise.

But he wasn't an architect. If he were, he would have made a different one.

I am the Architect.

A shiver coursed down Graham's spine, and try as he might, he couldn't blame it on the draft. It came from the sure knowledge that that thought was not just his own.

His limbs shook, making him reach to put a steadying hand on the wall. Plaster over brick. But not created for appearance, created for structure. Created for purpose. As its architect knew.

I am the Architect.

It had been misused, the building. But it wasn't the fault of its design. It wasn't the fault of the architect. One could argue that it was the fault of the owner, and one would have a point . . . but did that mean he deserved no mercy for his judgment? Did that mean Wilfred could turn around and blame the men who had built it fifty years before?

Senseless.

He sucked in a breath that smelled of snow and rotted leaves and machine oil and mildew. It smelled of intentions and failures. Of lives lived and lives mourned. But each brick had been laid with a purpose. Each line on the architect's blueprint had been for a reason. The bricklayers might not have known it. The owner might not have known it. Certainly the men who came later could have shrugged it off or called it unnecessary or needless.

But the architect knew. He knew what no other man who came after would ever see.

Tragedy didn't make sense. No logic or reason or maths or artistry could *ever* make sense of Jamie's death.

It didn't have to. *Trust me. I love you. Forever and a day.*

In this world, Graham understood buildings—stone and steel and wood. Symmetry and structure. Mathematics and art.

But he would never understand the grand design of the entire universe, all of history. And he didn't have to. That was why there was an Architect.

His fingers digging into damp, crumbling plaster, in his heart he reached out. And surrendered.

TWENTY-THREE

Gemma had been pacing their suite of rooms for the last twenty minutes, willing familiar footsteps to fall, stridently ignoring Marigold's continued reminders about watched pots and boiling water. The moment the key finally scraped in the lock and the door opened, she pounced, grabbing the unsuspecting Graham by the arm and pulling him inside, toeing the door shut again behind him.

"She was there. His daughter was there."

Graham swept his hat and his wig off his head. "Context, please, darling. I will assume you mean Astley's daughter, but where is *there*?"

"Matlock Textiles." She and Marigold said it at the same time—and let it be noted that her friend wasn't sitting calmly in a chair either. She'd been putting herself through a series of floor exercises that alternately had Gemma envious of her flexibility and wincing in imagined pain.

Spines weren't meant to bend that much. Not unless one was a cat.

Graham dropped the hat and wig to the floor. "Wait. By *there*, do you mean—"

"One of the children killed." Gemma rushed to get that out before Marigold, who was flipping upright.

His brows collided. "That makes no sense. Why would a baron's daughter be working at that factory?"

"The falling out, between him and her mother. They left, both of them. Returned to the village." When he moved to shrug out of his overcoat, Gemma slid around to his back to help him, like she'd done a thousand times before. "What Marigold and I discovered this afternoon is that the mother, Hannah, fell ill. She'd been working at the factory but couldn't. So her daughter, Agatha, took her place."

"She was old enough," Marigold said, voice bitter. "*Ten.* She had just turned ten." The legal age for a child to find employment.

Graham shrugged his suit jacket off, too, along with its padding. Then he rubbed a hand over his hair, his face. "Leopard stripes. That's it, then. That's our motive."

It was? Gemma looked to Marigold to see if she followed whatever clue Gemma must have missed, but her friend was frowning too. "His grief, you mean? Do you think it drove him to madness?"

"No. I think it drove him to revenge." He reached into the inner pocket of the overcoat Gemma still held and pulled out a piece of paper. "Wilfred owns Matlock Textiles. I found a report from a local architectural firm, recommending added support to the structure before the new machinery was installed. He rejected the advice."

Gemma had to press a hand to her chest to try to steady the wild beating of her heart. Wilfred was behind the tragedy that had taken Astley's daughter, however unintentionally. "Do you think Astley knows? That Wilfred knew the danger and did it anyway?"

"I daresay he did, given that the original ransom matches the amount of the proposed changes. Wilfred made a decision that cost Astley his daughter's life—and he wants him to pay."

"The legal proceedings that chap mentioned in the pub."

Gemma draped the coat over the back of a chair with more care than it really required. "I would bet Astley tried to get something started and either was shut down or lost."

"I don't know." Marigold stretched ceilingward. "A lawsuit would mean a lot of attention. From what we've gleaned, the Astleys have always avoided such things."

"Yes, well, this Astley kidnapped Wilfred's son, so I think it's safe to assume he's given up caring about his reputation." And perhaps his very life. He had to know there would be repercussions. He had to know Wilfred wouldn't let him get away with it. He must not care.

Gemma sank into the same chair she'd hung Graham's coat on. "So this really isn't about money. Not an investment he lent to Fitzroy and lost. He named such a ludicrous amount because he knew that delivering it, if he even tried, would be financial ruin. That's what he wants—Wilfred's ruin."

Graham's hand came to a rest on her shoulder. "I daresay it's more than that. I daresay he wants to make Wilfred hurt like *he* hurts."

"You don't think . . . he doesn't mean to kill them, does he?" Marigold dropped back down to the soles of her feet.

It was possible. That would certainly be the most thorough revenge. And yet if he meant to kill the boys, he could have done so. He wouldn't have provided Sidney with all the comforts one could stuff into a monk's cell. He wouldn't have then brought him back to his own home and likely to the comforts he'd provided his own child, once. Gemma shook her head. "Call it hope more than reason, but I don't think so."

"So many questions, though. If it was so personal, why did he ask for a money drop? And make no specification that Wilfred himself must be the one to deliver it? I would have thought he'd want to see Wilfred's anxiety." Graham's thumb pressed gently on the spot on her back where her tension always rode, rubbed it. "And what is he planning for tomorrow? He *knows* there won't be money coming—and he knows Wilfred's likely to have sorted out who's behind it, given his public appearances with Sidney and the sudden guards at his house."

"He doesn't care how it ends. Not for him. He—" Marigold stopped when a knock came at the door.

"Leopard stripes," Gemma muttered. She jumped to her feet and pushed Graham toward his bedroom. "Get out of sight. You're not in costume."

"It's only your friendly neighborhood investigators" came a Cockney voice through the door. Yates, obviously. Which was why they hadn't heard footsteps—he'd probably snuck up deliberately, just to startle them.

The boyish grin that peeked from beneath his greying moustache when Gemma pulled open the door certainly lent credence to the theory. Sir Merritt stood behind him too. He must have been taking his lessons on stealth seriously. A few months ago, he had no hope at all of sneaking up on them.

Gemma waved them both in, but rather than give them the latest update, she spun back to Marigold. "I think our plans need to remain intact. We need to visit the girl's mother. She and Astley were . . . *involved* for years. She must know him better than anyone."

"Put a pin in that." Yates scratched at his upper lip with one hand and held up a slip of paper in his other. "We need a sympathetic female to make a visit to the sister of our inside man—or woman, as it were." Directing his gaze to Marigold, he said, "The nursemaid. After she was sacked, she came directly here to Matlock, where her younger sister lives. The sister could know more details of the plan than Mrs. Christianson divulged. We managed to get the sister's name."

"I suppose we'll have to split up, then." Marigold reached for her dreary hat while Gemma plucked the paper from Yates's fingers. "I'll pay a visit to Hannah Thomas while you visit—"

"Hannah Thomas." Gemma read the paper three times to make certain she wasn't imagining it. Looked at Yates. At Marigold. "Wait. The mother of Astley's love child is the sister of Horace Wilfred's nurse?"

"It's a small county, I suppose." Sir Merritt had made his way to Marigold's side and slipped an arm about her waist.

"Actually, that makes perfect sense." Yates helped himself to one of the apples on the table. "That's why the nurse seemed so certain that Astley wouldn't hurt the boys. She knows how he loved his daughter—her niece. And no doubt she compared that to how coolly Wilfred treats his son and was easily convinced that the earl needed to be taught a lesson."

"Well. That simplifies the afternoon, anyway." Graham gave her a smile that was brighter than it should have been. No, calmer. No . . . more peaceful. That was it. If she'd been writing his description for a column, she would have said his eyes radiated an inner peace that overflowed into a smile. "You ladies can visit Hannah Thomas and see what you can learn. We gentlemen can compare notes on all the other facets of the case. Reconvene for dinner, and we'll make our plan for tomorrow."

Tomorrow—when Wilfred was supposed to deliver an undeliverable ransom or never see his son again. Eighteen hours from now. And they still had to sort out how to turn it all to their advantage.

Filing away Graham's smile for later examination, Gemma scooped up her own hat. "We'd better hurry."

Hannah Thomas lived in a small flat over a bakery that had no view and little space but the most delicious perfume wafting through it. Gemma drew in a deep breath of yeast and sugar and tried to pull her attention off her hostess's downstairs neighbor and onto the woman herself.

She'd let them in without any question as to what they wanted, which spoke to her graciousness. She pointed them to the sofa and offered them tea, which showed she had manners. She wore a simple, modest dress in navy blue that said she knew how to balance taste and a budget. And she met their gazes with an intelligence that said she knew a shoe was about to drop.

She was pretty, but not the sort of pretty Gemma had expected. She'd seen plenty of lords' mistresses in her line of work, and most of them fit a certain mold. Too beautiful, too flashy, too bold. This young woman looked like any other young woman. Perhaps thirty, average brown hair, pleasant features. The sort of woman no one minded looking at but no one stared at either.

Lord Astley must have loved her.

"Are you with Scotland Yard? Or the local constabulary?" Ms. Thomas smoothed her skirt over her legs, not even a tremor in her hands. "I'll be honest—I didn't think either were progressive enough to employ females."

"They're not—or rather, *we're* not. Both." Gemma smiled. "We're with a private investigation firm."

They'd debated what tack to take, and Marigold had decided this would be the best one. Ms. Thomas had to know, if she didn't already, what was at stake and why they were involved.

"Lord Wilfred has hired you." Ms. Thomas nodded at her own insight. "I've been expecting someone to come ever since they hauled Jill back to Fellsbourne this morning, saying she was wanted for questioning. I didn't catch the whole reason why, but she'd told me someone kidnapped young Horace. That's all she told me, though. If you're hoping she mentioned anything else, I'm very sorry to disappoint you. I would help if I could."

Gemma believed her.

Marigold must have too, given the relaxed line of her neck. "We think you *can* help, but not necessarily because of your sister. It's Lord Astley who took the boy."

"What?" That took her by surprise—proving her sister really had kept mum while she was here. "Franklin? Why would he . . . ?" Her face dropped with realization, and she fell back against the cushion of her chair. "No."

"You've made the connections we've made, I see." Gemma scooted forward a few inches. "It was Wilfred's factory. His decisions that led to the accident."

"I know. Everyone who lost someone knows." Ms. Thomas's eyes slid closed. She had the look of a puppet whose strings had been cut. But only for a moment. She roused herself, looking from one of them to the other. "I don't know how I can help, though. He won't see me—hasn't in years. He didn't—he didn't even come to the funeral."

"I'm sorry," Marigold murmured. "That must have hurt."

The turning of Ms. Thomas's mouth was more sorrow than smile. "It hurt *him*. That's what I regret. I know him. I know how it will have eaten him up."

"That's why we're here," Gemma said softly. "Because you know him. Perhaps, then, you'll be able to help *us* understand him so we can anticipate what he'll do. Is he . . . dangerous? Violent?"

A darker cousin of amusement flitted over Ms. Thomas's face. "No," she said in a breathy laugh. "I'd call the very suggestion ridiculous—except that he's apparently put himself in quite a spot of trouble, hasn't he?" She leaned forward again and rubbed at her temples. "But he isn't violent. He would never hurt anyone, certainly not a child. It was one of the things I loved about him—that he would sooner *be* hurt than to hurt another."

And yet he'd kept this seemingly well-bred young woman as a mistress for a decade without marrying her, had cast out both her and her child.

"Don't judge him too harshly." That sorrowful smile settled on their hostess's lips again. "He'd sworn to his mother on her deathbed that he wouldn't marry me. She knew we were in love and disapproved. I was only the daughter of a teacher, nothing more. Not a proper wife for a baron. He loved *her* too much to refuse her final wish."

Gemma had to press her lips together against the retort that wanted to spill out.

Ms. Thomas seemed to hear it anyway. "I was the one who suggested our arrangement. I knew it would mean ostracism for me, but . . . I was eighteen. I loved him more than I ever thought I could love another human being. I wanted to be with him, whatever the cost." She lifted a shoulder in a shrug that looked just as filled with regret as her eyes did. "Our story is not so unique in that regard, I imagine. I traded reputation for love. And for years, I was happy with my choice. Agatha came along, and he doted on her as if she were the only child in the world."

"His little duckling." Marigold pulled the toy from her bag and held it out.

Ms. Thomas took it with something like reverence. "Yes. And Agatha adored him. He was the best father any child could have asked for. It took me years to realize that he intended to make us his life. That when he agreed to my suggestion, he'd decided he would never marry. Never have children with anyone else. Never have an heir."

"You can't tell me that you *wanted* him to marry." No one was that good, to want to share the man they loved with another woman.

"Want it? No. But I'd assumed he would. I had braced myself for it, had known that eventually he'd have to move us to a little flat somewhere, that we wouldn't always have the run of Derwent. When I finally realized he meant to trade his family's legacy for me . . . it woke me up, I suppose you could say. I began to see that our choices had cost *him* something, not just me. And then I began to be aware of other costs—to our spirits, our souls. I wanted Agatha to be a good girl, a good woman. I wanted her to know right from wrong. But how could I teach her that when I was living as I was? Why would she ever believe me once she realized? Ever respect me?"

Had she been closer, Gemma would have reached out to take the woman's hand. "He didn't cast you out. You left."

She nodded. "He was so hurt. So angry. He said if I left, that would be the end of it forever. That he would offer no support for me or Agatha. That until I was ready to come home, he didn't even want to see us in passing. He only meant it as incentive to keep us there—I knew that even then. But he was a man of his word." A bittersweet laugh slipped out. "Always such a man of his word. He couldn't countenance breaking his oath to his mother, and he wouldn't go back on that threat either, I knew."

Gemma sighed. "Funny, isn't it? How you can both love and hate something about someone?"

Ms. Thomas nodded and let her fingers trace the contours of the faded yellow wood of the duck. "I think, in his mind, it cost him more than us. I think . . . he tried to do as he'd done with the promise to his mother and work around it. To arrange good, well-paying positions for me. Make a flat suddenly available for a pittance—as if I didn't know he was the landlord. But I knew I couldn't let him do that. I got a job at the Textile, found this little place. It was all I could do on my own, but I was determined."

"And the more you refused him, the more hurt he became?" Marigold said.

She tilted her head, neither in confirmation nor denial. "He kept trying. And the more he tried, the more stubborn it made me. We had tried once to have it both ways, and it had stolen something from me only God could restore. I didn't want to compromise again. I was afraid . . . I was afraid that would make it too easy to slip back into old sins. And he could have forgiven that, I think—until I fell ill two years ago and didn't tell him. Didn't go to him."

"You couldn't work." Gemma whispered the words, the information they'd already learned. Waited for Hannah Thomas to make sense of the next bit for them, because she couldn't fathom that this woman would have sent her ten-year-old daughter to the factory in her place, even given her own stubbornness and need to remain independent.

"I was . . . I don't even know what I was. I can scarcely remember that time. Delirium, fever—they stole the days from me, and my awareness. Whatever it was, it clung to me for weeks, and I couldn't shake it. Couldn't work, couldn't even get out of bed. I knew neighbors came in, that Agatha wasn't always there, but I think I must have assumed she was at school, as she should have been. I didn't realize she'd gone to work. That she thought she had to provide for *me*." Her eyes slid shut, but it did nothing to stop the tears that broke free. "When someone came and told me about the accident, told me Agatha had been there, that she'd been killed—I couldn't make sense of it. How could my baby have been in that place? *I* should have been, but her?"

Gemma's fingers curled into her palms. "She didn't think to go to her father? Or did he refuse her?"

"She never tried. He must have blamed me for that—for putting us, putting her in that position. Perhaps it was his anger with me that kept him from even coming to the funeral,

I don't know. Perhaps the grief was too deep. Perhaps he didn't want to show it to the neighborhood."

Gemma tried to keep the frown from her brow but failed. "He never came to see you, even after that? You've still never spoken to him?"

Wiping at the tears that kept flowing regardless, Ms. Thomas shook her head. "What could either of us have said?"

A million options flooded Gemma's mind all at once—words and phrases, some beautiful, some ugly. She could see different scenes playing out, everything from tearful reunions of healing to arguments not unlike the ones she and Graham had endured.

But it hadn't been her story to write. It still wasn't.

Ms. Thomas sank back again, the stringless puppet. "For the first year, I nearly drowned in my self-pity. In my self-recriminations. Then I began to look around me. To realize that I was far from the only woman mourning a child. I wasn't even the only one mourning the tragedy of that accident. It impacted nearly every family in the village in one way or another. I began to realize that the statistic I'd read in the paper once, about how one in ten children die in England before they reach their first birthday, was more than a number. That was grief for so many families. And that only counted children who lived to their own birth and died in that first year. It didn't count the children who died in later years. Or the precious babies like the two I lost after Agatha who were born into heaven instead of my arms. It certainly didn't count the ones lost in early adulthood, like one of my brothers, or the sister who died in childbirth when I was only a girl."

Weight settled on Gemma's chest, heavy but familiar. "Death is the only sure thing in life."

"No—death and the love of God." Marigold reached over and squeezed Gemma's hand.

Ms. Thomas dipped her head. "That was what I'd been

learning. That even when I embraced sin, God loved me. Even when I chose my own desires over Him, God loved me. Even when I was hungry and sick and lost the only person in the world who mattered, God loved me." The weight of it all pressed on her too, bowing her shoulders. "A lesson I don't think Franklin has learned. He always thought *he* was the one responsible for everything—that he had to fix every problem and meet every need."

They all sat in silence for a long moment, working through the implications of those words. This factory accident wasn't something he could fix. The loss of his daughter couldn't be undone. But clearly he would go to any extent to try.

Marigold finally voiced the question pulsing through Gemma's mind. "Do you think . . . is it revenge he's after, with Lord Wilfred? Will he seek it to the point of taking another child's life in exchange for Agatha's?"

The denial came quick and sure. "No. Never. If he has Horace, he's treating him well. He would never harm him." Then came that dreadful hesitation. "At least . . . the Franklin I knew wouldn't."

"The question, though, is who grief has turned him into." Gemma gave her best friend's fingers a squeeze and then pushed to her feet. "Thank you for your honesty with us, Ms. Thomas. You've been very helpful."

Ms. Thomas stood at the same moment Marigold did. "I wish I could do more. And I will, if you need me. I'll . . . I'll talk to him, if you think that will help."

Would it? Gemma couldn't say. How many times had Graham tried to speak with her in the last year? But she hadn't been ready to hear him. How could she know if facing Hannah Thomas again would help or hinder the situation with Astley?

Marigold, of course, just smiled. "Thank you. We'll certainly keep that in mind."

Hannah nodded, hesitated, and then said, "I heard he's hired guards, but I doubt they're covering my entrance."

Gemma had been ready to turn toward the door, but that brought her up short. "*Your* entrance?"

The woman nodded. "For the years I lived there, I didn't like to be seen coming and going. It made me far too aware of what everyone must think of me. I always used an old kitchen passageway that connected to the springhouse, and from there, a little path through the wood. Franklin thought it ridiculous. It was so roundabout, and I didn't go out often enough for the path to even truly be a path. It was little more than a deer trail."

Deer trails surely weren't being guarded, not unless he'd hired a whole army. And even though the guards were likely walking a patrol, if they could sneak into the springhouse . . .

Gemma's pulse kicked up, and she exchanged a glance with Marigold. "So if we made it to the kitchen . . ."

"There won't be any staff to stop you. He sent them all off for a long holiday right before the armed guards showed up, according to the gossip mill." Ms. Thomas met their respective gazes, her own steady and serene. "He'll have Horace in Agatha's rooms, I'd bet. I can tell you how to get there."

TWENTY-FOUR

*T*he suite of rooms that had seemed mockingly spacious for two people had become rather cramped. Graham cast a longing gaze toward his small bedchamber, which had been commandeered by Yates, and drummed his fingers on the small table in the joint sitting room.

When this was all over, he would need to sleep for a week—but that luxury would have to wait. He would be lucky to snatch a few hours in bed after Yates, Marigold, and Sir Merritt left to infiltrate Derwent Hall in the middle of the night and before he had to be up again to arrive at the factory before dawn.

Gemma paced the space behind him, having given her own room to the Livingstones. She looked, for the first time since they'd left London a week ago, like herself. The last of the beet-and-carrot-juice tincture had faded way with her bath that morning, and she'd tossed the black wig aside after dinner, when they deemed it unlikely anyone would come to the room and see her, and had changed into her own clothes. The skullcap she'd used to hold her real hair in place had been abandoned, and there'd been no purpose in styling her blond locks at this point in the day.

Which meant they tumbled free down her back, not even braided for the night yet. He wondered if he dared to run his fingers through the length of spun sunlight like he'd always loved to do. Did yesterday's kiss mean she'd welcome that now?

He had no idea. There'd been no real time to think or talk about their own lives. All their waking hours had been spent sorting through Astley's. Such as it was.

His stomach tightened at the thought of their villain, who didn't seem quite so villainous now, even given his actions. He seemed . . . broken. Distraught. With nothing left to lose.

That last bit could lead to fresh tragedy tomorrow if they didn't both rescue the boys *and* stay whatever plan he'd put in place.

The telegram that sat glaring at him from the table had arrived with dinner, sent by Carissa Horley to the Fairfax home in London and then forwarded to them by Neville. It was what had set Gemma to pacing and him to pitying.

F returned to W for New Year's. Flush. Pressed him last night after he was drunk and learned of payday from A, with more to come when named in will. Sick?

It hadn't required Sir Merritt's experience with decryption to understand what Mrs. Horley had found alarming enough to pass along to them. They had been wondering how Fitzroy fit in with all this, and the answer seemed simple enough: Astley had paid him for his help. For being shown to the monastery, and likely for otherwise turning a blind eye. Fitzroy was simply acting as Fitzroy always acted—willing to indulge in a little vice and sin if it meant money enough to take back to the games.

The will bit, though . . . that was what made Graham wish he could sit down and talk with Astley. Was he ill, as Mrs. Horley had wondered? Expecting to die of it soon? That could explain his willingness to take this last, unfathomable risk for some twisted sort of justice for his daughter.

Or . . . or he could simply not mean to leave the encounter tomorrow alive, one way or the other. They had all found it odd he'd never demanded the authorities be left out of things, even though Wilfred had seemed, according to Yates, only too happy to keep them out of the loop after their initial response. Astley might assume they'd be there. Assume he could provoke them to shoot him. End it all.

"If we had more time—another day—we could find whatever doctor he sees." Graham touched a finger to the yellow square of paper, turned it in a circle.

Gemma heaved a sigh and abandoned the window she'd paused beside. There wasn't much to see outside anyway. Winter's greedy night had already fallen, and it wouldn't sound its retreat for another fourteen hours.

Fourteen hours. All the time they had to rescue the boys and stop their kidnapper from doing something rash.

"I don't think he's sick. Not in body." She moved to his side and, after a brief hesitation, rested her arm over his shoulders and her head on his.

Graham anchored her with an arm around her waist. "That's even sadder. Assuming he really said that to Fitzroy and meant it."

"I can't believe Fitzroy didn't try to stop him. Talk him out of it. What sort of friend lets another use his family estate to hide a kidnapped child in exchange for a little cash?"

"Could have been a lot of cash." From what Yates and Merritt had gleaned in a second interview with Hannah's sister, Mrs. Christianson, she hadn't taken a dime for the information she provided on Horace's supposed whereabouts. She merely wanted the earl woken up to the son he was losing degree by degree. She had sent a message to alert Astley to his having napped the wrong kid but had only known to send it to Derwent, assuming someone would forward it. No one had. Which meant that he hadn't known about his mistake until he arrived home on Christmas. Which meant that Fitzroy had been the only one he'd paid for help at that juncture.

Graham shook his head, thinking of the charming wastrel. "Fitzroy cares more for drinking and gambling than anything else in life, I daresay." It was even more likely to his mind if Astley was ill—or had told Fitzroy he was. But whatever the truth, the result was the same. "Astley is a man with nothing to lose."

"He has everything to lose. He just can't see it through the pain of what he's already lost." Gemma lifted her head, tilted his chin up with a hand.

She was so beautiful. Had she ever been as beautiful as she was in that moment? He didn't understand how he could look at her so many times, how her features could become so familiar that he didn't even have to see them to know them, and yet be struck anew every time he glimpsed her with that soul-deep conviction. *Beautiful.*

Especially with that look on her face, so soft and welcoming. "Graham." They'd not been speaking at regular volume as it was, but now her voice was a breath across his brow. "I don't want to be like him. I don't want to miss the future because I've been crippled by the past."

He pressed a bit on her hip. Once upon a time, it had been his invitation for her to make herself comfortable on his lap, but he had no idea if she'd accept it now. Not until she settled across his legs, her arms wrapping his neck in a heady combination of love and—dare he hope?—forgiveness. "I don't either," he whispered.

"I want . . ." She closed her eyes. "I want to come home. When this is all over. If you can forgive me for leaving."

Forgive her? A quick claim that there was nothing to forgive sprang to his tongue. He swallowed it back. He had focused, as she had, on *his* bad choices that she couldn't forgive. But the truth was, she had hurt him too, when she left. When she cast all the blame on him. Whether he would forgive her had never been a question—but it still needed to be offered. She still needed to know it. "I forgive you, Gemma. Come home. Please come home."

"I forgive you too."

The words sounded as sweet as their first confession of love had, and just as difficult for her to say. She leaned toward him, and he met her there with a kiss to seal the oath. He wanted to pull her closer, kiss her soundly—but not here, not now. Not with their friends and family snatching sleep on either side of them, with the fate of two boys and one desperate man looming over them.

When their lips broke apart, she settled against him. "It won't be easy."

"No. It won't be," Graham agreed with a sigh. "He'll still be gone. It will still hurt. And you'll still be angry with me when you think about it. We'll still argue."

"We always did." A bit of a smile lifted her voice. "That never stopped us from loving each other, though. I shouldn't have let it stop us this time."

"We made mistakes. But God willing, we'll have the chance to rectify at least a few of them." That was all he said—one casual mention of the God before whom he'd laid down his heart, with all its doubts and anger. But she knew him. She knew the very ease with which he said it spoke of the reconciliation.

She hugged him tight, then pulled away with a long breath. "We won't have time to review anything after we've had our turn sleeping. We ought to go over it again now."

Part of him would have preferred to talk more about exactly what she meant by "coming home"—if she would take one of the spare rooms for a while or *truly* come home, to him. To let her press him for details about how he put his argument against God to rest, at least enough to trust Him. To kiss her again, no matter the people who could come out of the connected rooms at any moment.

But she was right. They were to wake the others at midnight and take their own turn sleeping while the team suited for such action stole back two kidnapped boys. They would have to wake up themselves at no later than three in order to first rendezvous with Wilfred and his crew and then get to the factory and into position several hours before daylight. That left now to review.

"All right." He pulled forward the papers on which they'd taken all their notes. "Lord Wilfred has scraped together some cash, Yates said. To have something to offer if money really is part of Astley's motivation." They'd questioned the earl about the lawsuit Matlock had been gossiping about, but the lord hadn't had any idea what they meant. He had never, he claimed, seen Astley's name on any suit against him.

"He wants to arrive before Astley, so he intends to get there around six." Gemma tapped a finger to that line. "He'll have the most recent set of blueprints with him for you to review."

He doubted he'd need them. He'd made his own when he got back to the hotel room after his scouting expedition. But it never hurt to compare the official ones with his observations. "That should give me enough information to know where to situate all his guards, and where we can hide to be unseen but able to see."

Wilfred had insisted he would provide the Imposters with weapons, but Graham had no intention of even chambering a round in the pistol Yates had entrusted to him. Sir Merritt had the distinction of being the only Imposter who ought to be entrusted with a gun. The rest of them had been trained on highwires and trapezes, on the stage and in the ring. He'd briefly tried his hand at sword swallowing and fire breathing, for one eyebrow-singeing weekend . . . but shooting had never been a desired skill set for any of them, and he knew he'd be more a danger than a help if he tried to take aim at anything other than the sky. "You know what would be handy? They should have brought Leonidas. He did a marvelous job of saving the day last spring."

Gemma chuckled. "I daresay that would take Astley by surprise. No one in England ever expects an old lion to leap out of the shadows."

"More fools, them." His eyes searched through the slap-dash notes, but he saw the factory more than Gemma's short-hand. "I think the basement will be our answer, so let's make certain we have fresh batteries in our torches."

"The basement?" Given her tone, Gemma didn't much like that suggestion. "As in, where the bulk of the wreckage is?"

"Exactly so. According to this report," he said, motioning to another of the documents Yates had brought back with him after his final visit to Lord Wilfred that evening, "every-thing is considered stable now. Not exactly *safe*, but stable. The wreckage hasn't shifted, so it ought to support us."

"Graham. Please tell me you don't mean for us to be climb-ing up the wreckage. Who do I look like, Penelope?"

He grinned at the reference to the capuchin monkey that called the Tower—and usually Yates's shoulder—home. "Well, you *did* have those matching skirts when you were nine."

She snorted a laugh. "Marigold's idea, I assure you."

"You know very well I won't let you step foot on anything that would put you at risk." He paused, let it sink in, waited to see if she would argue.

She didn't. She sighed. "Life comes with risks—as does rescuing someone else. If for some reason that means scaling an iron monster of a machine, then so be it."

Graham pulled his sketch of the building forward. "Here's the foreman's office." He tapped the small, blocked-off room.

"I think he chose it because it has an unhindered view of the disaster, being closest to it. Its door opens directly in front of the wreckage. If Wilfred goes in there, but if Astley positions himself here . . ." He paused to tap the edge of the hole in the floor, where he'd drawn the machinery, along with dotted lines to indicate the broken flooring, as best as he'd been able to map it. "He'll be boxing Wilfred in and also drawing his gaze to the disaster. Forcing him to see it. At the same time, the machinery will provide him cover."

He tapped the places they'd been considering for guards—every one of whom would have a line of sight blocked by the towering, canted machines. There was simply no other choice, not unless someone climbed up through the belly of the beast, and frankly he didn't trust a hired gun to be the one to do it.

"But he'll know Wilfred didn't come alone. He'll know the way out is blocked."

"Unless *he* intends to climb down the machines." Or, worse, throw himself down, without care as to whether he survived the fall. Another potential situation he hoped to head off by being there himself.

Gemma blew out a breath. "I really hope our assumption is right, and he doesn't mean to bring the boys with him."

"He didn't in Weymouth." It was the only pattern they had to compare it to. He'd left Sidney behind before. That's what they were counting on this time too—that after making certain the boys were in their room tonight, he wouldn't check again before leaving for his daybreak rendezvous and thus giving Yates, Marigold, and Merritt the opportunity they needed to get the boys out. "I think he wants to face Wilfred—make *him* face the disaster that resulted from a decision he made at his desk, hundreds of miles away. He wants to see him panicked over his son. He wants to make him hurt."

"Do you think he does?" Gemma turned enough to face him, her expression saying what he'd been wondering too. As incomprehensible as it felt to them, Wilfred didn't seem to value a relationship with his son. He wanted him back, yes. He had been willing to throw money at it, willing to provide them with his documents and resources.

But he hadn't been willing to listen to his boy before. He hadn't lifted a finger to help Horace's cousin and best friend. He hadn't done more than hire other people to protect him when he *knew* he was in danger.

And yet it had been his own idea to come tomorrow, rather than send someone else. To come with everything he could. Maybe that meant something more than pride and duty were at stake for him.

Graham hoped so. Prayed so.

Prayed that when—*please, God*—Horace was returned to Lord Wilfred safe and sound, it would mark something new in their family.

TWENTY-FIVE

*I*f he hadn't been born the heir to an earl, Yates suspected he would have made an excellent cat burglar—if the circus or theater career he'd dreamed of as a child didn't pan out. And if he hadn't been gifted by his saint of a mother with a healthy sense of morality.

As it was, he got to enjoy both the fun of sneaking about *and* the satisfaction of knowing he was doing it for a good cause. Win-win.

He crouched low at the edge of the wood, surveying the short distance between their current cover and their next. Hannah Thomas had been right in her suspicion that the once-was path wouldn't be guarded. She'd also been right in warning them that it would be so overgrown as to be scarcely identifiable, especially in the dark. The Lord had clearly been on their side, though—there were deer tracks they could follow from the opposite edge of the wood all the way to their current location.

There were plenty more tracks through the snow-covered expanse of lawn and garden, which was also a godsend. It meant theirs wouldn't be glaringly obvious to any guard who looked out a window and saw the footprints in the gleaming light of the moon.

Merritt took up position behind a tree trunk on Yates's right, Marigold hovered behind and to his left. Three sets of well-trained eyes surveying the still December landscape.

No lights glowed from the windows of the wing they were facing, the one that had once housed Ms. Thomas and her daughter. The scent of woodsmoke from the chimney drifted on the air, though, and made its own cloud against the star-studded sky. "Time?" he whispered. It had been nearly one by the time they started through the wood, and they'd had to move slowly for the sake of stealth and safety. But they'd known that and budgeted for it.

Merritt tilted his pocket watch's face toward the moon-light. "Ten after two."

Right on schedule. Yates nodded and waited another min-ute, his eyes alert to any movement.

A small animal scampered along the edge of the wood to the south. A bird circled, no doubt hunting it. The wind blew a few dried leaves in a dance over the snow.

The house remained still. Silent.

Annoying. He'd hoped that they would get here just as the guard posted outside came by on his rounds, so that they could give him a few minutes and then know they were in the clear. They hadn't had time to establish a record of his rou-tine, to know how long each tromp around the manor house took or when he was at each place. They only knew, from the reports in the village, that someone had the unenviable job.

There was nothing for it but to wait a few minutes. They couldn't risk being spotted. And again, they'd budgeted the time.

"Would have been more fun to scale the walls and go in through a window," Marigold whispered, her voice no louder than the breeze through the trees.

"But harder to get out again with the boys," Merritt replied.

Which Marigold would have known too. The tunnel from

springhouse to kitchen would be far better for their purposes. But Yates grinned beneath the fake moustache he'd pasted on again. The newest Imposter would have been relegated to lookout again, had they been scaling walls, so Yates knew he wasn't truly sorry.

Eight minutes had ticked by before he finally saw movement—a guard tromping steadily along the line of the house, ready to turn the corner.

Yates resisted the urge to move, to seek deeper cover—an instinct that would have served instead to provide motion to catch the guard's eye. No, he held absolutely still, trusting his dark clothing, dark hair, and the cover of the trees to do their work to hide him.

The guard never paused, never seemed to glance their way. He strode steadily along this wing of the house and then vanished around the corner.

Merritt had his watch out. Yates counted his own seconds to see how close he was when they hit the two-minute mark and Merritt gave the signal.

Merritt gave the signal.

Lionfeathers—he'd been off by three seconds. He'd have to work on that. Later. For now, he led the way in a low lope across the open space, toward the springhouse. Upon reaching its squat back wall, he paused, waiting for Marigold and Merritt to draw up alongside.

Then the slow, careful easing around the corner, the next, and a tug on the door.

His heart stuck in his throat when the door didn't budge. Locked? Not usually a concern with a springhouse, but this one had a passage connecting it to the house, so it was possible.

"Frozen," his sister whispered.

Frozen—quite right. The latch had no lock, but the sun had thawed much of the snow during the day, only for the dripping water to refreeze once night returned. Brute force, then—along with a prayer that brute force wouldn't be too loud. He gave a hefty tug, paused, then another. The door clearly hadn't been opened since Christmas, given the iced-over snow blocking its arc, but he bullied it into giving them enough room to slip inside.

Marigold had her electric torch ready and flashed it over the small space the moment he closed the door again.

They didn't have a springhouse at Fairfax Tower, but he'd seen a few over the years, and this one offered little to surprise him. Damp, warmer-than-the-winter air matched the gurgling of the spring that welled up at the back of the house and then vanished again. A few jars lined a row of shelves, and wrapped meats hung from the ceiling.

He was most interested, though, in the carved-out stairs that led downward. Upon spotting them, he nodded to the others and then crouched down to untie his boots as they did the same. Sturdy footwear had been essential for the outdoor portion of the evening, but from here onward, stealth was key.

He didn't know which Astley ancestor had insisted on a covered, underground walkway between kitchen and springhouse, but he praised him or her mentally and padded down, careful to duck his head to avoid slamming into the low threshold.

The passage smelled of damp earth, cool water, and a hint of mold. He was a fairly good judge of distance based on his own steps, so though he could see only the few feet in front of him that Marigold's light touched, he kept a mental count of how far they'd gone and how far that left. At last, a wooden door appeared in the circle of the torch.

He'd known from Ms. Thomas's account and Graham's schematics that the kitchen at Astley Hall had an older basement portion and then a newer ground-floor addition.

Even so, it seemed strange to open a door underground and step into a serviceable room full of workbenches and pots and dried herbs. The hearth was dormant but clean, and no cooked-food smells lingered down there.

Narrow stairs stretched upward to the right. He paused at the bottom, straining, listening. No sounds filtered down to warn him of guards having a cup of something hot or a nighttime snack during their rounds. A bit of moonlight stretched down the stairs, but no gas or electric.

Good. Empty. And when he climbed the service stairs, he saw an electric cookstove, other appliances Yates had never even seen, and a line of iceboxes.

He cleared out of the way of his companions and used the moonlight slanting through the bank of windows to look for the door into the rest of the house. They certainly couldn't stay here long. Those guards could pop in for a nip or a nibble at any moment.

"Left" came Marigold's whispered reminder once they'd tiptoed out the kitchen door and paused in the service corridor.

He knew that, but he never minded her verifying his memory. He had studied the drawings Graham had done, put together from the old books and records in the Archives, his own observations, and Ms. Thomas's descriptions.

Alertness kept every muscle coiled as they moved silently on stocking-clad feet, from one puddle of moonlight to the next. They soon arrived safely through the main part of the house and to the wing at which they were aiming.

Voices. Coming from behind, in the main house, so Yates rounded the corner before flattening himself to the wall, Marigold and Merritt dashing around to do the same. For another moment, the voices were more echo and impression than words, then they must have passed some barrier. Syllables emerged, in masculine tones.

". . . tomorrow. I'd keep walking around this bloke's house doing nothing for another month if he wanted to put up the money."

A laugh. "No good thing lasts forever. I'll be glad to get back to civilization. These country estates are too quiet."

"Still don't know why he hired us. Twelve of us to guard one of him and an empty house?"

"I think Joe's right—worried about break-ins, with all the staff given a holiday. A lot of stuff in here that would fetch a pretty price with the right fence."

"You ever take a look at that sculpture in the gallery? My brother-in-law, he . . ."

The voices moved off again, and Yates drew in a deeper breath. The exchange had answered one question for him, anyway. Now he knew that the hired muscle didn't know Astley was holding two kidnapped boys hostage here. That might mean that they could expect no more guards in the wing where they were being held. Surely if they patrolled the halls, they'd hear Horace and Sidney or see food being brought to them.

No reason to get careless, though. They started moving again, sticking to the deepest shadows, never so much as whispering. With only outdated information on which doors were likely to be unlocked if they needed to duck through one for cover, Yates would just as soon avoid the need to hide.

They encountered no other people, though, before they reached the set of stairs Ms. Thomas had described to Marigold and Gemma. They had only to climb them, then move down to the rooms at the end of the corridor. Those—the ones on both left and right and end—had been Agatha's. Her bedroom with its private lavatory, her schoolroom, her playroom. All connected to one another, the outer doors all sharing the same key. Ms. Thomas hadn't had one anymore, but his sister had assured her that wouldn't be a problem.

It wouldn't. Marigold had her master keys in her pocket, and if those failed, Yates had his set of picks in his own.

Upon reaching the end rooms, they fanned out, each pressing an ear to a door. Yates ended up at the room filled with toys and games, where the boys likely spent their daylight hours, but he wasn't surprised to hear nothing through it now. Even so, he twisted the knob.

Locked.

They all were, but the wave of Marigold's hand signaled that she heard something within, so Yates stole across to her. He pressed his own ear to the door rather than ask what she'd heard.

He'd expected to hear deep breathing, snores perhaps, the rustle of bedclothes. Instead, he heard light footsteps and quiet mumbling in a boyish tone that he had to strain to make out. Only a few words came through the door clearly.

"No. I'm going to tell his *mum*, that's what I'm going to do. Stupid, stupid, stupid."

Leopard stripes. They'd imagined the boys would be in bed at this hour, asleep. That would allow them to slip into the room, cover the boys' mouths gently while they woke them up and explained they were there on behalf of their parents, and convince them to come along.

Slipping in now, with at least one of them awake, made it far too likely that he'd scream when he saw strangers in his room, and that it would be loud enough to grab the attention of either the patrol or Astley.

He could tell from the purse of Marigold's lips and Merritt's frown that they were thinking the same thing. Though the answer was obvious. He grinned at his sister and motioned for her to take off the black knit cap covering her hair. They'd just send her in. No one would be afraid of *Marigold*, with her long braid and gentle features. She looked like the personification of a sweet, trustworthy friend.

She scowled.

He motioned to his own frame—not exactly diminutive and non-threatening. And then waved an illustrative hand toward Merritt, who had the bearing of England's most elite band of warriors. Did she really think sending either of *them* in would work?

Even in the dim light, he could see the roll of her eyes. She got out her key, though, and fitted it in the lock. All three of them winced at the sound of the tumblers clicking, loud as a gong in the otherwise quiet hallway.

The noises from inside stopped.

Lionfeathers. Yates sent a few frantic, wordless prayers heavenward.

Marigold, sensible and sweet and trustworthy girl that she was, tapped a finger on the door, soft and polite, like a servant warning a guest that she was about to enter.

Yates and Merritt both flattened themselves against the wall to stay out of view when she eased the door open.

"Shh," she said as she stepped in, in such a sweet, gentle tone that naturally there was no scream.

See? Wise decision.

"I'm here to help. Are you Horace? Sidney?"

"I knew it!" Whichever-Boy-He-Was whisper-shouted. "I *knew* someone would come! Did my father send you? I *told* him."

"Shh," Marigold said again, and he could imagine her pressing a finger to her lips or motioning for him to remain calm. "Are you Horace, then?"

"Yes."

"Good. Horace, my husband and brother are here with me, and we're going to help you and your cousin escape. Is it all right if they come in?"

They scarcely waited for his permission before slipping into the room. Dark, but for the generous light of the moon and one candle set on the floor and dim enough that they must not have been able to see it through the window. It was enough to make out everything in the room, though. The wide canopied bed, the chairs and bookcase, the child-sized writing desk and shelves filled with porcelain dolls.

A little girl's dream . . . but not so alluring to two boys.

Speaking of which. He looked from bed to chairs to the closed doors that presumably led to the lavatory and the other rooms in the suite. "Where's Sidney?"

Horace sniffed. Snuffled. Gasped.

Not a good sign. Dread pooling in his stomach, Yates crouched down so as not to be towering over the boy. Still, he could blame the lad neither for trying to knuckle away the tears nor for giving up and rushing toward Marigold, burying his face in her stomach.

"Shh." This time, it was comfort. She ran a hand over his head, down his back. "What's happened, sweetling? Where's your cousin?"

"I—don't know. He—he *took* him."

"Lord Astley did?" she whispered to the boy but sent a confused look to him and Merritt.

"He thought . . . Sid said . . . said he was *me*. He got into . . . into my clothes. While I was sleeping. Put his . . . on me. I tried to tell him!" Horace tilted his face back, the dim light magnifying his horror. "I tried to tell him *I* was Horace!"

"All right." Voice soothing, Marigold pressed a hand to his round cheek. "All right. We'll find him too. Why was Astley taking him? Why did he claim to be you?"

"Because." Horace wiped at his face again, but he didn't step away from Marigold. "He said he wanted to teach Father a lesson. Wanted him to know how it felt."

Leopard stripes. This wasn't good.

The boy knew it. He moved his gaze from Marigold to Merritt to Yates. "He's going to kill him, isn't he? Because he thinks he's me. He's been kind up until now, but that's all over. Because he wants to punish Father. He's going to kill Sidney, and Sidney *knew* it, and he pretended anyway. To save *me*." His bottom lip trembled.

Yates's might have done too. "You're a blessed lad to have such a friend. Such a cousin. That said." He stood to his full height, rather *hoping* he looked intimidating now, and held out a hand. "Let's go foil that plan, shall we?"

Marigold whooshed out a breath. "We can try. But I think we'll stand a better chance if we recruit some help."

TWENTY-SIX

*G*emma, once more decked out in her costume, knew all their careful planning had been neatly sidestepped when they arrived at the place in the fencing Graham had slipped through the day before and found it hammered back into place. No easy way to slip in and out without being observed. A horse's low whinny from within the locked compound only weighted the dread even more.

They had assumed that by arriving so many hours early, they would have ample time to get in position and hide themselves before Astley arrived. But clearly he'd had the same idea.

"Blast," Graham muttered at her side.

Funny. Sharing this particular burden didn't lessen it at all.

Behind them, Wilfred pivoted. "Well then. The front gate it is. Richardson—the keys."

The head of Lord Wilfred's guards produced a ring of them with a jangle, and the group of eight—Wilfred, the Harts, and five guards—all moved back toward the front of the grounds.

"I don't like it," Gemma murmured, even though it was as obvious a statement as "the snow is cold." She didn't turn to follow Wilfred and the others, not yet.

Graham sighed, his gloved fingers finding hers. "I knew we should have set up camp here last night."

At the time, getting a few hours of rest first in their nice, warm hotel rooms had seemed wise. Especially since Astley hadn't shown up to the first rendezvous early.

She didn't like the implications. "If he's variating from his behavior in this . . . ?"

Graham's fingers squeezed hers. "Father God." It took her a moment to realize he was praying. He'd rarely done so out loud, even before his yearlong argument with God. "Go before us. Prepare a way for us. Help us to bring these boys safely back to their parents. Amen."

"Amen."

Another jangle and a clank had them both turning, the groan of long-unused hinges their serenade as they hurried back around the corner.

There certainly wasn't any sneaking up on the place now, but the moment they slipped onto the property behind the knot of guards, Graham pulled her off to the side. "Let them gain the attention of Astley and any guards he brought. We'll still try for stealth."

She nodded, content to scurry along the shadows of the fence while Wilfred's men strode toward each set of the factory doors, keys in hand.

Graham, she knew, had the one key he wanted—the one for the basement door. It was located at the back of the factory, deep in the shadows of one of its warehouses. By the time they reached it and padded down the snow-crusted concrete steps—the snow was still pristine, which was encouraging—the sounds of other doors opening and closing echoed throughout the building, along with the brick-muffled call of Lord Wilfred.

"Astley? I've come. Where's my son?"

They both paused, Graham's hand on the door. Waiting.

No voice echoed back from within. Gemma knew that according to Graham's theory, Astley wouldn't present himself until Wilfred was exactly where he wanted him, in the foreman's office. To her mind, it remained a question of whether he would panic when he realized so many other people had come too. Her husband's intuition seemed to be proven right thus far though, or at least not proven wrong.

Her husband. Strange how the phrase she'd worked to obliterate from her thoughts in the last year could feel so much like home when she thought it again now. Strange how even this horrible situation, with danger and the threat of violence, could be underscored by peace.

Her husband was back in the arms of God—and she was back in the arms of her husband. If the worst happened and everything went wrong and they ended up in the path of a madman's bullets tonight, she could find solace in knowing that they'd made their peace.

Even so, she sent a silent prayer for protection heavenward as Graham unlocked the door. There had been tragedy enough. She prayed God's will was for life. Reconciliation. Joy.

The basement door creaked too, but there were enough noises from footsteps and Wilfred's continued shouting for Astley to show himself that she doubted anyone would have heard it. Gemma trailed Graham inside, glad to be out of the wintry breeze. She reached for the electric torch in her pocket.

Before she could even pull it out, lights blazed. Electric lights, all coming on at once in a flood from the main factory floor and spilling down through the broken beams and gaping hole into the basement as well.

Graham halted them both in the shadows near the wall. She could feel the tension in the arm he'd put around her, holding her back.

Full light hadn't been in the plan. Had Astley thrown them on?

No. Wilfred's voice rang out again. "There will be no hiding, Astley! Show yourself—now. Where is my son?" He must have either had the electricity turned back on, or it had never been fully off.

"Leopard stripes. That man won't follow any plan he didn't himself originate, will he?" Gemma breathed the words just loudly enough for Graham to hear.

His tightly pressed lips said he agreed. The lines that sprang to life around his eyes and mouth said he didn't much appreciate the deviation from their script, even granting the spanner Astley had already thrown in the works.

Although silence greeted Wilfred's demand. Maybe . . . was it possible that Astley wasn't here yet after all? Perhaps he'd wanted to force them through the front for some reason but had made the preparations yesterday. It could still be that they'd arrived first.

That hope was dashed as Graham led her carefully toward the edge of the destruction. Dashed not by Astley's voice, but by one far younger. Coming, it seemed, from the heart of the broken machinery, and sounding more defiant than scared.

"I'm in here! But he's here too, be—"

The lad's voice—Horace? Sidney?—cut off as quickly as it had pierced the night.

"Horace?" Wilfred, panic-laced rage in his tone.

"Sidney!" The Harts, together, with relief and desperation.

Sidney, then, she would guess. They seemed the more likely ones to recognize their son's voice. Though that made precious little sense. Why would Astley have brought Sidney? He must have them both up there and had simply removed a gag from the mouth of one at random.

"I have proven him alive." Astley's voice also came from

the mountain of twisted metal. Though even as Gemma watched, his figure, dark as the iron, emerged from the grotesque sculpture and leapt onto the jagged teeth of the broken floorboards, facing where the parents' voices had come from. The foreman's office, presumably.

Graham touched her arm to get her attention and motioned toward the base of the machinery, where it had dug into the earth and come to a crooked rest. She nodded.

They moved forward silently, gazes leaping along the cogs and levers and grooves, looking for a likely way up to where the boys were. Wherever that might be. Gemma knew neither she nor Graham were the wall-scalers the Fairfax siblings were, but they'd both climbed their share of ladders and ropes and poles as children too. She nodded that she'd found a likely way up even as Graham gave a silent signal of his own.

While she put the first hand on icy metal, the players a level up didn't exactly fall silent.

"I brought what I could scratch together on such short notice." Lord Wilfred let his bag full of cash fall to the floor with a thud. Astley wouldn't miss the contempt in his voice, though. It rang through the factory as loud as the looms must have done.

"Good." Astley's voice had a dark sort of pleasure. "Whatever amount it is, it will help the families of your victims. Too many of them have all but been reduced to begging after losing parents and income."

"*Victims?*" Wilfred spat out. "It was an *accident*, Astley. A tragic one, yes, but to imply that I purposefully—"

"You *knew*! The proof is right there in the foreman's office. You knew the structure couldn't support the new machines, but you had them installed anyway! I saw it—I saw the note from your company on the architect's advice and proposal when I came in here on the anniversary of the accident two months ago. You *knew*!"

"I had *one* architect recommend a refit, and two others assuring me it would be fine! I had contracts I would lose and two hundred people who would be out of work for months. In retrospect, yes, I should have chosen differently. But I could not have known that at the time."

Even through her gloves, the metal was so cold it bit, but Gemma gripped one length whose purpose she couldn't have defined and used it to hoist herself up until her feet rested on another unidentifiable protrusion.

"Does that excuse help you sleep at night? When dozens of families are still mourning the loss of their mothers? Their fathers? Their *children?*"

Wilfred hissed out a breath. "Curses, man, who are you to judge me so harshly? I realize many of them were your tenants, but if you feel so sorry for their lost income, *you* can—"

"You killed my daughter!"

The words echoed through the building, shivering down the metal and straight into Gemma's fingers. The pain in them traveled up her nerves and straight to her heart.

"You don't have a daughter."

"Not anymore, thanks to *you*. But I did. Agatha Thomas. It was only her seventh day working, taking her mother's place when Hannah—"

"Your mistress? And her illegitimate brat? Is *that* what this is about?"

"Don't call her that." Astley's voice was now a low thrum, threatening for its very lack of volume.

Gemma squeezed through an opening that would provide her some cover as she climbed when Graham did the same thing on the opposite side. She glanced up, able to see boy-sized shoes above her.

"And tell your men to stay back or I shoot the boy here and now."

"No!" The twin shouts were again from the Harts.

Gemma paused. Had he seen her? Graham? But no, Wilfred barked out, "Richardson, Stanley—fall back. Now."

"Care enough for that, do you? I was beginning to wonder. Beginning to doubt you had any paternal instinct in that miserly heart of yours. Any shred of human sympathy, much less decency."

Gemma exchanged a glance with Graham and moved another few inches upward. Through some of the slats, she could see the back of Astley's legs and shoes. Good. That meant he was facing the offices and Wilfred and wouldn't be keeping so close an eye on the machines that their movements within them would catch his attention.

"Don't pretend to know me," Wilfred snapped in reply. "Nor presume to judge *my* affections. *I* am not the one who refused to marry the woman I loved because she wasn't from the right family. *I* didn't consign my child to living with that stain because I was too weak-willed to restrain my passions otherwise."

Gemma barely kept her own breath from hissing out. What was Wilfred *doing*? Was he *trying* to provoke Astley into shooting?

"You've scarcely even looked your son in the eyes since his mother died!"

"And *you*—"

"Stop it! Both of you, *please*." Mrs. Hart's voice ripped through the tension, tears at once clogging it and yet making it that much more resounding. "Lord Astley, whatever your complaint with my brother-in-law, you must grant that it isn't the fault of the boys. Please, return them to us. I beg of you. Don't harm them."

A thump of silence, then another to match the beating of Gemma's heart as she raised herself up another little bit. She could angle herself to see up the shaft on which Sidney was standing, and just enough light wove its way through the bits and pieces that she could make out the ropes tying his hands together and the gag in his mouth.

Lionfeathers. They'd have to undo those if they meant to have the boy help in his own escape—and since neither of them were Yates, able to carry and climb at once, that would be necessary. She hoped Graham had his pen-knife on him.

"Sidney's mother, I presume? Madam, I assure you, your son is safe at my home. I haven't harmed a hair on his head and have taken the greatest care to see to his comfort. Causing him distress was never my aim."

"My lord, you're mistaken. My son is behind you, he—"

"Nonsense. It's Horace with me now, and I haven't harmed him either. Nor do I intend to if his father will simply admit to his sins."

"*My* sins?" Wilfred suddenly sounded as though he was more likely to tell his men to open fire on the man, never mind the danger to his son or anyone else. "*You* are the one with the mistress and illegitimate child. *You* are the one who kidnapped both my son and his cousin. *You* are the one who tried to extort my entire fortune from me—"

"Because money is the only language you speak! Tell me, Wilfred, what would you have done had I simply shown up and demanded an apology?" A beat of silence, swollen with dread. "I'll tell you. I'll tell you exactly what *did* happen. When I sent a letter to your solicitor, he told me that you denied all responsibility, that it was an 'act of God.' That if I intended to bring a suit, it would be long and drawn out and costly because you had no intention of offering any settlement." A harsh, brittle laugh. "It was an act of *you*. That's what it was, and everyone in Derbyshire knows it. *Your* hubris. *Your* greed. *Your* ambition. You never care who else gets hurt so long as *you* turn a profit."

Graham had climbed high enough that he was able to wave a hand and get Sidney's attention, so that he didn't scream or make some other noise to give them away as they climbed up beside him. Gemma maneuvered herself into place on one side of him, holding him steady while Graham sawed at the ropes. She gently moved the gag down, though she pressed a finger to her lips. He nodded, his eyes wide.

Astley still lobbed his verbal accusations. "You proved my point, didn't you, when you refused to intervene on Christmas Eve? At first I thought you a true monster, refusing to rescue your own son. But no, I had the wrong boy. Your own flesh and blood gets a nod, but not your nephew. Your *nephew*, you lout!"

"What do you want, Astley?" Finally, a bit of anxiety snuck through Wilfred's anger. "Money? It's here. An apology? Fine. I'm sorry the accident stole your daughter."

"Not enough! *You. You* admit to the guilt! It isn't enough to be sorry for it, you need to beg *forgiveness* for it. You need to open your eyes and actually *look* at what you've done! Do you see this?"

Oh no. He was turning to wave at the mangled mess of metal, and given that he knew exactly where Sidney was, it would be easy for him to check on his captive. To spot her and Graham. *Lord, shield us!*

"Of course I see it, as I did the day after it happened." Did Wilfred speak so quickly to regain Astley's attention? "Do you think I was untouched by it? For months, my managers were parrying journalists and barristers and architects, and it was all my people could do to keep my name from being dragged—"

A dry laugh from Astley cut him off, but at least the man had spun to face him again. "Even now," he said, his voice sounding . . . sad. "Even now it is only about *you*. About the cost to *you*. Why did you not so much as send your condolences to the families, Wilfred? Why did you not attend the funerals? Why did you not see they were provided for, at least for a week or a month? Why did you not offer the displaced survivors positions in the new factory you built outside Sheffield instead of abandoning them as you did this property? You only see pound signs when you look at this, not the lives torn apart. *That* is the cost of this accident."

Graham had the ropes cut and had begun backing down, motioning for Sidney to follow. Gemma crouched in place, waiting to see if she should go down the same way in case she could be of help or backtrack on her own path.

She peered out again and caught Wilfred's eye. He was looking right at where they'd been and must have seen that Sidney—Horace, in his mind—had moved down with Graham. Something shifted in his face, and not in a way that brought Gemma any relief.

He went harder. "What I see is a pathetic excuse for a man who ruined his own life and now seeks to cast all the blame on another. What did you intend here, Astley? To make me watch while you killed my son because you blame me for the death of your daughter?"

"No." Astley sounded genuinely disturbed at the suggestion. "I only want you to face it. To consider, for once, a life and fortune other than your own."

"Oh, I have. I've considered what I'm going to do to *you* once my son is safe." Hard. Cold. Cruel. "I'm going to tear to pieces everything that matters to you. Rip your legacy apart bit by bit. You'll be a pariah in society. No one will speak to you, no one will listen to a word you say. You'll—what's so amusing?"

Gemma hadn't even realized that the rasping sound that made her hold tight to her perch instead of climbing back down was a laugh. Much like the moan to follow barely seemed a voice. "You already *have*. Don't you see? You've already taken everything that matters. There's nothing left. Nothing."

From the little window between the metal, Gemma saw

him lift his hand, saw the electric lights glint off the polished metal barrel of his gun. Saw him lift it.

Her heart caught in her throat. If he spun, pointed it at where Sidney had been, *she* would be the one in its path—a thought that flashed through her mind in half a second, leaving another half for her to pray a lifetime of prayers.

If I die, Lord, protect Graham's heart. Hold him close. Help him see this isn't your fault, that you still love him. Tell him we'll be together again in a blink of the eye in Paradise, with Jamie. Tell him every minute I had with him was joy and that I'm sorry for the ones I missed.

Then she saw the dark shadow of satisfaction settle on Wilfred's face, even before her gaze refocused on Astley.

He wasn't turning. Wasn't aiming at her location, nor at any of the guards, nor at Wilfred. He'd raised the gun to his own head.

"No!" Gemma screamed from within the dormant monster that had stolen his daughter. She surged up another few pieces, emerging into lamplight. "My lord, don't!"

Wilfred looked as though he was about to call his guards down on *her*, but she hadn't the attention to spare him. Hers was all on the man so filled with despair that death seemed preferable to life.

He spun, confusion warring with that empty determination but not enticing him to lower the gun.

In a breath, he saw part of the picture—his hostage, gone. Her in his place. He narrowed his eyes, clearly trying to place her, but then seemed to give up. What did it matter, after all? She wasn't important, not to him. Not to his decision.

Her hand fell to her pocket, brushing over the comfort of notepad and pencil, wishing it had some happily-ever-after to give to him, some words that could make it better, some clue to help him make sense of these senseless tragedies that befell them all.

Maybe it did. She drew it out.

"Why not?" Hollow. Colorless. More pain than voice. "There's nothing left. Even revenge is empty. No one will care; no one will mourn me."

"*Everyone* will mourn you. Everyone in Matlock, in the villages. They love you." She lifted the innocent little pages, thumbed to the last one when those words pinged off him like sleet. "Hannah will mourn you."

His face twisted. "She won't. She hates me. If I'd protected our daughter, provided for her instead of making that stupid threat—"

"She knows why you did it. She told me so herself. Listen." She read Hannah's own words back to him, word for word. Marigold had memorized the entire exchange, like she always did, and Gemma had scribbled the whole conversation down as soon as they left, in shorthand. Like she always did, for their files.

And perhaps, maybe, if God poured out his mercy on this man and his heart was soft enough to receive it, for some better purpose this time. *Agatha adored him. . . . He was the best father any child could have. . . . He tried to take care of us. . . .*

Astley's eyes slid shut, but he seemed to be pressing the gun even harder to his temple. "I failed them. Both of them. I couldn't even face her at the funeral, knowing what she must think of me. Knowing how I hurt her."

"She loves you." Maybe she shouldn't proclaim it for another woman. But it was true. She knew it, even after having only talked to Hannah Thomas once. "She said so. She said one of the things she always loved best about you was that you would sooner *be* hurt than to hurt another. But don't you see? You'll be hurting *her* if you pull that trigger."

His closed eyes squeezed tight, his face twisted with the tears that eked out. "No. I'll be freeing her. Helping her. I've left enough for her in my will to see that she never wants again, and she won't refuse it if I'm gone. If it doesn't mean more sin, falling back into that."

"It was never your money, Franklin!" The new voice came from the door still standing open, where Hannah Thomas stood looking as though she'd barely paused to put on a coat after being roused from bed. "It was *you*. You know that. You *know* I would rather a lifetime of poverty than knowing I benefited because you hurt yourself. Please."

Motion caught her eye, and Gemma lifted a hand, sending a glare at the guards that were creeping closer.

Astley was shaking. "I failed you. I failed our sweet Agatha. She's dead because I didn't provide, because I tried to force you to stay when you knew it was wrong, because—"

"My love." Hannah hurried around the gaping boards, her arms outstretched. Only when they'd closed around him did she say, "She's dead because a terrible accident happened. That's all. There is no point in casting blame. It won't bring her back."

A cry ripping from his throat, he folded himself around Hannah.

She held him tight. "I would trade my life for hers in a moment if I could. And I know you would too—but we can't. We can only go on. We can live, and we can remember her, and we can honor the bright, loving child she was. You know how she loved you. If she thought you were going to harm yourself for her sake . . ."

Gemma recognized the convulsions that overtook him—the same sobbing that had racked her as the bells tolled and the snow fell. The kind that broke a grieving heart into pieces.

Graham had been there in her broken moment; Hannah was here now for his. Gemma easily jumped across to the floor and gently took the gun from his fingers. He gave it up without a fuss.

She checked the barrel of the revolver. One round. He'd never intended to ward off any guards, nor to harm anyone else. Only himself. She slid the bullet out and tucked the weapon into the waistband of her black trousers.

Stopping him, though, wouldn't set his world to rights. Reconciling with Hannah Thomas wouldn't either. The fierce look on Wilfred's face said he intended to have every legal book in England thrown at him, and quite possibly a few more creative ones besides.

Justice . . . but not mercy. Not forgiveness. And that made her heart ache. Astley had committed a crime. Two boys would have to work through the mental anguish he'd caused for years to come, and yet she was still left feeling as though Wilfred was the villain. The only one who hadn't learned a lesson.

Maybe he had. Maybe the scare of losing his son had affected him more than it appeared. Certainly he was looking around now, those rapacious eyes searching.

Graham and the boy came running up the basement steps, the younger calling, "Papa!"

Both Wilfred and Matthew Hart turned, both faces lighting up.

Then Mrs. Hart pushed past them both, and the boy cried, "Mama!" and all but flew into her arms. She caught him up, and Mr. Hart folded them both into his embrace, laughing and weeping from joy.

Lord Wilfred froze. Uncertainty flickered in his eyes, over his face. And for the first time since they entered the building, his shoulders sagged. Only because Gemma was standing so close could she hear his broken whisper.

"He was right. I didn't . . . I didn't even know my own son." The realization must have struck him like a fist. It left his eyes dazed and unfocused, his breath a wheezing exhale, and he sank down right there in the office doorway until he came to an undignified seat on the floor.

She glanced toward the exterior door again, somehow not surprised to see that Marigold was lounging there. She must have been the one to wake Hannah Thomas and bring her here. She must have known, assuming they'd rescued Horace and realized Astley had Sidney here, that it would take something more than logic or cunning to steer the lord away from his goal.

It would take the forgiveness of the only one left on earth who he loved.

A faint, "All clear?" came from outside in Yates's familiar tones, his Cockney in place. Marigold leaned back out the door and called back that it was safe.

And then more steps, and more familiar forms. A costumed Sir Merritt and Yates, who had another child, nearly identical to the one embracing the Harts, by the hand. He let the lad go, and Horace blinked against the lights for a moment.

He spotted his father, and she saw the joy that sprang up—and quickly shuttered. She saw the careful armor that replaced it. He was bracing himself for a far different reunion than the one his cousin had received.

And it broke her heart. Were it her story to write, she'd pen an ending full of repentance and vows to do better, of another weeping reunion and all charges dropped and a long-awaited marriage proposal from Astley to Ms. Thomas.

She slid her notepad back into her pocket. This wasn't her story. But she put it into the hands of the Author of Life and, with a small smile for Graham, moved over to Lord Wilfred. "My lord."

He didn't even look up.

She crouched down beside him and touched a hand to his shoulder. That got his attention, so she simply pointed toward the door. Toward his son, who stood there, waiting. Not knowing whether his father cared that he was alive and well.

"Horace!" Wilfred pushed back to his feet, face at once brightening and yet touched with a sorrow not so easily dispelled. He lunged forward, staggered around the Harts, his gaze on the boy.

On the boy. Not on where his feet landed.

He stepped too close to the jagged edge, a dreadful crack of splintering wood filled the air, and Gemma swore time slowed to a drift like crystals of snow. Each moment frozen, twirling, falling.

She saw the wood give.

She saw Wilfred lose his balance, his arms wheeling in an attempt to find something, some purchase.

She saw the guards, Yates, Graham, everyone lurch into motion.

She saw the distance between them all and knew they'd be too far away.

She saw Wilfred's body tilt, sway, gravity taking hold.

And then, when she was certain the silent prayer she screamed would be answered in one more tragedy, she saw another lurch. Another arm reaching out. This one close enough to grab hold of Wilfred's flailing hand.

Astley not only caught on; he had the presence of mind to lean backward, away from the hole, and pull Wilfred down with him. Back to safety.

"Papa!" Horace finally moved—on stable ground—running to his father. Wilfred pushed to his knees.

Arms open. Eyes closed. Relief too deep for a smile on his face as his son fell into his embrace.

Graham helped Gemma to her feet, and she slid her arms around his waist as Wilfred murmured something about fresh starts and second chances. But she came to attention again when the lord looked up, over his son's head, toward his neighbor. "You," he croaked, voice hoarse. "You could have let me fall."

Astley had stood again, but he made no move to leave. "No, I couldn't. I never wished you harm, Wilfred. I just . . . I just wanted you to *see*."

As Wilfred's eyes slid shut, Gemma had a feeling he finally did.

"I'll submit myself to the authorities," Astley added softly.

Wilfred shook his head. "No one needs the circus that would bring down on us. We'll sort it out between us."

Gemma didn't know what that would entail. And didn't think about it overlong.

Yates had pasted a look of exaggerated offense on his still-disguised face and said, "I beg your pardon. What's so terrible about a circus?"

Only the Imposters got the joke, but their quintet of laughter was enough to bring the others into the chorus too.

TWENTY-SEVEN

2 January 1910
London

The wind-bells spun in the breeze, dancing and singing all at once. Graham watched them, smiling at the memory of little hands trying to reach for them, at the laughter that far eclipsed the chimes in sweetness. He glanced down at Gemma, who made no attempt to move onward. Not yet.

She watched the dance. But he knew she, too, was hearing a different music. It brought tears glistening to her eyes, but they didn't fall. Not yet.

They would. But that was good. She would need to cry over each memory as she took it in her hands. It wouldn't make it easier, really . . . but it would be necessary nonetheless. A part of accepting. A part of living life now without Jamie. A part of taking hold of what remained.

He kept his arm around her, not rushing her inside despite the bite of the wind. When she moved toward the door, though, he kept pace. Beside her, not pushing her. That was going to have to be the byword for this whole homecoming, he knew. And he could only hope he didn't look as frightened of making a mess of it as Lord Wilfred had when he promised his son things would be different from then on, that he'd be a better father.

At least it had only taken *near* tragedy to wake him up. He'd praise God for that.

He unlocked the door, smiling when heat wafted out to greet them, along with the scents of dinner. He'd wired her brother and aunt when they were leaving Northumberland after the New Year celebration they'd shared with his family, asking if perhaps they could see that the house was prepared for the return of its mistress. He half-expected James and Priss to be here to greet them, honestly . . . but they must have forced a bit of restraint. Tomorrow, though, they'd no doubt descend upon them. They would be welcome.

She stepped inside without hesitation but not exactly quickly. The way she looked around the entryway reminded him of how she'd done so the very first time they entered, before they were married, when they were picking out where they'd live. Where they'd raise their family. Whether this place could be home.

Now, like then, appreciation lit her eyes, and something more. Recognition. She unwound the scarf from her neck and dropped it onto the coat-tree as Graham set his hat on its usual hook. He helped her with her coat—habit and pleasure both—and hung it up with his own.

A year's absence wasn't enough that she'd have forgotten anything, not really. But she moved from room to room, running her hand along the chair rail and her favorite pieces of furniture, smoothing out the blanket that draped her chair, the lace doily under the lamp.

He could tell each time she spotted something that reminded her of Jamie when her breath caught. A few tears fell. But she was smiling too.

They were good memories. Even if there should have been

more of them, the ones they had were good. Sweet. Worth remembering.

She meandered into the kitchen long enough to lift the lid of the pot on the stove and smile at whatever her aunt had made for them. The lid went back down in the next moment, though, and she spun to take in the row of teacups and their matching pot. The pattern she'd chosen. The pieces she'd wanted.

Why did she purse her lips? Was something amiss?

"What do you think of a tea set as a wedding gift?" she asked before he could do more than send a furtive glance around the room in search of out-of-place china. "For Lord Astley and Ms. Thomas?"

He puffed out his breath. "I think Derwent Hall probably has half a dozen sets or more already."

"That doesn't mean she won't want one that's *theirs*. Without the associations of his family that didn't approve or the years she regrets. Something for their new house."

He still found it a bit amusing that their answer to those regrets had been to build a new house on the edge of Derwent Hall's land—where they'd found the duck, Agatha's favorite spot. But who was he to argue? Yates, still dressed as Mr. C, had passed them one of Graham's cards and told them they wouldn't do better for an architect. According to the telegram from his firm two days ago, an inquiry had already come in, Lord Astley claiming to have met him over the holidays at Weywent. He'd heard, he'd gone on to say, that no one was better at matching existing historical architecture, which was what they wanted.

Good thing the lord had been too teary-eyed over Wilfred's offer of—and request for—forgiveness to get a good look at Graham's face under his wig at the factory. The Imposters had all happily melted into the shadows after the children had been restored to their parents, and he was glad. He didn't really fancy explaining why the architect Astley had met in Weymouth had been helping search for the kidnapped boys.

As for a tea set, Graham grinned. "Perhaps she would. I'll leave that to you, darling. You've always had impeccable taste in such things."

Her smile was warm despite her glassy eyes. "Which is to say, you don't much care what we send so long as I sign your name as well."

"Which is to say, wait to see if I land the contract before you decide on a whole tea *set*. If I don't, perhaps a spoon or two."

She chuckled and started moving again. "You'll secure it. Though you had better get the library project finished up first."

"Mm." They'd covered all those basic updates on life during their stay in Northumberland and on the train ride home, sitting up long into the night over mugs of tea and crackling fires on New Year's Eve while his cousins attended the Children's Ball in York. His work, hers. The demands of their superiors, the jokes of their colleagues. All the things they'd missed. They'd talked and laughed and spent enough time kissing that he'd felt like an eighteen-year-old all over again, yearning for what he couldn't have quite yet.

He wasn't going to push her. He *wasn't*, despite the fire that heated his blood every time he touched her. The one thing they hadn't talked about yet was whether *home* meant their shared room or a guest room for one or another of them for a while. He didn't know how to bring it up now either.

So, she could take the lead. He'd walk beside her. Not pushing.

Walk again she did, through the rest of the main floor and then, after a deep breath, up the stairs. Toward the nursery and the bedrooms. Toward the rocking chair where she'd put their son to sleep every night, the toys still in their baskets, that lingering scent of talcum powder and lavender.

Graham leaned his shoulder into the doorframe as she moved from item to item. Touching, lifting, smelling. Crying. He was too, and he made no objection when she came and slid her arms around his waist and buried her face in his chest and sobbed. He sobbed with her.

It wasn't the same, their mourning. The grief of a mother and the grief of a father—they weren't the same. But sharing them made them a little bit easier to bear. He held her tight long after the tears dried, pressing his lips to the top of her head and resting his chin there.

"I don't want to forget," she finally whispered against him. "I think that's my biggest fear. That we'll have other children, and they'll fill this room, and new memories will push out the old ones. We'll start to forget there was a Jamie before there were the others. I don't want those new memories to be a betrayal of the old ones. I don't want to not *make* the new memories for fear of it. I want . . . I want to be both. His mother *and* the mother of whatever other children God may give us."

His heart cinched tight. It was a fear he understood all the way down to his bones. He was Jamie's father. That would never—*could* never—change. Jamie would always be his firstborn son. "We'll tell them stories. Celebrate his birthday in some quiet way. We'll make certain they know, and yet make certain they don't resent him. We'll never let them think they're any less loved."

She nodded, tilting her face toward his. "We will. Somehow."

They didn't need to know how yet. Intention was enough. God would have to help them through the details.

Sniffing back his tears, Graham let go of her so he could reach to the silver chain fastened around his neck. He unclasped it, took it off, and smiled at Gemma's look of confusion. He would put the cross back on it—one sign of faith. But first, he slipped off the other one and held it up.

Her lips trembled their way into a smile. "You kept my ring."

He breathed a laugh. "Of course I did." His brows lifted. "But I don't want to keep it anymore. I want it back where it belongs."

"I want that too." In proof, she lifted her hand. But in even greater proof, she didn't take her gaze from his. "I love you, Graham. For better or worse."

"In good times and in bad. Forever and a day." He slipped the circle of gold back onto her left ring finger and kissed it into place.

Gemma curled her fingers into her palm, as if locking it there. Stretching onto her toes, she pressed a kiss to his lips, at once fierce and sweet. Then she wiped at her face, tried to blow a stray lock of golden hair from her eyes, and finally stepped away. "I'm going to tidy up a bit."

"All right." He could probably use a tidying too. For now, though, he contented himself with leaning against the banister. Looking across the familiar rooms on the first floor, down to the familiar landing on the ground floor. His house—home again with her in it. That was all he needed today. Gemma, his Gemma. Home.

Minutes later, the lavatory door squeaked open, and he heard her steps moving toward their room. Graham's throat went tight. Given the way she hummed that particular hum that always accompanied her toeing off her shoes, he didn't have to wonder where *she* meant to sleep tonight. Just where she wanted *him* to, then.

"Darling?"

He turned to face her, his feet even drawing him a few steps closer to her. Couldn't help it. Though her eyes were

A Noble Scheme

still puffy and her hair had escaped its pins and her dress was webbed with travel wrinkles, it didn't change the simple fact.

She was still the most beautiful woman in the world.

With a crook of her finger, she drew him nearer still, until her arms were looped around his neck and her lips were pressed to his. He kissed her, his shirt still wet from her tears and his cheeks sticky from his own, and he knew with every pounding heartbeat that God had brought them back to where they needed to be: together. He could wish that it hadn't taken two kidnapped children and quite a few Imposter schemes to get here, but it didn't matter now. They were home.

He made himself pull away when he wanted to walk her backward instead, made himself cup her cheeks instead of reaching for her buttons. He met her gaze. "I don't want to rush you, love. Two weeks ago, you weren't even speaking to me. This is enough for now. I need you to know that."

Gemma gave him that challenging grin she'd been using on him since they were kids to get her own way. "Darling," she said, pulling his mouth down to hers again. "Do shut up."

Read on

FOR A SNEAK PEEK AT

An

HONORABLE
DECEPTION

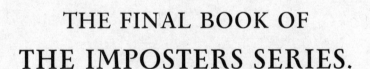

THE FINAL BOOK OF
THE IMPOSTERS SERIES.

AVAILABLE NOVEMBER 2024.

ONE

15 August 1910
Fairfax House
London, England

Yates let the barbell clang back into its brackets and sat up, his eyes searching for the utilitarian clock on the wall. Sweat dripped from his brow, forcing him to wipe it off before he could make sense of the time. Three in the afternoon. He had just enough time to bathe and dress before he had to get to James's church on the other side of the city for his appointment with a potential client. If he didn't roast to death in the meantime.

He moved to the open window, but the breeze that trickled through did little to cool him. London was often miserable in the summer, but today it was doing a fair imitation of the pits of the netherworld. And it would only get worse once his sister and her husband left for Northumberland tomorrow.

It was absolutely not fair that they got to escape the city while he was stuck here, sitting in Sessions and voting on bills he scarcely cared about and working on Imposters business while they had their holiday at home at Fairfax Tower.

Positively unfair. They'd already made him suffer two

months of solitude after the wedding, before they agreed to move back to the London House and let Merritt's rented townhome go. It was just cruel to subject him to his own company again now.

Lionfeathers, but it was hot. He mopped his face off with a towel and charged from the room, ready to find Marigold wherever she was and let her know, yet again, what a horrible, horrible sister she was to abandon him like this and go back to the cool sea breezes and comforts of home without him. Wasn't it bad enough that she only kept him company in the gymnasium for half an hour a day lately, and then only to do the lightest and easiest of exercises?

He followed her voice to the drawing room, pausing when he caught tones that were neither hers, nor Clementina's, nor Gemma's. Did she actually have a guest? One who would be outraged if he barged in wearing only his leotard and pajama-style trousers he wore when taking his exercise?

He listened a moment more and then relaxed. It was only Lavinia. She may be as much a lady as his own sister, being the daughter of Earl Hemming as she was, but she was also their closest neighbor in Northumberland and had seen him in every possible mode of dress over the years. He barreled through the door, perhaps with a bit more gusto than it really demanded.

"Cruel creature," he pronounced upon entering, scowling at his sister.

She sat on the couch, her hair still done up in an elaborate braided coiffure, one of her magnificently ridiculous hats on the cushion beside her, and her dress looking straight from the highest of haute couture boutiques in Paris, despite having actually come from their own attic. She was setting tongues ablaze, he knew, daring to wear fashionable ensembles when she was in a delicate condition as she was.

Three more months, by the doctor's estimation, before she

presented him with his first niece or nephew. He alternated between unbridled joy and unfettered panic at the thought.

Everything was going to change. Everything already had. No trapeze acts just now, no acrobatics that required two people in their investigations. What's worse, she looked so blasted *tired*, and her face was pale beneath her smile.

She quirked a brow at him. "Are you still pouting about staying in London?"

"Of course I am." It was his sworn duty as her pesky little brother, after all, to complain to her. "It's hot as blazes."

She chuckled. But even that sounded tired. "So come with us."

If only he could. Were it only the Sessions, he might well choose to duck out of them. There was nothing really urgent up for vote—not that his vote mattered on, anyway. But there was still a case that needed wrapping up, and the appointment later today could well result in another. And rarely did their cases allow for investigation in their own home county.

And the last one that did had been anything but pleasant. Which reminded him to send a smile to their guest. "Hello, Lavinia."

Only when he glanced at her did he realize that she'd been looking at *him* ever since he barged in, an amused look on her face. "Yates."

Lady Lavinia Hemming was, without question, beautiful. And he could admit—to his sister, anyway—that he'd been in love with her for a good portion of his life. But that was before he realized his father had left him without so much as a tuppence with which to run the estate, before they'd had to let all their servants go and—*gasp*—learn to cook their own food and take on work to make ends meet. He'd known as he sat in the solicitor's office beside Marigold and heard that there was nothing left of the Fairfax fortune that

Lavinia was never going to be his wife. Then she'd caught scarlet fever, had nearly died, and had been all but bedridden for years from the ensuing heart condition. He'd scarcely seen her for years.

And he'd had to focus on earning his family enough income to survive on.

Six years later, he'd learned to look at her without that punch to his gut. Which was good, since she'd been courted by no fewer than a half-dozen leading gentlemen since she finally came out last year, after her recovery. Most of them just this summer, when she returned to London after the horrible months of grief from losing her mother—first to betrayal, then to death.

She wasn't exactly glowing with the societal success, though. If anything, she looked as weary as Marigold, and without the handy excuse. He frowned. "You look like a stout wind could blow you over. Have you been sleeping?"

Lavinia rolled her green eyes. "Yes, Father."

"Eating?"

"*Yes.*"

"Exercising?"

At that, she let out a huff. "My physicians have cautioned me not to overexert myself. You know that."

"*Over*exert, yes. But a bit of exertion is necessary for regaining one's strength."

The glance she gave his arms wasn't exactly admiring. "I suppose you think yourself the expert, Mr. Strongman?"

His lips twitched upward. "That's *Lord* Strongman to you. And I'll have you know that after my devastating wound, which I took saving *your* life—"

"You did not!" It got her laughing, anyway. If they could laugh about it now, that surely meant her heart was recovering from the blow her mother had dealt it. "*I* saved *you!*"

He waved away that little detail. "While recuperating, I

definitely found it of the utmost importance to push myself a little more each day in order to truly recover."

Lavinia rolled her eyes again. "It was barely a scratch."

"I took a dagger to the leg! Eight stitches!" But he grinned and flopped down beside her on her sofa, leaning in and draping a sweaty arm around her just to watch her flinch away and wrinkle her nose. "Come on, my lady. Join me in the gymnasium. I'll have your heart as healthy as Leonidas's in a month."

"Tempting as that is . . ." Lavinia nodded toward Marigold. "I've come today to beg your sister to let me go home with her and keep her company at the Tower until Papa decides to return to Northumberland. I've found I've had my fill of Town."

It had tired her too quickly, she meant. The late nights, the rich foods, the stress of gossip—and there had been no shortage of that. The country air would restore her, though. As would his sister's company. Yates nodded, reclaimed his arm, and pushed back to his feet. "Good. Any gents you want me to look into while you're gone?"

She didn't know about their private investigation firm, The Imposters, Ltd. But she *did* know he was a friend and that he'd make sure anyone she was considering was deserving of her.

Lavinia shook her head. "No. They're all . . . no."

Leopard stripes. There was a world of meaning in that sigh she let out that he didn't have time to explore right now. But Marigold would take care of it. He moved toward the door. "Well, I know you two will cry over it, but I have an appointment to keep. Enjoy your trip north tomorrow. I am consumed with envy."

Their laughter followed as he vaulted up the stairs, and he made quick work of his ablutions so that he could slide down the banister and hurry out the door.

Hot, damp air swamped him the moment he stepped outside. The thermometer read ninety degrees, but the dratted uniform of the gentry—shirt, waistcoat, tie, jacket—made it feel about twice that. What he wouldn't give to be able to leave the house in his exercise garb.

Usually he'd walk to a Tube station farther from home just to stretch his legs, but today he opted for the Underground as quickly as possible, and he thanked the good Lord for the coolness of the cavernous cathedral when he stepped inside its back door twenty minutes later. Voices from James's office said he must be with a parishioner, which was a shame. Yates always enjoyed popping in and chatting with their former steward's son whenever he could. James didn't know *precisely* why he lent them the old confessional for their meetings. But he knew they focused on truth and justice, so he made it available whenever Yates needed it.

He slipped into the confessor's side of the booth, indulging in a long breath and the loosening of his necktie. He pulled a slender tome of poetry from his pocket, though he didn't open it yet. He closed his eyes. He breathed out a prayer. And he looked deep into himself.

Ever since he started meeting potential clients in this booth, he'd made a habit of examining his own conscience first. To make certain he was always working for good, that he didn't fall into judgment as he investigated truths that were often ugly. And to ensure that though every other foundation he ever took for granted shook, his faith didn't.

Today, he looked back over his life of the past week and had to purse his lips. Had his complaining moved from joking to truth? Probably. And Gemma hadn't taken it well when he jested about how she seemed bent on catching Marigold up with the size of her stomach, though her own pregnancy was a month behind. He ought to apologize for that. He'd fallen into worry again on Friday when he was reviewing their accounts, which he knew was a lack of trust in God's provision.

And they weren't doing *badly*. They just weren't doing as well as he'd hoped they'd be. Cases always slowed down as the weather cooled and society left London for their country homes, and he'd hoped to have a bit more of a cushion for the winter this year, what with his sister and Gemma both with child. What if they needed a doctor? Hospital? Medicine?

He gave that again to the Lord and said a prayer, while he was at it, for the health of both mothers and babies. For his sister, but then for Gemma, especially. She and Graham had already lost a child. If anything were to happen to this babe . . . it didn't bear thinking about.

Another few minutes of prayer, and then he cracked open his Tennyson and read until he heard the large front doors squeak open. He glanced at his watch. Must be the potential client, who had signed the note the urchins had delivered to him simply as *A. B.* Not exactly a lot to go on, that, but the hand had been feminine.

Not exactly *unusual*. But not the most common. The cards he placed at the Marlborough brought far more clients their way than the ones his sister and Gemma left at the ladies' clubs—a fact that he rubbed their noses in regularly, out of brotherly duty. And when women *did* hire them, all too often it was to investigate a spouse they suspected of infidelity. Not his favorite task, because far too often they proved exactly what the ladies feared.

He didn't know if he had another such investigation in him, when he wouldn't have Marigold on hand to joke with and help him keep his spirits up. But then, winter was coming, and he'd just as soon it not be too lean.

The steps were definitely feminine—but quick. He heard a few moments of hesitation as the woman searched the massive chamber for the confessional, but once she spotted it, her stride became as sure as it was fast. The door to the penitent's side opened, shut again, and someone sat on the bench, nothing but a vague silhouette through the screen.

"We are such stuff . . ." she said, as he'd instructed her to.

Yates smiled and pulled forward the accent he'd decided on today—a Scottish burr. " . . . as dreams are made of. Good day . . . miss?"

Her voice sounded young—not childish, but certainly not matronly. Were he to guess, he'd have put her somewhere in the general range of his own twenty-three years, give or take a few. But he'd found it always wisest to err on the side of youth when addressing women he didn't know. Give a *madam* to the wrong one, and you'd earn quite a scowl.

"Miss will suffice. Miss B."

His lips twitched. A cagey one, then. He could understand that, on the one hand. But if she really thought she could hire a PI without her own identity becoming known, she was in for a surprise. "All right, then. Mr. A. How can I help you today, Miss B?"

The woman drew in a deep breath and let it slowly out. "I would like to hire you to find someone."

He frowned. The last time they'd been hired to find someone, it had been a kidnapped boy, and it had turned challenging in a hurry. "Missing person?"

"Not . . . exactly. At least, I don't know that she is. Everyone says she isn't. Except she *is*."

"Uh-huh." That clarified things. Yates leaned back against the wall of the booth, imagining himself a Scottish laird of centuries gone by. "I'd love to say I ken what you mean, Miss B, but a bit more information wouldn't go awry, aye?"

Another sigh. "All right. It's my *ayah*, from when I was a girl."

Yates sat up again, his brows furrowing, even though his guest wouldn't see it. "You grew up in India?"

"I did, yes, until I was twelve. When we came back to England, my childhood ayah opted to travel with us, rather than my parents hiring a stranger for the task. She left us once we reached London, of course, but she hired on with another family returning to India. I believe at this point she's made the journey five or six times, roundtrip."

Not uncommon, he knew. Families coming from India were happy to hire cheap nannies to keep track of their children on the journey, but rarely were they interested in keeping such unfashionable help while they were in England. And if the women couldn't find a journey home, they were often left to fend for themselves in London. It had been enough of a problem a decade or two ago that charities had sprung up to house them and manage funding to send them to and from England.

This was the first he'd heard of a grown child wanting to find her ayah, though. "And . . . you wish to reconnect? After how many years?" He'd have to determine if the woman was even in England, or back in India, or somewhere on a steamer in between.

"It isn't like that." Her words came out in a snap, then she sucked in a breath. "Forgive me. My parents . . . wouldn't exactly encourage this search."

Unmarried, then, most likely, if she was worrying with her parents' opinion more than a husband's. He hadn't been willing to accept as much just by the "Miss B" bit. "No forgiveness necessary. But if you could answer the question?"

"We've kept in touch all along. Whenever she's back in London, I've managed to visit her. Only, this last time, when I went to the home, she wasn't there. Or so they said. Even though it's the one she said she'd be at. I've visited the others, too, and no one reports seeing her. It isn't exactly something I can take to the police, though, is it?"

"Mm. I see your point." Scotland Yard rarely wanted to

bother with transients from India, especially when all they'd have to go on was one young lady's concern. "Aye, then. What can you tell me about her?"

"She's thirty years old—"

"Only thirty?" He couldn't keep the surprise from his tone. Even if Miss B was only eighteen, that would have been six years since her first transit, which would have put the nanny in her early-to-mid-twenties when she worked for the B family. Unusual, indeed. Most ayahs were middle-aged or older.

"She is only eight years my elder. It was why we were so close." Defensiveness colored her tone, yes. And something more.

Fear. Genuine, heartbroken fear.

Noted. This wasn't idle curiosity. This was a young woman seeking one of her dearest friends. He nodded. "Go on."

"I went to the home on Mare Street, in Hackney, first. That's where she always went. But when I got there, they—"

The front doors creaked open again—but not just a creak. They banged against the wall, startling Yates off his bench. Doors that size didn't just swing about in a breeze. To hit the wall with such intensity, they'd have had to be thrown with considerable force.

Footsteps, at least three sets of them. Heavy. Running.

Lionfeathers. What was going on? He held his breath, knowing that no one ever really thought to look in the old, abandoned confessional if they were searching for someone. If hiding was necessary, this was the best place to do it.

Though James was just back the hall in his office, and a parishioner with him. Was *he* in danger? Yates sent a prayer heavenward.

Miss B apparently didn't work through his same logic. She drew in a startled breath, and he saw her lurch toward her door.

No! He didn't dare scream it, though he willed it at her

342

as loudly as he could and reached toward the screen separating them.

Too late. She was already out, already screaming, "You!"

Yates clenched his teeth, his hands, and tried to peer through the grate without giving himself away. He couldn't just burst out to see what was going on. He had no disguise on, and no one could know that Mr. A of the Imposters was in fact Lord Yates Fairfax, ninth Earl Fairfax. Anonymity was the key to their entire success.

Which mattered for exactly three more seconds. And then the unthinkable sounded.

Gunshots, there in James's church.

The next moments were a blur. He burst out, but only in time to see two men running for the doors again. He made note of their relative heights, their clothing, the color of hair he could just make out under their hats, but he didn't run after them—not given the moan from the floor.

He fell to his knees beside the young woman. Her eyes were shut, blood staining her clothes in three places. He checked for her pulse, found it present, and took stock of the wounds as he distantly noted more footsteps coming from the direction of the office.

One in her shoulder—through and through. One in her side—he prayed it had missed any vital organs. One in her leg. Whoever those men had been, they either had lousy aim or hadn't meant to kill her, only to wound her.

"Yates!"

"Blast it, James." His friend knew better than to call him by name in the presence of a client. But then, he was under duress, understandably. And Yates was out here in the open, face undisguised, so what did it matter? Besides, the girl was unconscious. He'd need to examine her head, see if she'd struck it on the stone of the floor as she fell. "I'm fine. It's the girl."

He looked down at her again, and recognition hit him—twice. First, the recognition that she was beautiful—beyond beautiful. And second, that it was a thought he'd had about her before—when he'd seen her in the society columns, next to photographs of his sister.

She wasn't *Miss* anything. She was Lady Alethia Barremore, daughter of the previous viceroy of India.

And if she opened her eyes, she'd know his deepest secret.

AUTHOR'S NOTE

I didn't know when I first proposed this story that it would be one about parents' grief. I didn't know when I first wrote Marigold and Sir Merritt's story in *A Beautiful Disguise* that the rift between two of the Imposters was so deep, over something so serious. I didn't know until I was taking a walk on the beach with my husband a few weeks after turning book one in, brainstorming what this book could be about, and I caught a glimpse of the ragged, bone-deep story behind Gemma's biting tongue and Graham's anger with God.

I think, in part, their story turned into what it is because in the months leading up to its writing, I worked on a book called *Grief Exposed: Giving a Voice to the Unspeakable* by Mike Sollom and, through the process, I gained a friend who feels like family, even though we've yet to meet in person. He and his wife, LuAnn, lost a son to cancer in 2004. That son was my age.

As I read the words that Mike had journaled through ten years of grieving, and as we turned them into a book meant to tell other grieving parents that grief doesn't have to be excused or ignored or glossed over, that their feelings are *allowed* and can be as ugly as they need to be, I began to understand how deep a parent's love really is.

And I was so, so struck by one of his observations: that while he and LuAnn grieved together, their grief was *not* the same. It couldn't be. Grief is both the most universal human experience and the most insular. It is individual. It *must* be individual. That's both what makes it so hard and what makes it so universal.

For the sake of fitting everything into one story, I did compress the likely timeline of grief and reconciliation. What took Graham and Gemma a year is far more likely to take several. I made every effort to respect the pain and process, even as I shortened how long a process that can really be.

On a lighter note, Gemma and Graham were actually the story that inspired this whole series. It's the only book I've written thus far that was inspired by a dream. I woke up one morning with a vague recollection of the story that had played out in my mind: Edwardian in setting, aristocratic in leaning, but about private investigators who called themselves The Imposters. The twist, I knew even then, was that they were already married, although I knew there were siblings in there somewhere too.

As I debated how to turn this random snippet of a premise into a whole series, I decided theirs wasn't the first story, and they weren't the actual nobility . . . but that made it all the more fun to plant them in book one and establish the tension between them. Then, of course, figure out how to put them together in book two.

I know this story wasn't a light one, but I hope you enjoyed the adventure, the reconciliation, and the journey they traveled. I hope, too, you're looking forward to book three. It is time for Yates to move to center stage—because let's be honest, he's been wanting to elbow his way into the spotlight all along. We'll be back at the Tower for that one, with the circus animals and the trapeze . . . and with a new, interim Imposter filling in while some ladies take a maternity leave. I hope you're as excited for it as I am!

As always, I enjoyed delving into some of the fun history and architectural tidbits that Graham and company made use of, especially the hides and tunnels that monks had used to escape marauding Vikings in eras past. Ruins from those old buildings really do lurk under many modern estates, and we're only beginning to rediscover some of them with technology like lidar and ground-penetrating radar.

And if you're intrigued by the world of the Imposters, I hope you'll pop over to my website, where you can learn more about them and their skills, play games, read Lady M's fashion advice, let Graham take you on a tour of the neighborhoods in the books, test your investigative skills, and learn some shorthand from Gemma. Check out all that and more at RoseannaMWhite.com/imposters.

DISCUSSION QUESTIONS

1. Gemma is a woman used to playing roles in order to do her job. What did you think of her "Gabrielle" character? If you had to keep up a different accent for a few days, which one would you pick?

2. Gemma has to change her appearance several times in the book. Did you like her disguises? If you had to go incognito to help someone, what disguise would you choose?

3. Graham's Imposter skill is knowledge of architecture and his intuition about buildings. What did you think of his skills and the ways they were used in the story, including his discoveries? Are you intrigued by architecture and its oddities? Do stories of hidden rooms and tunnels excite you? Have you ever explored any "secret" areas?

4. Yates provides the comic relief in a story otherwise quite serious and heavy. What was your favorite scene or dialogue from him? What did you think of his "Mr. C" confrontation with Lord Wilfred?

5. Who was your favorite character and why? Your least favorite?

6. Were you surprised by the revelations about Gemma and Graham's relationship and family? Grief is very personal and often makes us react in ways unexpected by both ourselves and others. What is one reaction you've experienced in your own time of grief that you wouldn't have expected of yourself?

7. "Faithless is faithless" is an accusation both Gemma and Graham throw at each other. What do you think of their arguments, and of how loss and love, faith and anger with God played out in their hearts? Have you ever had difficulty reconciling your faith in a good God with your circumstances, or with the behavior of a loved one?

8. Who do you think the true villain was in this story? Did you feel sorry for Astley? For Lord Wilfred? What do you think life has in store for all the families impacted by these lords' choices?

9. Hannah Thomas shares that one out of ten children in England don't live to see their first birthday—an accurate statistic for 1909. Does knowing that fact change how you look at historical people? How do you think the changes to infant mortality rates have changed our culture? What did you think of Hannah's character?

10. What was your favorite scene in the book? Which relationships were your favorite?

11. Book three in the Imposters, *An Honorable Deception*, will be about Yates; his childhood friend Lavinia (who you met in *A Beautiful Disguise*), who steps in as an interim Imposter; and a compelling new client, Lady Alethia. What do you hope to see in his story?

Roseanna M. White is a bestselling, Christy Award–winning author who has long claimed that words are the air she breathes. She pens her novels beneath her Betsy Ross flag, with her Jane Austen action figure watching over her. When not writing fiction, she's homeschooling, editing and designing, and pretending her house will clean itself. Roseanna is the author of numerous novels, ranging from biblical fiction to American-set romances to Edwardian British series. Roseanna lives with her family in West Virginia. Learn more at RoseannaMWhite.com.

Sign Up for Roseanna's Newsletter

Keep up to date with Roseanna's latest news on book releases and events by signing up for her email list at the link below.

RoseannaMWhite.com

More from Roseanna M. White

Dire straits force Lady Marigold Fairfax and her brother to become private investigators in London. When Sir Merrick Livingstone hires them to look into the father of Marigold's best friend for suspected international espionage, she is determined to discover the truth and even more determined to keep her heart from getting involved.

A Beautiful Disguise

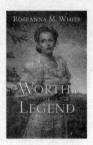

In Edwardian England, on the beautiful Isles of Scilly, three women are swept away by ancient legends and hidden treasures. As they navigate the treacherous waters of secrets left behind, they uncover the most mysterious phenomenon of all: love.

Secrets of The Isles:
The Nature of a Lady, To Treasure an Heiress, Worthy of Legend

 BETHANYHOUSE

 Bethany House Fiction

 @BethanyHouseFiction

 @Bethany_House

@BethanyHouseFiction

 Free exclusive resources for your book group at BethanyHouseOpenBook.com

 Sign up for our fiction newsletter today at BethanyHouse.com